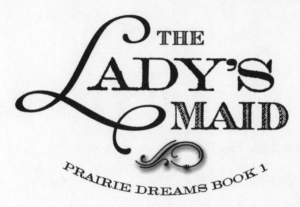

# THE LADY'S MAID

## PRAIRIE DREAMS BOOK 1

# SUSAN PAGE DAVIS

BARBOUR
PUBLISHING

ISBN 978-1-61626-439-0

For more information about Susan Page Davis, please access the author's website at the following Internet address: www.susanpagedavis.com

All scripture quotations are taken from the King James Version of the Bible.

This book is a work of fiction. Names, characters, places, and incidents are either products of the author's imagination or used fictitiously.

Cover design: Müllerhaus Publishing Arts, Inc., www.Mullerhaus.net

Published by Barbour Publishing, Inc., P.O. Box 719, Uhrichsville, OH 44683, www.barbourbooks.com

*Our mission is to publish and distribute inspirational products offering exceptional value and biblical encouragement to the masses.*

ecpa Member of the
Evangelical Christian
Publishers Association

Printed in the United States of America.

# CHAPTER 1

"Come with me, Elise. I can't face him alone."

Lady Anne gripped her hand so hard that Elise Finster winced. She would do anything to make this day easier for her young mistress.

"Of course, my lady, if they'll let me."

They walked down the sweeping staircase together, their silk skirts swishing and the hems of their crinolines nudging each other. Lady Anne kept her hold on Elise's hand until they reached the high-ceilinged hall below.

At the doorway to the morning room, Lady Anne straightened her shoulders. A pang of sympathy lanced Elise's heart, but she couldn't bear this burden in the young woman's place. Anne Stone had to face the future herself.

"Good day, ladies." Andrew Conrad, the Stone family's aging solicitor, rose from the velvet-upholstered sofa and bowed. "Lady Anne, you look charming. Miss Finster."

Elise murmured, "Hello, sir," while Lady Anne allowed Conrad to take her hand and bow over it.

From near the window, a tall, angular man walked forward—Anne's second cousin, Randolph Stone. Ten years older than Anne, the studious man lived in a modest country home with his wife and two young children and eked out a living on the interest of his father's meager fortune. Elise gritted her teeth, a reaction he always induced in her. With great effort, she had managed to keep Lady Anne from guessing how much she loathed Randolph.

3

"Anne." Stone took his cousin's hand and kissed it perfunctorily. He nodded in Elise's direction but didn't greet her.

"Randolph. I didn't expect to see you here." Lady Anne arched her delicate eyebrows at the solicitor.

"Mr. Stone had some questions, and I invited him to come with me today so I could explain the situation to both of you."

Lady Anne said nothing for a long moment then nodded.

"Er, if it pleases you, my lady, this is confidential business." Conrad shot a meaningful glance Elise's way.

Elise felt her face flush but held her ground. She wouldn't leave until Lady Anne told her plainly to do so. Besides, he'd brought along an extra person. Why shouldn't Lady Anne have that right as well?

"I would like Elise to stay." The lady smiled but with a firmness to her jaw befitting the daughter of an earl.

Conrad nodded. "As you wish. Shall we begin, then?"

Lady Anne sat on the upholstered Hepplewhite settee and signaled for Elise to sit beside her. Elise arranged her voluminous skirt and lowered herself, avoiding the direct gaze of Randolph Stone. He didn't care for her either, and Elise knew exactly why, but she didn't believe in letting past discord interfere with the future.

"You must have news," Lady Anne said. "Otherwise, you wouldn't have come."

"That is astute of you, my lady." Conrad reached inside his coat and brought out an envelope. "I've had news that is not really news at all from America."

"America?" Lady Anne's tone changed, and she tensed. "Is it my uncle David?"

Conrad sighed and extracted a sheet of coarse rag paper from the envelope. "You are aware, dear lady, that I sent letters the week after your father died, hoping to locate your uncle—that is, David Stone."

"Earl of Stoneford," Lady Anne said gently.

"Yes, well, that's the point, isn't it?" Conrad sounded tired and the tiniest bit cross, as though he hated being beaten by the Atlantic

4

Ocean and the American postal system. "If your uncle were alive, and if he were here, he would inherit your father's estate and be acknowledged as earl of Stoneford, it's true. But after three months of dillydallying, all we have is a letter from the postmaster in St. Louis, Missouri, declaring that while a Mr. David Stone did reside in the city some ten to fifteen years ago and apparently ran a business at that time, no one by that name lives there now."

Anne's shoulders sagged. "Surely they're mistaken. The last word we had from him came from there."

Conrad shook his head. "I'm afraid we've reached the end of our resources, my lady. I had that letter a couple of weeks ago stating that the city had no death record for your uncle."

"That was a relief," Lady Anne said.

"Yes, but all it tells us is that he did not die in St. Louis. Now, the courts agree on the procedure. The trustees will continue managing your father's estate, but the peerage will remain dormant until your uncle is either found or proven to be deceased."

Lady Anne stirred. "And why is Randolph here?"

"You cousin is next in the line of succession, provided David Stone is proven dead and does not have a male heir. However, it is my duty to tell you both that those things may be impossible to prove."

"And the title will stay dormant and the estate unclaimed for how long?"

"As long as it takes." Conrad brought out a handkerchief and patted his dewy brow. "There are titles that have been dormant for decades—one for more than a hundred years. It will probably never be claimed."

"But the estate, the property—"

"The Crown may decide to dispose of it in time."

"Surely not, if Uncle David is still out there."

"The trustees will not spend your father's fortune in an attempt to find his heir. If you or Mr. Randolph Stone wants to spend your own money trying, that is your affair."

Lady Anne and her cousin glanced at each other. Randolph looked away first.

"And my situation is as you indicated previously," Lady Anne said.

"Yes. You will have the modest fortune your father left to you. The bulk of the estate will remain in trust for the proven heir."

"Then I cannot stay here any longer."

Conrad lifted a hand. "The trustees might allow it, but you would have to pay all household expenses and the wages of any staff you wished to keep, other than the minimum they would retain to maintain the property."

Elise schooled her features to remain impassive, as she'd been taught since she entered domestic service more than two decades ago, but her heart was in turmoil. Her own fate was closely entwined with Lady Anne's. Her mistress's inheritance would hardly enable her to keep living in this huge manor house or to pay the staff that would require. She and Lady Anne had discussed it several times in the past three months, since the earl's death. The young mistress would probably lease a cottage somewhere or go to stay for a while with friends.

"I cannot do that," Lady Anne said. "I shall have to make other arrangements."

Randolph leaned forward. "Surely you've been expecting this outcome, Anne."

Lady Anne's chin shot up. "No. I did not expect it at all. What I expected was that my uncle would be found and that he would come home and take his rightful place as head of the family."

"That isn't going to happen," Randolph said.

"It seems most unlikely." Conrad's voice held a tinge of regret.

Elise felt great sadness for her young mistress, but she could do nothing but sit beside her now and be available later when she cried.

Randolph shook his head. "So there's no hope of my ever inheriting."

"None, unless you can prove that David Stone is dead and has no male children."

They sat in silence for half a minute.

"Your uncle David was much loved," Conrad said at last. "Let me

6

add my condolences, my lady. This must seem a fresh bereavement to you, on the heels of your father's death. I had hoped for a better outcome."

"As did we all," Randolph said hastily.

Lady Anne looked impassively at Conrad. "I shall let you know what I decide to do."

"Thank you. Then I shall be going." Conrad rose.

Elise stood, along with Lady Anne and her cousin.

"Thank you for your work on this," her mistress told Conrad.

Again he bowed over Lady Anne's hand. "I hope I can continue to be of service, my lady."

Elise stood slightly behind Lady Anne and did not offer her hand. It wasn't her place.

Randolph said, "I wish it were otherwise, Anne."

"Of course you do."

Randolph's mouth twitched, but he didn't respond other than to clasp her hand and take his leave with Conrad. How was his wife taking the news, Elise wondered. In the past year, since Anne's other uncle, John, had died in battle, Randolph and Merrileigh must have speculated much on their chances of becoming Earl and Lady Stone. Now it seemed that would not come about. Merrileigh, who loved to entertain beyond the means her husband's current income afforded, must be distraught.

Elise walked into the great hall with the visitors and opened the front door, rather than summoning the one remaining housemaid to show them out. The butler and three quarters of the staff had already left to seek other positions before the money ran out, and Lady Anne had bid them sincere good-byes and Godspeeds. Some had served the family all their lives—and many since before Anne's birth.

Elise herself had started as a parlor maid at sixteen, hired by Anne's mother. What days those were! Elegant house parties at Stoneford and social seasons at the town house in London. When the mistress died three years ago, the family had lost much of its sparkle, but Elise had stayed on with Anne out of love as much as convenience. The seventeen-year-old girl had blossomed into a lovely, refined woman of twenty, and Elise felt that Anne relied on her almost as much as she once had her mother.

When she got back to the morning room, Anne sat once more on the settee. She looked up at Elise with a thoughtful gaze. "I shall have to make plans, Elise. I should have before now, but I couldn't believe Uncle David wouldn't turn up."

"He'd have let you stay here," Elise said.

"Perhaps. Who knows? And I admit I've never given much thought to his hypothetical offspring."

"No need to."

"Isn't there?" Lady's Anne's brown eyes widened. "Uncle David might be dead, though I don't want to think that. Still, he could have children. Father didn't hear from him once in the last ten years. He might have married and settled down to raise a passel of little Yankee Stones. There could be half a dozen of them out there, standing between Cousin Randolph and the peerage, though they have no inkling."

Elise cringed at the mention of Randolph's name. She'd done rather well in concealing her dislike of him while he was in the room, but she couldn't hold it in forever. Best to change the subject.

"Would you like your tea now, my lady?"

"I can't stay here, Elise."

For a long moment neither of them spoke. At last, Elise said, "I understand."

This was Lady Anne's way of saying she could no longer afford to keep her on. Elise's wages were near the top of the scale for lady's maids. The Stones had always prided themselves on paying their staff well and treating them humanely. Should she offer to work for less? If she took another position—and Elise had no doubt she could find one, with Lady Anne's recommendation—Anne could hire both a general maid and perhaps a cook-housekeeper, though not a very good one, for the price. If she wanted to keep a frugal household in the country, Anne could live in comparative comfort. Nothing like what she was used to of course, but she could be independent.

Lady Anne rose. "I believe I shall lie down. If I don't ring for you, please wake me in an hour. I shall take my tea then and—and lay plans."

"Yes, my lady."

Anne walked slowly into the hall and up the stairs. Her steps dragged, and her chin nearly touched her chest. Her heart aching, Elise descended to the servants' hall, where the last kitchen maid jumped up from a chair in the corner. Her eyelids were puffy from weeping.

"The mistress will take tea in an hour," Elise said.

"Yes, mum." Patsy sniffed and wrung her hands in her apron. Her hair looked disheveled, and several strands hung down from her cap. "What's to do, Miss Finster? Should I give my notice?"

"If you hear of another opening, it might be wise."

"Would you tell me if you learn something, mum?"

"Yes."

Patsy nodded. "Thank you."

Elise suggested Patsy serve a simple meal of fruit, cheese, and scones. "If there's any butter or honey in the pantry, so much the better. If not, perhaps Hannah could run to the grocer's."

"Hannah's left, mum, and Lucy is packing."

"Indeed?" That was bad news. They would be left in the huge house without servants—only Patsy. "Is Michael still out at the stable?"

"He came in for breakfast this morning, but he said if the mistress hasn't any horses to keep, he might as well go with the rest. He went out to look for a new position."

Elise went up to her room, her heart heavy, opened the doors of the large cedar wardrobe, and took out her best silk and wool gown. If Lady Anne was going to move to different quarters, Elise would have to pack all of her mistress's clothing, which comprised much more than her own. She might as well pack her personal things now and have it out of the way, so that she could give her full attention to Lady Anne's wardrobe when the time came.

How would she bring up the subject of a letter of

recommendation? She hated to ask, but certainly Lady Anne would give her one. And she probably knew of several highborn ladies who would love to have a maid of Elise's experience—although lady's maids usually retired by the time they reached Elise's age. Ladies going out in society liked to have a pretty young woman accompany them.

Elise tried to put that depressing though out of her mind. Lady Anne had once told her she wouldn't part with her no matter what the fashions were. But now, Elise was nearing forty. Her savings wouldn't be enough to retire on, and she had no prospects of marriage. Necessity would force her to remain in service, but in what capacity? She didn't know if she had the energy to work as a housemaid. Perhaps one of Lady Anne's acquaintances was in need of a companion or a governess. Neither would pay much, but she'd be comfortable and have lighter duties than most house servants.

Elise shook off the thoughts and went to the large room down the hall designated as Lady Anne's wardrobe. The room was filled with racks of gowns and petticoats. Cupboards along one wall held shoes, lingerie, and tools of the lady's maid's trade. Elise fetched a bundle of tissue paper and carried it to her room. She had a valise in her armoire, but she'd have to get a trunk down from the attic. Too bad she hadn't thought of getting out the trunks before all the menservants left. Perhaps she and Patsy could manage.

She put the clothing from her dresser into the valise and nestled the gown on top. The rest of her dresses and other clothing would go into her trunk.

Of course Lady Anne hadn't instructed her to pack, but what else could she expect? The earl was dead, and Anne would inherit nothing but the meager fund her father had set up for her. He'd expected his only daughter to marry a rich man before he died, and failing that, to have her two uncles to depend on.

Tears spilled over. *David, David, why did you leave us?* And now John was gone, too. And the earl—Anne's father and the eldest of the three brothers—had succumbed to pneumonia three months past, and Anne was alone. But Elise was alone as well—and perhaps in a worse predicament. She snatched a handkerchief from her dressing table and blotted her cheeks carefully before reaching for her rouge pot. She would *not* feel sorry for herself.

A quick tap on her door stayed her hand, and she turned toward it, recognizing Lady Anne's method of announcing herself when she was in a hurry, rather than using the bell pull in her chamber. So close they'd become that this seemed normal. Elise would have to get used to new ways and a new mistress, one who would probably not be so lenient and informal as Lady Anne.

She opened the door. "What is it, my lady?"

Anne stood in the doorway, her chin high. Her eyes gleamed, though the whites were reddened from her recent weeping and her eyelids puffier than usual.

"Elise, I need your help."

"Anything, my lady."

Lady Anne's gaze lit on the piles of garments scattered over the bed and Elise's open valise. "What are you doing?"

"Packing. I assumed. . . ." Elise faltered to a stop.

"But. . . You can't leave me now!"

"Of course not, my lady. I'll stay with you for as long as you wish."

Lady Anne sobbed and lurched forward into Elise's arms.

"There, there, my dear." Elise patted her heaving shoulders. "I shan't leave you unless I have to. Nothing would please me more than to stay with you. I only assumed. . . ."

Lady Anne sniffed and pulled away, wiping her face with the back of her hand. "You assumed I'd toss you out? I should hope not."

Elise grabbed one of her daintiest lawn handkerchiefs from the stack on the dressing table and held it out to her. "I'm sorry. I know things will be difficult for you, and I didn't want you to feel guilty if you couldn't keep me on."

"Not keep you on? Elise, I should die without you. How would I live?"

It was true, Lady Anne depended on her lady's maid a great deal—perhaps overmuch. The thought of the twenty-year-old, pampered girl facing the harsh world alone made Elise shudder. Yet she hadn't dared hope Lady Anne would find a way to support them both, let alone maintain the lifestyle she'd lived since birth.

"I'm sure I don't know," Elise murmured. "Should I unpack, then?"

Lady Anne sighed and wiped the tear streaks from her cheeks. "I wish I could say yes, but you heard what Mr. Conrad said. Though we throw in our fates together, we cannot stay here. I'm afraid my income won't stretch to cover the coal and servants' wages."

"Yes, I suspected that." Elise frowned. "What do you suggest, then?"

"Let's go down to the little drawing room, shall we? I think a cup of tea would do us both good, and I shall tell you what is on my mind."

"That sounds most practical, my lady. I've told Patsy to have tea ready about now."

"Ah, so Patsy hasn't left us yet?"

"No, she's out in the kitchen, alone and frightened about to death. She asked me if she ought to give her notice, too. I counseled her not to ignore any opportunities that came her way. Perhaps I spoke amiss."

Lady Anne sighed. "I wish I could keep her, though she's clumsy. She has a good heart. But I fear she'd be better off if I give her a referral. And Michael is going to the Blithes."

"He's spoken to you?" Elise asked.

"Yes, he came in a few minutes ago and asked to see me. Hemmed and hawed, and I told him to speak up. I gave him his wages and a sovereign extra. I'm glad he's found a place."

Elise nodded. Michael would be happy with the Blithes. The viscount was fond of racing and owned several blood horses. It seemed all the Stones' domestics were landing on their feet, and she was glad.

A few minutes later, Elise and her mistress sat opposite each other on rosewood chairs before a very small coal fire, each sipping tea from a delicate china cup. Elise was thankful for both the tea and the coal, and for the fact that she hadn't been forced to make the tea herself.

Lady Anne set her cup and saucer on the side table with a gentle sigh. "Elise, the thought that you might leave me terrified me."

"I shall stay at your side as long as you want me, my dear."

"Thank you. I believe you and I may continue to dwell together—quite frugally of course." She waved a hand, encompassing the elegant room. "We'd have none of this, but we could take a small house together, and I believe we'd have enough to get by, just the two of us."

Relief washed through Elise. Security was high on her list of life goals. "But would you have to give up your place in society, my lady?"

Lady Anne shrugged. "We shall see. I suppose some of my friends will invite me to house parties and such, but maybe not, now that Father is gone. I may have to wear this year's gowns for several seasons." She gave Elise a rueful smile. "Perhaps I shall learn now who are my true friends."

"To be sure." The idea of setting out as two independent, if impoverished, women, had a certain appeal that bolstered Elise's stifled longing for adventure. That side of her nature seldom stood up and spoke to her, but she felt almost as excited as she had twenty-four years ago when she'd boarded the ship that brought her here from Germany to enter domestic service at Stoneford. And Elise had often been certain that Anne longed to defy convention and try an adventure of her own. Life with Lady Anne, outside the strict confines of high society, might be rather fun.

"There's another, more pressing matter," Lady Anne said.

"Oh?" Elise watched her over the rim of her cup as she sipped her tea.

"Yes. You know the situation Mr. Conrad detailed to me today, and you are aware that my father had two brothers."

"Yes." Elise hoped she wouldn't flush at the mention of Lady Anne's uncles. So unseemly.

"Since my uncle John died last summer—"

"That awful battle in the Crimea. So tragic."

Lady Anne nodded. "So that leaves David."

Now the telltale blush crept into Elise's cheeks. She could feel it spread upward and quickly raised her cup again.

"David is now the earl of Stoneford," Anne said. "At least he is if he can be found."

"Ah. But David Stone hasn't set foot in England, so far as we know, for twenty years." Elise set the cup back on the pink-and-white saucer with a slight clatter. "It was my impression that Mr. Conrad intended not to expend further energy looking for your uncle."

"That is true." Anne looked down at her cup, as though studying the bits of tea leaves as they settled in the bottom, to seek her future there. "And yet, so many lives are affected by his existence—or lack of it."

Elise swallowed with difficulty. Throughout these twenty years, she'd pined for David. For Anne it was perhaps a more academic matter, since she was an infant when David sailed for America. Of course she'd heard stories of her dashing young uncle, then third in line for the earldom. But Elise had known him personally, had thrilled to the timbre of his voice, had delighted in every glimpse of him when he came to his brother's house. Her lip quivered, and she thought it best to remain silent.

"Perhaps I'm not thinking clearly," Lady Anne said, "but I see only one course of action."

That caught Elise's attention. The young mistress had considered her options and had already made a decision. A cottage in some small village, no doubt. They could be quite cozy together, as Lady Anne had said.

"What course is that, my lady?" she dared to ask.

Lady Anne raised her chin and looked Elise in the eye. "We must find him, of course. Elise, you and I are bound for America."

# CHAPTER 2

March 1855
St. Louis, Missouri

Elise held to the railing as she moved down the gangplank from the crowded riverboat. After the jolting, plunging river crossing, her gratitude on landing dwarfed all else.

"Elise?"

Lady Anne's wail brought her up short before her feet touched dry land. She turned and peered up the gangplank. Her mistress stood at the top, clutching the railing. The cold wind tossed the young woman's light veil and fluttered the decorative capes on her overcoat.

"Come along, my—my dear. It's perfectly safe."

Lady Anne's face held remnants of the terror she'd expressed on the ocean voyage. Elise shifted her valise to her other hand and hurried back up the ramp. With her large skirt, distended by six stiff petticoats and whalebone hoops, Lady Anne had effectively blocked all the other passengers' exit from the river steamer.

"Take my hand, dear." After a week's practice, Elise could still barely restrain her tongue from uttering "my lady" each time she addressed Anne. But the behavior they'd experienced in New York had made it clear that they'd be wise to travel as friends, not titled lady and servant. People who perceived that Anne was wealthy—something Elise would debate, depending on the definition of wealth—did their utmost to extract her fortune from her. As just plain Miss Anne Stone, she was less likely to be extorted.

Elise reached out and pried Anne's gloved fingers from the rail. "It's all right," she said softly. "Just a few steps and we'll be on good, solid earth again. Don't look over the side." She tugged gently on Anne's hand.

Anne took one mechanical step.

"That's good. Let's go." Elise tucked her hand firmly under Anne's elbow and threw an apologetic glance at the couple standing behind them. She couldn't help but notice the man behind them in line. He was staring at her, and Elise shivered. She'd seen him on the train yesterday, and again on the steamboat that brought them across the Mississippi. He seemed to lurk wherever she and Anne went on the steamer—in the cabin or up on deck, it didn't matter. He was always there: a thin man with an equally thin mustache. He hadn't approached them, but his presence made her uneasy. The best thing she could do was get Anne off the gangplank and into a hackney.

"Come along now, dear." Each step took an effort on Anne's part and constant praise from Elise, but at last their shoes—sturdy walking shoes Elise had insisted upon, but fine quality—touched the ground.

"Good day, ladies." One of the ship's stewards stood at the foot of the ramp, for all the good he'd done.

Elise nodded to him and pulled her mistress hastily to one side so that the other passengers could disembark. The couple bustled on toward a liveried coachman waiting with an open carriage. The thin man who'd watched them strode on and disappeared in the crowd. Elise hoped she'd never see him again.

"We're finally here." Anne looked about the busy wharf.

"Indeed, we are. St. Louis, Missouri." Elise noted that most of the passengers climbed into carriages, some of which appeared to be hackneys. "Come. I think we can find transportation."

A disembarking gentleman spoke to the steward, and the steward hurried out among the conveyances and returned a moment later.

"Right over there, sir. The team of black horses."

The gentleman passed him a coin.

"Thank you, sir. Have a good journey." The steward smiled as he tucked away the coin.

Elise opened her reticule. "Pardon me, but my companion and I shall need a hack that can take us and our luggage to a suitable hostelry."

"Yes, ma'am. Wait right here, and I'll fetch someone for you."

While he was gone, Elise fingered her available coins. She was still getting used to the American currency. The train trip from New York to the Mississippi had given her a quick if spotty education, and she selected a quarter dollar. She would have to give the fellow who loaded the luggage even more. When they reached their hotel, she must ask Lady Anne for more pocket money so that she could continue dealing with the laborers they found necessary to their journey.

"Here you go, ma'am. This fellow will take you in his cab to any hotel you please."

"Thank you." Elise slipped the quarter into the steward's hand, and he promptly pocketed it and abandoned her.

The newcomer, a short, lithe man of indeterminate age dressed in a rough jacket and trousers, whipped off his shapeless cloth cap, exposing a head of thick, dark hair.

"Afternoon, ma'am. At your service."

"Thank you." Elise pulled Anne forward. "This lady and I want you to collect our baggage and drive us to a decent hotel. Not the most expensive in the city, you understand, but a *nice* one."

"Yes, ma'am. I understand perfectly. You got trunks?"

"Er—yes." Elise peered down the wharf to where the stevedores were unloading luggage from the hold of the steamer. "Perhaps we could put the lady into your cab first? Then I could go with you to claim our things."

He nodded. "That's it right there, with the horses tied to the lamppost."

Elise lowered her voice. "Would the lady be safe if we left her there?"

"I think so."

"I'm feeling much better now," Anne said. Her face still looked pale, but she managed a smile. She'd always been a sturdy, healthy girl. Who would have thought she'd have gone all green about the gills as soon as they left the dock in England?

Elise had waited on her constantly for a week before Anne had gotten her sea legs, and they'd thought all was well. The voyage could have been worse, though they were always cold, and the ship's plunging still sent Anne to her berth on occasion. After landing in New York, they'd endured a jolting, smoke-filled journey on the train to the bank of the Mississippi and spent a night in a marginally clean hotel in the riverside town. But when they'd embarked on the river steamer that morning, Anne's queasiness had returned in full force.

Elise took her elbow. "Let's get you into the hackney."

She and the cabby put Anne in his coach and ventured onto the pier. The wind seemed to grow stronger as they got farther from shore, pulling at Elise's full skirts. She was grateful for the hatpins that securely anchored her chapeau.

The cab driver set a brisk pace to where the travelers' chests were piled. Elise pointed out her own steamer trunk and Anne's three. From another pile, she collected four smaller bags. The driver eyed the heap askance.

"I'll have to get a handcart. Are you sure this is everything?"

Elise almost thought he was joking. "Quite."

He nodded. "You go get in my cab. I'll be there shortly."

Elise didn't wait to see what heroics he'd have to perform to get a cart and load their trunks. She thrust a dollar into his hand and hurried back down the wharf.

Reaching the cab, she opened the door and gathered her skirts as best she could. She placed her foot on the step. The hoops in the hems of her petticoats eased through the doorway. She thought she was safe when she stumbled and catapulted into the coach, landing unceremoniously across Anne's lap.

Anne gasped. "Are you all right?"

"I believe so. Let's close the door so that I can bear my humiliation in relative privacy."

Anne giggled. "I'm sorry, but you did look funny." She managed to grab the door handle and swing it closed. The absence of wind immediately brought a comforting sense of warmth.

"Elise." Anne frowned and stared out the window.

"What is it, my lady?"

"Aside from the fact that you're not supposed to call me that, did you notice that man?"

"What man?"

"I thought I saw that annoying gentleman from the train—the one who ogled us so rudely."

Elise hesitated. She'd hoped Anne hadn't noticed him on the steamer. "What about him?"

"I thought I saw him just now—across the way. He was talking to another man—a tall, gangly fellow."

Elise leaned forward and peered from the side of the window opening.

"He's gone," Anne said.

Leaning back against the seat, Elise tried to breathe calmly. She'd told herself not to be suspicious when she saw the man on the steamer. Many people probably took the same train they had and then crossed the river to St. Louis. But this man had lingered about the docks while their luggage was being fetched.

"I expect it's nothing," she murmured, but her chest felt tight.

Wheels rattled nearby over the cobbles. The carriage swayed, and she grabbed the edge of the seat.

"Up, up," said a man's voice outside. "Heavy, ain't it?"

Elise caught her breath. Anne's eyes were wide with alarm.

"That's our cabby," Elise said. "He's loading our trunks, I'm sure."

"Of course." Anne took off her hat and smoothed her hair. "I admit I'm tired of traveling."

"We should be able to stay in St. Louis a few days," Elise said. "We'll rest this evening and put out inquiries for your uncle tomorrow."

All indicators pointed to David having left St. Louis several years ago, but it was their only clue. Had he gone back to the Atlantic coast, where business might be brisker? Or had he pushed on, into the western frontier?

"There should be some people in St. Louis who remember him," she said. "People the postmaster didn't talk to. Perhaps we can stop here a few days just to get our feet back under us."

"That sounds attractive. I wouldn't have thought it, but I'm quite exhausted."

The coach dipped on its springs and swayed again. A few moments later, the cabby appeared outside their door, smiling.

"All loaded, ladies. And where did you say I will be taking you?"

Elise smiled at his cheerful voice and Irish cant. "Well, sir, we hoped you could suggest a place." She looked around. "Suggest it quietly though, if you please. We do not wish to broadcast our lodging place."

Anne leaned forward. "Surely you know of a nice, clean place where ladies can stay without worrying every minute."

"To be sure," the cabby said. "I'll have you there in twenty minutes."

He disappeared, and the springs gave as he climbed to his perch on the driver's box. The horses set out at a good clip, and the cab rolled along with a minimum of jostling. Elise sank back with a sigh. Weariness seeped through every muscle. She closed her eyes and opened them, startled, when Anne spoke.

"Do you think we'll find him?"

Elise fought back her sleepiness and sat straighter. "Yes, I do."

"We've both prayed so hard," Anne said.

"The Lord will honor that."

"I wish I fully believed that. But if not, perhaps we can at least get the documentation needed for the peerage to remain active. It would be a pity for the house to sit there empty until the Crown takes it over and for Randolph to miss out on the title if it truly should be his." Anne reached out a hand as though to stop Elise's thoughts from running astray. "I haven't always been courteous to Randolph. For some reason I always found it difficult to like him."

*Not "for some reason,"* Elise thought. *There are plenty of reasons, and I could personally name half a dozen.* But she wouldn't. Anne's vague dislike of her cousin was far better than certain knowledge that the man was a scoundrel.

The cab slowed, made a turn, and at last rolled to a stop.

"There we go, ladies. If this place is not to your liking, there's another not far from here that we can try. But this one is very genteel, they say."

Elise took the hand the cabby offered and climbed down, wishing she weren't so stiff. These long days of travel made her feel like an old woman. She surveyed the hotel as he helped Anne down. The broad, three-story clapboard building had a wide covered porch. Two elderly women sat there in rocking chairs, bundled up against the cool late March air, and a man in a beige suit lounged against the pillar near them. Shrubs lined the walk to the steps, and baskets of budding plants sat on the window ledges. A sign at the edge of the lawn read CINDERS HOTEL.

"It looks well kept," Elise ventured. "Shall we go in and see what it's like inside?"

"Would you like me to accompany you?" the cabby asked. "If you take a room, I'll come back out and unload your trunks."

"Splendid." Elise was thankful they'd found a reliable man. So far the Americans she'd dealt with ranged from blatant rapscallions to suave gentlemen. The cabby, to all appearances, was an honest and hardworking fellow.

Twenty minutes later, she and Anne had been shown to rooms on the second floor, and the hotel owner's son, with the cabby's help, had delivered their ample baggage. Elise tipped them generously and looked about Anne's room as the lady removed her hat and gloves.

"Perhaps we should have taken but one room," Elise said. "We need to conserve your funds."

"We may come to that," Anne said, gazing at the stack of trunks. "But for now, at least, we'll maintain our privacy."

"As you wish. But do tell me when we need to make a change." Elise walked over to her. "Here, my lady. Let me help you undress and get to bed. I'll have some supper brought up for you."

"I'm so tired," Anne admitted. She held up her arms and allowed Elise to pull her gown over her head. "Thank you. I know I shall feel better once I'm out of these crinolines and my corset."

As quickly as she could, Elise helped her change into a nightdress and wrapper then sat her mistress down so she could brush her hair.

"I could have a bath drawn for you."

"No, I'll wait until tomorrow. I want only to sink into that bed."

The single beds in both rooms had iron head- and footboards. Elise wasn't sure how comfortable they would be, but they did seem to have plump mattresses, and the bedding looked clean.

She helped her mistress into bed and turned the lamp low then walked down to the dining room where only a few customers lingered.

"Am I too late to dine?" she asked the waitress.

"No, ma'am. We've got roast beef and potatoes, or chicken stew. Take a seat anywhere you like."

"Thank you. And could I get a tray afterward for Miss Stone?"

"You sure can."

Elise hid her smile at the woman's broad accent. She supposed that she and Lady Anne sounded odd to these Yankees.

As she waited for her meal, she observed the other diners. None of them, to her relief, resembled the man she and Anne had seen earlier—*Mustache*, as she'd begun to think of him.

She supposed her suspicions were brought on by fatigue. He was only a traveler, like her, headed in the same direction. She unfolded her napkin and laid it across her lap, determined to think of more pleasant things.

David Stone, for instance. "Tell me about Uncle David," Lady Anne had said on the train. Elise had gathered her rioting thoughts and complied. David Stone was a handsome young man when last she'd seen him. Anne, of course, was too young to remember him, but she'd seen his portraits countless times. One of the three brothers hung in the hall at Stoneford—Richard, the eldest, at twenty-one, John at nineteen in his uniform, and David a lad of fourteen. He was the fairest, the most likable, and the most charming.

A second portrait of David hung in the small drawing room. He had sat for it the winter before he left England. He had grown only more handsome in the intervening eight years.

"Everyone liked him," Elise had told Anne. It was true. David had myriad friends and no enemies. Every woman who laid eyes on David Stone adored him. Elise was no exception.

But she was only the maid. At that time, she'd served Anne's mother, Lady Elizabeth Stone. She'd loved her mistress. And her mistress's brother-in-law.

David hadn't really noticed Elise—not in that way. He'd always been nice to her and even joked with her occasionally, but he'd never approached her romantically. The one man in the world she wished would do so treated her like a sister. On the other hand, Elise had needed to fight his cousin off whenever Randolph visited Stoneford.

Life wasn't fair.

Her meal came, and she savored it. The long, arduous day had taken its toll. She almost doubted she'd be able to waken Lady Anne long enough for the young woman to eat her dinner, but the plain, tasty food would be worth it and would give her strength for tomorrow—no doubt another long day.

Would they find David tomorrow?

Elise's pulse raced, though she calmly cut her roast beef and chewed one small bite at a time. It was unlikely that they'd catch up to him so soon. David had lived in this city for several years, but then he'd written to his brother Richard that he was moving on. The earl hadn't heard from him again, or if he had, the rest of the household wasn't told. If David had moved back to St. Louis, the postmaster would have informed Mr. Conrad. He must have gone somewhere else. But still. . .they might find some hint of his whereabouts among people in the city who knew him. Someday, and soon, God willing, they would find him.

Would she shortly stand face-to-face with the man she'd held in her heart all this time? David would have changed—Elise understood that. And if he'd changed for the worse, perhaps seeing him again would cleanse her mind of him. Maybe she'd be able to think about someone else now, after all these years.

She wanted a love. She wanted a home of her own. Perhaps it was too late to hope for children. But with Lady Anne's change in circumstances, Elise felt free to decide her own future. Would she remain with Anne for the rest of her life and serve her quietly? Or did something bigger await her? David? Or someone else?

# CHAPTER 3

W e'll start with the last known address," Lady Anne said the next morning.

They'd both slept late and had breakfast sent to their rooms. Then they'd bathed and taken great care with their morning toilette. It was nearly noon before both felt ready to venture out and begin their search.

The hotel's owner came from behind his desk, smiling as they descended the stairs.

"Good day, ladies. How lovely you both look."

"Thank you," Elise said. Lady Anne merely nodded with a faint smile.

"How may I help you?" Mr. Williams asked.

Elise drew a slip of paper from her pocket, though she knew the address by heart. "Perhaps you could tell us where Union Street is. If it's not far, we might walk there."

"To be sure, ma'am. If you go down to the corner and turn left, then go two blocks—you might want to cross the street though, because it's muddy, and there's no cobbles here and no sidewalk on the near side—and get down to Walnut and turn again. Then it's not far. You'll see a laundry on the corner. That's the street you want."

Elise nodded slowly.

"And the livery?" Anne asked. "How far is that?"

"Perhaps half a mile."

After more discussion and repetition of the directions, the two ladies opted to walk rather than hire a hackney or a buggy. They set out on foot for the address where David had lived ten years ago, with Elise carrying a furled umbrella. The early morning fog had lifted some, but gray clouds hung low overhead. The streets were already muddy from the last shower, and the ladies were grateful for the board sidewalks that led from the hotel to the corner. As Mr. Williams had foretold, however, on the next street they were forced to pick their way across the muddy thoroughfare, and the hems of their skirts grew filthy.

At last they arrived at the address, only to find that it was occupied by a tobacco shop. Lady Anne looked at Elise in dismay.

"Have we got it wrong?"

"I don't think so. The city is growing quickly. It's more likely that sometime in the last ten years your uncle's old house was torn down and this shop put here in its place."

Rain pattered down on them, and Elise raised the umbrella. "I suppose we can ask the shopkeeper if he knows anything about the building's history." The rain increased as she spoke, and that sealed their choice for taking shelter inside the shop.

No one stood behind the counter in the small store, but two men sat in chairs near an upright heating stove, and a third stood nearby, in conversation with them. All three had their pipes lit, and the air was hazy with aromatic smoke.

"Well, ladies!" One of the men, with luxuriant gray hair and a short-cropped beard, stood and gave a slight bow. "How may I assist you, or are you merely seeking a roof until the rain stops?"

Elise handed the collapsed umbrella to Lady Anne and stepped toward him. "We're looking for a gentleman who used to live at this address."

"Ah, an English lady seeking a gentleman." He smiled and ran a hand over his beard. "How long ago did your friend reside here?"

"At least ten years. This was the address he gave."

"Probably dead," the man still seated said dolefully. "Them was rough times."

The man who had first addressed Elise scowled at him and cleared his throat. "Pay no mind to him. This did used to be a private residence. I bought it about four years back. Before my shop, it was a bakery, or so I'm told. But it was a house once." He nodded, looking around him as though expecting to see the old furniture and residents emerge through the smoke.

"How would I find out more about the man who used to live here?" Elise could scarcely credit David, the son of an earl, living in such a small, rough building, but what did she know of life on the edge of civilization? David might have lived in poverty and not hinted of it to his family.

"What's his name?" the man asked.

"David Stone."

"Don't know him." The bearded man took a puff on his pipe and looked at his two companions, but they shook their heads.

"Might ask at the post office," said the younger man, who still stood by the stove.

Elise nodded and did not volunteer that the Stones' solicitor had done that already.

"You could ask around," said the third man. "Old Henry Cobb across the street has been here as long as anyone."

"Thank you."

Lady Anne began to cough. Rain or no rain, Elise decided it was time to get out of the tainted air.

"Good day, gentlemen." She took the umbrella and opened the door. Anne dived through it as though desperate to escape.

As she closed the door behind them, Elise heard the seated man say, "Dutch, you're lettin' 'em get away."

The wind blew a torrent of raindrops over them, and Elise angled the umbrella against it.

"What do you think, my lady? Should we seek out this man named Henry Cobb?"

"I'd feel we were remiss if we didn't." Anne had to raise her voice against the wind.

"I don't want you to catch a chill," Elise said.

The wind whipped Lady Anne's short veil and a few tendrils of hair escaping from beneath her hat. The fetching bonnet would be ruined if they stayed out long in this weather.

"Perhaps we should go back to the hotel until this blows over."

"No," Anne said. "I want to find Uncle David as quickly as possible."

"All right, then we'll make inquiries across the street."

Smoke rose from the chimney of the house directly across. The two women picked their way between ruts and puddles. They were nearly across when a laden wagon slogged down the way, throwing muddy water across the lower half of Elise's skirt. The driver shrugged and lifted his hat, grinning.

Elise held in the response she wanted to make and took Lady's Anne's elbow, guiding her up onto the stoop of an unpainted house that looked as though the wind might blow it down.

Anne rapped timidly with her gloved hand.

After a few seconds, Elise said, "We shall have to knock louder, I'm afraid." She used the umbrella handle to rap smartly on the weathered planks of the door.

She saw movement through a window to one side and waited, with the rain sheeting off the umbrella. The door swung open.

"Ladies! How may I help you?" An elderly man with several teeth missing and thinning white hair appraised them with an eager smile.

"Mr. Cobb?" Elise asked.

"Yes. Come in. Don't get company often, and the day's not fit for a three-legged dog. Come in and dry off, ladies."

Grateful for the prospect of a few minutes' warmth, Elise stepped in cautiously. She saw nothing to alarm her and beckoned to Anne to follow. With the door closed, the heat of the small room enveloped them. A fire blazed in a brick hearth, and a lamp burned on a small, bare table.

"Will you take a seat?" Cobb gestured toward a rocker positioned near the fireplace and a ladder-back chair near the table.

"Oh, no, thank you," Elise said. "We only wanted to inquire for my friend's uncle." She turned and nodded toward Anne. Despite her normal reserve, the lady had drifted toward the hearth and stood shivering before the fire.

"The young lady's uncle?" Cobb asked. "Do I know him?"

"Well, we hope so," Elise replied. "He used to live across the way, where the tobacconist's shop is now."

"Ah, that would be in the old days. And his name?"

"David Stone."

Cobb's brow furrowed. "Did he speak cockney like you?"

Elise flushed. The man obviously had no idea of the differences between a cockney accent and that of a cultured English gentleman, let alone a woman whose German tongue had taken on the British slant. "He was English, yes."

"Ah. Seems like I recall a gent living yonder."

"His family had a letter from him about ten years ago. Do you know when he left, or where he went?"

Cobb shook his head. "He's been gone a good many years. Ten sounds about right. Talked about going farther west, I think."

"Farther west?" Elise swallowed hard. Their journey had already taken them into conditions more primitive than she had ever imagined. St. Louis was reportedly one of the jumping-off points for even wilder country. "Do you have any idea how we can find out where he went? Were there other people he was friendly with?"

"I'm sorry, ma'am. I can't help you there." A gleam came into Cobb's eyes. "But I can offer you a glass of ale and a biscuit."

Lady Anne actually raised her chin at his words, and Elise realized she was exhausted and famished. "Uh, no, but thank you kindly, sir."

He winked at her. "If you're in town long, come back and visit with Henry Cobb. I always have a jug of ale put by."

The ladies ventured out again. The rain had slackened, but the drizzle and the deep mud made their trip back to the hotel miserable.

"I'm going to put you right to bed for a nap, and we'll continue our inquiries tomorrow," Elise said as they climbed the stairs. "In a few hours, we'll go down to dinner, or I can bring up a tray."

"I'm sure I'll be fine by then," Lady Anne said, but as Elise unlocked their door, she let out a delicate sneeze.

Elise spent an hour removing the mud from their skirts and petticoats. The hotel owner allowed her into the kitchen to use a flatiron, after which she returned to her room to clean and oil their shoes.

She ended up dining alone that evening and carrying up a bowl of soup, a coarse bread roll the Americans called a biscuit, and a cup of strong tea. After half the soup was gone, Lady Anne insisted she couldn't eat another bite. She rolled over and went back to sleep.

Elise turned down the lamp and went to her own room, where she undressed wearily in semidarkness. She prayed silently that her mistress would not be very ill. She'd been foolish to take Lady Anne out in such foul weather.

*Dear Lord,* she pleaded as she climbed into the narrow bed and drew up the piecework comforter, *please, please, let us find David soon.*

⸎

Thomas G. Costigan leaned on the bar in the Horsehead Saloon, sipping a beer. He couldn't afford whiskey anymore, so he bought beer one glass at a time and drank it slowly. He wished he'd never come east of Fort Laramie.

"You Costigan?"

He turned at the voice and faced a stranger. This fellow looked like a dandy—not unusual for St. Louis—but generally his kind patronized a higher class of watering hole. The slender man wore a suit and necktie and a bowler hat. On his feet were low-cut shoes, not boots. His mustache was more of a dark ink line across his top lip. A sissy mustache. Still, could be trouble.

"Who wants to know?" Thomas asked.

"My name is Peterson."

Thomas thought he caught a hint of New York in his accent, but he wasn't sure. Folks came to Saint Louie from all over.

"What do you want from me?"

Peterson gestured to a table at the side of the room. "Care to sit and discuss it? I'll stand you another one of those." He nodded toward Thomas's glass.

"Make it whiskey."

"Certainly."

Thomas stood and shuffled toward the empty table, taking his beer with him. A moment later, Peterson joined him and set down

29

two glasses. Abandoning his beer, Thomas took a small sip. Now that was the real thing.

He set the glass down and looked at Peterson. "So what do you want?"

"I need a man to do a job, and I was told you might be the one."

Thomas wasn't against working, though he'd rather it didn't get too strenuous. But who would recommend him for a job? And what sort? He'd been in the brig for two days once at Fort Benton—up in Montana. Didn't like it and had determined never to be confined again. That experience had grown a little caution inside him.

"Depends. What do you need done?"

"It's what you might call a surveillance job."

Thomas squinted at him. "What's that?"

"Where you watch someone and report on their activities."

"Is that against the law?"

"No, absolutely not." Peterson seemed almost happy about it. "You simply follow the person about—without them realizing it of course—and make note of where they go, to whom they speak, and so on. Then you tell your employer what you've learned, and you get paid. Simple."

Thomas hesitated. It sounded like a job that would require staying sober, but he never got thoroughly drunk, anyway. That would likely end him up in some jail.

"How much?"

"Oh, I'll make it worth your while. Two dollars a day, plus any legitimate expenses you incur. And it won't be an unpleasant job. The people I need you to observe are quite pleasant to look at."

"That so?" The man wasn't making a lot of sense, to Thomas's way of thinking. Seemed like good wages for easy work. He took another sip of the whiskey.

"Are you interested?"

"I might be."

"Absolute confidentiality is required. You must tell no one either whom you are following or to whom you are reporting. Understood?"

"And how long does this go on?"

"I don't know yet. Perhaps a week or more."

Thomas nodded. "Sounds all right. But I can quit any time I choose."

"So long as you inform me. Don't just stop shadowing them without letting me know."

Thomas nodded.

Peterson slid a dollar across the table. "That's in advance. I'll pay you again at the end of a week or when the job ends, whichever comes sooner."

"All right—so who's the gent I'm following?"

Peterson smiled.

# CHAPTER 4

**E**lise opened the door between her hotel room and Lady Anne's carefully, but it creaked on its hinges anyway.

"Welcome. Did you learn anything?" Lady Anne smiled at her from the chair by the window, where she sat fully clothed. Her prayer book lay open on the small table before her.

Elise closed the door and stripped off her gloves. "I'm afraid not. The postmaster was no help, as we feared. He only repeated what he'd said in his letter to Mr. Conrad. There's no record of David inquiring for general delivery mail since he left the city ten years ago. The postmaster did send me to the police station, however."

"The police?" Anne's rich brown eyes darkened in dismay.

"Only because he thought they would have a record if anything untoward had happened to your uncle. I spoke to one of the constables there, but they knew even less than the postmaster. The consensus is that your uncle David left St. Louis of his own free will and either returned to England or went farther west."

Lady Anne sighed. "Well, we know he didn't go back to England."

"Do we?"

Her young mistress considered that while Elise opened her reticule and took out the folded sheet of paper on which she'd written the names of the people she'd questioned.

"We know he never contacted the family again," Lady Anne said at last. "I can't imagine Uncle David setting foot in England again without letting Father know."

"I agree. So, barring a shipwreck, he's still in America someplace, and that place is most likely westward." *Whether dead or alive,* Elise added to herself, but she wouldn't speak the thought to poor Anne, who had already lost so many loved ones.

"Why west? Isn't it possible he went back to New York or one of the other cities on the East Coast?"

"Yes," Elise said, "but everyone seems to think his more probable course was westward. I found out where his store was located. It was a sort of general store, selling a variety of goods—groceries, tools, yard goods."

Lady Anne inhaled deeply and leaned her head back, closing her eyes for a moment. "So what do we do now?"

Elise took the Windsor chair opposite her and spread her skirts around her. "I have a few suggestions. Some may be practical, some not."

Anne studied her face. "Proceed."

"We can inquire of the people who now run the store. It's given over to furniture and cabinetry now, but it's possible they might know something. And the constable suggested we send letters to officials in several western cities—San Francisco, Oregon City, and so on—making inquiries about David Stone. That would take time—we'd have to wait here for replies—and is a very uncertain method of locating a person of whose whereabouts we have no clue."

"True. Unless we find evidence that he went to a particular location—"

"Precisely." Elise smiled at her. "Which is why I recommend a different course. If we stay in St. Louis a couple of weeks, we can make a more thorough inquiry. We know David left here ten years ago, but we still might turn up someone who knew him better than Mr. Cobb or the postmaster. Someone to whom he mentioned his plans."

"How likely is that after all this time?"

"I don't know. However. . ." Elise leaned toward her, holding Anne's gaze. "The constable told me that wagon trains will be forming as soon as the ground is dried up enough for travel westward. Most of them leave from Independence or St. Joseph, which are two other towns on the western edge of Missouri. But many people will pass through here on their way to the encampments. Hundreds of families will be crossing the Great Plains, going to Oregon or

California, and we might make inquiries among them."

Anne cocked her head to one side, causing her fetching curls to sway. "Why would people going west know about someone who went ten years ago?"

"Not them. The ones organizing the wagon trains. The outfitters."

"I see. Uncle David may have gone west on a wagon train."

"Yes, and one of the outfitters may have met him or perhaps even guided him. Or they might have met him in their travels, since some of these men go back and forth across the plains almost yearly."

"I like it," Anne said.

"Good. Then we need to bide our time, decide whether to keep these lodgings or look for something more economical, and inquire at places like stables and wainwrights' shops about how to contact the outfitters. As a start, I saw a broadside hanging outside the emporium today, announcing a gathering of emigrants in Independence the first week in April. Those interested in joining the expedition were urged to contact a Mr. Robert Whistler, who will be at the Riverside Hotel afternoons this week. He will take a small caravan of people to Independence soon, where they'll join a larger group."

Lady Anne clapped her hands together. "Elise, you are so clever. Whatever should I have done without you? Surely if we seek out these wagon guides, we'll learn something."

"I hope so. And in the meantime, we pray."

"Of course. And eat. Are you hungry, my dear?"

"Yes. Are you?" Elise asked.

"Starved."

"You look much better than you did yesterday."

"I feel better, too. I would like to go down to the dining room with you and partake of luncheon there."

"All right. Just let me freshen up." Elise stood and went to the door.

"Elise," Lady Anne said.

"Yes?"

"Did you have a third plan?"

Elise chuckled self-consciously. "I did have a rather nebulous thought—but it's so farfetched that I wasn't going to suggest it unless this other plan fails."

"Oh?" Lady Anne nodded slowly. "Perhaps that is best. We have our course laid out for us."

Thomas G. Costigan sat on a keg of nails in Wyatt's General Merchandise, laconically watching the checker game in progress a few feet away and absorbing heat radiated by the tall stove in the center of the store. As long as the clutch of loiterers didn't get too big, the owner of the store encouraged them to stop by and socialize. That suited Thomas's plans perfectly.

His seat on a keg at the fringe of the hardware area allowed him a clear view of the counter to his right and several aisles of merchandise that ran the length of the store. James Wyatt, the store owner, had deliberately placed the most frequently purchased items at the far end of the room so that people in need of flour, cornmeal, or rolled oats had to walk through the store and pass displays of his most alluring merchandise—colorful woolen fabrics from New England; bulk tea and spices from the Far East; new books; medicines for man and beast; ready-made shoes; and the latest gadgets, tools, and notions.

Thomas could hear not only the talk around the stove, but also much of what was said at the counter without appearing to eavesdrop. And he could keep an eye on the tall woman with the brown hat as she moved about the store.

On this chilly morning in late March, the stunning woman had entered the store alone. He'd never seen her before. He would have remembered. But from the description Peterson had given him, he was sure. The cut of her clothes and her accent gave her away. She was the older of the two. The younger woman might have come out of the hotel and gone somewhere on her own—he had no idea. But he could only follow one at a time.

She browsed the textile display while Wyatt helped another customer, but she kept looking toward the counter. Thomas had no

35

doubt she'd step up to have a word with the storekeeper as soon as he was free.

She stood halfway down the store and one aisle over from where Thomas sat. Even when she walked behind a tall rack of ready-made garments, he could see the top of her distinctive hat. She rounded the display and headed across the row, past the bolts of cloth, high-topped shoes, and bins of ginger roots and walnuts. When she glanced his way, Thomas averted his gaze to the checker game. The checker players and the hangers-on were watching her, too. A faint scent wafted toward him, overcoming the cinnamon, coffee, and pickle brine just for a moment. Lilacs?

Thomas sneaked another glance. In the dim recesses of the emporium, her hair looked to be a light, golden brown, but he'd be willing to bet that on a sunny day outside, it was more blond. The woman carried herself well. Thomas was thirty-nine. She looked to be a little younger, but she also seemed to be one who took care of herself.

The checker players resumed their game. One of them made a move, and the spectators crowed. The other customer went out the door, and the woman strode toward the counter. Thomas strained to hear what the lovely lady said to James Wyatt.

"Oh, he's been gone a long time, ma'am," Wyatt said. "I do remember him. He was my competition for a while. He must have been in business about five years. He seemed to be doing all right. They say he imported some fancy goods from England, and some of the ladies liked his shop because of that. But one day, he decided to close up and leave."

"Did he sell the store?"

"I don't think he owned the building. It's a furniture store now." She nodded.

"Seems to me he held a sale when he went out of business, to sell off his inventory. That was a slow week for me, but I knew that once he was gone, I'd pick up some of his regular customers, so I rode it out."

"You've no idea where he went, or if he opened another store somewhere else?" the woman said.

The lady had a pronounced English accent—though a cultured one—and it was difficult to catch some of her words. To make matters worse, the chatter around the stove grew loud again.

Thomas stood and eased into the tool aisle and sauntered casually toward the entrance, keeping the row of display shelves between him and the counter. He paused before a rack of harness fittings, about four yards from where the lady stood. Her pinkish-tan skirt stood out around her. It looked to be velvet, or maybe a soft woolen material. Only the well-to-do women of St. Louis would wear something as fashionable. The poorer housewives wore plain wool or cotton dresses without those puffy petticoats underneath.

Over her dress, she wore a dark-brown, caped overcoat, and the matching brown hat sat atop her golden hair. She looked better than the sugar buns in Lars Neilsen's bakery window.

"I wish I could help you," Wyatt said, "but when Mr. Stone left, I didn't hear where he was going. Did you say you're a relation of his?"

"No," the lady said. "I'm a friend of his family. They've been trying to locate him for some time."

Wyatt nodded sympathetically. "I suppose you asked the postmaster if he left a forwarding address."

"Yes, that was one of the first things we did." The lady bowed her head for a moment. "Thank you for your time. Would you have any advice for someone in my situation?"

Wyatt shook his head. "Sorry, ma'am. If I was to guess, I'd have thought he went back to England. But from what you say, I'll have to change my theory. He might have gone west. Could have gone to California during the gold rush a few years back—lots of men did. And there's a lot of things that can keep a man from coming back."

A middle-aged woman with her arms full of sewing notions swooped down the center aisle toward the counter. Miss Finster, the Englishwoman, paid for a small purchase she'd apparently picked up during her wait. Thomas slipped out the door and across the street.

He leaned against the wall of a dentist's office and waited. A minute later, he was rewarded.

The Englishwoman came out of the emporium, carrying a small parcel wrapped in brown paper. She headed up the boardwalk. Thomas followed on his side of the street. When she turned a corner, he dashed across the cobbled thoroughfare and up onto the sidewalk where she'd been. Around the corner, he quickened his steps. For a moment, he'd lost her in a rash of pedestrians. Then he saw her again, near the end of the block. She walked quickly. No nonsense, that gal.

He hurried along, careful not to break into a run and attract attention. Three blocks later, he slowed. She'd turned in at a doorway. He sauntered along until he could read the sign clearly: Missouri Democrat. She'd gone into a newspaper office. Across the street was a bakery. The scents of yeast and chocolate hung in the air. Just the place he needed to keep watch in comfort.

Ten minutes later, Miss Finster came out of the *Democrat* office and retraced her steps a few blocks. Thomas had finished his sweet rolls and kept her in sight without difficulty. When she'd made two turns, he slowed down with a satisfied smile. She was headed for the Cinders, as he'd expected. Not the most plush hostelry, but a cut above what he'd be willing to pay for, and two above what most of the poor emigrants heading west could afford. He wondered if the younger woman, Miss Stone, was still inside. He looked around for a spot out of the wind where he could wait.

⁂

Eb Bentley sauntered across the paved street to the Riverside Hotel. He hated cobblestones. Hated cities. Hated big buildings. Give him the open West. Big sky, a good horse, distant mountains, and home waiting at the end of the day. Why had he let Rob Whistler talk him into doing this again, anyway?

As he dodged wagons and horsemen, he knew the answer. He needed the money. Enough to buy cattle to stock his ranch. The land was his, and his little house was built, but he needed cattle and fencing and a bigger barn and a thousand other things. Seemed the surest way to accomplish that was to do one more run across the plains with a wagon train—or perhaps a crawl across the plains was more accurate. Nothing moved slower than an emigrant wagon pulled by oxen.

He strode up the steps and into the hotel's lobby, taking his hat off as he ducked instinctively beneath the lintel. He rarely bumped his head on doorways here, but it had become a habit from entering small cabins and low-ceilinged ranch houses.

"Eb. Over here."

He swung toward the familiar voice. Rob was sitting on a horsehair sofa in an alcove across from the front desk, talking to two men in rough clothes. They all stood as Eb approached them.

"This is our scout, Eb Bentley," Rob told the others. "He'll be with us from Independence all the way to Oregon City."

The two nodded at him, and Eb sized them up. Farmers, both with brown hair and eyes, both solidly built. Brothers, maybe.

"These gentlemen are outfitting their wagons here. They want to bring their families with me to Independence," Rob said.

Eb nodded, keeping his own counsel. Most folks took the riverboat to Independence, up the Missouri. But some—usually those trying to save money—drove their wagons the two hundred miles across the state. The river journey on a steamer was certainly easier, and faster, too. But it did cost money, and some people didn't want to be confined so closely with others that long. He recalled a few years back when cholera ran through the ranks of emigrants and decimated the passenger population on the riverboats. Personally, he'd rather take his horse and make his own peaceful way to the rendezvous. Never liked boats much.

"Well, sir, I guess we'll see you tonight," one of the men said.

"Sure enough. Be at the field where I told you by sunset. Eb and I will come around and make sure everyone's ready. We head out at dawn." Rob shook hands with the two men and waved them off as they left the hotel.

"How many wagons?" Eb asked, plopping down in the chair one

of the men had vacated.

"Eight so far, and I've sent several families on ahead by boat."

"There'll be three or four times that waiting when we get to Independence."

"I expect so." Rob put two fingers in his vest pocket and extracted a folded paper. He opened it and squinted down at the writing. "I've had thirty-three families speak for a place on the train so far. There'll be more, and some of them will have more than one wagon."

"Don't let it get too big," Eb said.

"I plan to cut it off at fifty."

"Lot of wagons, even so. It'll be hard to find grazing."

"We'll be one of the first trains out."

Eb shook his head. "I dunno, Rob. You go too early, and there's no grass yet."

"Go too late, and it's all eaten up," his friend retorted. "It's all in the timing, and I think we've planned it just right this time. Not like last year. Waited too long last year, that's for sure. Now, I'll head out with these eight wagons tomorrow morning, and you make sure you're here every afternoon for three more days, in case anyone else comes to see about joining the train."

Eb nodded. They'd been over the plan a dozen times. Any latecomers would have to take the riverboat to Independence or catch a later wagon train.

Rob's forehead wrinkled as he gazed toward the entrance.

Eb swung around and looked over the back of his armchair. Rob was watching two women who had come into the lobby and now approached the desk.

They looked like quality—Eb wasn't an expert, but the fabric of their skirts looked rich and ample. They wore the spreading crinoline skirts that at first had seemed to him such an outlandish fashion. Every time he came to a city, he had to get used to the style again. The ladies seemed to puff their skirts out wider every year. They must have to work hard, carrying all those starched petticoats around with them. It made him wonder if the ladies wore those huge skirts to keep fellows a good distance away. They both wore bonnets, too. Not cotton poke bonnets, like the women on the wagon trains would wear, but fancy things with short netting veils and furbelows that probably served no practical function. Those hats wouldn't keep either sun or rain off the women's faces, so what good were they?

"That's a sight to behold," Rob said softly.

"You got no call to stare."

"No, you don't." Rob chuckled. "Did you get our supplies all laid by?"

"Sure did. I got a little extra horse feed."

"Good. We'd pay more in Independence. I've arranged with one of the wagon owners—a Mr. Leonard—to stow our grub in his wagon. It's just him traveling alone. He was glad to get a bit of cash for the space."

Rob raised his chin and stopped talking. Eb turned to see what he was staring at now.

The two women had walked over and now stood close behind Eb's chair. One hung back, a young woman of twenty or so, and pretty as a spring morning in the mountains, with dark hair, huge brown eyes, and a flawless complexion, so far as he could tell through the little veil. The older woman was past the flower of youth, but she'd held on to her beauty, with golden hair and rosy cheeks. Handsome woman, some would say.

"Mr. Whistler?"

Rob jumped up. "Yes, ma'am, I'm Robert Whistler."

Eb unfolded his long frame and stood, too.

"I am Elise Finster." The older woman sounded just a mite stuck-up, but in a flash Eb realized it was her accent. She sounded like a Britisher. She held out her gloved hand, and Rob took it—just the fingertips—and nodded.

"Ma'am."

"My friend and I"—she glanced fleetingly at the young woman—"have come to inquire about the wagon trains."

Eb almost choked. These two? On a wagon train?

Rob kept his composure. "Won't you sit down, ma'am? I'd be happy to answer any questions you may have."

Before Eb could have tightened a saddle cinch, the two ladies were seated on the chairs the farmers had sat in earlier. Rob resumed his seat, but Eb moved over near the wall and leaned against it, studying the two women. True quality, unless he was missing something, and definitely English. What on earth were they doing here?

"Allow me to introduce our scout, Mr. Edwin Bentley, usually known by his initials as 'Eb.'"

Both women looked at him. Eb nodded but said nothing. When he caught the older woman's frank gaze, he wished he'd put on his other shirt and washed off a layer of trail dust. Blue eyes with mysterious shadows in them—like the Blue Mountains in eastern Oregon, when you saw them from a distance.

"We understand you've led many wagon trains over the plains, Mr. Whistler," Miss Finster said.

"That's right." Rob leaned back a little and smiled. "This summer's trip will be my ninth across the plains." He craned his neck around. "What is it for you, Eb?"

"Seven."

Rob nodded. "Between us, we've got more experience than most anyone else you'll find, ma'am."

"That is just what we hoped for. You see, we're seeking a gentleman—my companion's uncle, actually—who we believe may have immigrated to Oregon. Or California. Or. . .well, you see our dilemma. We don't know exactly where he's gone. But we hoped you might, in all of your travels, have come across him."

Eb let out a deep sigh. So they weren't planning on going west themselves. That was a huge relief. All he and Rob needed was a couple of tender-skinned ladies to look after on the trail. But Rob wouldn't accept women unless they had men to drive and do for them. They'd talked about that after their first trip together and decided it was imperative that every wagon have at least one man attached to it.

"Ah, so you don't wish to make the journey yourselves," Rob said.

"Oh no, sir."

Rob nodded. "What is the name of the man you're looking for?"

"David Stone."

Rob's brow furrowed, and he shook his head slowly. "I don't recall anyone by that name." He looked over at Eb again. "Eb? Have you—"

"Don't think so. What'd he look like?"

Miss Finster smiled. "Miss Stone has a small portrait. Of course, the picture was made twenty years ago."

The younger woman opened a fancy mesh handbag and extracted a framed miniature portrait. Her friend took it and handed it to Rob.

"He's tall," Miss Finster said. "Your height or taller, and a very handsome young man. Well proportioned."

Was she blushing? What stake did she have in this quest other than acting as spokesman for the man's niece, who seemed quite timid?

"Did he have an English accent?" Eb asked.

Both women stared at him.

"Well, yes," Miss Finster said. "I suppose he did, though by then he'd been in America ten years or more. He owned a store here in St. Louis for a few years." She glanced at the younger woman and went on. "You see, he left England shortly after his niece was born. The family had several letters from him over a period of ten years. Half a dozen in all, perhaps. And then they stopped. The last one came from St. Louis, in early 1845."

Miss Stone nodded. "That's correct. We haven't heard a word from Uncle David since then."

Rob leaned back in his chair. "Ladies, I wish I could give you some definite news. I don't recall having this man along on any of my emigrant trains, and I think I'd remember an Englishman like that. But I have met a few English fellows in my travels." He turned to Eb. "Do you recall those two fellows who tagged along with us in 1850 until we came to the cutoff? They were headed for California, hoping to find gold."

"Irish," Eb said.

Rob frowned. "Are you sure? I thought they were from England."

Eb shook his head.

Rob shrugged. "Oh well. There are a lot of British people out in Oregon. England used to lay claim to the territory, you know."

Something stirred in Eb's memory. "I remember one fellow who had a general store in Oregon City for a while. You said this Mr. Stone ran a store here in Saint Louie?"

Both women turned eager faces toward him, and Eb's heart twanged. *Lord, don't let these ladies land on a wagon train. None of the men would want to do a lick of work between here and the Columbia. They'd all stand around gawking at the pretty faces.*

"The last time I was in that store must have been two or three years ago." Eb rubbed his chin and frowned, trying to think what the man had looked like.

"Do you recall his name?" Miss Finster asked.

"No, ma'am."

Rob said, "You must mean the man at Valley Mercantile."

"Right." There was no use getting the ladies' hopes up, but still . . .it could be the man they were looking for. Miss Stone's poignant expression heightened Eb's anxiety.

*Nope, can't let our herdsmen get a look at these two.*

Rob's face wrinkled. "I only saw that fellow once or twice."

"Same here," Eb said. "But he was tall, ma'am. Had light hair."

"That sounds like Uncle David," Miss Stone said.

Eb shrugged. "I don't know if he looked like that picture you have. Of course, I didn't know him well. I went in his store a couple of times. But it almost seems as though the last time I went in, somebody new was running the place."

Rob said, "You ladies are welcome to talk to the folks preparing to go with us on the wagon train. They're forming up at a field west of town."

"When will you leave?" Miss Finster asked.

"Early in the morning. It's not likely any of them knows Mr. Stone, but you never can tell who has connections out West these days."

Eb pushed away from the wall. "One other thing you could do."

"Yes?" Miss Finster and Miss Stone swiveled toward him.

"Seems to me that one Englishman would gravitate toward another. You could ask around for other English folks in the city. They might know your gentleman."

"Yes," said Miss Finster. "We could ask the hotel keeper and the postmaster and the police department for names of other British people. That makes sense, Mr. Bentley." She gathered her skirts and stood. "Thank you so much, gentlemen."

Miss Stone rose as well, holding her ridiculously tiny handbag before her.

"You're very welcome, ladies," Rob said heartily as he rose. "If you want to go out to the rendezvous field this afternoon, you'll find several emigrant families there you can talk to, but you might have better luck following Eb's suggestion. We pull out for Independence at dawn. That is, I do. Eb will be here a few more days, and then he'll catch up to us at Independence. If he can be of further assistance to you, just come here between one and four in the afternoon."

Miss Finster shook his hand as Rob rambled. Then she turned toward Eb and held out her dainty hand. He looked down at her spotless white glove and slowly reached out to grasp her fingers.

"Thank you, too, Mr. Bentley. You've been most helpful."

"It's nothing."

"Oh, it's something indeed. It's sound advice and courage you've given us. Isn't that right, Anne?"

The girl nodded—she wasn't much more than a girl. Though she was pretty, Eb felt she hadn't the substance her companion had. Miss Finster might be a highfalutin' lady, but there was something real about her. She probably couldn't make pie worth eating, but she wasn't going to quit looking for this David Stone until she'd exhausted all avenues. Whether her resolve was for the young lady's sake or her own, he couldn't tell.

"Good day, gentlemen, and thank you," Miss Stone said.

Neither Rob nor Eb pretended not to watch them as they glided smoothly toward the hotel entrance.

Rob let out a deep breath. "Now, those were ladies, Eb."

# CHAPTER 5

W e have to go to Oregon."

Lady Anne nodded slowly, surveying Elise with troubled eyes.

"That was my third plan all along," Elise said. "I know it's crazy, but we've tried everything else." She sat on the patchwork counterpane in her hotel room and spoke earnestly. If she couldn't persuade Anne now, the adventure was over, and David's fate would remain unknown. "We can't learn any more here, and we can't go home empty handed."

Lady Anne swallowed hard. "It's such a foreboding thought. I don't know if. . ."

"If what, dear?" Elise rose and went to stand beside her. They'd drawn so close over the last few weeks, sharing close quarters and their hopes and dreams. She laid a hand gently on Anne's shoulder. "What is it?"

Lady Anne's eyes glistened. "I'm not sure I'm strong enough."

Elise pressed her lips together for a moment, considering what she was asking of the young woman. "Before we left England, I might have agreed, but you're stronger than you were. I have confidence that you'll be able to find David. You were magnificent when we questioned all those people yesterday. I could see how the gentlemen at the newspaper office admired your pluck."

"I did feel as though they truly wanted to help us. It's a shame no one answered your advertisement."

"Yes. I had such hopes for that possibility." It seemed David Stone was forgotten in St. Louis. Elise tried to summon her own courage so she could keep buttressing Anne. "My dear, I don't think you could be content to go back across the ocean without knowing you'd tried everything."

Lady Anne drew in a shaky breath. "Perhaps you're right. But

I was so seasick. . . ."

"You're over that now."

"I know, but to catch Mr. Whistler and his caravan, we'd have to go to Independence. The only way to get there quickly and have time to buy a wagon and outfit it would be to go by riverboat, and I'm afraid I'd be ill again."

"The trip to Independence is only a few days. You can survive that. And you've done so much better since we arrived in St. Louis. Well, except for that one rainy day."

"Yes. Since the sun came out, I've felt quite well." Lady Anne stood and walked to the window. "Do you really think we could survive the rigors of the trail, Elise? The men we've spoken to have talked about huge mountains, and wolves, and—and Indians." She swung around and faced Elise. "What about the savages? Do you believe the stories?"

"I'm not sure."

Anne's eyes brightened. "Maybe we could go see Mr. Bentley again. We could ask him how difficult the trip really is."

"I fear we're too late. They said he'd be at the hotel three more afternoons. Wasn't today his last day?"

"Too bad."

"Yes. But Mr. Whistler's made the journey nine times." Elise smiled. "Either those men are superhuman, or the trip is doable for mortals like you and me."

Lady Anne squared her shoulders. "Well, we can't give up now. If we sail to Independence and can't find Uncle David, we have no other choice. We haven't any other promising leads. Only the man who rented the store to him."

"Yes." The man running the furniture store had directed them to his landlord, and that man had remembered one vital bit of information. "He sent David some money in Independence."

"But that doesn't mean he stayed there." Anne eyed her bleakly.

"No, and the store owner thought he recalled David saying he wanted to see Oregon. He sold the last of David's inventory for him and posted David's share to him in Independence. It's the first clue we'd found that named a destination."

Anne grimaced. "I had hoped that couple from Dorset could be of more help to us. And the newspaper ad didn't help. I'm sure if Uncle David was still in the vicinity, we'd have caught wind of him by now."

"I think so, too. So then. . .we're agreed?" Elise watched Lady Anne's face carefully.

Her young mistress nodded. "I only hope I shall not fail you, Elise. You've done so much for me."

"But this is for you. For the Stone family."

Lady Anne's smooth brow furrowed. "It's for both of us. I dare you to say otherwise."

Thomas G. Costigan looked over his shoulder before entering the Horsehead. No one was following him—but then, why would they? He smiled grimly and ducked inside. The low-ceilinged room was dim and smoky. He saw Peterson at a small table in the back corner. Thomas stopped at the bar for a glass of whiskey and carried it to the table and sat down.

"Well?" Peterson asked.

"They've made inquiries all over town, but they haven't turned up anything solid."

Peterson swore. "My own efforts have been no more successful. Where did they go today?"

"They hired a buggy and driver and went to several private residences and a few shops. And they went back to the newspaper office. I was able to hear a snatch of their conversation when they left there. Seems that ad they took out a few days ago hasn't gained them anything."

"I was hoping."

Thomas fished a folded piece of paper from his pocket and passed it to Peterson. "Here's where they went today." He smiled at the memory of the afternoon he'd spent trailing them about the city. "The older one—Miss Finster?"

Peterson nodded.

"She had the driver give her a lesson on the way back to the livery."

"Really? A lesson in driving?"

"Yup. Independent, that one. She's a fine-looking woman though. They both are." Thomas had to wonder why the handsome Miss Finster was still unmarried. Those fellows in England must be blind.

Peterson lifted his glass and took a swallow. "All right, stay on the job."

Thomas nodded. "They seem to make an early night of it."

"As proper ladies should."

Peterson didn't suggest that he should keep watch once the ladies retired to the hotel in the evening, and Thomas was glad of that.

"What if they give up and go back to England?"

"Then your job ends." Peterson scowled. "And mine will have only begun."

Thomas inhaled slowly as he watched the thin man. Peterson definitely hoped these two women would lead him to David Stone. But why? What was so important that this man would continue the search even if Stone's loved ones gave it up?

<hr />

Independence was a rough and rowdy town with growing pains. No cobblestones here. No horse cars or fancy shops.

Eb's boot heels thudded on the bare boards as he mounted the steps to the Kenton House. Rob Whistler was still on the road with the emigrant train they'd formed in St. Louis. He didn't need Eb to scout for them on this leg, so he'd ridden past the caravan and on ahead to check on the rendezvous field and secure permission to use the hotel lobby as an office for a few days.

"Mr. Bentley!" The desk clerk's call drew Eb's attention, and he strode over to see what the fellow wanted.

The short man behind the desk smiled at him. "You have some callers."

"Already?" Eb wished they'd wait for Rob to arrive. He didn't have the easy manner with farmers and haberdashers that Rob had.

The clerk nodded toward the sitting area behind him. "Yonder. I must say they're classy ladies."

Ladies? Eb turned slowly. A woman in a gray-and-cream-striped silk dress with an emerald-green cape and a green hat rose from one of the chairs and smiled at him. Her full skirt swayed gently, and her blue eyes sparkled.

"Hello, Mr. Bentley."

"Miss Finster?"

She nodded. Beyond her, Miss Stone sat demurely on another chair.

A week had passed since he'd seen the two women in St. Louis, but here they were in Independence, looking as lovely and well groomed as ever. He'd been sure they'd give up the search for Miss Stone's uncle.

"We decided to continue our journey," Miss Finster said.

Eb did some quick calculations. He'd have seen them on the road if they'd driven. "You must have taken the steamer."

"That's correct." Miss Finster's face skewed for a moment, and he gathered that the voyage had been cramped and unpleasant, but she said no more about it. "The best information we could gather was from you, sir, with your description of the Englishman in Oregon City. That and a possible clue from the gentleman who owns the building David Stone leased for his store in St. Louis. We've pinned our hopes on those bits of news."

Eb's heart sank. He didn't want to be responsible for their disillusionment. "Now, ma'am, you've got to understand, I'm not at all sure that was him. I don't know his name or where he went to or anything."

"We realize that. But La—that is, my companion, Miss Stone, feels very strongly that she must do everything within her power to locate David. It's a family matter, you see."

Eb didn't see at all. He had a raft of cousins back in New Hampshire himself, but he didn't feel compelled to go see them.

He'd had no news of his family in years.

Miss Stone came over to stand beside her friend. "We did seek out other British citizens as you suggested. We found several during our time in St. Louis. One woman who married an American attorney remembered David Stone."

"Well now. I expect that was an encouragement."

"Yes."

Miss Finster smiled, and the transformation of her face almost made Eb glad she'd found him again. Her features formed such a pleasant view that he could stand and watch her face for a long time, the way he did sometimes in the Cascades, watching the sun dip behind the high peaks, leaving purple and orange streaks on the snowcaps.

"Indeed it was, sir. Mrs. Stanley told us that she and her husband invited Mr. Stone to dinner once so that they could talk about England, and a pleasant evening they had."

"But she didn't know what became of him?" Eb asked.

"We feel that what she told us confirms—or at least adds to—what you said. David Stone decided about ten years ago to sell his business and go farther west." Miss Finster shrugged. "The Stanleys couldn't tell us any more. They'd never heard from David after he left, but they were sure he would head for the Pacific and probably open a store there, as he'd done fairly well here in that line."

"I guess that makes sense, but I still—"

"Which is why we want to join the wagon train for Oregon." Miss Stone's eyes widened as though she was shocked at her outburst. Her gloved hand flew to her lips.

Miss Finster smiled. "Yes. That's exactly what we want to do. It's why we came here to see you, Mr. Bentley. What do we need to do to join your wagon company?"

Eb stared at her. "You. . .uh. . .you want to—" A vision of the two refined ladies gathering buffalo chips for their campfire flickered across his mind. "Oh no, ma'am. That's not possible."

"The nerve of that man." Elise could barely contain her ire as she and Lady Anne marched down the boardwalk in search of a livery stable. "He has no right to tell us we can't go."

Lady Anne scurried to catch up.

"I'm sorry." Elise slowed her pace. "I'm so incensed with that—that—scout."

Lady Anne chuckled. "Dear Elise. I felt certain you'd come out with some vulgar name, but it isn't in you, is it?"

"I guess not, but if we start hobnobbing with teamsters, I may learn a few earthy expressions to use on Mr. Bentley."

"I know it's upsetting," Anne said, "but if it's Mr. Whistler's policy, we'll have to abide by it."

"I think Eb Bentley's making it up." Elise paused at the end of the boardwalk and peered at the rutted dirt street below them. At least the roadway they had to cross wasn't a river of mud like the one they'd encountered in St. Louis two weeks ago.

"He said Mr. Whistler has made it his policy since his first trip across the plains, when he had so much trouble with a widow woman who couldn't control her own livestock." Lady Anne's reminder came out gently, in a ladylike tone.

Elise frowned. "I know, but I intend to go ahead with our plans. If we need a man to drive our wagon, we'll hire one." She threw Anne an apologetic glance. "That is, if you wish to and you think we can afford it."

"I believe we can. Once we know how much a wagon and team will cost, we'll have a better idea."

Elise nodded. Lady Anne would not be able to collect more money from her trust until the first of the year—a long nine months from now. She'd taken all she could from the bank before they left England. They had to plan carefully, or they might run out of funds in the middle of the wilderness. If only they didn't need to hire a man. She'd learned the rudiments of driving a horse. Surely it couldn't be that difficult—after all, the wagons would move slowly.

"Well, Mr. Whistler should be in Independence the day after tomorrow. We'll get the full story from him on what's required."

"Yes. I'm sure he'll let us go if we just adhere to his rules." Lady Anne patted her arm.

"There's a bakery shop," Elise said. "Let's stop there and ask directions to the nearest stable. That Eb Bentley was rather vague about where we could buy our equipment. I'll tell you right now, I don't trust him."

# CHAPTER 6

**E**b was surprised at the relief he felt when the wagon train came in sight. He'd ridden out two miles from town to meet Rob and the emigrants. The white dots crawling down a hill in the distance were covered wagons approaching from the east. He trotted his spotted gelding, Speck, toward them and soon distinguished Rob's form at the head of the convoy. The man on the tall chestnut horse wore his usual wide-brimmed black hat and a red neckerchief that stood out from the dullness of the scene.

Speck cantered willingly toward the train. Eb pulled him up and swung around to ride side by side with Rob.

"Howdy," Rob said.

"You made it."

"Sure did."

Eb looked over his shoulder at the wagons that were strung out single file behind them. "Looks like more than eight wagons."

Rob grinned. "Twelve. The Harkness family added one, so they've got three in all, and the Adams brothers each have their own wagon. We added two more families between St. Louis and here."

Eb nodded. It happened a lot. Families who'd been waiting for the season to start joined up with the first train that came through.

"There's already twenty-eight at the field. More coming in every day."

"Good," Rob said. "Can we pull out Monday?"

Eb grimaced. "Not sure. Several people have come to ask me about going. Some of them aren't ready."

"Did you give them the list of supplies and equipment?"

"Yup."

Rob nodded. "If they're ready by next Monday, we'll take 'em. But I won't let anyone start off half-cocked. Not on my train."

"Well. . ."

Rob's eyes narrowed as he studied Eb. "What?"

"Those ladies."

"What ladies?" Rob scowled at him fiercely—a sure indicator his patience was wearing thin—probably as thin as the seat of the twill pants Rob favored when he rode horseback all day. Not a good sign when they hadn't even reached Independence.

"The English ones."

"English?" Rob pulled his head back, and his eyebrows nearly collided. "You mean those two gals in St. Louis? Miss Stone and Miss. . .Miss Finster, wasn't it?"

"They're the ones. Only they're not in St. Louis anymore. They're here."

Rob jerked back on his reins, and his chestnut stopped abruptly. "How can they be here? I left them healthy and beautiful in Saint Louie last week."

"Took the steamer." Eb let Speck keep walking, and Rob had to trot Bailey to catch up with him.

"All right, so they're here. What's going on? Are they still looking for Miss Stone's uncle?"

"Yup."

They went on in silence for a few steps.

"Well?" Rob's voice rose.

"Well, what?"

"Edwin Bentley, you are the most irritating man I know. If you weren't such a good scout, I'd trade you in for someone else. Someone who'd speak up and say what he meant instead of dropping little nuggets on the trail."

Eb had to chuckle at that. "You know me, Rob. I ain't no prospector, and I ain't a big talker."

"You're also not usually a man who butchers the English language. What's up with those English ladies? There's got to be some reason you brought up the subject, or were you just awestruck by their pulchritude and had to share your devotion with me?"

"Haw. They want to get a wagon and go west."

Rob's jaw dropped.

Eb said quickly, "I told them you'd say no, on account of they've got no man to drive them."

"Whoa, whoa, whoa." Rob's gelding stopped dead. "Not you, you lunkheaded nag!" He kicked Bailey, and the chestnut began walking again.

Eb shoved his hat back. "They're single ladies. I told them it's your longstanding policy not to let women attempt the crossing without a man to handle their livestock."

"Well, yes, but—"

"What do you mean, 'but'?" Eb glared at him. He'd had a bad feeling about this. Ever since they'd met the ladies, Rob had kept bringing up how dainty and courteous they were, almost like he wished he'd see more of them, which didn't make sense, because Rob had a perfectly good wife waiting for him at home in Oregon. Maybe Miss Stone's story had stirred his heart and he was feeling magnanimous. Eb hoped it wasn't something more than that.

Ever since he'd gotten his wife, Dulcie, safely to Oregon a couple of years ago, Rob had hinted that Eb should find married bliss as well. He wouldn't be thinking along those lines now, would he? Miss Stone was too young for men their age—Eb was pushing forty pretty hard, and Rob was a couple of years older. But Miss Finster—well, if the herd was culled according to age, he suspected she'd be in the holding pen with him and Rob. And if Rob was getting notions about having an eligible woman in Eb's age range along on the trek to Oregon, he would have to put a stop to that right now.

"You can't think of letting them set out alone. Why, those women have never done a lick of work in their lives. They're ladies."

Rob smiled. "Oh, I suspect they can ply a needle and maybe even bake a cake."

"Ha! Not likely."

Rob was unsuspecting; that was it. When it came to dealing with men, he knew a pickpocket or a professional gambler when he saw one, and he could weed out the greenhorns on the wagon train quicker than you could wolf down a flapjack. But women? His friend had a soft spot. He always voted in favor of helping widows and ladies in distress. And when a woman started crying, watch out! That's why Rob had made the policy in the first place—so he could invoke it when his emotions threatened to beat the stuffing out of his logic.

"So you discouraged them?" Rob asked.

Eb thought about that. The ladies hadn't looked too glum when they'd left him. In fact, Miss Finster had an irate spark in her eye that made her look, if anything, more handsome.

"It wouldn't surprise me if they came 'round to question you about your rules. They're set on going out to look for Mr. Stone."

"They should go by ship," Rob said.

"Around the horn?" Eb couldn't imagine the proper ladies undergoing that ordeal.

Rob shrugged. "They sailed across the Atlantic, and you said they took the steamer here. Sounds like they're right at home on boats."

"Why don't you suggest that to them?"

"Maybe I will."

"Good."

The buildings on the outskirts of Independence came into view, and Eb shot Rob another glance. Better be on hand when the ladies confronted him, or that old soft spot might come to the fore. And Eb was determined not to guide a gaggle of helpless females through Indian Territory.

Try as she might, Elise hadn't been able to discover where the wagon master and his scout were lodging. She'd thought they must be at the Kenton House, since that was where she and Anne had found Mr. Bentley a couple of days ago. But this morning the clerk told her the gentlemen weren't actually staying at the hotel, and he didn't think they'd be in today.

The town was half-grown and a bit on the wild side. The ladies had traipsed about to several hotels and boardinghouses and found no trace of Whistler and Bentley.

"You might try out at the rendezvous field," the owner at the last place had suggested. "If they've got a wagon train that's leaving soon, they're probably sleeping right there on the ground."

And so they went to the livery stable and inquired about renting a horse and buggy with a driver.

"Got no driver available," the liveryman said.

Elise swallowed hard. "Well, then I suppose I shall have to drive myself."

Anne's eyes grew round, but she kept her peace, for which Elise was thankful.

The liveryman looked her over doubtfully. "Are you sure, ma'am?"

"Yes, sir, I am. I should like a well-behaved horse though."

"Yes, ma'am." He named a price which seemed to Elise exorbitant.

"That's more than we paid in St. Louis, with a driver included."

The man spat on the ground. "This ain't Saint Louie, ma'am. Do you want the rig or not?"

"Yes."

Elise and Anne waited while the man harnessed the horse to a small single-seat buggy with a black cloth top. At least they would have some protection from the fickle sun.

"Are you certain it's safe to go alone?" Anne whispered.

"I learned the rudiments of driving," Elise said. "We need to consult Mr. Whistler today. I don't feel we have another choice. And with a calm horse, what can go wrong?"

The owner led out the sorriest-looking animal Elise had ever seen. Its back curved lower than normal, and she could easily count its ribs behind the leather tugs.

Anne, who had regularly ridden her father's hunters to hounds, also eyed the horse askance. "That animal doesn't look healthy," she ventured.

"Take it or leave it."

Anne looked to Elise with questioning eyes.

"We'll take it." Elise was surprised by her own grim determination. She went to the buggy, held up her skirt, and climbed in. The liveryman had the grace to give Anne a hand up on the other side.

"Good day, ladies. I'll expect you and Prince back before sunset."

Elise decided it would do no good to comment on the pitiful horse's regal name. "Shouldn't I have a whip or something?"

The man frowned at her. "Naw, you'll be all right. Just snap the reins on his flanks and he'll go."

"All right," she said dubiously. "And if you'd be so kind, sir, would you repeat the directions to the wagon train's field for me one more time?" He did, and Elise tried to memorize the roads and landmarks he named.

"You can't miss it," he concluded.

Elise gathered the reins. With her mouth, she made the clicking sound she'd heard coachmen make many times. When Prince didn't move, she jiggled the reins and then flicked them so that they slapped against the horse's thin rump. Prince walked toward the street.

"There." Elise smiled over at Anne. "We should be there in no time."

She soon discovered that Prince had a mind of his own. Whenever Elise pulled on one rein, indicating he should turn, he obstinately tried to continue in a straight path. If they came to a broad, open place, he curved around, trying to head back toward the livery stable.

As they reached the outskirts of town, the horse veered to the edge of the road to avoid an oncoming wagon and sent one wheel off the edge and into a shallow ditch. Elise gasped and snapped the reins.

"Get up, you!"

Startled, Prince leaped forward and hauled the buggy back onto the roadway. Elise let him continue at a trot and concentrated on keeping him moving straight. After a few yards, however, he dropped back into his sluggish walk.

She looked over at Anne, who still clutched her hat to her head. "All right?"

Anne nodded and straightened on the seat. Her countenance smoothed out. "I'm sure we're fine."

They continued on sedately, but the moment's terror was not easily forgotten. Elise's confidence flagged. Her arms ached from tugging on the lines and flicking them often in her futile efforts to convince the horse to trot again.

They'd been out an hour when Anne looked uneasily toward the small copse of trees they were passing. "Perhaps we missed it after all. They can't be this far out of town, can they?"

"As soon as I find a place wide enough, I shall turn this animal around." Elise gritted her teeth. There might be highwaymen lurking about, or even savages. She'd been foolish not to insist on a driver, even if that meant finding a different livery stable. The open country seemed limitless, and she shivered.

She found a place where she could turn safely off the road and guide the horse around in a wide circle. When they had lurched back onto the road, she flicked the reins. Pointed toward home once more, Prince stepped out in a smarter walk.

Eb was checking over a New York family's oxen when the buggy rolled into the field. He nodded to Mr. Woolman and wandered over to where Rob was talking to the Adams brothers. Eb began whistling "London Bridge Is Falling Down."

"Hmm?" Rob arched his eyebrows at Eb then looked beyond him. "Aha." He strolled toward the buggy, driven by a windblown and very attractive Miss Finster.

Eb tore his gaze away and nodded to the Adamses. "So, you got your supplies all laid in?"

"Mostly," said Hector, the elder brother. "We need to pick up a few more foodstuffs between now and Monday." The "boys" were in their thirties, and Daniel usually let his brother do the talking while he stood by and nodded.

"Good work." Eb ambled on to the next wagon, a little closer to where Rob was engrossed in conversation with Miss Finster and Miss Stone. He stooped and pretended to examine the axle nut on the wagon's front wheel.

"Well, now, Eb tells me he informed you about my rule," Rob said. "Ladies who haven't got a man along to drive and do the heavy work for them aren't allowed."

"He did mention it," Miss Finster replied, "but you must have a way for women to circumvent that. There must be women who need to go out and join their husbands, or widows who want to take their families out and begin farming."

"Not so many as you'd think," Rob said. "They know how hard it is without a man along. I've had a few instances where a man died along the trail and his womenfolk had to continue on without him. That's a little different. But it's always hard, and it puts hardship on the others in the train to look out for them."

"We're self-sufficient, I assure you, sir."

Rob shook his head. "I'm sorry, ladies, but it would be asking for trouble. Neither of you has much experience in overland travel, and it would slow us down. Maybe you should think about going downriver to New Orleans and taking a ship."

"What if we could hire a man to go along and work for us?" Miss Finster asked. "Is that ever done? Get someone who can tend to the animals and do some of the driving?"

Rob pushed his hat back on his head. "Well, yes, it's possible. You might find a man who wants to go west but hasn't the money to outfit a wagon for himself. But you need to make sure you get someone you can trust and who'll work hard."

Miss Finster glanced toward her companion and cleared her throat. "That's what we'll do. Can you recommend someone?"

"Why, ma'am, I don't live here. I don't know too many people in town. But you could ask at the livery or put up a broadside at the post office. But you'll have to get right on it. We pull out Monday morning, no matter what."

"Oh dear," said Miss Stone.

"That is soon," Miss Finster agreed. "What exactly would we need, assuming we found a driver?"

"Well, ma'am, I can give you a list of supplies. You'd have to figure foodstuffs for yourselves and your hired hand. Of course, the first thing you'd need would be a wagon and a team of oxen or mules."

Eb straightened and stared at Rob's back. He couldn't be doing this—but he was. Probably they'd wind up with a couple of old mules with heaves. Someone wanting to unload some bad stock would see them as an easy mark. The swaybacked horse they drove today was proof of that.

Rob left them and strode to where he'd tied his saddled horse. Eb intercepted him while he fished in his saddlebag.

"What on earth are you doing, Rob?"

"I'm getting a copy of the supply list for the ladies."

"You can't let them go with us."

"They said they'd hire a driver."

"Oh, I suppose they'll find a man of sterling character on three days' notice."

Rob shrugged. "I can't refuse them if they meet the requirements."

"Of course you can."

"I won't."

Eb nodded in silence. Rob had tossed his good judgment aside because of a couple of pretty faces with a tragic story. Poor Miss Stone had her heart set on finding her long lost uncle, and they'd convinced Rob that, with his help, they could find him.

"Excuse me," Rob said with exaggerated politeness. "I need to explain to these ladies what they need to do in order to join this wagon train."

Eb watched him go. The ladies bowed and simpered when he gave them the paper—or so it seemed to Eb.

Miss Finster's smile faded as she perused the list. "Oxen? Oh dear. Must we?"

"Or mules," Rob said affably. "Oxen cost less and hold up better on grass. Mules generally need some grain, so you'd have to buy that and carry it along."

"Neither of us has much experience with cattle," Miss Finster said.

Her young companion asked, "Couldn't we use horses, Mr. Whistler? I've been around horses since I was a child."

Rob shook his head. "Horses don't generally last well on the trail. It's a very rough trip, pulling a heavy wagon. They need too much feed and too much rest. Sounds like you'd do best with mules though, if you've never been around cattle."

"Mules would do the job, would they?" Miss Finster asked. "Aren't they balky?"

"They can be, but generally they'll follow along if the other animals are moving."

"Where would we buy a mule team?" Miss Stone asked.

"There's a couple of livery stables in Independence, and you'll find other traders about if you look. But be careful they don't try and fleece you."

The two women looked at each other doubtfully.

"How would we know?" Miss Finster asked.

"Well, right now a good mule oughtn't to cost you more than seventy-five or eighty dollars. Oh, they up the prices out here. You might have done better in Saint Louie."

"Yes, but we didn't know for certain then that we wanted to make the trip." Miss Finster looked so sad that Eb almost wished he could cheer her up. But he didn't really want to mix with them any more than he had to. He still hoped they would see the folly of attempting this adventure and back down.

"Of course, if you use mules, you'll need harness, too," Rob said. "All of that costs money."

"Oh well, that. . ." Miss Finster threw Miss Stone a quick glance. "I believe we're all right in that department, sir."

Rob looked over his shoulder and called, "Say, Eb."

Eb kicked himself for not making himself scarce. He walked over and touched the brim of his hat.

"Good day, Mr. Bentley." Miss Finster almost smiled but then seemed to think better of it. No doubt she remembered his words of discouragement.

"Eb, you told me which stores have the packages of supplies all made up for the emigrants," Rob said. "Whyn't you tell these ladies so they can save some time over shopping for all the individual items?"

"Well now, that'd be Ingram's or Blevin's. Of course, they don't sell wagons or livestock."

"No, but once they have their wagon, they'll need to fill it quickly, so they'll be ready to pull out with us."

Eb nodded, still unconvinced. "You ladies sure you're up to this? It's an arduous undertaking."

"Why yes, Mr. Bentley, I believe we are. I guess our ability to find and outfit a wagon in the next few days will be a test of sorts." Miss Finster's blue eyes held a spark, or maybe they just caught the glint of the sun.

"I guess it will." Eb held her determined gaze.

Miss Stone leaned toward her friend and peered at the list. "Bacon. Do we really need that much?"

"Well, bacon will keep a long time if you pack it right," Rob said. "The men on the train will hunt some fresh meat, but it's good to have enough staples along in case we don't get any game for a while."

"What about chicken?" Miss Finster looked at the younger woman with a worried frown—almost like a mother worrying over her child.

"Some folks take chickens in a coop tied to the side of their wagons," Eb said. "But are you ladies up to butchering your own fowl?"

Miss Finster glared at him. "We dainty things are up to whatever is necessary, Mr. Bentley."

"I see." Eb glared back, until Rob jabbed him in the ribs with his bony elbow.

"One hundred fifty pounds of flour. . .each?" Miss Stone turned her questioning gaze from the list to the wagon master.

"That's right." Rob shrugged. "Of course, that's an average. You ladies might need a bit less, but to be on the safe side. . . And that way, if you have a little extra, you can share with those who meet with misfortune."

"Corn *and* cornmeal," Miss Stone muttered. "Saleratus?" She looked up at Rob with a look of confusion.

"For cooking, miss. Baking soda."

"Oh."

"And we need all these tools?" Miss Finster asked.

"Every wagon needs to carry spare parts and tools to fix their gear with," Rob said. "But since you ladies don't plan to settle in Oregon, you won't be hauling furniture or farming equipment like some do. You might be able to sleep in your wagon all the way, but I'd bring a tent. An extra wagon cover, too."

"Such a lot of stuff," Miss Finster said as she looked down at the paper.

Miss Stone caught her breath.

"What is it?" Miss Finster asked.

Miss Stone pointed to the list. "It says women may take two dresses. Two." She stared into her friend's eyes. "And woolen at that."

"Well now, that's not chiseled in stone," Rob said, "though you do want to keep your wagon as light as possible. Woolen material holds up well, and the nights will be cold."

Miss Finster cleared her throat. "Since we won't have any furniture or a plow in our wagon, perhaps we'll be able to expand the wardrobe option a bit." She and Miss Stone continued to study the list.

Eb turned away, unable to stay put until they read the underwear allowance and howled in protest. Those ladies would probably bring an extra wagon along just to hold their extra petticoats.

As he walked away toward where he'd left Speck, he heard Miss Stone tell Rob solemnly, "I assure you, Mr. Whistler, we shall succeed in being good travelers, and we won't slow down the wagon train."

Eb scooped up his horse's reins and hopped into the saddle, not sure where he was going. Anyplace where those refined, would-be pioneer ladies couldn't see him steam.

He headed for the path that led to the creek. Before he entered the scattering of trees, he looked back. Apparently Rob was done giving advice. Miss Finster urged the horse into a reluctant walk. The buggy made a wide turn and nearly clipped one of the wagons before they were headed back toward Independence.

Eb shook his head. "Come on, Speck. Let's get you a drink." More than ever, he wished he'd stayed in Oregon on his little ranch. But he was in it now.

Rob found him a quarter of an hour later, helping a family completely repack their wagon. The greenhorns had no idea of how to go about it. Heaviest stuff on the bottom, along with the bacon and other food supplies that needed to stay as cool as possible. Lightweight stuff on top. Eb had tried to talk them out of taking a big cupboard, but the wife insisted it was going with her.

"My grandmother brought it from Cornwall," Mrs. Harkness declared. "If I can't take it to Oregon with me, I'm not going."

"Then lay it down in the wagon bed and fill it with your tools and other heavy stuff."

"Books?" Mr. Harkness asked.

"You're taking books?" Eb asked.

"Only one crate." Mr. Harkness touched the wooden box in question with the toe of his shoe.

"That's a big box."

"We have to have books." Mrs. Harkness's voice grew more shrill each time she spoke. "How will the children do their schooling without books?"

Eb was relieved to see Rob approaching. "Well, whyn't you ask the wagon master? You folks have three wagons, and you're loading them mighty heavy. Those river crossings and mountain passes will do you in."

"Eb's right," Rob said, as if he'd heard the entire conversation—but then, he had, a hundred times. "You'd do better to sell some things here and have the cash than to leave them beside the trail in the Rocky Mountains."

"Oh no, not the books." Mrs. Harkness put her foot up on the crate and folded her arms across her chest.

"All right then," Rob said. "Make sure your wagon box is watertight, and stow that crate low in the wagon, like Eb said."

They helped heft cargo for the Harknesses and walked away a half hour later, tired to the bone.

"Mr. Leonard's wagon is yonder," Rob said. "What say we get our bedrolls out and have something to eat?"

They walked to Abe Leonard's wagon and pulled out their bundles.

"Where you want to make camp?" Rob asked.

"I slept over there last night." Eb pointed. "Made a fire pit." As they walked toward it, he said, "You should have turned them down flat, you know."

"Who? The Harkness family?"

"No, the English ladies. They'll never make it to Oregon."

"If they hire a man to handle the livestock for them, I can't see why we should object to having them along."

"Oh, you don't, do you? Isn't it obvious that they've never done a lick of work in their lives? Those are highborn women, used to being waited on hand and foot."

"You don't know that."

"Oh don't I just?" They reached Eb's fire pit, and he kicked at the charcoal in the bottom. "They can't harness a team."

"Miss Stone said she'd been around horses."

"Oh sure. Likely riding sidesaddle in the park, wearing a fancy velvet habit. And you can bet your boots she had a groom tacking up the horse for her."

"Well, Eb, they're healthy women, and apparently they have the means to buy a stout rig. I won't deny them a place on the train, and I don't see why you're so upset about this."

"I'll tell you why. You've always insisted that the best way to get everyone through to Oregon is to not accept any weaklings in the first place. Those women are trouble. They'll mean more work for us and possibly tragic results. But that doesn't matter to you. Two pretty ladies smile at you and charm you with their cute accents, and you're falling over backward to accommodate them."

"I resent that."

"Sure you do. Dulcie would have your hide if she knew."

"Dulcie knows how hard the trail is, but she wouldn't deny those women a place in our company. Not if they obey the rules. I expect she'd cheer them on. And I might add, it's encouraging to me that you noticed how pretty they are. Maybe there's hope for you yet."

Eb scowled at him. "Just watch yourself, Robert."

Rob pulled his hat off and wiped his brow with his sleeve. "All right, Eb. Let's leave Dulcie out of this. My wife has nothing to worry about. And if those ladies come back without an able-bodied man, I won't let them go."

"Promise?"

"You have my word."

"All right, but when they need help hauling water or starting a fire or plucking one of their precious chickens, I won't be the one helping them, ya hear?"

"I hear you. Now, why don't you fetch us some kindling, and I'll set up to cook supper. Mrs. Libby gave me some dried apple pastries. Might be a while before we taste that kind of cooking again."

Eb went off to the edge of the field to look for some dry twigs. Within a couple of weeks, the area would be bare of anything burnable. People would have to buy firewood from enterprising locals who came around to peddle it while folks camped here and waited for their wagon trains to pull out.

He mulled over what Rob had said, and he still didn't like it. Not one bit.

But he wasn't in charge, and that was his choice. Eb didn't like being in charge because the wagon master had to deal with all the complaints and the people who broke the rules. The scout got to ride ahead and get away from the grumblers all day if he had a mind to. In order to hold that position, he had to let Rob be in charge.

# CHAPTER 7

Elise opened one eye. Indirect sunlight seeped through the thin muslin curtain at the window and filled the room. She sat up cautiously so as not to fall off the edge of the narrow bed. All night she'd kept as far over as she could, trying to avoid touching her mistress.

Lady Anne rolled over with a little moan and opened her lovely brown eyes. "Is it morning?"

"Yes, my dear. I'm afraid you haven't slept well, and I apologize."

"For what?"

Elise grimaced. "For having to share a bed with you, and such a small one at that."

Lady Anne sat up and shoved the blanket aside. "It's not your fault."

"This room isn't fit for a lady of consequence."

Her mistress chuckled. "I'm afraid any 'consequence' I once had is gone, Elise. And I chose to come to this wild place, remember? I intend to show you and those—those frontiersmen that I'm made of as stern stuff as the American women."

"Frontiersmen? Oh, you mean Mr. Whistler and Mr. Bentley."

"Yes, those two. They seem to think we're made of glass. That Eb Bentley has taken a notion that we can't either one of us cook or drive a wagon or do anything else useful."

"Well. . ." Elise swallowed hard. "I must admit that cooking is not my strongest talent. I can make tea and scones and boil an egg. That's about it."

"It's more than I can do." Lady Anne blinked at her. "Do you think he's right? Are we useless?"

"Not at all. Because we can learn. When we go to the general store today, I shall ask if they have a cookery book. One that tells you how to make meals over an open fire." She rubbed her sore arms and forbore to mention her newly acquired driving skills.

"That's a good idea." Lady Anne scooted to the edge of the bed and swung her legs down. "Oh Elise, we've got to fit our trunks in."

"Never fear, my dear. We shall have our fripperies and enough foodstuffs to get us across the continent. I'm not sure about chickens though. Mr. Bentley might have a point there."

"Nonsense," Anne said. "We just need to find a man who can butcher *and* drive mules. Surely that's not too much to ask."

"Perhaps you're right. But we need to find someone today. We've only four days to prepare, and one of those is the Lord's Day."

The hotel served a sketchy breakfast of pancakes, sausage, and coffee. Elise choked down half a sausage patty and left the rest on her plate, instead filling her stomach with the bland pancakes. Lady Anne delicately spooned applesauce over her pancake, something she would never have done in the breakfast room at Stoneford, and poured a generous dollop of milk into her mug of coffee. Elise only hoped they could find better fare somewhere else at lunchtime.

They headed for the livery stable first, but Elise wondered if Mr. Pottle was the man they ought to buy from. Mr. Whistler had said there were other places in town. It might be worth their while to seek them out.

"I believe we should continue to keep my connections quiet," Anne said as they walked.

"You mean—"

"I mean that I shall continue to be plain 'Miss Stone.' It's served us well so far, and we don't want to appear pretentious. If the tradesmen knew my father was an earl, they would probably ask more for everything."

"I agree with you there."

"And on the wagon train," Lady Anne persisted. "This man we're about to hire, for instance. He mustn't know."

"Agreed." Elise wrinkled her nose. "It's bad enough that Eb Bentley thinks we're helpless. But if everyone on the wagon train thinks we are *rich* and helpless, that will be even worse."

"Yes. The other emigrants will be our neighbors for the next few months. We need to be friendly and make sure they see us doing our share of the chores. And you must always call me Anne, as you have been, never using my title."

Though Elise had played down their relationship since they boarded the ship in England, she didn't approve of familiarity between a domestic and her mistress.

"It's difficult sometimes to remember."

"We must," Anne said. "Imagine how they'd sneer at us if they thought we—that is *I*—was putting on airs. There is no aristocracy here, and I'm sure Americans disdain anyone who claims to be above them in any way."

"But you're not like that," Elise protested. "You're the kindest, most compassionate girl I know. Woman, that is. I'm proud of the way you've grown up, my lady."

"Thank you, but you must never say those words again, so long as we are in America. I am no longer your lady, and you are not my maid. You are my friend and a bit of a mentor/chaperone, I think. And I am very fond of you. That is no pretense."

"And I of you," Elise said. "I shall do my best not to betray the secret of your birth."

Lady Anne presented such a charming picture of an English lady, one born to the manor and reared in luxury, though not always conscious of it. Could anyone possibly think she was anything else?

"Perhaps we should go into the emporium on the way to the livery and speak for our supplies."

"I thought I would go by myself this afternoon while you rest," Elise said. "I'm sure it will be tedious, my—my dear." Lady Anne had never bargained with a tradesman in her life, and Elise would feel freer to dicker without her elegantly gowned mistress standing beside her.

"I think we should stay together. This town has such a ragtag bunch of people, I worry when you go out alone. Men wearing guns, and people flying out of saloons on every corner."

Anne had a point. There was a measure of safety in numbers, and they had no time to waste. If they spoke for their equipment now, it would perhaps save a trip later in the day. "All right."

Ingram's general store was smaller and less organized than the one they'd patronized in St. Louis. Sacks of provisions were stacked nearly to the ceiling. Boots and iron kettles lay in jumbled heaps. Every square inch of wall and rafter was hung with harness, tools, and cooking implements.

Elise took out the list of supplies they needed and approached a man who stood on a ladder placing canned goods on a high shelf.

"Excuse me, sir. I'm told you sell lots of supplies for emigrants."

"That's right." He looked down at her. His jaw dropped as he stared for a moment. He came down the two steps to the floor and brushed his hands on the front of his apron. "You can't mean you ladies are joining one of the wagon trains?"

"Yes, we are." Elise raised her chin. "Why not, sir?"

"Well, it's just. . .you're just so. . .so. . . You don't look like most of the women heading west, that's all."

Elise glared at him. "What business is that of yours?"

Anne cleared her throat. "We have a list."

Her soft-spoken words reminded Elise that efficiency was more important than respect at the moment. She lowered her lashes. "Yes, and your establishment was recommended to us by the wagon master, Mr. Whistler."

The man eyed her for a moment then nodded. "Rob Whistler sends folks my way. He's an honest man. I guess if anyone can get you to Oregon, he can." He ignored the list Elise held out and turned to the counter. "Here's my usual outfit for a wagon. For each extra person, I'll add on these extra supplies." He pointed as he spoke to a notice tacked to the front edge of the counter.

"I'm sure that's fine," Anne said, looking uncertainly at Elise.

Elise hesitated. "We have yet to procure our team and wagon, but we won't need anything besides the basics."

"I'll set everything out on the back porch. You can pick it up there, and if there's anything you don't want, you can tell me then and I'll deduct it."

His plan sounded reasonable, and Elise nodded. "Fine. And we're thinking of taking a few laying hens."

"I haven't got any of those, ma'am. I can pack some eggs in a bucket of lard for you. They'll keep fresh a long time."

"Well. . ." Elise knew Anne had hoped for fresh fowl along the way. "I suppose that's the best we can do on short notice. We've no time to track down a farmer who can sell us chickens."

Thomas Costigan ducked inside the general store and peered around. The two Englishwomen were talking to the storekeeper. He gravitated toward the stove, though the day was fairly warm. An elderly man with a flowing white beard sat near it with a checkerboard set up on top of a nail keg.

"Hey there, young feller. Feel like a game?"

"Sure." Thomas sat down opposite him and cocked one ear toward the two ladies.

"All right, provisions for two adults," the storekeeper said to the English ladies.

"No, three," said Miss Finster. "We'll be hiring someone to tend our livestock for us."

The younger woman—Miss Stone—spoke up. "You don't know anyone, do you, sir? A healthy, honest man who'd like to work his way west?"

It was all Thomas could do not to turn and gape at them. They were heading farther west? Those two prim and proper ladies?

"Your turn," the old man said.

Thomas shoved a checker forward with his index finger.

"Lots of folks want to go west," the storekeeper said. "You might ask at the saloons. They tend to hang about there, waiting for someone to come in and ask."

"We will not be entering a saloon," Miss Finster said firmly.

"Oh, well then, you might check the porch posts outside. Some folks post notices out front here, or in front of the saloons, or at the post office."

"The post office. We'll try there." Miss Finster sounded as though she was drowning and lunging for a piece of flotsam. "When will our order to be ready?"

"Well now, that depends." The storekeeper scratched his head and eyed their list. "You said you want triple everything on food?"

The two women looked at each other.

"I doubt we'll need that much bacon," Miss Stone said.

"Is there anything we can substitute for bacon?" asked Miss Finster.

"You have to understand, ma'am, the things the wagon masters recommend are things that won't spoil quickly."

"Well, yes. There is that. But my friend is not fond of bacon. We'd like a little more variety, if possible."

"I could give you some dried beef. And how about some dried peas? They're not on the list."

Miss Finster said something Thomas couldn't catch, but the storekeeper responded with, "Canned food? Well, yes, we've got oysters and some soup. I've had peaches and a few vegetables before, but they're expensive compared to dried foods, and of course, they weigh more. Some folks are leery of them."

"May we see what you have?"

During the next ten minutes, the ladies examined various wares and discussed the safety, reliability, and price of tinned foods. Thomas kept the checker game moving and listened with half an ear. At last, Miss Finster said, "We'll take all of those you have."

"Yes, ma'am." The storekeeper's tone revealed his pleasure in the transaction. Thomas wondered how long those tinned oysters had sat on his shelf.

"And more tea than it says here. Double, if you please. Instead of the coffee."

"Our hired man might like coffee better," Miss Stone said.

Miss Finster nodded. "You're right. I suppose we'll need both. Now about the tea. Do you have good quality black tea from India? What we had at our hotel this morning was abominable."

Thomas chuckled.

The old man sitting opposite him smiled. "Those ladies are a bit finicky, wouldn't you say?"

"Just a tad." Thomas made his next move.

By the time the ladies had worked their way down the entire list, questioning the quality, price, and need for every item, several more customers were waiting in line behind them. Some didn't trouble to conceal their impatience. Finally the storekeeper excused himself, went through a doorway, and returned a minute later with a woman whom Thomas supposed was his wife. He went back to total up the English ladies' order and sent the woman to deal with the other patrons.

At last Miss Stone and Miss Finster left the general store.

Thomas stood and handed the old man a nickel. "Looks like you're winning this round, and I need to get going. Buy yourself a bun or something."

"Thanks, young fella."

The women were still visible down the street, and Thomas ambled after them. They turned at the corner. He followed at a leisurely pace. He had a feeling he knew where they were headed.

Sure enough, they wended their way to the livery stable where they'd rented their rig the day before. Thomas leaned against the side of a barbershop half a block away and crossed his arms. The nebulous plan that had begun forming in his mind was beginning to crystallize. If it worked, he'd have to get word to Peterson.

# CHAPTER 8

The big barn door of the livery stable stood open, and two men worked inside. The bearded owner leaned on a paddock fence outside, talking to another man. He looked up as they approached and swept off his hat.

"Good morning, ladies."

"Good morning, Mr. Pottle," Elise said.

"Do you need a rig again today?"

"No, thank you, sir. We're here to purchase."

"Oh?" Pottle straightened and eyed her thoughtfully. "And what are you purchasing, ma'am?"

"A team of stout mules, please."

He let out a guffaw and tried too late to swallow it. "Pardon me, ma'am, but you wish to buy a span of mules?"

"However many it takes to pull a wagon over the plains to Oregon."

Pottle stared at her.

"Well, I never," said his companion.

"Let me get this straight." Pottle stepped toward her, frowning. "You ladies intend to take the Oregon Trail."

"Indeed we do, sir."

"Well now." Pottle shook his head.

"Oxen," said the other man. "That's what you want. Easy keepers, and if things go wrong, you can eat 'em."

"Oh, hush, Newt. Don't go scaring the ladies. H'ain't nothing going to go wrong for them. I expect they'll have a nice trip."

"In a pig's eye," his friend said. "My cousin went on a wagon train two years ago. The Injuns ran off their herd of milk cows, and they lost one of their kids crossing the Platte."

"Would you hush?" Pottle glared at him.

"Sure. I'll talk to you later, Ralph," the other man said. "Sounds like you've got some business to do." As he walked away, he said, "Wait till the boys hear this."

Elise gritted her teeth, suspecting that she and Lady Anne were about to become the subject of conversation in the nearest saloon.

"If you please, Mr. Pottle, we've been advised that mules will do us nicely. Since we have more experience with horses than cattle, we thought mules might be best. We intend to hire a driver, but we realize we may need to handle the animals in an emergency ourselves."

"Makes sense to me." Pottle walked over to the open barn door and called, "Benjy, bring those mules up from the lower pen. I've got a wagon train customer here."

He turned and smiled at Elise. "Now, these here are Missouri mules, ma'am. They're strong and they're tough. Tougher than most. They'll take you across the plains slicker'n greased lightning."

"How many mules do we need?" Elise asked.

"I'm thinking eight, ma'am."

"So many?"

"Well, you could haul your wagon with less, but if they get tired out, or if you need replacements. . .and of course, you could always sell one or two to someone less fortunate than yourselves, if'n theirs give out and they didn't bring any extry."

"I'm not sure we need so many," Elise said.

"Suit yourself. Come on through the barn, if you will, and have a look at 'em. Oh, watch your step there."

Elise hopped to one side and avoided a pile of fresh manure, but Lady Anne was not so fortunate. She stepped squarely in it and stopped, holding up her skirt and staring down at the mess surrounding her calfskin shoe. Her face turned a garish green.

"Quick, my—Anne! Come over here, my dear." Elise grabbed her mistress's wrist and all but yanked her to one side. "Now wipe your shoe on that straw." Glaring at the liveryman, she snapped, "What's the matter with you? Get a rag and clean off my lady's shoe."

"Oh, a little of that won't hurt her none," Pottle said. "If'n you ladies are serious about crossing the plains, you'd better get over lettin' a little horse manure frazzle you. Now these mules are the best you'll find in Independence...."

Elise stared after him but didn't follow. "Are you all right?"

Anne's face was still pale, but she diligently rubbed her foot in the straw, trying to scrape off the manure. "He's right, you know. I've got to toughen up, like those mules of his, if I want to make it to Oregon."

"Well, you don't have to do it all in five minutes." Elise pulled out her handkerchief and knelt in the straw.

"Oh, don't," Anne cried. "You'll ruin it. I'll have my shoes cleaned tonight at the hotel. I can stand it until then."

Elise gave in and stood, but privately she doubted their spartan hotel offered niceties like shining shoes.

They caught up with Pottle outside the back door. The mules his hired men were herding into the small corral from a larger pasture looked enormous.

"They can pull all day," Pottle said with evident pride. "You give them a little grain when you stop for nooning of course."

"Ah, of course." Elise studied his face but couldn't read his expression through his bushy beard. "Mr. Pottle, if I may be so bold, how much are these mules?"

"A hunnerd dollars each, ma'am, and that's a bargain."

"A hundred?" Elise stared at him, outraged.

"Perhaps we should buy the oxen instead," Anne murmured.

"Oxen? Oh no, you ladies don't want oxen," Pottle said.

"Why not?" Elise asked, hiking her chin up a half inch. She suspected that Mr. Pottle didn't deal in oxen and didn't want to lose the sale of his high-priced Missouri mules.

"These mules are much better for your purposes," he said.

"Morning, Pottle. Ladies."

Elise whirled at the sound of the lazy voice. Eb Bentley touched his hat brim as he emerged from the back door of the livery stable.

"Mr. Bentley!" For some reason she couldn't fathom, Elise felt both chagrin and relief at his appearance.

"Eb," said Mr. Pottle with a nod.

"Buying some livestock, are you?" Eb asked in Elise and Anne's general direction.

"Yes, they are," Pottle said, "and if you don't mind, we're in the middle of a transaction."

"Mr. Bentley." Anne reached for his arm and gazed up at him with her huge brown eyes. "Sir, was I mistaken, or did Mr. Whistler tell me a good mule would cost us around seventy-five dollars?"

Elise schooled her features not to show her feelings. Anne would do much better not to get too close to the rough-and-ready scout. On the other hand, perhaps she should take a lesson from Anne. In this situation, Eb Bentley might take their side, and right about now, she and Anne could use an ally.

"I believe he said something along those lines, miss." Eb's color heightened as he looked down at the beautiful young woman.

"That's what I thought." Anne turned her sweet smile on Pottle. "Could you show us some of those seventy-five-dollar mules, please, Mr. Pottle?"

The owner's face clouded.

Elise mustered her courage and stepped closer to Eb. "Mr. Bentley, I know that Mr. Whistler said horses aren't as hardy as mules, but Miss Stone and I would both feel more at home with horses, I'm sure. Even those big draft horses—they're quite gentle, aren't they?"

"Yes, ma'am," Eb said, "but they'd eat you out of house and home. There's no guarantee of good grazing along the way, and horses have to eat often. You'd need to carry a wagon full of feed just for them. It's not practical."

Elise sighed. "Then mules it is, I guess." She turned back to Pottle. "I believe you said we need eight?"

"Eight mules?" Eb asked. "Four will pull a regular wagon just fine. You might want to get a couple of spares though, and have the drovers bring them along with the other loose livestock."

Elise arched her eyebrows at Mr. Pottle. "Is that right?"

"Oh, well, I thought you was pulling a Conestoga wagon, miss. It's an honest mistake."

Scowling, Eb stepped toward the livery owner. "You use these ladies right, Pottle. You're not the only horse-and-mule trader in town. If you can't find them a team of six good, strong mules for four hundred dollars, I'll take them over to Parley Rider's place."

"Four—that's way too cheap." Pottle glowered at him. "I have to make a living, you know, Bentley."

"I'm sure Rider can make that deal for my friends. And if you've got a set of harness, add another hundred, but if you try to cheat these ladies, you'll have to answer to me." Eb looked toward the mules milling in the nearest corral. "Those look sound from here. Do I need to climb in through the fence and check their teeth?"

"No," Pottle nearly snarled.

"Good. Because Rob Whistler and I have sent you a lot of trade lately. You treat our people right if you expect it to continue." He turned and said to Anne, "Have you bought your wagon yet, ma'am?"

"No, we haven't."

He nodded. "Well, there's a woman over at a boardinghouse on Mill Street who has one for sale. She was going to go with us, but her husband died suddenly. She's already sold her ox team, but I told her to hold the wagon for an hour in case you wanted it."

"That's kind of you," Anne said.

He shrugged. "Make sure you don't pay more than seventy-five dollars for it. That's a fair price for a good, sturdy wagon with a watertight bed and bows to hold the canvas. And make sure you buy an extra canvas cover at the store. I don't think she has but one."

"We surely will," Anne said.

It dawned on Elise that he was not only ignoring her—he knew that Anne was the one holding the purse strings. Even though Elise had done most of the negotiating throughout their trip and tried to protect Lady Anne from having to deal with coarse tradesmen, Eb had somehow discerned that Anne would pay for their wagon and team. She wasn't sure whether to be apprehensive or to respect his acumen.

He lifted his hat and included her in his parting words. "Good day, ladies."

"Thank you, Mr. Bentley," Anne said with a smile.

"We'll see you in a day or two," Elise added.

"Looks that way." Eb glanced at the mules once more. "Pottle, don't give them that one with the notched ear. He's favoring his off hind foot." He strode away through the barn.

Elise stared after him, watching his tall, straight form as he moved through the shadowy stable and out into the sunlit street beyond.

"What are you thinking?" Anne asked softly.

"I'm wondering what he came here for."

"To tell us about the wagon?"

Elise frowned. "How did he know where to find us?"

"I'm sure I don't know. But let's finish our business with Mr. Pottle and get over to the widow's boardinghouse."

They walked together to the corral fence. Mr. Pottle was inside with the mules.

"All right, ladies, I've picked out six of the best for you. If you want the harness and collars with them, that'll be five hundred dollars cash."

"Is the harness in good repair?" Elise asked.

He hesitated. "Sure it is."

"Perhaps we should purchase a new set at the emporium," Anne said.

"No, no, I'll make sure it's ready for the trail." Pottle scratched his chin through his beard and waited for her verdict.

"All right then." Anne turned away and removed her chain-link purse from her skirt pocket and counted out the odd-looking American bills. With what they'd paid the emporium's owner, their bankroll looked very small.

"Are we doing all right?" Elise murmured.

"I believe so."

Five minutes later they left, with an understanding that they would be back for their new team and harness later. As they walked toward Mill Street, Anne said, "Seventy-five dollars seems like a huge price for a wagon. What is that in pounds?"

Elise quickly figured the price. "Mr. Bentley said it's fair."

"But you don't trust him."

Elise ruefully shook her head. "Isn't it funny how things change? Compared to Mr. Pottle, I'd trust Mr. Bentley with my life. But next to your father? No. I'd take one Stone man for ten Eb Bentleys any day of the week."

# CHAPTER 9

Thomas followed the two women as they left the livery stable. He'd had to scramble for cover in the shadowy barn when the man from the wagon train came through and helped the women with their dealing, but he was pretty sure the scout hadn't seen him. He tailed the women out to the street and waited until they were out of sight of the establishment. He caught up to them on the sidewalk.

"Pardon me, ma'am," he said when he was within a couple of steps of their swaying skirts.

The two women spun around in a flurry of colliding crinolines.

"Yes, sir?" asked the older one, looking down her nose just a bit.

Thomas supposed he looked a bit shopworn to the meticulously gowned and coiffed ladies. He straightened his shoulders and cleared his throat.

"I ran into that fella from the wagon train a few minutes ago, and he said you were looking for someone to drive your team when you take to the trail."

"Do you mean Mr. Bentley?" the woman asked.

"Sure. He told me that if I was to ask, you might hire me. See, I want to go to Oregon, but I don't have the money for my own rig. I'm a hard worker. If you was to take me along and stake me for my grub, I could hitch up for you every day and drive if you need me to, and I could help you load and unload things and haul water—things like that."

The two women looked at each other.

"What is your name, sir?" asked the younger one. She was a regular stunner.

"Thomas G. Costigan, at your service." He doffed his hat and gave a little bow.

"I am Miss Finster," said the older one, "and this is Miss Stone.

We are on our way to see about a wagon now. Could you begin work today?"

"Oh yes, ma'am, I surely could."

"And where would you sleep?" she asked.

"Oh, I'd bed down with the herdsmen, I suppose. Most wagon trains have a herd of extra animals—milk cows and extra horses and mules and oxen—and they have men to herd them along behind the wagons. I could spread my bedroll with them."

The woman still seemed undecided.

"Excuse us a moment, won't you?" Miss Finster asked.

"Of course."

The two women stepped to one side and conferred in low tones. Thomas caught only a few words—"recommended," "proper," and something that might have been "scruffy."

Miss Finster turned back toward him after a few minutes. "Mr. Costigan, we have agreed to give you a trial. We hope to have a wagon to collect and load today. If you do well with that job, we'll hire you. In any case, we'll pay you for your time."

Thomas smiled and ducked his head. "Why, thank you, ma'am. That sounds fair and reasonable."

"And where shall we find you if we buy the wagon?" Miss Finster asked.

"How about at the livery, ma'am? You'll have to fetch your team."

Her eyebrows shot up. "Our team?"

"Uh. . .well. . .I assumed. . .uh. . .you said you were on your way to buy a wagon. I assumed you'd get mules. . .or, uh, oxen. . .from the . . .uh. . .unless the wagon owner is selling you his team, too."

She appraised him coolly for a long moment. "At Pottle's livery stable, then. In three hours."

"Very good, ma'am." He touched his forelock and backed away, bowing and trying not to fall off the edge of the boardwalk. He'd almost botched that interview—which would have ruined his entire plan.

The ladies walked away. He ducked into a doorway and watched surreptitiously. Sure enough, Miss Finster looked back at the edge of the block. He pulled back before she saw him and counted to ten. When he peered out again, they were gone. He ran down the boardwalk and halted at the corner. He looked ahead, then left, then right. There they were. Those huge skirts were hard to miss. Men were dodging into the rutted street to keep out of their way.

Thomas turned and made a beeline for the nearest saloon. They were headed for the place the scout had mentioned. He needed to get word to Peterson and make sure the man wanted him to do this. So long as the ladies hired him, he'd be set for the next few months, but he'd ask Peterson for advance pay and have a free trip west. Thanks to the wagon master, who was a bit of a stickler, things looked pretty good on that front. Just to be sure the women had no complaints, he would limit himself to one drink and make sure he turned up a few minutes early at the livery. Thomas G. Costigan believed in covering all contingencies.

✒

Elise and Anne located a Rooms to Let sign in the yard of a substantial wood-frame house. A woman of about fifty opened the door and showed them to a small but clean parlor. When she'd left them, Anne sat down on a threadbare settee, and Elise took a straight chair by the window.

A few minutes later, a thin young woman entered, holding a wailing bundle on her shoulder. A toddler clutched a handful of her skirt and, when she stopped walking, wrapped his little arms around her legs. The woman's dress was a nondescript cotton that hung limp on her frame. Her hair and her tanned skin were almost the same color as the dress. The only splash of color was the small pieced quilt she held close about the crying baby.

"You're here about the wagon?" she asked.

"Yes." Elise stood and spoke loudly over the baby's cries. "I'm Miss Finster."

The young woman nodded. "Sallie Deaver. Eb Bentley said you folks need a wagon."

"That's right. We're joining the wagon train."

Sallie patted the baby and shook her head. "We was, too, but

85

Ronny up and got himself killed yesterday."

Anne came and stood beside Elise. "I'm so sorry, Mrs. Deaver."

Sallie shrugged. "I'm going back to my folks in Connecticut. I sold the team already."

"Yes, it's just the wagon we're interested in," Elise said.

"You can have it for a hunnert. I advise you to be careful packing it. Ronny fell off and busted his neck."

"I see." Elise shot a quick glance at Anne, who was frowning at her. It was a ladylike frown, but still an indicator of her displeasure. Elise drew in a deep breath. "Well, Mr. Bentley told us it was worth seventy-five dollars. I assumed you'd sell it for that."

"I need money to get home."

"I'm sure you do...." Elise glanced at Anne, who gave the tiniest of shrugs. If she didn't close the deal quickly, Elise was afraid her tenderhearted mistress would give away money they would need on the journey. "Seventy-five is all we have laid aside for this purchase, Mrs. Deaver. If that's not agreeable to you, I'm sorry we've bothered you."

Elise turned to her chair, where she'd laid off her cloak.

"Don't be so hasty, now." The baby gave a belch, and Sallie stopped patting him. "I'll take eighty-five."

Elise smiled, but not too congenially. "I'm sure we can buy a new one for less than that."

Sallie's mouth drooped. "You ladies have got them fancy clothes. I'm sure you can afford a few extra bucks. Me, I've got this dress and one other to my name, and this is the best one."

Elise eyed her thoughtfully. "Would you excuse us just a moment? I'd like to speak to Miss Stone privately."

Anne followed her into the hall, and Elise shut the door. "My lady, she might take a dress instead of the extra money. I'd offer one of my own, but she's so thin, I doubt mine would fit her."

Anne's face lit up. "Why didn't I think of that? I've got trunks full of dresses!"

"Yes. One of your morning dresses, perhaps. A simple style."

"There's that sprigged muslin that I only wear at Stoneford when we've no company."

"Perfect. I'll make the offer."

They returned to the parlor. Sallie was sitting on the settee with the baby in her arms and the toddler curled up beside her.

"Mrs. Deaver, you're right that we have been blessed with more clothing than you. Would you take seventy-five dollars and one good day dress for the wagon?"

Sallie eyes widened. "I might. Something pretty?"

"Oh yes. It's one that suits Miss Stone admirably, and it has a lot of wear left in it."

"And gloves?" Sallie asked, gazing pointedly at Elise's delicate crocheted pair. "I want to look proper when I go to Connecticut."

"Certainly." Elise didn't bother to check with Anne. She had a dozen pairs in her own trunk, and Anne had two or three times as many.

Sallie stood. "All right then. Do you have the money on you?"

"Yes," Elise said. "We'll bring the dress and gloves later today, when we come with our mule team to get the wagon."

"Fine by me."

Anne opened her purse and counted out the money. "I wish you well, Mrs. Deaver."

They left the boardinghouse and walked toward the hotel.

"Are you all right?" Elise asked.

"I'm fine," Anne said. "I'm glad things are working out for the journey. I feel sure God will bless us and we'll find Uncle David."

"I pray you are right."

Though their steps dragged, Elise wouldn't ask for a hackney unless Anne showed great fatigue. Anne had obtained her complete allowance for the remainder of the year from Mr. Conrad, and that would have to last them. Elise carried a portion pinned into her corset cover, and her mistress did the same, with enough to carry out today's transactions in her reticule. Elise kept reminding herself that they must keep back enough for a return trip, either by wagon or by ship. She refused to think about how long the overland trip would take. At least their transportation to Oregon was paid for, along with the supplies they would need along the way.

They stopped to dine at a rough eatery on the way. The plain food filled them up, but Elise wondered how Lady Anne would do when forced to eat their trail rations for months.

Back in the cramped hotel room, Anne lay down on the bed. Elise removed her outer skirt and her top petticoat, with its stiff whalebone hoop in the hem, and sat down to write to her sister in Germany:

*Dear Gretl,*

*I am about to set out on an adventure unlike anything I've ever done. My mistress and I have traveled from New York, where I last wrote to you, and come westward. We stopped in the city of St. Louis for a week, but now have come even farther, to a smaller, wilder town called Independence. Lady Anne and I have come to a momentous decision: we will push on to the Pacific in search of her uncle.*

*I know this is shocking. The two of us would never under ordinary circumstances consider throwing aside the comforts and security of polite society. My mistress, however, is determined to locate her uncle, inform him of her father's passing, and persuade him to claim his title and estate in England.*

*But alas! David Stone is reported to have gone to Oregon Territory. Because communication is so fractured here in America, she has no recourse but to go in search of him. Letters have not reached him, and we've not found a trustworthy way to get him word, so we shall carry it ourselves.*

Elise went on to describe the arrangements they had made, and even their dickering session with Sallie Deaver. She hoped her family would see the humor of the situation, though it might lose some of that as she translated her thoughts into German. Unfortunately, over the last twenty years, her English had become stronger than her command of her native tongue. It took her nearly an hour to compose the letter. She hadn't seen her sister in six years. Would she ever see her again?

She closed the letter by admitting that she was a bit frightened by what lay ahead, yet excited about the possibilities. What she didn't express was the weight of responsibility she felt. Lady Anne's well-being lay squarely on her shoulders.

Had she made a mistake by falling in with Lady Anne's whim? No, she couldn't think that. The young woman was determined to find her uncle. If Elise had refused to go with her, Anne would have found another companion.

The scout's bluntness and the daunting list of provisions had nearly overwhelmed her, and she couldn't imagine how they'd have come through bargaining for a team and wagon had Eb Bentley not stepped in. There was no turning back now. Lady Anne was set on finding the new earl of Stoneford. And if that proved impossible, she would need someone there to comfort her at the end of the trail.

Anne stirred and sat up, stretching her creamy white arms.

"Feel better, my lady?" Elise asked.

"A bit. But you must stop calling me that, even in private. Sometime you'll slip in front of people."

"I'll try. And now I'll get the dress you're giving to Mrs. Deaver. It's nearly time for us to go and meet Mr. Costigan."

Elise opened the trunk that she thought held the dress in question. One of Lady Anne's finest ball gowns was folded in a sheet on top.

"Elise, why did I bring so many fancy dresses?" Anne asked, watching from her seat on the edge of the bed.

"I believe the logic was that one never knows whom one will meet aboard ship—or in New York or St. Louis."

Anne chuckled. "Well, Mrs. Deaver can't use a watered silk ball gown."

"This is the one I was thinking of." Elise pulled out the white muslin dress sprigged with embroidered pink flowers. The summer-weight dress looked darling on Anne, and Elise hesitated. "I hate to give it to her, you look so well in it."

"Perhaps I should save my plainest dresses to wear on the wagon train." Anne reached out and fingered the snowy material. "This one wouldn't be very useful though. In one day it would be ruined."

"Your woolen dresses will hold up better, as Mr. Whistler said."

"I suppose you're right. Let's give her the muslin. Or do you think—I did bring one mourning costume."

"No, she wants something pretty. I'll contribute a pair of my cotton gloves." Elise draped the dress over her arm and closed Anne's trunk.

"I've thought of another way we could save money." Anne's voice was a bit timid, and Elise turned to observe her face.

"I've thought along those lines, too. We mustn't spend all you have getting to Oregon, or we shan't be able to come back."

"Yes. So I thought that after Mr. Costigan loads our wagon today, we could move out to the field with the other emigrants. That way, we wouldn't have to spend any more for the hotel room."

"Such as it is. This room probably isn't much more comfortable than our beds in the wagon will be," Elise said. "But we'd be outside of town. Do you really want to be away from the shops and other conveniences?"

Anne shrugged. "It would help prepare us for what's ahead."

"I suppose that's true, though I hate to take you away from comparative ease. You do realize we'll have to cook for ourselves once we leave here?"

Anne gritted her teeth. "That's true. But it might be shrewd to discover our shortcomings before we're too far from civilization."

"Let's think about it and see how Mr. Costigan does." Elise didn't mention it, but she also had concerns about the security of their belongings once they were loaded in the wagon. Could they trust Costigan to guard it for them?

∼◯

Costigan sat on a barrel outside the livery stable as the two ladies approached. Elise was glad, though she'd half expected him not to show up, and something perverse in her nature would have been gratified to know her suspicions were founded.

She caught Anne's eye. "Well, he's here."

"Yes. That's a good omen."

He hopped down when he saw them and tipped his hat. "Afternoon, ladies. Pottle's out back, rounding up your mules. He says you bought six stout ones."

"That's right," Elise said. "Can you drive them for us to the place where we'll get our wagon?"

"Yes'm. How far is it?"

"About half a mile."

"Then I'll just hitch 'em up and ground drive 'em over there. If you want, you can just tell me where it is, and I'll go fetch the wagon and bring it to your lodgings so we can load it."

"Well. . ." Elise hesitated. To outward appearances, Costigan wanted to please and was willing to work hard. Why couldn't she just trust him? Was it because he'd been recommended by Eb Bentley? Or was it her conservative, cautious nature and her compulsion to keep Lady Anne safe?

"We need to deliver the bundle to Mrs. Deaver," Anne said, nodding toward the package Elise carried.

"That is correct." Elise was a bit relieved for the excuse to go along and observe Costigan's behavior. "Let me speak to Mr. Pottle. He can help you harness the team, and Miss Stone and I will set out for the boardinghouse on Mill Street and deliver the package. When you have the team hitched, drive over, and we'll see you there."

The sun shone brightly, and a light breeze blew as she and Anne walked toward Mrs. Deaver's lodgings. Perfect weather for drying up mud and making grass grow. Elise felt stirrings of wanderlust. This journey could be the best time of her life, if she'd let it. She must help Anne see it that way, too.

She remembered the countless outings she'd taken Anne on when her mistress was a child. She'd tried to approach each day as an adventure and an opportunity to learn. Was this any different? They would see sights most Englishwomen couldn't imagine.

"You must make sketches of our journey," she said to Anne. "You draw so beautifully."

"Thank you. I believe I'll do that. I bought a new sketchbook in St. Louis for the purpose. It will help me remember the places we see." Anne tipped her head and looked at Elise from beneath the brim of her hat. "What do you think of Mr. Costigan now?"

"Still undecided," Elise admitted.

"I think he knows what he's doing," Anne said. "We're fortunate to have found a man so knowledgeable about horses and willing to go for low wages."

"We shall see."

The landlady admitted them to her parlor and went to fetch Sallie. The young woman entered a few minutes later with her little boy clinging to her hand. *The baby must be sleeping,* Elise thought. At least they didn't have to put up with the infant's wails again.

Anne stood and held out the package. "Here are the dress and gloves we promised you, Mrs. Deaver. I hope they please you."

Sallie sat down on the settee, and Anne placed the package in her lap. Sallie laid back the edge of the wrapping paper and gasped. Elise feared at first that she would say the dress wasn't suitable.

Sallie fingered the soft muslin folds. Her lips trembled.

"It's prettier'n anything I've ever owned." She looked up at Anne. "Thank you, but you could have given me something plainer."

Elise smiled wryly, thinking, *No, Sallie, she couldn't.*

"If it doesn't suit you, they have some ready-made dresses in Ingram's store," Anne said.

"Oh no." Sallie hugged the dress to her bosom. "This is the beatingest dress I ever saw. I can wear it when I get off the train in Hartford. Maybe my folks will quit saying that Ronny didn't take good care of me."

Elise forbore commenting on the skewed logic of her statement. Instead she slid the white gloves out from between the folds of the skirt. "Here are your gloves, Sallie."

"Oh my! They look brand new."

Elise cleared her throat. "Our driver will be here soon with the mule team. We'd like him to hitch up the wagon and take it to our hotel. Is there anything else you need from us?"

"I don't think so. I'm leaving for Connecticut tomorrow."

"We wish you a safe journey," Anne said.

They left Sallie to admire her new dress and headed back up the street. At the corner, they met Thomas Costigan, who was driving the team down the street, walking about six feet behind the last two mules and holding the long leather lines. The mules' feet and Thomas's boots squelched in mud with every step.

"How do, ladies!" He shuffled the reins and lifted his hat for a moment and then dropped it back onto his brow.

"Good day, Mr. Costigan," Elise called. "We shall be at the Kenton House Hotel. Mrs. Deaver and her landlady know you're coming."

He nodded.

"There now," Anne said as they resumed their walk. "If he's not dependable, I don't know what is."

Elise smiled. "Yes, it seems we've got the beatingest hired man in Missouri."

The ladies spent the next hour repacking their belongings and deciding what to keep in their satchels so that they'd have all essentials accessible. Thomas arrived with the wagon, and they went out to inspect it. Elise was impressed by the solid look of it, but Anne bemoaned the lack of space inside.

"How shall we get everything from the store in and still live in there?"

"Most folks take a tent and sleep in that," Thomas said. "Of course, you'll use your foodstuffs on the way, and you'll gain space every time you eat something."

The bows were in place above the wagon bed. With a little assistance out of Anne's reticule, Thomas found a couple of lads to help him carry the trunks down the stairs of the hotel and load them into the wagon. Then they spread the canvas top over the bows and tied it down.

"Well," Anne said dubiously, "there is our home on wheels."

"Yes. Are you sure you don't want to stay at the hotel one more night?" Elise expected her to vacillate, but Anne shook her head vigorously.

"No, I think we should move right to the field. We can get to know the other travelers sooner if we do. And as you said yesterday, if we've forgotten anything, we'll soon find out. Better now than a hundred miles out on the trail."

"All right, Thomas," Elise said. "We'll go pay the hotel bill, and you can bring out the last bits of our luggage. Are you prepared to stay at the field with the team tonight?"

"Yes, ma'am. I'll fetch my bedroll after we go to the store for your supplies."

Loading the provisions they'd purchased at the emporium took another two hours. They added a tent and a second wagon cover, along with a few sundries the ladies thought might be useful. For some reason, Thomas kept putting items in the wagon, taking them out, and rearranging them. Elise gathered it had something to do with the balance of the load. That and her occasional protests that some item or other had to travel where she and Anne could reach it easily.

"We can't be pawing through a ton of crates and bundles to find our cooking utensils," she told him at one point.

"No, ma'am, you can't." He hauled out the box of pans, ladles, and spatulas and positioned it on top of one of the trunks. "Now, where's your tinderbox? We may as well put that in with the cooking gear."

Elise gulped. She'd never mastered the art of fire building. There was so much she had yet to learn. Perhaps Thomas could tutor her and Anne in the fine points of trail living. They must become self-sufficient if they intended to survive this jaunt.

# CHAPTER 10

Elise awoke for the twentieth time to find that at last the walls of their canvas tent were growing lighter. The sun must be rising. Unable to stand another moment on the hard, damp ground inside the tent, she sat up and rubbed her hip.

Shivering, she hauled her satchel onto her lap and groped inside for her clothing.

Anne rolled over and pulled the blanket close to her chin. "It's freezing!"

"Just about." Elise's teeth chattered as she fumbled with her clean stockings. Her fingers ached. The storekeeper had included two wool blankets in their kit—Thomas had declined one, saying he had his own bedroll. They had proven far from adequate for the cold night air. The women ended up adding extra flannel petticoats beneath their nightdresses. They laid one blanket beneath them and spread the second one over them and huddled together like children in an ice-cold nursery.

"We'll need to go back for more blankets." Anne tucked in the edges of the top one, now that Elise was out from under it.

"Yes, and a couple of feather ticks if you think we can stuff them into that wagon."

"I'm sure there's some reason why they didn't include proper bedding in our list of supplies." Anne's voice was muffled by the blanket.

Elise sighed as she tried to figure out which side of her corset went where in the semidarkness. "Men. They always think they have a good reason for everything." Immediately she felt guilty. "I'm sorry, my dear. I shouldn't complain. This is exactly why you wanted to come out here yesterday, and it's a good thing we did. We've already learned a great deal."

Anne poked her nose out of the blanket nest. "Yes. We learned that we have no hope of raising this tent without Thomas, and that there's not enough room for us to sleep in the wagon, even after we take out the tent and blankets. And that apparently western people don't use sheets. Or do you think Mr. Ingram just forgot to put them in?"

"No. I think they consider sheets to be superfluous on the trail."

Anne sat up, clutching the blanket about her. "Are they really so vulgar? These wool blankets are itchy."

"I'm so sorry, my dear. Of course they've irritated your sensitive skin all night long. We've simply got to find a solution to this bedding problem today." At last her corset seemed to be in place. "Forgive my asking, but could you. . . ?"

"Of course." Anne let go of the blanket and pulled Elise's corset strings. "It's hard to get it tight when my hands are cold."

"I believe I'll wear a dress that doesn't require hoop petticoats today," Elise said. "But of course, the one I want is in the wagon."

"I think I'll wear my cashmere since it's so cold," Anne said. "But none of the women in the encampment seem to be wearing wide skirts. Do you think we should forgo our crinolines altogether? It seems scandalous, but. . ."

"But I had the distinct impression yesterday that we were being sneered at," Elise finished for her. "Are we insane to carry fashionable clothing across the plains?"

"But what if we got to Oregon and found that everyone was wearing crinolines?"

"I don't know. From what I'm hearing, we'll spend a lot of time walking, and it will be dusty and dirty. We'll be doing our own laundry and cooking. We can't wear our good quality clothing for that." Enough light came into the tent now that she could see Anne's troubled face. "Perhaps we need some plain dresses in calico or printed muslin."

Anne sighed. "Like the one I gave away yesterday."

"No, not white. I think we should look carefully at what the other women on the wagon train are wearing. Most seem to favor a full skirt with a basque that buttons up the front."

"I'm not sure I'm ready to give up my crinolines," Anne said.

"Well, I'm going to go and root through my trunk for something more suitable, and then I'll start breakfast." Elise patted about in search of her shoes.

"I shall help you." Anne crawled out of the blankets. "Brrr. But if I'm going to be a true pioneer woman, I need to brave the cold and learn to cook."

"Call to me when you're ready for me to help you with your corset."

Elise crawled out of the tent, stood up, and lowered the flap. She looked around at the camp. Every wagon but theirs had a fire burning near it, and women hovered over them. Children scampered about, and dogs woofed. Men walked purposefully with buckets of water and armloads of firewood.

"Morning, ma'am."

Elise turned and found herself face-to-face with Thomas. "Hello. Early risers here, aren't they?"

He chuckled. "That's the usual, ma'am. Once we're on the trail, we'll get up even earlier than this. We'll most likely pull out at sunup every day. That means we've got to have breakfast over with and the dishes packed up and the team harnessed and ready to move."

Elise eyed him with wonder. "Indeed."

With new determination, she found the dress she'd all but ruined on the ship coming over. She'd mended a tear, but the stains from food and tea spilled during a storm had refused to come out. She'd almost discarded it after they landed, but kept it, thinking she might be able to salvage the material. Out here, no one would care about stains, and the huge apron she'd purchased at the emporium would engulf her, covering most of them.

She changed in the wagon, donning the old dress, and climbed down. The final step was a good eighteen inches, and she plunged to earth and staggered. Thomas was lighting the fire and didn't seem to notice. After she caught her breath, she hurried to the tent door.

"Anne? Do you need my assistance?"

"Yes please."

Anne had on her stockings and cotton drawers. Elise helped her mistress get into her garters and chemise. Next came the corset. She fastened it in front then turned Anne around so she could pull the strings tight.

"Do you want your petticoat with the smaller hoop in the hem today?" Elise whispered.

Anne looked over the streamlined silhouette Elise had chosen. "Yes, I think so. I'm sure we'll be less of a curiosity if we leave off our wide hoops."

Lady Anne's plainest walking costume was still much more elegant than anything the other women wore. Elise helped her adjust the bodice and skirt.

"Where's my hat?" Anne asked.

Elise hesitated. The hat that matched the costume was very ornate, suitable for a promenade in Hyde Park.

"I thought perhaps we'd wear bonnets today. You have a lovely blue-and-white one that will shade your face from the sun."

"Oh. All right, if you think it best. I don't suppose I'll meet any dowagers of the ton today."

"My thought precisely. Fashion might not be an asset on the wagon train."

Cooking breakfast was an ordeal, especially with Thomas lingering about, looking ravenous.

Elise cut several slabs of bacon and put them in the cast-iron skillet. It had little legs that allowed her to set it over the fire, but the pan was extremely heavy.

"I can watch the bacon," Anne said. "How hard can it be?"

Elise handed her a long-handled fork. "Just be careful your skirt doesn't come near the fire." She got out the cookery book and ingredients for what the Americans called "biscuits." The biscuits Elise knew were small, shaped sweets, but the waiter in St. Louis had informed her that those were known in this country as "cookies." Their biscuits were more like round, flaky scones. Prepared well, they were very tasty, and Elise wanted to learn to make what seemed to be a staple of the American diet.

She read through the recipe, feeling increasingly helpless. Cut lard into flour. How did one do that? With a knife? She could make scones—maybe she'd better stick to those. But there was no recipe for scones in the book, and she didn't think she could do it from memory. She drew in a deep breath and measured out the flour for a batch of biscuits. From a small keg, she scooped a blob of lard into her pottery bowl with the flour. Next she took a knife and fork and carved at the lard over and over, pressing the small pieces into the flour.

She was still at it when Rob Whistler came by ten minutes later. He greeted Anne first.

"Looks like your fire's getting low, ma'am. Would you like me to add some wood?"

"Oh, thank you." Anne stepped aside and watched him work.

Mr. Whistler lifted the spider off the coals with ease, added three short sticks of wood, then replaced the spider. He stood and brushed off his hands.

"How are you ladies getting along?"

"Fine, thank you," Anne said.

"Miss Finster?" he asked.

"I...uh....I'm cooking biscuits."

He nodded. "Most of the ladies make a big batch whenever they cook on the trail. That way, you have enough for a cold meal at nooning."

"That's good to know." Elise looked down at her bowl. "I'm not sure I'm doing this correctly. American cooking seems to be different from English, and so many things go by different names."

Whistler smiled. "I'm sure you'll get the hang of it. And Mrs. Harkness, over yonder"—he pointed across the encampment to where three wagons were drawn close together—"makes fine biscuits. She gave a few to Eb and me last night. I'm sure she'd be happy to give you some pointers."

"Thank you." Elise's independent streak vied with a rush of relief. Perhaps the other women on the wagon train would offer assistance, and even friendship, to her and Anne.

"How's that hired man working out?" Whistler asked.

"Fine. He brought us firewood this morning."

"Well, let me know if you need anything." Whistler nodded at her and Anne and strode off toward the next wagon.

"He's such a nice man," Anne said. "I think he likes you."

"Nonsense," Elise said. "He's only trying to enhance our chances of completing the trip successfully in order to save face with Eb Bentley."

"Whatever do you mean?" Anne stepped closer, her face troubled.

"Isn't it obvious? Mr. Bentley never wanted us along. He's sure we'll drop out or at best slow down the caravan. He probably thinks we'll die along the trail because we're so inept. Well, I intend to prove him wrong."

"Oh, I see." Anne nodded, still watching Elise's face.

Whatever was she hinting at?

A sudden crackling behind Anne drew Elise's attention. The flames of the campfire leaped high, and black smoke roiled skyward.

"Oh! The bacon!" Elise ran to the fire and grabbed the pot holder Anne had left on one of the rocks of their fire ring. When she reached for the spider's handle, the huge flames drove her back. She lunged in again, grabbed the handle, and tried to drag the heavy spider off the fire. She only succeeded in tipping it.

Hot grease spilled over onto the flames, and the fire roared higher.

Someone grabbed her from behind and yanked her back. Elise tumbled to the ground and gasped.

"You want to catch your clothes on fire?"

She looked up into the irate face of Eb Bentley.

***

Eb stomped on the smoldering edge of the Finster woman's hem and glared down at her. How ignorant could an obviously intelligent woman possibly be?

She sat up, patting vaguely at her skirt, and looked from him to the fire pit, where the blaze still roared. Miss Stone stood by staring, her face pale, with one hand clapped to her mouth.

"I suppose I should thank you," Miss Finster said doubtfully.

Eb sighed and offered his hand to help her up. She grasped it firmly and rose, batting at her ridiculous dress.

"Fires and full skirts don't mix, ma'am," he said. "Especially when you throw a pint of grease on the fire."

Her eyes blazed. "What do you know about it?"

"I know how to cook bacon."

She huffed out a breath and flounced away from him, toward the fire.

"I'd let that burn down and then start over," Eb called after her.

Miss Stone seemed to have found her wits at last. "Thomas's breakfast is ruined, and it's my fault. I suppose we'll need a new spider."

"Nah," Eb said. "Just take it to the creek and scrub it out good. But don't try to take it out of the fire until it's cooled down. And I suggest you give your hired man a cold breakfast this morning."

Miss Finster looked over her shoulder at him. "But I have the dough for the scones nearly mixed. Biscuits, that is."

Eb shook his head. "Whyn't you ask Mrs. Harkness yonder if she'll let you bake them over there? Her fire's down to coals. I expect they ate breakfast an hour ago."

Miss Finster's cheeks went red. "For your information, that fire was fine until your boss came along a few minutes ago and put more wood on it."

"My boss? Oh, you mean Rob?" Eb chuckled. "He's not my boss. Nobody's my boss, lady."

Her jaw tightened. "I beg your pardon. That should have been obvious." She marched to the back of the wagon, where she'd set out her cooking things, and began working furiously at some mixture she had in a pottery bowl.

Eb looked over at Miss Stone and shrugged.

"Thank you for your assistance, Mr. Bentley," the young woman said earnestly. "I'm sure that when the shock has passed, Miss Finster will realize how opportune your intervention was."

Eb stared at her for a moment and decided she wasn't poking fun at him. "Think nothing of it, miss. But I would get rid of those high-toned fashions if I were you. Hard enough getting in and out of a wagon in a dress, or so I imagine, but cooking around an open fire—well, you're just asking for trouble."

"Perhaps you're right. My friend and I will discuss it. Thank you very much."

Eb nodded and glanced at Miss Finster. She ignored him as she pored over a cookery book—or maybe the recipe really fascinated her. Eb touched his hat brim in Miss Stone's direction and ambled on toward the next wagon.

Daniel Adams, the owner, was loading a wooden box of pans into the back of his rig.

"Morning, Dan."

"Hey, Eb. Everything all right with the English ladies?"

"Oh, yeah. They just don't have much experience camping." Eb chatted for a moment then went on to the wagon belonging to Dan's brother. Hector was seated on a small keg, braiding some strands of twine together. Eb was about to speak to him when he noticed Costigan coming along the path from the creek that flowed into the Missouri River.

"Hey."

Costigan looked toward him and shifted his pail of water to his other hand.

"Yeah?"

"Your employers had a scare with their fire. You might want to help the ladies clean up the mess and teach them how to lay a fire that will give them some good coals for cooking."

Costigan frowned. "The fire was fine when I left to get the water."

"Took you long enough to fetch it," Eb noted.

Costigan said nothing but lurched on toward the women's wagon. Eb wondered how he'd react when he learned the ladies had nothing prepared for him to eat.

He walked back to where he and Rob had spread their bedrolls the night before. Rob was saddling his horse.

"Heading into town?" Eb asked.

"Yeah, there's always a few last-minute folks who want to join up. I reckon we could take two or three more families. Need anything from town?"

"Nope. But I wish you'd turned those Englishwomen out."

"What do you mean? Throw them off the train? Why?"

"That Miss Finster almost burnt herself up this morning. If I hadn't happened along at the right moment, she'd have gone up in flames."

Rob frowned. "I was by their camp a little while ago and added a couple of sticks to their fire, but it wasn't out of control."

"Oh, she's blaming you for the incident. I don't know what happened for sure, but she managed to tip the spider over and dump the bacon grease on the fire. Her skirt was starting to catch when I grabbed her away."

Rob shook his head. "They just need to get their trail legs, so to speak. Good thing you came along."

"Ha!" Eb leaned toward his friend. "I almost wish I hadn't saved her. If she'd burnt herself to a crisp, we wouldn't have to stop along the way long enough to bury her."

"You don't mean that." Rob looked rather shocked at his bald statement.

Eb rubbed the back of his neck. "No, of course I don't. But, Rob, you've got to tell them they can't go."

"On what grounds?"

"They're. . .they're. . . Oh, you know! They're *ladies*."

Rob laughed. "Is that the worst thing you can say about them?"

"You know what I mean. They're the sort of ladies who haven't a notion of how to do for themselves. That means trouble on a wagon train. Sooner or later—and probably sooner—there's going to be an accident, and someone's going to get hurt."

"Settle down. I'll ask Mrs. Harkness to stop by and see if she can help them with their cooking setup. Miss Finster and Miss Stone could have stayed at the hotel until Sunday, Eb, but they didn't. They want to learn how to live out of a wagon before they hit the trail, and I have to admire them for that. They're *trying*."

Eb slapped his hat against his thigh. "Oh, they're trying, all right. Trying my patience."

# CHAPTER 11

Mrs. Harkness looked up from her sewing as Elise and Anne approached the large family's encampment.

"Well, hello, ladies! I was thinking of coming over to meet you later. I'm Rebecca." She stuck her needle into her project and rose from the rocking chair that sat on the ground beside one of the wagons.

Elise introduced herself and Anne. "We wondered if you might be willing to help us. . . ." She stopped, embarrassed to admit their shortcomings. "Well, you see, neither one of us has ever had much instruction on cooking, particularly over an open fire."

Mrs. Harkness eyed her dubiously. "Surely you ladies have baked bread before?"

"Actually, we haven't."

The older woman made a *tsk* sound. "Your mothers didn't teach you?"

Elise felt her cheeks flush. "Miss Stone's mother died several years ago, and I. . .well, I began earning my living when I was quite young, and cooking was not one of my duties."

"Oh my."

"I can do passably well on a stove," Elise added hastily. "Basic meals and refreshments. But this is a new experience, working over the open flames and having a hungry hired man to feed. We thought you might be able to share your knowledge with us."

"I'd be happy to. Would you like me to come over to your wagon? It might be best if you learned using your own dishes and such."

"That sounds reasonable," Elise said.

"And most kind of you," Anne added.

Rebecca's cordial reception encouraged Elise, and she was able to overlook any differences between them. Fashion and "station" didn't matter as they went about the task of preparing a cook fire for baking.

Only an hour had passed since Eb Bentley had jerked her so rudely away from her fireside. Elise was still angry at him, though the sight of her singed hem had tempered her ire. That dress was ruined—unless she decided to shorten it. She had put it away in her trunk, out of sight until she had time to think about it.

First Mrs. Harkness showed them how to mix a simple batter for cornbread, or "johnnycake" as she called it. That was easier and quicker to prepare than biscuits, she pointed out. The ladies could always fall back on it when time was short, though it took an egg. Elise assured her they had several dozen among their stores, preserved in lard.

Baking the johnnycake in the dutch oven over the coals proved to be tricky. Mrs. Harkness had mastered the process from forty years or so of practice. She showed Elise and Anne how to situate the cast-iron pot on a bed of coals and then shovel more coals on top of the lid.

"But how do you know when the coals are ready—not too hot, but still hot enough?" Anne asked.

"They just look right," Rebecca said with a frown. "Dear me, I don't know."

They left the johnnycake to bake slowly while she showed them how to prepare passable biscuit dough. Anne insisted on learning, too. Elise was gratified to see that for the most part, she'd made her dough correctly. Their teacher pointed out that biscuits had the advantage of not needing eggs.

Again, the baking was the difficult part. They'd made four batches before Mrs. Harkness pronounced them "proper" biscuits. Elise was going to throw out the first three batches, but Mrs. Harkness protested.

"You're going to throw them away? That's scandalous! Even the ones you blackened, the oxen will eat. And I daresay that hired man of yours can stomach the others."

When they were alone, Elise and Anne agreed to give Thomas

the best biscuits and eat the trial batches themselves. It was a type of frontier penance, Elise supposed. And as Mrs. Harkness had reminded them, "Waste not, want not."

They parted cheerfully at the end of the lesson, and Rebecca offered to send her "big girl," Lavinia, over in the morning if they needed help at breakfast time, but Elise was now so confident that she was certain they wouldn't need Lavinia's assistance. And she most assuredly would not need Eb Bentley's aid.

On Saturday morning, Elise awoke while it was still dark. She lay in the tent listening for sounds of activity. Soon she caught faint rustles and a thud as one of the Adams brothers lowered the hinged back of his wagon. She sat up and groped for the clothing she'd carefully set out the night before, close at hand so she could find it easily. The dress was one of her plainer ones. She'd spent the previous afternoon taking in the skirt and shortening the hem so that she could wear it without hoops and full underskirts and yet not have it dragging on the ground. Even so, it hung longer than most of the emigrant women wore their dresses.

She emerged from the tent to the first birdcalls of dawn. Already wood smoke hung in the air. The glow of four campfires was visible from where she stood.

*It's simply a matter of adapting to the schedule,* she told herself. Breakfast at daybreak, bedtime at sundown or shortly after. She could make that adjustment and thrive on it.

Poor Anne found everything about the trip more daunting than Elise did. Elise felt they could overcome each difficulty, one task at a time. But for Anne, life in the encampment was completely foreign. Tending the fire, preparing meals, keeping their clothing clean and in good repair, not to mention the dirt, the smoke, and the drudgery of it all—these were things she'd never been asked to deal with before. Servants performed the menial labor, and her family and Elise had shrouded her from all unpleasantness. She'd put on a brave front during their entire trip, but at several points yesterday, Elise could tell she was on the verge of tears. Perhaps she was reconsidering her decision to find her uncle, no matter how hard the quest.

But just as Anne started to realize the sheer enormity of their undertaking, Elise began to revel in it. They would have to make changes. They must cast aside many assumptions and embrace the more casual ways of America—in short, the freedom. If they could do that, they could enjoy this new life. She would try to help Anne come to that point of view. Giving up the journey now was unthinkable.

In the gray morning light, Elise hurried to the wagon and took out the box she'd stocked the evening before with the utensils she would need for making breakfast, as well as the leftover biscuits they'd deemed edible. She resolved to cook bacon this morning without burning it or spilling the grease into the fire, and to fry a few eggs for Thomas out of those the storekeeper had packed so carefully for them a few days back. She hoped the eggs would mollify Thomas enough that he wouldn't notice their biscuits' imperfections.

As she stirred the ashes of last night's fire, she wondered how she would ever get the blaze going. Mrs. Harkness had told her to cover the live coals with ashes at night, to "bank" the fire. Elise had done that, but now there seemed to be only a few tiny orange coals left in the mess. She took a couple of sticks off the wood pile, but she didn't think they'd catch from the meager embers. She wished she had some paper to burn.

Where was Thomas, anyway? Maybe he'd gotten used to the idea that she wouldn't get up until the sun was high above the horizon and figured there was no sense building the fire too early.

She knelt and blew on the pile but only succeeded in blowing ashes over her precious coals. She brushed them away and blew again. The coals shone brightly while her breath lasted, but the large sticks showed no disposition to catching fire.

Eb Bentley came around the end of the wagon, strolling as though he had not a care in the world.

"Morning, miss. Let me make that up for you?"

Elise clenched her teeth. Why did it have to be him? And if he disdained her and Anne so much, why was he offering to do this for her? Wouldn't he rather see her fail and give up?

She rose and brushed off her skirt, resolved to learn to cope, no matter who the instructor. "Thank you, Mr. Bentley. Could you please show me how it's done? I'd like to become proficient at this, but there don't seem to be many live coals left."

"Oh, they're in there, miss. You've got to stir around in the ashes and pull together any little bits that glow."

He reached down and removed the large sticks she'd set in the fireplace. Tapping them together, he let the ashes fall off them into the pit.

"And you need some tinder—anything small that will burn well." He looked toward the edge of the field. "Anytime you're near pine trees, you can usually find little twigs underneath the overhanging branches. They're small enough to light from a match, and they usually keep dry, even when it's wet out." He strode purposefully toward the trees.

Elise placed her hands on her hips and gazed after him. Should she have offered to go? She probably wouldn't have been able to find the right twigs.

She wanted to. She wanted to know exactly what to use. This would make her and Anne more independent. She hurried after him, holding her skirt up and hoping he didn't turn and see her engaging in such unladylike behavior.

He reached a pine tree on the edge of the sparse woods. The emigrants were forbidden to cut down the trees. If they did, the man who owned the land would make them leave and would never allow another wagon train to form there. Anne had paid for enough split wood in town to give them a small woodpile. Once they hit the trail, Elise had no idea how they would find more, but they couldn't haul enough to feed their cook fires all the way to Oregon.

Eb lifted a low-hanging pine branch and ducked beneath it. Elise came up behind him.

"Will any pine tree do?"

He looked up with a flicker of surprise on his face. "Unless someone else beat you to it. See here?" He pointed to some small twigs sticking out from the trunk—smaller around than her knitting needles. "A handful of those will work."

"What about pine needles?"

He shrugged. "If they're dry, they'll catch fast, but they'll burn quick, too. Maybe quicker than you want them to. Get a bunch of these twigs, and then something a little bigger—that's your kindling—and put your fuel wood on last, once the little stuff is burning."

She nodded, hoping she could remember the steps. She would *not* call him back to demonstrate again. He gathered a few small branches off the ground inside the tree line, passed them to her, and then broke a few more dry twigs off the bole of another pine tree.

"All right, that should be enough."

She tried to match his long strides as they walked back to the wagon. He set down his load and picked up the crooked stick she'd used to stir the fire. Kneeling before the stone circle, he used the stick to probe the ashes until he found the little embers and herded them together. In a couple of minutes, he had a small cluster of them.

"Tinder." He held up his hand.

Elise placed a clump of the pine twigs in it. Eb bent and put them on top of the coals, heaped up above them in a loose bunch.

"More."

When he'd used all the little twigs, he took the larger dead branches, broke them in short lengths, and stood them up in a little pyramid over the pile, like the frames the gardener at Stoneford used to make over the bean plants. Eb stooped low and blew gently on the embers.

Nothing happened at first. Elise was disappointed. Apparently Eb didn't have the secret down as well as he thought.

Suddenly a flame shot up and licked the twigs. Eb kept blowing softly until the whole thing caught. He sat up and watched the kindling begin to burn.

Elise laughed. "I'm sure I would have given up."

"Are you carrying any matches?"

"Yes, we have a few, and a flint and steel."

He reached for some larger sticks from her woodpile. "You never need to be without fire, then. If you've got no coals, just set it up and light a match."

"Thank you."

"Not much to it. You'll be an expert inside a week."

"Maybe. I do want to learn how to do things for myself."

He nodded. "I see that. It's a commendable attitude." He added a few more sticks. "Let that burn down some before you try to cook. You don't want to put your pots over high flames like that. Wait until it's settled down and you have a bed of coals."

"Yes. Rebecca Harkness showed us what to look for yesterday." Though Elise still wasn't completely sure she'd know the exact moment to begin her cooking.

He stood and glanced toward her wagon. "Do you have a grate?"

"I. . .don't think so. Should I?"

"It'd make things easier. You can put it on top of the stones if you shape your fireplace right, and your pots will sit up above the fire. That's good for frying things."

She nodded. "I guess we could get one at the general store."

"Could be."

Anne poked her head out of the tent. "Good morning, Mr. Bentley."

He turned toward her and smiled. "Morning, Miss Stone. Miss Finster's going to have your coffee ready in two shakes."

"Oh, Miss Stone prefers tea," Elise said.

"Your tea, then." Eb looked at Elise. "You can set your pot of water in there. Can't burn water. And while it heats and the fire burns down to where you can cook over it, maybe I can give your wagon a last once-over."

"I beg your pardon?" Elise's urge to defend herself and point out that she was not the one who burned the bacon yesterday dissipated as she took in his last remark. "You intend to look into our wagon?"

"Yes, ma'am. Rob and I will inspect all the wagons today and tomorrow. We don't want anyone setting out unprepared."

"I assure you, we have all the equipment specified on the list."

"I'm sure you do," Eb said. "And I saw your wagon before you bought it, so I know it's in good shape. But have you loaded your goods to advantage?"

She wasn't sure what he meant by that last question, but Thomas had seemed to know how to load a wagon, so she looked him in the eye and said, "I believe we have."

"Good. Let's take a look."

He walked to the back of their wagon and stood expectantly, waiting for Elise to open up the rear flap. Elise glanced at Anne.

Anne shrugged. "If they're doing this to everyone. . .I mean, it's better to know now if we need to buy anything else. Isn't it?"

Elise tried to keep a neutral expression as she tied the flap back and lowered the tailboard of the wagon.

Eb peered inside then climbed up and began poking about.

Anne came to stand by Elise. "He's not opening our chests, is he?"

"No. If he did, I should protest loudly."

"I wish we could know that this is worth it—that we'll find Uncle David in Oregon."

"There are no guarantees."

Anne let out a sigh. "I suppose not. But it will take us months to make ourselves presentable again when we go back to England. I've already broken most of my nails, and I despair of ever feeling truly clean again. And we've not even set out yet!"

Elise slipped her arm around the girl—for Anne did seem like a girl to her still. Most days she kept her "mature young woman" mask in place, but Elise knew the child within.

"My dear, we can't turn back now. Think of the regret you'd suffer and the renewed agony of not knowing what became of David."

"Yes, you're right."

Eb climbed out at the front of the wagon and walked slowly to them, eyeing the buckets and tools they had tied to the side of the wagon.

When he reached them, he nodded soberly. "You ladies seem to have everything necessary for supplies. I suggest you lighten the load a bit. You're using mules, and they can only pull so much weight up the mountains."

"Lighten the load?" Anne stared at him with round eyes.

"Yes, miss. If I were you, I'd toss out a couple of those heavy trunks."

Outrage welled in Elise's breast. "Those trunks hold Lady—" She stopped short as she realized her mistake. Blood rushed to her cheeks, and her face felt like it was on fire. "I wouldn't think of asking Miss Stone to appear in Oregon City society, however provincial it may be, without a proper wardrobe, sir. You don't know what you're asking."

He shot her a keen glance then addressed Anne.

"I'm not saying you should get rid of everything, miss, but if you want to get to Oregon without killing those mules of yours, you'd do well to reduce your load."

Anne swallowed hard and turned to Elise. "Perhaps we should sell some of my clothing and buy plain calico dresses like the other women are wearing. We've talked about it. . . ."

"Yes, we have." Elise shuddered at the thought of Lady Anne in such drab dresses, but she could see the practicality of getting rid of the laces and flounces. In addition to blending in better with the farmers' wives, they'd be able to cook and tend livestock more safely in plain clothing. "I suppose we might be able to do with a bit less, and we could buy more once we arrived."

"Certainly." Anne's face brightened.

"Besides," Eb said drily, "Oregon City society may not be all you're thinking it is."

# CHAPTER 12

Elise and Anne went about breakfast preparation with grim resolution. In only an hour, they were able to present Thomas with a plate full of biscuits (left from their lesson the day before), bacon (not burned), and eggs (cooked carefully by Anne in the bacon grease and only a little browned). While Elise took the dishes to the creek to wash them, Anne supervised the unloading of two of her trunks.

The rest of their morning was occupied in sorting through both women's gowns. After much deliberation, Anne closed the hasps on the smallest of her three trunks.

"I suppose if we're going to try this, we need to do it this afternoon. Tomorrow is the Lord's Day, and we can't be transacting business then."

Elise nodded. She wished they could have thinned their wardrobes even more. Most of the items they'd agreed to dispose of belonged to her mistress, but she'd added a dress from her own collection that required several petticoats to support it. Anne was giving up five gowns. Between them, they would relieve the mule team of more than fifty pounds of goods to haul, including the weight of the chest.

"Wilbur Harkness says he'll take us to town with it in his farm wagon," Elise said.

"Should we post a letter to Mr. Conrad or Cousin Randolph?" Anne asked.

"What for? We've nothing to tell them."

Anne nodded, but her brow puckered. "I felt a bit guilty not revealing our plans to Randolph before we left."

"You told Mr. Conrad. That's enough."

Elise had felt it needful for someone in England to know where they'd gone, in case tragedy befell them during their travels. But

Anne hadn't wanted to broadcast her plans to the world, and so they'd left England quietly. Elise hoped they could complete their mission and return in triumph.

The Harkness family had two wagons covered with canvas and stuffed with their goods, but Wilbur, the couple's eldest son of twenty-two years, had convinced his father to hold off on covering the smaller farm wagon.

"He told his pa they should put the canvas on last thing, and stow the tools and animal feed in it," Rebecca confided to Elise as they watched Wilbur and his younger brother load Anne's trunk. "That way we've been able to keep using the small wagon to fetch stuff."

"That's been a blessing to others," Elise said.

"Oh yes. Several families have needed to go into town for some last-minute business and found it very helpful not to have to take their ox teams and covered wagons."

Elise determined to pay Wilbur something and not take advantage of the family's generosity, but he wouldn't hear of it.

"We're neighbors for the next five or six months, ma'am. I wouldn't think of charging a neighbor when I'm going into town anyway."

It was more than most people would do, Elise was sure. Wilbur's mother and her two eldest daughters, Lavinia and fourteen-year-old Abby, rode with them and the trunk. Wilbur exhibited his courtliest manners, especially when Anne was close by.

At the general store, the owner reluctantly came out to inspect the merchandise they offered. He shook his head as Elise held up one gown after another.

"I dunno, ladies. I can't imagine the women of this town buying such fancy duds. And women going west sure won't want 'em. I get a lot of stuff people can't take with 'em, but I don't know if I can take these. The trunk, maybe, if you want to empty it out."

"Why would we want to sell you a trunk and keep the things in it?" Elise placed her hands on her hips and scowled at him.

He shrugged. "You could set up on the corner and ask folks if they'd like to buy, I s'pose. 'Scuse me, I got payin' customers inside." He ambled into his store.

Anne's eyes glimmered with unshed tears. "What shall we do now?"

"I could ask him if he'd trade these gowns for cotton and woolen dress goods," Elise suggested.

"Didn't sound hopeful." Lavinia grimaced in sympathy.

"You could try doing what he said," Mrs. Harkness told Elise. "Set the trunk down on the boardwalk here and sell to people going into the store."

"Ma, I like that lilac dress," Lavinia said, leaning over the open trunk. "Do you think we could buy it?"

"Don't talk nonsense, child. We don't have a spare nickel. Your father would rant from here to Sunday if we came back with a fancy dress like that."

"But Mr. Whistler said maybe there'll be dancing some nights—especially when we get to Independence Rock."

"And you'll wear your green cotton, not some outlandish fashion from Europe." Mrs. Harkness gathered her skirt and lifted it slightly. "I wish you good fortune, ladies. Come, Lavinia. Abby. Let's go get those things we came to get." They went into the store.

Wilbur, who'd stood by in silence during this exchange, said, "I've got to get over to the wainwright's and pick up our extra wagon rims. Do you ladies want me to hoist that chest out onto the sidewalk for you?"

"I suppose we've no other option," Elise said. At least the store owner had given tacit permission for them to set up their clothing business outside his establishment.

A few minutes later, two women who were walking toward the general store diverted their steps to see what the finely groomed ladies were offering out of a steamer trunk.

"Oh, how lovely," one of them said, her eyes softening. She fingered the folds of the golden satin gown Anne had worn to Lady Erskine's ball the previous spring. "So impractical though."

Her companion's lip curled. "Where would you ever wear it, Mary?"

"You never spoke a truer word."

The two women turned away.

A man and his wife slowed to take a quick look.

"Imagine spending good money on something like that," the man said. "You can't wear that to the chicken coop."

One somber woman turned up her nose and muttered, "The idea. Women out peddling their clothing on the street. It isn't proper."

Anne had again reached the verge of tears. Elise handed her a lace-edged lawn handkerchief. "There, my dear. Don't be discouraged. If no one wants them, you'll get to keep them—there's always a bright side."

"Oh Elise, you always say the right thing." Anne gave her a watery smile.

"Well, maybe I haven't said the right thing all day." Elise squeezed her arm. "I should have suggested that we pray about this venture before we ever set out on it. If the Lord wants us to sell dresses, He'll bring along buyers, now won't He?"

"Afternoon, ladies."

They looked up into the face of a cheerful young man in overalls. He smiled broadly through his russet beard. "Whatcha sellin'?"

Was this the answer to the prayers they had not yet voiced? Elise said, "Only the finest gowns you'll see this side of London. They were made by a fine seamstress there, sir. You must have a lady in your life who'd like to wear a dress of the best quality—something she couldn't find out here on the frontier."

He gulped and stole a glance at Anne then looked at the trunk. "Well, I do have someone, ma'am, but she's back in Boston. I had to leave her there while I came out to Missouri to start my farm. But I'm ready to go back and claim her now."

"How sweet," Elise said. "And she's been waiting for you."

"Yes'm. Two years. I reckon I'm ready to bring her out here now. We've set the wedding for June the twelfth, and I'm leaving as soon as I get my crop in the ground."

"Oh sir," Anne said, reaching into the trunk, "wouldn't your young lady like to have a pure silk gown? She could wear it when you take her to church in Boston."

"Or at the fete her parents throw before the wedding," Elise said. "Tell me, is she slender like my friend? Anne has the most beautiful gown in there that's gathered and flounced. The slate-blue one, Anne."

"Yes, ma'am, she's about the size of this young lady."

Anne delved into the trunk and brought out the gown Elise had mentioned.

"I could picture her in a dress like that."

"Are they wearing hoop petticoats in Boston?" Elise asked.

The young man's face went scarlet. "I'm sure I don't know."

"It's the height of fashion in London."

Five minutes later, the man carried Anne's gown and crinoline to his wagon, and she tucked the money he'd parted with into her reticule.

"I'm not used to the mathematics of the currency yet," Anne said, "but I don't think we got a quarter of what that gown cost new."

Elise smiled serenely. "You didn't, but you got some good wear out of it, and it's for a good cause. You know Mr. Bentley won't let us start out with an overloaded wagon."

"True. And we might need the money desperately before our journey is done."

"Let us give thanks," Elise said.

⁂

When Rebecca Harkness and her daughters returned, Lavinia carried a small bundle wrapped in brown paper.

"Sold anything?" she asked.

"One gown," Anne said.

Lavinia shrugged. "Better than nothing."

"Here comes Wilbur," her mother said. "Are you ladies ready to go back to the field?"

Elise looked at Anne. "It's getting late."

Anne glanced anxiously toward the door of the general store.

"Yes, and we hoped to have time to buy some suitable ready-made travel dresses to replace these. Perhaps we should ask the store owner again if he'd take the rest of the gowns. . .for a very small price."

"I saw a dressmaker's sign down the street," Lavinia said.

Elise looked where she pointed. "That's a thought. She may have customers who would buy our things."

"If you ladies want to go talk to her, I'll tell Wilbur," Rebecca said. "We can wait a few minutes."

"I'll show you where it is," Lavinia offered.

Elise smiled at Anne. "Why don't you stay here with Mrs. Harkness and Abby. I'll go with Lavinia and see if I can convince the seamstress to come look at the dresses."

"Maybe Miss Anne would like to go into the general store and look over the dresses they've got," Rebecca said. "If you're getting rid of your finery, you'll want something plain to wear on the trail."

Anne looked relieved. "I could go in and see what's available."

"That's probably a good idea," Elise said.

"Yes, and with Rebecca here to advise me, I'm sure I wouldn't purchase the wrong thing."

Mrs. Harkness's tanned face split in a big smile at Anne's expression of trust.

Lavinia led Elise down the street to a house with a modest sign out front. They found the gray-haired seamstress in the front room, where she apparently did most of her work. A rocking chair sat by the window with a work basket nearby, and a low table covered with folded lengths of fabric and pattern pieces cut from newspapers.

"Don't know if I can use any ready-mades." She peered at Elise and Lavinia through small, oval spectacles.

Before Elise could speak, Lavinia jumped in. "Oh ma'am, you've got to see them. These aren't any common dresses. They're beautiful ball gowns. Some famous tailor in England made 'em."

"Seamstress," Elise said gently. "But yes, we have a satin ball gown, and a couple of day dresses that any lady would be proud to wear to church, or to a wedding, or some other event. They're extremely well made. We wouldn't be selling them, except that my friend and I are heading for Oregon, and the wagon master says we must reduce our load before we set out."

"Hmm." The woman frowned. "I guess I can look 'em over. Can you bring 'em here? I've got a customer coming for a fitting any minute."

"Oh, well—"

"Of course we can," Lavinia said.

Elise arched her eyebrows.

"I'll make my brother drive the wagon down here with the trunk in it."

"All right, just be quick." The seamstress all but pushed them out the door.

They bustled down the sidewalk to the general store. Rebecca was unsuccessfully declaring the merits of Elise's promenade dress to two women who shook their heads and walked away as Lavinia and Elise approached.

"Pack them in the trunk, Ma," Lavinia called. "Wilbur, load it in the wagon. If we take these things to the seamstress's door, I think she'll buy them."

"Abigail, quick," Rebecca told her younger daughter. "Run into the store and tell Miss Anne." She and Elise hastily folded the gowns into the chest and closed it.

A moment later, as Wilbur tugged the trunk toward the rear of the wagon, Anne emerged from the store with an armful of calico. She lifted a questioning gaze to Elise.

"Don't count your shillings yet," Elise said, "but it's a possibility the seamstress with oblige us."

Wilbur called, "Come on, Liv, get on the other end."

Lavinia took one handle and helped Wilbur hoist it onto the wagon bed. A few minutes later, Elise knocked again on the seamstress's door.

"My customer is here." She glanced over her shoulder. "I told her I had someone bringing a few things to sell, and she said she'd wait. Bring them in. It's possible she might be interested in something."

Elise hurried back to the wagon, where Wilbur had already set the trunk onto the sidewalk.

"We're to take them in. Shall I help?"

Wilbur shook his head. "I think I can get it, if you hold the door."

Anne hopped out of the wagon and followed him up the steps. He set the trunk down just inside the threshold. "I'll wait for you."

Elise nodded and turned toward the seamstress. Anne closed the door discreetly behind them.

"Well, let's see what you got," the woman said.

Anne bent to undo the hasp. Elise glanced beyond the mistress of the house, curious about the customer who might buy the dresses. At once she averted her gaze. The woman standing in the far corner wore an extremely short red dress with a neckline cut so low Elise felt the blood rush to her cheeks. She was thankful that Wilbur had not ventured farther into the room. She helped Anne take out her satin ball gown first.

The seamstress bent close and fingered the material. "Hmm. Let me examine the stitching."

Elise helped her carry the mound of slippery material over to the window. The seamstress sat down and adjusted her spectacles. She proceeded to turn the bodice inside out and peer at the seams. She let go and pulled up the skirt until she found the hem and turned it for a critical look.

The woman in the corner stepped forward. "Now, that looks like high-toned cloth, don't it?"

Elise had to force herself to keep from staring at the customer's heavily powdered and rouged face. She looked over at Anne, but her mistress was delving into the trunk for another dress.

"I don't mean to hurry you, ma'am," Anne said, "but our driver is waiting. This lovely promenade gown belongs to Miss Finster, so it's a little longer than the others. It's a fine silk and woolen blend. I recollect her wearing it when we attended the Great Exhibition in London."

The seamstress grunted, but the other woman hung on Anne's every word, her lips parted and her eyes round.

"It were something special?"

"Oh yes," Anne said. "The Crystal Palace was a wonder on its own, but the exhibits and vendors from all around the world—it was truly amazing."

The woman sighed.

"And this was one of my day dresses." Anne pulled out their final offering. The customer's eyes gleamed when she saw the rich plum-colored fabric and silver braid.

"How much you want for these?" the seamstress asked.

Elise named a rather high price, she thought, in American dollars.

The seamstress scowled. "That's too much."

"Take them," said the customer. "Take them all, if you think you can let out that satin enough to fit me. In fact, if you can't, that's all right. I'm sure it would fit Velvet. She's scrawny as a stray cat." She stepped forward and touched the plum dress. "You'll have to alter this one, but I expect you won't have any trouble taking out a bit around the neck."

Anne gulped and turned a helpless expression Elise's way.

Elise reached out and patted her shoulder. "We are agreed, then."

The seamstress got up, still scowling, and folded the dress she held back into the trunk.

"And did you want the trunk as well?" Elise dared to ask.

The old woman squinted at her. "How much?"

Anne said, "Two dollars."

Muttering, the seamstress hobbled out of the room.

"It is a lot for the dresses," the customer said, "but I'm sure you ladies wouldn't cheat that old woman."

Anne's face flushed at the very suggestion.

"Certainly not," Elise said. "The price we're asking isn't half what Miss Stone paid in England."

"Yes, I can see it's all quality goods."

The seamstress came back and handed Elise a gold coin and several paper bills. "There. That'll buy you some cornmeal and bacon."

"Do you have any more?" the customer asked.

"Uh. . .nothing else for sale." Elise glanced at Anne, who shook her head vigorously.

They thanked the women and hurried outside. The sun had set, and the air was noticeably cooler.

"Well, now. Success?" Rebecca asked.

"Yes, thank you," Elise said. "And thank you, Wilbur, for waiting." She climbed into the back of the wagon with a little help from Lavinia. They each tugged at one of Anne's arms and got her up with them.

"There be a rug or two back there," Rebecca called from the seat beside her son as he flicked the reins and signaled the mules to move out.

"Elise," Anne whispered as Lavinia unfolded the thick wool blankets for them. "That woman..."

"Yes?"

"Was she...an actress?"

"Best not to ask, I felt. After all, does it really matter who wears our dresses?"

"Last chance to go to church for a long time, ladies." Wilbur Harkness grinned at them. "We've got room in the wagon for you—just."

Anne looked at Elise with longing. "I know God will go with us, but I shall miss being able to attend worship."

"Of course we'll go," Elise said.

That morning they'd donned their new calico dresses. The light material swirled about their legs. It felt odd, with only one petticoat and a pair of pantalets beneath it. Rebecca had warned them that the thin cotton wouldn't be enough to shield them from the sun in midsummer, but for now Elise reveled in the ease of movement the light garments gave her.

"Should we wear these dresses?" she asked Anne when Wilbur had left.

"I hardly think so." Anne's face looked pained. "Last week we attended services at the Episcopal church, and I didn't think our costumes were out of place."

"That is true." Elise reached for her satchel.

The Harkness family planned to attend the Methodist church, but Wilbur assured them that they could drop the ladies in front of the towering Episcopal building. As they left the field that now bulged with canvas-topped wagons, Elise spotted Eb Bentley saddling his horse. He looked at bit more dapper than usual, and she wondered if he was also headed into town to worship.

At noon, as the Episcopal church's bells rang the end of services, the two ladies emerged and stood on the sidewalk while the congregants dispersed.

"Wilbur said it will probably be twenty minutes or so," Elise said.

"Yes. I'm glad it's not so cold today."

Elise reached over and adjusted the soft muffler Lady Anne had tucked about her neck. She mustn't allow her mistress to become ill now. Taking care of Anne on the ship or in a hotel had been difficult enough, but she couldn't ask her to endure sickness in the discomfort of a covered wagon.

At last the Harkness family arrived. Wilbur and his father hopped down and assisted the ladies into the wagon. Even though they'd given up the broadest of their fashionable skirts, the women's dresses took up a large share of the wagon bed. The younger children crowded against the sideboards to give them space.

Mr. Harkness drove them down one of the less desirable streets of Independence, in a direct line toward the rendezvous field. To Elise's horror, the saloons that had been quiet when they arrived that morning were now open, and a few men drifted toward their doors.

Anne caught her eye and made a face. "It's Sunday," she hissed.

Elise nodded. Unthinkable—and yet, there it was. Apparently a large contingent of Americans did not observe the Lord's Day.

The door of a rundown establishment opened wide as they passed, and a woman minced out onto the boardwalk before it. Elise sucked in a breath. The dress the woman wore was of the same deep gold satin as Anne's ball gown—the one they'd sold yesterday. But the neckline of this dress plunged indecently, and the skirt was caught up with rosettes, exposing the woman's lower limbs and the edge of a black net petticoat.

Elise looked over at her companion. Anne's face had gone a

stark white. She stared at the woman until they reached the corner and Mr. Harkness drove the wagon into another street.

Anne turned around slowly and sank down into a heap.

"Are you all right?" Elise whispered.

Anne nodded, but her breathing was shallow, and she closed her eyes.

A few minutes later, after they'd entered a more respectable neighborhood, Elise realized they were drawing near the hotel where they'd stayed on their arrival in Independence. "Perhaps we could stay in town tonight," she said softly. "You could sleep in a real bed one last time." *And have less chance of becoming ill on the eve of our journey,* she thought.

Anne obviously wavered at the suggestion. The whole scheme of toughening up for the trip had worked to a point; they now knew better what to expect in their daily routine and the hardships of keeping food prepared and their clothing cared for. But roughing it might be better faced tomorrow morning if they'd had a good night's sleep.

"We might even get a hot bath," Elise said.

Anne smiled. "I suppose so. We'd have to rise terribly early to get to the field on time though."

Elise didn't bother to debate that. She called to Mr. Harkness, "Would you mind stopping at the hotel up ahead? I'd like to see if Miss Stone and I could stay there tonight."

"Oh, you'd miss the forming of the train," Rebecca said with a frown.

"I think we could rise early enough," Elise said. "Our hired man could hitch the team and get it into line for us."

Mr. Harkness pulled his wagon up before the hotel, and Elise climbed down and hurried inside. Knots of people, mostly men, stood about talking to each other. She excused herself repeatedly until they cleared a path for her. Again she was struck by how primitive the establishment was. Why exactly did she think this would be more comfortable than their bedrolls in the tent at the field? And there seemed to be far more patrons now than there had been a few days ago.

The landlord came from another room with an armful of blankets.

"Mr. Lewis," Elise called. "Would you have a room for Miss Stone and me tonight?"

"Oh Miss Finster. I'm sorry. You two were very nice customers, but, ma'am, we're full to bursting. Folks have started cramming into town for the emigrant trains. I reckon yours will be the first out, but I've got at least four people in every room right now, and gents sleeping on the floor down here."

Elise turned away disappointed yet with a sense of rightness. *This is Your will, Lord,* she prayed. *Thank You for giving us this clear direction. We'll stay with the wagon tonight.*

"Oh ma'am," Lewis called before she could reach the door.

Elise paused and looked back. "Yes?"

"You might want to meet this gentleman." He gestured toward a tall, shaggy-looking man coming down the stairs. "Mr. Hoyle is the captain of a train leaving next week. I know you like to talk to everyone you can who's been out West, about that fella you're looking for."

"Why yes. Thank you."

The man had heard the landlord's comment and eyed Elise curiously as he finished his descent. He walked over to her and bowed his head slightly.

"Ma'am. I'm Ted Hoyle. Can I help you?" His gaze roved briefly over her, and Elise guessed he was weighing her station, income, age, and stamina.

"I'm searching for a man I believe may have gone west a few years ago—David Stone. He formerly resided in St. Louis, and he then came here. We've lost track of him, and his family in England would like very much to locate Mr. Stone."

"Stone, eh?" Hoyle rubbed his bristly jaw. "Sure, I remember him."

# CHAPTER 13

Elise's heart raced, and she felt a little giddy. "You say you knew Mr. Stone?"

"There was a man a few years back," Ted Hoyle said. "An Englishman, that is. He took three wagons. Said he was going to open a haberdashery."

Elise caught her breath. "Are you sure it was David Stone?"

"I think that was his name. Let's see, it would have been '51 . . .no, '50. That's it. The spring of 1850. He joined my outfit for California."

"California?" Elise let that sink in. "Then we're joining the wrong expedition."

"Where you headed?" Hoyle's brow furrowed as he again eyed the gown, hat, and coat she'd worn to church.

"Oregon."

"Well then, you're headed to the right place. See, the trails are the same for a while. A good while. And besides, unless I'm mistaken, that fella didn't go all the way to the coast with me."

"He didn't? What happened?"

"Changed his mind somewhere along the way. Split off when we got to the cutoff and went with another train headed for Oregon." Hoyle rubbed his chin again as if that would improve his memory. "Yes, I'm sure that's what he did. I talked to him a few times while we were crossing the plains. Said he'd tried farming for a while, but he wasn't very good at it. I guess he'd had a store before that—"

"Yes, he did," Elise said. "In St. Louis."

"Well, I guess he thought he was a better shopkeeper than he was a farmer."

"I don't suppose you know where in Oregon he planned to settle?"

"No, I don't, ma'am. Sorry."

"That's all right. You've been very helpful."

Elise rushed out to the wagon and called to Anne, "You'll never guess! I've got some solid word on your uncle at last."

Anne rose to her knees and clutched the wagon's sideboard. "No! Really?"

Elise nodded and lifted her skirt in preparation for climbing in at the back of the wagon. Abby and Ben, the brother between Wilbur and Lavinia in age, reached for her arms and hoisted her up.

"This gentleman is another wagon master, and he says David went with him on a train five years ago, headed for Oregon. We're on the right trail, Anne!"

"Well now," Rebecca said with a nod. "Your persistence paid off."

"Finally." Anne sank back and stared at Elise with wide eyes. "But. . .five years ago?"

"That's what the gentleman said, and he seemed quite certain. He thought David had been farming for a few years before he joined the wagon train."

"Well, think of that," said Rebecca.

"Are you staying here tonight?" Mr. Harkness asked.

"Oh. No, we're not. I'm sorry—I should have told you that at once. The hotel is full." Elise smoothed her skirt as the wagon lurched forward. Somehow beds and baths didn't matter anymore. They'd had word of David, and they would find him.

The night was still inky black when a piercing horn sounded across the field, signaling that it was time to rise and prepare to move out.

Eb was already poking at the embers in the rock fireplace where he and Rob cooked their meals when they weren't invited to share with one of the emigrant families. Rob came back from the center of the camp, where he'd blown the alert, smiling and polishing the bugle with his sleeve.

"You like that thing entirely too much," Eb said.

128

"It is a beauty. Traded a pair of beaded Blackfoot moccasins for it."

"You've told me that story a thousand times."

Rob sighed and stooped to tuck the bugle into one of his saddlebags. "It feels good to be getting onto the trail again."

Eb grunted and reached for the battered coffeepot. He'd feel a lot better when they reached Oregon. "I'll fetch some water."

"Got some yonder." Rob nodded toward where a galvanized bucket stood with a feed sack draped over it.

By the time Eb had the coffee on, Rob had four eggs, a slab of bacon, a frying pan, and some stale johnnycake laid out.

"May as well use the last of the eggs."

Eb frowned. "Guess we forgot to get more. Only a couple of people have laying hens along."

"We'll live." Rob squatted before the fire and fed two more sticks onto it. "I can tend breakfast if you want to make sure the drovers are rounding up the mules and oxen."

Eb walked out to the corral where they'd penned the animals the night before. Farmers and hired hands were sorting out the teams for each wagon. On the trail, they'd have to use the wagons themselves to form an enclosure for the stock, but here at the departure place they had the luxury of a separate fenced area. Mules neighed and shifted about inside. A horse nickered, and oxen lowed. The sprinkling of cows mooed to let their owners know they were ready to be milked. The men dodged about among the animals.

"Everything going all right?" Eb called to Abe Leonard.

"We'll figure it out."

Eb smiled and went back to the campfire.

"That was quick," Rob said. "I haven't even cooked the eggs yet."

"I'll go back in a few minutes if they haven't started to bring the teams in and hitch up. Looked like they had enough men out there in the dark."

"The sun'll be up before you know it," Rob said.

Eb squinted eastward, toward the river. He could discern a lighter gray band of sky on the horizon. "Wonder how Miss Finster and her young friend are doing."

As soon as he'd spoken, he wished he hadn't. Rob already ragged him mercilessly about the Englishwomen, teasing him about what he perceived as Eb's regard for Miss Finster.

"I'm sure the ladies will be fine," Rob said. "I haven't talked much with the man they hired, but he seems capable."

"I'll go by their wagon later," Eb said. He thought about shaving. He usually let his beard grow while they were on the trail. Maybe he'd start it today. Or maybe not.

He walked over to his pile of gear and pulled out his soap and razor.

"You can handle it," Peterson said. He passed Costigan a handful of bills. "You know people all the way along the trail from here to Oregon. I'm sure you can get word of this man. Just make sure you know where he is before his relatives do, and get the job done."

Thomas tried to count the money in the semidarkness.

"That's all you'll get until you report something definite," Peterson said. "Send word as quick as you can, so the boss knows."

Thomas gave up trying to see the denominations. It looked like enough, seeing as how his food and a small salary were being paid by the ladies. He'd never before heard of a job where you got paid twice. He shoved the money in his pocket and looked anxiously toward the road.

"I've got to get back there. Whistler's horn blew ten minutes ago. If I don't get the mule team up, he'll be suspicious and the ladies will be out of sorts."

"Go. Just don't forget to send word along the way, as often as you can without making it noticeable."

Peterson mounted his horse and trotted off toward Independence.

"What shall we do?" Anne wrung her hands as she paced beside the wagon, looking toward the corral.

The men of the company had driven most of the pulling teams into the encampment and were busy hitching them to their wagons.

Anne and Elise had eaten and cleaned up afterward. Elise had held back a plate for Thomas and couldn't pack the dish box away until his cup, plate, and fork were in it. The coffeepot still steamed over the dying fire, and the grate was cooling so they could pack it.

But Thomas Costigan had not shown his face that morning. The sun was rising, and everyone else seemed nearly ready to pull out, but their mule team was still in the corral with the extra livestock.

"I suppose we'd better go find those mules." Elise made the decision as she spoke. She hitched up her skirt. "We can't let everyone else be ready before us. We told Mr. Whistler and Mr. Bentley we wouldn't slow them down."

"That's true. And we wanted to come without hiring a man, so even without Thomas, we should be ready when the others are." Anne tied her shawl about her shoulders so she could use both hands to work. "Let's go."

They set off briskly to the corral. Nick Foster, the fifteen-year-old son of a farmer, was milking his family's cow just inside the gate.

"Good morning, Nicholas," Elise said. "We need to get our mules. I wonder if you could tend the gate for us."

"Surely, ma'am. One moment while I finish here."

"Perhaps we can go locate the team while you do that," Anne said.

Elise walked to the gate. It was fastened with a simple loop of twine over both the gatepost and an upright pole on the gate. She lifted the loop and swung the gate open.

"Careful," Nick called. "Don't let the other cattle out."

Elise quickly drew the gate back until it was open only far enough for her to step inside. She and Anne squeezed into the corral, and she turned to replace the twine.

Anne's sharp intake of breath made her whirl around. A huge ox ambled toward them, his head wagging from side to side. Anne clutched Elise's arm.

"Will he hurt us?"

"I don't think so." Elise's pulse roared as the ox came closer. Her mouth went dry, and her stomach flipped. "Nicholas?"

Nick called, "Oh, don't worry about him. That's just Bright. He's one of my father's extra oxen."

Even though all the other teams had been removed, a large herd of animals remained in the pen. Elise tried to ignore Bright, who now stood solidly a yard in front of her.

"Do you see our mules?"

"I'm not sure I'd know them from anyone else's." Anne's voice had a pronounced tremor.

"I believe Mr. Costigan marked the straps on their halters," Elise ventured. She should have paid more attention to the livestock question, but she'd gladly given the matter over to Thomas.

She grasped Anne's hand and led her cautiously around Bright. The big ox lowered his head and let out a thunderous bellow. Anne yelped.

"Nicholas," Elise shouted.

He strode quickly into the pen with something that looked suspiciously like a smirk on his lips.

"I'm here, ma'am. How can I help you?"

"We. . .need to locate our mules."

"Yes'm. How many you got?"

"Six," Elise said, "but we only want to hitch up four of them." Nick nodded and set off across the corral.

Elise held her skirt up and followed. "Watch your step, Anne."

"This one's yours," Nick called, and Elise hurried toward him.

"Can you take two at a time?" he asked.

"Umm. . ."

The young man shook his head as though she were helpless. Elise hated the feeling of inadequacy. They hadn't even started the journey, and already she'd proven incompetent.

"Take this one. I'll bring two. Miss Stone, can you take one?"

"I think so." Anne sounded hesitant.

"Lead him over to the gate," Nick said to Elise. "If you don't think you can get him to your wagon, I'll come back. You didn't bring any lead ropes, did you?"

"No," Elise said.

"All right. I'll grab those two mules over there. Let's go."

Leading the mule to the camp was terrifying yet exhilarating. Elise flinched every time the beast moved his head, afraid she'd lose her hold on the halter. The path seemed much longer than it had when they'd approached the corral, but at last she and the mule, whom she'd mentally nicknamed Challenger, arrived at the wagon.

"You present a challenge," she said softly to the big mule. "If I can't meet it, I shall have failed Anne and debased the purpose of our journey. Therefore, I shall face this challenge, and I shall win."

There were the lead ropes she and Anne should have taken, hanging from the back of the wagon. She held firmly to Challenger's halter. Anne had fallen back about ten yards and seemed to be struggling with the mule she led. Elise grabbed a rope, hooked it to Challenger's halter, tied the other end to an iron ring on the frame of the wagon, and grabbed a second rope. She hurried back to help Anne.

"Here we go." She clipped the rope to the smaller brown mule's halter. "I'll take him."

Anne let go of the strap and stepped back with a sigh. "Thank you. He stepped on my foot twice."

Nick passed her, leading two more mules.

"There are ropes at the back of the wagon," Elise called.

"Where's your harness?"

"Oh. In the wagon."

"Best get it out," Nick said.

Grateful beyond words, Elise decided the best way to thank him would be to secure Anne's beast and get the harness ready. She found it easily, in a large wooden crate inside the wagon, near the back opening.

"Anne," she called out through the gap in the canvas.

"I'm here." Anne stepped up close to the tailboard.

"Let me hand down the collars to you, and I'll try to get the harness."

Elise passed two of the padded leather collars out.

133

"Wait," Anne said. "I don't think I can carry any more." She disappeared.

Elise set the others out, ready to pass down on Anne's return. She reached into the crate for the huge mass of straps and buckles that was the harness. Long sticks with brass knobs on the end seemed to be a part of it. What were those things called? Perhaps Nick could tell her. She tugged at a wide leather strap, but it all seemed connected.

"Ready for more," Anne called from outside.

"Oh, here." Elise handed her the other two collars. "I'm not sure I can get the harness out by myself."

"I'll be right back."

A minute later, Anne clambered in at the front of the wagon and crawled over their trunks, sacks, and bundles to where Elise was working. Together they managed to haul the harness out of the crate and tip it out the back of the wagon into a heap on the trampled grass.

"Which two mules are the wheelers?" Nick yelled from the front of the wagon.

"I. . .have no idea," Elise confessed.

"We'll put the biggest ones at the back, then."

"Nicholas!" The strident female voice reached them from halfway across the bustling encampment.

Nick turned toward it, shielding his eyes. "Yeah, Ma?"

"Where's the milk?"

"Down to the corral. I had to help these ladies get their team up."

"Well, you go get it, young man! The idea! You need to do for your own family this morning, not those fancy ladies."

"All right, Ma."

Nick turned back to Elise with gritted teeth. "Sorry."

"It's all right," Elise said. "You go and do as your mother says. We can do the rest."

It was a gross overstatement, as Elise knew, but Nick hurried away toward the pen.

Anne's lips trembled, and Elise wondered if they had the same thought. The way Mrs. Foster said "fancy ladies" sounded vulgar. Could she possibly be casting aspersions on their morals? The American women didn't seem know what to make of them. Their accents and clothing set them apart. Mrs. Foster and the other forty or so women on the wagon train were trying to classify them.

She drew in a deep breath. "All right, Anne. Let's see if we can separate the harnesses and lay them out in one pile for each mule."

Anne seemed relieved to be given a task that didn't involve touching the animals again. It took them ten minutes to figure out that they had six sets of harness in the mound, not four.

"That's right," Anne said meekly. "Mr. Pottle insisted we might need to harness all six when we reach the mountains."

Elise removed two complete sets—as nearly as she could tell—and put them back in the crate. They laid out one set on the ground. Elise looked from Challenger to the harness and back.

"I think this is the front," she said at last.

"Need some help, ma'am?"

Elise's heart sank. Of all the people she did *not* want to see her in this weak position, Eb Bentley had to come along. On the other hand, just seeing the man's rugged face at this trying moment sent a wave of relief cascading over her.

Anne jumped in and saved Elise the embarrassment of admitting their predicament.

"Oh Mr. Bentley, that's very kind of you. I'm afraid our hired man has been delayed. . .somewhere. Miss Finster and I are trying to make sense of all this harness. Perhaps you would be so kind. . ." She smiled up at the scout.

Apparently her hopeful face was enough to sway Eb. "Sure, I'll help you. We need to get this train moving. But you know you need your man along."

Elise cleared her throat. "Yes, sir, we understand. We're hoping he'll arrive at any moment. I can't understand why he's not here this morning."

"Perhaps he mistook the day," Anne said.

"Perhaps." Elise was certain Thomas knew what day it was and that the wagon train was supposed to have moved out at daybreak. What if he'd decided to take the small advance payment they'd given him and desert them?

Across the field, Rob Whistler yelled, "Put your wagon next in line, Mr. Clark. Then you, Binchley."

"Here," Eb said. "This set of harness looks to be adjusted the longest on the sides. We'll put it on the big fella there."

He set about tossing the bundle of leather over Challenger's back, and miraculously, the straps fell into place on the mule's body. Eb quickly fastened a couple of buckles.

"Ever harnessed a horse?" he asked.

"No, but I'll try," Elise said.

He pointed to another mule, almost as large as Challenger. "Do him next."

Elise picked up another set of harness. She could barely lift it as high as the mule's back.

Anne came and stood beside her. "How can I help?"

"Let's see. . ." Elise looked over at the harness on Challenger to see how Eb had positioned it. "I'm not sure where this buckle goes. Can you go around and look on the other side and try to find where Mr. Bentley put it?"

Anne was gone for a minute, and Elise struggled to find a spot to attach every free end of leather. Anne came back carrying two of the wooden pieces with round brass balls on the ends.

"He says these are hames and they go on each side of the collar. The tugs hitch to them."

Elise hadn't expected that. She looked under her mule's neck and over at Challenger. Did she need to remove the collar? By this time Eb was putting on the big mule's bridle.

She tiptoed over and peered closely at the collar and hames.

"Got it?" Eb asked.

"I think so." She went back to Challenger and fumbled about until she felt that part was right. Now to fix the straps of the harness to the hames. By the time she had most of it done, Eb had harnessed mule number three and positioned him in front of Challenger.

"What's this?" Anne held up a rounded piece of leather. Straps with buckles hung from it, but Elise couldn't imagine where it should go.

"I'm not sure." Elise scrutinized Eb's work again but couldn't spot a piece similar to Anne's. She took it and held it up, frowning.

"That's the crupper, ma'am."

Elise jumped and looked up into Eb's face. He was closer than she'd thought, and she stepped away, bumping the mule's flank. The animal let out a snort of protest.

"The what?" she asked.

"The crupper. It goes under his tail."

Elise glanced toward the mule's rear end. With a grimace she headed back there. Eb seemed amused. He walked to the harness they'd left on the grass and picked up the last bundle.

She could see now one tab of leather on the mule's near side that must attach to this buckle. But how did one get the tail to lie over the crupper? She stared at Challenger's rump, frowning.

Suddenly Eb was beside her again.

"Allow me, ma'am." As he took the offending piece of leather from her, his large, tanned hand touched her fingers. Elise relinquished the crupper as if it had burned her.

"Thank you."

"Maybe you can bring up the last mule from the back of the wagon."

Five minutes later, they had all four mules in place, and Eb was making a final check of all the harness connections. Rob Whistler rode up on his horse.

"Eb, where you been?"

"More like where's their hired man been."

Eb definitely sounded grumpy. Elise exchanged a look with Anne.

"Costigan's not here?" Rob asked. "We're supposed to have pulled out half an hour ago."

"I know it," Eb said. "Can't be helped."

"Well, it's often this way on the first day." Whistler smiled down at Elise and Anne.

"I don't know about that fella," Eb said. "I asked about him at the livery. Pottle didn't seem to think much of him."

Anne's eyes widened. "Do you mean Mr. Costigan?"

"He's the one." Eb straightened and slapped the near lead mule on the shoulder. "You're all set, if you have a driver."

"But. . .you recommended Mr. Costigan," Anne said.

"Me?" Eb swung around to look at her. "I never did. In fact, I never saw him before he showed up with your wagon a few days ago."

Anne looked helplessly at her, and Elise hauled in a deep breath.

"I believe what he actually said the day we met him was, 'that wagon train fella' had told him we needed a man to go with us on the journey. He asked for the job."

Eb pursed his lips then glanced up at Whistler. "Did you talk to him, Rob?"

"I never. Not before he was hired."

Eb's eyebrows drew together. "Well, lookee yonder."

They all turned toward the road. Thomas Costigan walked quickly toward them.

"I reckon your driver's here," Eb said. "But I'll be watching him."

Rob nodded. "Me, too. Come on, Eb. We need to finish setting the lineup. Miss Finster, have Costigan put your wagon last in line. After we stop at nooning, you'll move up." He touched his hat brim and rode off.

"I'll check in on you later, ladies," Eb said. He didn't wait for Thomas to get there but strode away instead.

Elise clenched her jaw. Eb had neglected his usual duties to help them. They'd fulfilled his dire predictions about them—the ones she'd vowed would not come true. She and Anne had delayed the starting of the train and made extra work for the scout. Those reflections did not put her in a kindly mood toward Thomas.

"Mr. Costigan." She stood in his path with her hands on her hips. "We needed you, and you weren't here."

"I'm sorry, ma'am. I got called away last night, and I thought

I'd be back before—"

"Called away? By whom? We have a business agreement." *At least he's sober,* Elise told herself, but she wasn't going to let him off too easy.

"Sorry, ma'am." His confident tone had sunk to a mumble. He shot a glance in Anne's direction. "I couldn't help it, but I'm ready to go now."

"I should hope so," Elise said. "We have four of the mules hitched, as you can see. I wasn't sure which two you wanted to keep in reserve."

Thomas did a quick survey of the team. "This will do, except I put Bumper there in as a leader, him being so independent and all."

"Bumper?" Elise asked.

He slapped the near wheeler on the withers. "This one right here." He looked over the mules' backs toward where the lead wagons were rolling out onto the road westward. "No time to switch them now. Probably won't matter."

Elise made a mental note to learn the peculiarities of all their mules soon, in case Thomas proved unreliable again.

"Your breakfast is cold, but it's waiting for you on the other side of the wagon. As soon as you get your coffee, I'll pack up the coffeepot."

"Thank you, ma'am."

Anne sidled up to her as Thomas disappeared around the wagon. "He seems contrite enough."

"Yes." Elise frowned. "I don't know what to think. It's too late to change our plans and find another man, but we'd best learn all we can about caring for mules."

"Yes, and I'd like to learn to drive," Anne said.

"Excellent idea."

More than half the wagons had lumbered out of the field onto the roadway. Rob Whistler cantered toward them on his chestnut horse.

"You ready?"

"Next to it."

"Where's Costigan?"

Thomas came around the back of the wagon carrying his tin plate and cup. "I'm here."

"Get your wagon into the last place in line. Let's not have any stragglers the first day."

Thomas shoved his empty plate into Elise's hands. "Thanks, ma'am. Not half-bad this morning."

Elise supposed that was a compliment. "Just don't be tardy again." She hurried to put the dirty dishes away. No time to clean them now. They'd have to do them at noon, and she hoped the egg wouldn't stick too badly.

To her surprise, Anne was dumping the dregs of the coffee onto the smoldering remains of their campfire.

"Is there anything else?" she asked.

"Just that box. I hung the grate on the wagon."

Elise flung the dish box in over the tailboard as the mules leaned into their collars and pulled. The two women stood for a moment catching their breath and watching their wagon pull away from them.

"Oh." Anne looked down at the coffeepot in her hand.

"Come on," Elise said. "I don't suppose it will take us ten seconds to catch up."

They set out on their first day on the Oregon Trail, walking fifty feet behind the last wagon.

Elise heard a commotion behind, and she swung around.

"Oh my! Hurry, Anne."

The herd of milk cows and extra oxen and mules surged up the trail from the corral. Elise and Anne turned and ran for the back of their wagon.

# CHAPTER 14

Elise sat on the wagon tongue, finishing her sewing before the last rays of daylight faded. They'd been on the trail three days, and she was weary beyond expression. Anne had already retired inside their tent.

"Everything all right over here?"

She looked up to see Rebecca Harkness approaching with Mrs. Legity, a widow traveling with her daughter, son-in-law, and their three children.

"Yes, thank you," Elise said.

Rebecca nodded. "Thought I smelt something burning over here earlier."

"Oh, well. . ." Heat rushed to Elise's cheeks. "Miss Stone and I are still learning to use the dutch oven to good advantage."

Rebecca smiled, and it transformed her careworn, critical visage into the pleasant face of a friend. "Would you like another lesson? Tomorrow evening if we stop in good time, perhaps we could bake gingerbread after supper."

"That sounds lovely."

Mrs. Legity snorted. "Don't know why you two thought you could head out for parts unknown without knowing so much as how to bake biscuits."

"There now, Agnes, likely these ladies had people to do for them back in England."

Elise swallowed hard. She didn't want to go into their former situation. "We would both like to increase our knowledge of household tasks."

Mrs. Legity snorted again, but Rebecca smiled.

"There now. When you talk, Miss Finster, it's like music. And Miss Stone—why, her voice is like honey."

"She is sweet," Elise said.

"Yes, and Wilbur's like a bee drawn to her," Mrs. Legity said.

Elise stared at her for a moment then averted her gaze. "Wilbur has been nothing but courteous in our presence."

"That's good to hear," Rebecca said. "I'm sure Miss Stone does seem like an angel to him. She's so pretty and dainty."

"She'll never make a farm wife."

Mrs. Legity's sour comments hurt, but Elise knew better than to show her reaction. In England, she'd have given any woman who spoke so a proper set-down. But these women, rough and dour as they were, held a trove of wisdom Elise envied. She had to live with them for the next five or six months, and she could either learn from them or turn up her nose and be snubbed. She chose to make friends.

"Mrs. Legity, I admire the fine stitching on your buttonholes. Did you make them yourself?"

"Aye. And I see you've been sewing this evening."

Elise nodded. "A small mending job. I tore a sleeve yesterday."

"You'd do well to take up your skirts while you're at it."

Elise hesitated, unsure how to respond. The pioneer women all seemed to wear their skirts scandalously short, exposing their ankles. Lavinia Harkness's were among the worst, but her mother didn't seem to care that Lavinia and her sisters sometimes showed the edges of their petticoats and even a bit of stocking.

"The fashions do change," she murmured.

"It's nothing to do with fashion," Mrs. Legity said. "If you're going to walk miles every day and cook over an open fire, you'd best have skirts that won't get in your way."

Elise recalled her near accident with the fire the week before, and the way Eb Bentley had hauled her away from the blaze with his well-muscled arms. Her face flushed anew.

"Perhaps you are right." Climbing in and out of the wagon was another activity where full skirts hindered her, and she'd noticed Anne impatiently yanking hers upward before she mounted the wagon step. A couple of inches off the hemline might in reality

142

allow them more modesty if it meant less hiking up their skirts. "I shall speak to Anne about it tomorrow."

Rebecca nodded. "That's the spirit."

Mrs. Legity had found the charred pot Elise had set aside. She'd hoped Thomas would carry the heavy iron kettle to the stream and scour it out with sand, but Thomas had disappeared as soon as he'd eaten. That seemed to be his pattern, and Elise had mulled how to keep him around camp for a few chores each evening, but she hadn't worked up her courage to speak to him about it yet.

Now Mrs. Legity peered into the dutch oven and wrinkled her nose. Elise felt compelled to say something.

"I hoped to take care of that earlier, but I needed to use the daylight for my sewing."

"Have you plenty of water?" Rebecca looked pointedly at the nearly empty bucket by the wagon's rear wheel.

"Uh. . .Mr. Costigan. . ." Elise glanced about, but Thomas was still absent.

"Don't go to fetch water by yourself," Mrs. Legity said darkly.

"Do you suppose we'll be able to do a washing soon?" Elise asked.

"It might be weeks afore we do," Mrs. Legity said.

Rebecca shrugged. "Mr. Whistler won't want to stop long enough for that until we get to Fort Kearny, I'll wager."

"Oh." Elise didn't consider herself overly fastidious, but already she was running out of clean stockings and underthings. Lady Anne had certainly never been so long without a bath.

"Well, we'd best get back to our wagons," Rebecca said. "Take care, Miss Finster, and do come by tomorrow evening if you're not too busy. We'll do a baking."

"Thank you, and perhaps you can share that knitting pattern you mentioned to me."

"I'd be happy to."

As the two women turned away, Elise caught an incredulous glance from Mrs. Legity. Probably she couldn't believe Elise actually knew how to knit, though it was something she'd learned in childhood.

Mrs. Legity offered not so much as a farewell, and the two walked away in the twilight. Elise sat down again and took up her needle, but it was so dark she couldn't see the thread against the fabric. With a sigh, she stuck the needle through the cloth, rose, and tucked the dress inside the wagon.

The next morning Thomas brought up the two mules that pulled in the wheel position while Elise stood over the bacon and Anne set out the dishes.

"Thomas, we'll need more water," Elise called.

"Got to get these mules hitched."

"But toting wood and water is part of your job."

Thomas frowned. "Don't remember that."

Elise gritted her teeth. No use asking him to clean the burned-on dutch oven. He would surely balk at that. "It is indeed part of the job, and if you need to rise earlier to do those chores, then so be it, but I'm sure you could bring a little extra fuel and water in the evening."

He tied the two mules to the wagon frame and walked out into the center of the camp again, where the loose livestock were confined at night.

"That man is starting to irritate me," Elise said to Anne.

"I understand, but here's the rub—he's the only man we've got or are able to have at this point."

"Yes. I'm beginning to feel he's taken advantage of us. He does hitch the team each morning—aside from that first day—and he drives all day, sitting on the wagon seat, while we have to walk. Then he unhitches at night, eats his supper, and disappears."

Anne carefully removed the coffeepot from the fire. She set it down on top of the dish crate and turned to Elise.

"We must learn to drive well. Both of us."

"I've been thinking the same." So far Anne had not asked Thomas to teach her, and neither of the ladies had taken the reins of the mule team. "It would be wise of us to master the skill—and any others we might have to perform if our hired man abandons us along the way."

Anne's forehead wrinkled. "Where would he go? We've passed a few farms and that one little village yesterday, but I believe we're quite beyond civilization now."

"He says he knows people along the trail. There must be trading stations. And—and forts."

Anne nodded. "I did hear Mr. Whistler mention some forts. He said our first major destination is Fort Kearny. We'll stop there a few days to rest and trade, he said."

"Ma'am?"

Elise whirled to find Thomas standing behind her. With each hand he held the halter of another mule. His shirt was fastened by the two top buttons but hung open below them.

"Really, Thomas, your shirt," Elise said.

"Yes'm. Bumper here took off a couple of buttons. Thought maybe you could help me out."

"Do you have the buttons?"

He shook his head. "No chance to look for 'em."

Elise sighed. The buttons in her limited sewing kit were mostly small mother-of-pearl disks for mending her own clothing and Anne's. She also had a few cloth-covered ones that matched some of their dresses.

"Change your shirt after you hitch the mules. I'll see what I can come up with."

When he was out of earshot, Anne said, "I think he's only got two shirts to his name."

"And I've no masculine shirt buttons."

"Perhaps Mrs. Harkness would trade for something," Anne suggested. "She has several men to sew and mend for."

"That's good thinking. What shall I offer in trade?"

Anne smiled. "A yard of lace to put about the neck and sleeves of one of her dresses. She may fuss about fripperies, but I daresay she'd love to have some."

"Perhaps you're right. If that doesn't do the trick, I'll see if she has plenty of spices. I really think we purchased more than we'll use between here and Oregon."

"Yes, but if we're going to trade our supplies for Thomas's upkeep, we need to come to an understanding with him."

"True." Elise looked toward where he was fitting Challenger's collar over the mule's head. "I believe I can do that now. Mending wasn't mentioned when we hired him. But I shall be glad to do it—after I see a full water pail and a good-sized woodpile this evening." She turned over a slice of bacon. "I'm getting the knack for this, Anne."

"Wonderful! And I believe we should use our bargaining position to make Thomas agree to driving lessons as well."

"Hmm." Elise turned another piece of bacon. It looked quite appetizing, and the smell of it cooking made her stomach rumble. "Perhaps the time to broach that subject is when we present him with a large slice of hot gingerbread."

*

"My dears, I'm so worn out, I've got to go to bed after this batch is done baking, whether it's edible or not." Rebecca eyed the dutch oven doubtfully.

"I'm so sorry I ruined the last batch," Anne said contritely.

"There, there, it wasn't your fault." Rebecca patted her shoulder.

"That's right. Anyone might mistake saleratus for salt," Lavinia said stoutly, though Elise didn't see how that could be true. Still, she admired Lavinia for sticking up for Anne. The poor young lady's confidence was now lower than Bumper's shoe nails.

"We wanted a good batch tonight, so we could bribe Thomas," Anne confessed, "but he's probably asleep by now."

Rebecca laughed. "So that's why the baking lesson was so important. Well, it's a shame you ruined two cakes' worth of supplies, but I do believe this one will turn out all right. If he's gone to bed, you can give it to him at nooning tomorrow. He'll be surprised, you can be certain of that."

"That should work fine," Elise said, though she and Anne had hoped to extract a good amount of wood and water out of Thomas before then. "We're grateful to you for your patience, Rebecca. I know you're tired." She finished the row she was knitting, turned the beginnings of a sock, and started on the next row. Perhaps a pair of woolen socks would help win Thomas over as well.

"It's not as though we're completely helpless," Anne said with a stubborn lift of her aristocratic chin. "I'm sure Elise could cook fine if she had a stove."

"Maybe," Elise said. *A stove and a couple of kitchen maids.*

"I do believe it may be ready." Rebecca handed Anne her cooking paddle. "Scrape off the coals, dearie, and make sure you don't dump any ashes on your gingerbread when you take the lid off."

"You're lucky to have enough wood tonight," Lavinia said.

*If you only knew,* Elise thought. She'd bargained with Thomas for replacing his buttons, and he'd grudgingly gone for more sticks.

"Yes, we'll soon have to start gathering buffalo chips, they tell me," Rebecca said.

"Buffalo chips?" Elise didn't like the sound of that.

"Is it wood chips?" Anne asked.

Rebecca and Lavinia laughed. "No, my dear, it's not, but it will burn clean if you get nice, dry ones. They say the buffalo aren't as plentiful as they used to be, but I expect, since we're one of the first trains this year, we'll find enough of their leavings."

Anne's mouth skewed. "You mean—oh, I say."

"Yes, that's what I mean." Rebecca passed her a pot holder. "All right, let's see if your gingerbread is edible."

<hr />

"Mr. Whistler says we'll get to Fort Kearny tomorrow," Lavinia said on the first day of May, as she and Elise walked along beside the Harknesses' wagons. "That means we'll rest a couple of days and do a big washing and visit the trading post and dance in the evening."

"We're all looking forward to it," Elise said. They'd been on the trail more than a month and had come three hundred miles from

Independence. Elise was content with the life they now lived, if not always comfortable.

The warm winds already carried the dust stirred up by the wagons. She hadn't expected that until high summer. The dust sifted into the wagons no matter how tightly they tied the flaps down. Everything bore a coating of dust, and it sometimes blew so thick that they could barely see the wagons ahead of them.

Elise and Anne, along with the other women, had found that walking a few yards off the trail, to the side of the line of wagons, made it easier to breathe. It also afforded them a chance to pick up fuel.

The Harkness family carried a small barrow in one of their wagons. It was up to Lavinia and her younger siblings to fill the barrow twice a day and stow the dried buffalo chips they collected in the family's third wagon—the one that carried tools and animal feed. Once the two wheelbarrows full were stashed, the children could explore and play, so long as they stayed within calling distance of the wagons.

This afternoon, Anne was having a driving lesson from Thomas, and therefore had the luxury of riding on the wagon seat. Elise and Anne had taken turns over the last few weeks, and both were becoming fair drivers. Elise could now harness a mule in less than five minutes, and she was perhaps inordinately proud of that accomplishment.

"I can't wait to see what you and Miss Anne wear to the dance." Lavinia smiled as she trudged along.

"What will *you* wear?" Elise asked.

Lavinia laughed. "I've only this or my brown dress."

Elise found that tragic—that a girl of seventeen should have such a limited wardrobe. Even though she and Anne had eliminated one trunk back in Independence, they still had an extensive wardrobe stowed in their wagon. She almost opened her mouth to offer Lavinia the use of one of their gowns but stopped. Rebecca might not approve. And would such an act cause problems among the other women of the wagon train? She didn't want to prompt any jealousies. She and Anne were snubbed already, apparently because their clothes were finer than the others' and because they had more of them. Even Rebecca, who had befriended them from the beginning, laughed at their continued use of parasols and gloves.

"A woman expects her face and hands to be tanned when she crosses the plains," Rebecca had said, "and carrying a parasol—well, that just means you're using your hands to carry something frivolous, instead of to work."

Elise didn't see it that way. Safeguarding her mistress's complexion—and her own of course—was an important part of a lady's maid's duties. In England they'd haunted London's exclusive shops for Lady Anne's cosmetics, and Elise had prepared lotions and emollients from recipes guarded closely among personal servants.

Out here there was nothing to work with, and she could only hope the cosmetics they'd brought with them would last throughout the journey. As a precaution, she'd picked up a few extra items before they left St. Louis, but she hadn't been able to obtain the high quality products available in London. If only she'd realized in New York how long their journey would last and that it would take them into the wilderness.

She sighed heavily. No use regretting such things at this point. Instead she would have to make the supplies they had last and find substitutes for those that gave out. Lavinia used lard to keep her lips from cracking. The idea of Lady Anne smearing lard on her lips repelled Elise. She was grateful that she had a good supply of the beeswax and rosewater concoction she and Anne preferred.

"Will you wear one of your Paris gowns?" Lavinia asked. "Miss Anne told me some of her dresses were made there."

"I expect that would make us complete outcasts," Elise said.

"Oh no, why should it? We'd all love to see them. I heard you have three trunks bursting with gowns."

"Mr. Bentley was probably right to advise us to get rid of most of it."

"As you've told me more than once, there's no telling whom

one will meet in Oregon City. Why, even at Fort Kearny there'll be army officers and their wives, and other folks who are traveling." Lavinia glanced at Elise's dress. "Even your calicos that you and Miss Anne bought in Independence are much prettier than what Ma and I have."

Elise put a hand up to the ribbon at the neckline of her bodice. After hard use on the trail, the dress was showing wear, but she knew Lavinia was right. She and Anne had bought the best quality they could find in Independence—sturdy fabrics with tight stitching, and in cheerful colors. By comparison, some of the emigrant women wore drab, shapeless garments that were heavily mended and wearing thin.

"Here comes Mr. Bentley," Lavinia said.

Elise kept her head down and refused to follow the natural inclination to look. Eb Bentley had become the bane of her life, second only to Thomas Costigan. Thomas was lazy, she'd concluded weeks ago. He refused to gather chips once they were beyond accessible wood, and he hauled water only if she bullied him mercilessly. That was too tiring. Her attempts at bribing him produced limited results. He still went off with the other single men whenever he got a chance and left the women to their own devices. Usually he showed up for meals, but sometimes he didn't. Elise concluded that he found sustenance at other campfires on those occasions, though once or twice she was certain their cache of leftovers had been plundered during the confusion of the early morning time when the team was hitched.

Elise had discussed the situation with Anne, but so far they'd kept their suspicions and their difficulties in dealing with Thomas to themselves.

Eb Bentley was another case entirely. He seemed to know everything about traveling overland in the American West, and his very omniscience on the topic annoyed her. Even worse, he seemed to show up just at the moment she exhibited her own ignorance. He'd ridden by on that oddly colored horse yesterday morning as Elise was scraping out yet another burned meal—her attempt at flapjacks for breakfast. He'd shaken his head sadly and moved on without comment, but the incident had blackened Elise's day.

Now he rode along on his horse—white with large, reddish-brown spots—inspecting each wagon as he passed. Eb Bentley's eyes saw everything. If an ox limped even slightly, Eb spoke to the driver. If a strap hung loose on a mule's harness, he let the owner know. If a wheel squeaked too loudly or a bundle hung precariously on the side of a wagon, Eb brought it to the guilty party's attention.

Elise supposed that was his duty, and he was good at it. But she always felt like a naughty schoolchild when he came around, because she was sure he'd find several things amiss with the wagon she and Anne owned.

To her horror, he turned aside from the line of wagons and headed toward her and Lavinia.

"Afternoon, ladies." He tugged at his hat brim.

"Hello, Mr. Bentley," Lavinia called gaily.

"Good afternoon, sir." Elise wanted to admire the rugged figure he cut on horseback. His worn clothing—dark trousers and a blue shirt, with a soft leather vest over it, and that droopy, grayish hat he always wore low over his brow—enhanced that image. But she wouldn't allow herself to admire such a man. It was unthinkable. His long legs hung comfortably against the horse's sides, ending in well-worn leather boots coated with trail dust.

"You ladies doing all right?"

"Quite well, thank you," Elise said.

"Don't forget to drink something every now and again."

He smiled down at her and Lavinia, and Elise almost gave in. It was hard not to admire a man who stopped to see if you were comfortable, especially one with a smile like that. Eb's smile rarely saw daylight, but when it did, he very nearly inspired confidence in her. Was that admiration? He was a good man, and he only wanted the best for the people on the wagon train. Of that she was sure. So why did she dislike him?

Was it because he made her feel incompetent? Because she still felt he barely tolerated her presence and Anne's and was certain they'd fall by the wayside before they crossed the mountains ahead? Or was it because he was so different from David Stone?

That thought alarmed her, and she quickly shoved it down and smothered it. She'd tried not to dwell on thoughts of David these past few weeks. Besides, her reaction to Eb Bentley had nothing to do with her esteem for David Stone.

"We will," Lavinia said. "Thank you, Mr. Bentley."

He touched his hat brim again, his gaze lingering on Elise for a moment. She peered up at him from beneath the edge of her silk parasol.

"I'm surprised the wind hasn't grabbed that little thing away from you."

It took Elise a moment to realize he was teasing. Was this the frontier version of flirtation?

"I have a death grip on the handle," she said.

Eb laughed. "Well, if the wind gets to be too much, you might have to start wearing a poke bonnet like Miss Lavinia here."

Elise raised her chin. The limp, wide-brimmed bonnets the emigrant women had adopted were, in her opinion, the most unbecoming headgear she'd ever seen. Her London-bought chapeaus might be out of place on the plains, but she would never submit to a fashion as ugly as the poke bonnet.

Eb nodded, rather grimly this time. "I suspect you've got a death grip on your dignity, too, ma'am."

He rode off before Elise could think of a suitable retort.

"Of all the nerve," she said.

Lavinia giggled. "I think Mr. Bentley's funny. He doesn't usually say much, but when he does, it's anything but usual."

Elise cocked her head to one side and surveyed her young friend. "Lavinia, I expect you'd cause a sensation if you attended an assembly in London."

"What's that?"

"It's a social gathering."

"Hmm." Lavinia shrugged. "The most social gatherings I'll ever see will probably be at the forts or the dancing we have when we get to Independence Rock. You and Miss Anne will dance, won't you?"

"I haven't given it much thought."

"If you do, I'll bet Mr. Bentley will ask you to dance with him."

Elise stared at her for a moment then turned and looked down the line of wagons again. Eb's spotted horse was clearly visible—the patches on its rump made it stand out even at a distance. She had danced with gentlemen—even an earl once—at Almack's Assembly Rooms when she'd accompanied Lady Elizabeth Stone. What would it be like to dance with a man who worked for a living? A wild, western scout like Eb Bentley?

She realized Lavinia was waiting for a response.

"Indeed. We'll see about that."

"Yes," said Lavinia. "I expect we will."

# CHAPTER 15

When the wagons formed their circle that night, the livestock was again turned loose inside. The women would do their cooking and set up their tent just outside the circle. Elise never felt truly secure out there, especially as they were now within Indian Territory, though she'd only seen a few of the native people in the distance. Guards patrolled the camp all night, but even so, she longed for the day they'd used enough mule feed and cornmeal to make space for sleeping in the wagon.

"I'll be glad when we get to the fort," Anne said as they got out their dishes and foodstuffs for supper.

"Yes. I'm told they have good grazing there, and the herdsmen can keep the animals away from the wagons."

"That will be wonderful," Anne said. "The lowing and snorting keep me awake at night." She took the pottery bowl from the dish crate. "So. . .biscuits tonight?"

"I suppose so, and let's use a can of peaches." Elise took the tinderbox to the spot they'd decided to have their fire. For once, Thomas had arranged a fire pit without being told. Rocks were scarce on the grassy prairie, so he used the shovel to dig away the grass in a small area. His ministrations didn't extend to making the fire, so Elise prepared to do that. She headed back to the wagon for some tinder and the sack of buffalo chips she'd gathered earlier.

A sharp scream from Anne made her heart pound.

"What is it?" Elise dashed to the tailboard. "Anne? What happened?"

Anne appeared, white faced, at the canvas flap. "Bugs. Worms."

"Where?"

"In the flour."

"Oh." Elise had hoped they'd avoided that complication by

storing their food in tin boxes and small kegs, but apparently not. "Why don't you make the fire, and I'll sift them out?"

Anne climbed down shakily, and Elise took over the unpleasant task. The flour keg seemed to be thoroughly infested. Her inclination was to throw out the flour, but in the last month, she'd learned better.

"That's what we have sifters for," Rebecca had told her with a shrug. "You can't keep them out, try as you might, so you sift before you bake."

So far, Elise's vigilance had seemed to be working, but that was past. She steeled herself for the chore. If she could only see it as one more task, and not as the removal of vermin from the food she would eat an hour hence, it would help. Even so, her stomach roiled as she peered into the flour keg.

She scooped the bowl half-full of wriggling flour and backed out of the wagon.

"Where's our sifter?" she called to Anne, who was struggling with the tinderbox.

"I'm not sure we have one."

"What? Wasn't it on the list?"

"I looked for one when we first started making biscuits, but I didn't see one. The flour seemed to work without being sifted, so I didn't worry about it."

Elise sighed. "Perhaps I can borrow Rebecca's."

"Must we?" Anne asked. "After an entire month on the road, I hate appearing ignorant."

Elise knew that exact feeling. "Well. . .do we have something else we could use? Some sort of screen or. . ."

"Or netting?" Anne asked.

"Yes, that might do, if we stretched it over a bowl. Have we any in the sewing basket?"

"I don't know." Anne started to rise.

"No, keep on with the fire. We need that. I'll go and look for something."

Eb made his rounds at a leisurely pace. Rob had started in the opposite direction. They would visit each wagon with instructions on getting the water each family needed for the night, and they'd meet halfway around the circle and go back to their campfire spot for supper.

As he approached the Englishwomen's wagon, he paused for a moment and admired the view. Miss Stone, in her red calico dress, knelt on the turf and was industriously trying to build a campfire. As he watched, she succeeded in getting sparks from the flint and steel she held and blew them gently into a small blaze. These ladies had come a long way since Independence, and he didn't mean in miles.

Miss Finster, wearing an eye-pleasing plaid dress, sat on a box sifting flour. As Eb watched, he noticed the rather curious apparatus she used and stepped closer so he could see it better.

Miss Finster glanced up as his shadow fell across her work and flinched.

"Mr. Bentley."

"Good evening, ma'am. That's quite a fancy sifter you have there."

She glanced down at the black netting edged with jet beads. It was stretched over the lip of a large bowl, held in place with clothespins.

"Well, yes, we've had to improvise."

"May I ask. . . ?"

She sighed and let her shoulders slump. "It's the veil off Miss Stone's mourning hat."

"Mourning?"

Miss Finster shot a quick glance toward her friend, but Miss Stone was absorbed in building the fire bigger. "Her father died last fall. She put aside her mourning attire when we left England."

Eb gazed at the dark-haired young woman. "I'm sorry. I didn't know."

"She didn't want people to know. But she brought a complete outfit along, in case. . .well, her uncle. . ."

Eb nodded. "She's got spunk."

"Yes. I'm glad you realize that." Miss Finster looked up into his eyes, and Eb's stomach did a somersault.

"You've both done well on this undertaking."

She smiled faintly. "Better than you expected?"

"Yes, I'll admit it."

She picked up the bowl, tipped it, and brushed a few worms off the net onto the ground. "I believe it's done us both good."

"I expect you're right." Eb cleared his throat. "We've sent four men with a wagon to haul some water tonight. They'll bring it in barrels, and everyone can go and get a bucketful."

"What about the livestock?"

"The drovers took them to a spot on the river about half a mile from here. But the water's pretty muddy, and Rob and I thought it would be better to bring some from a creek a couple of miles away for drinking."

"That's very kind of you gentlemen," Miss Finster said.

"Just trying to keep everyone healthy."

Eb touched his hat brim and turned away. Miss Stone was now putting a large, flaky buffalo chip on her fire. She stepped back and wiped her hands on her apron.

"Evening, Mr. Bentley."

"Miss Stone."

He nodded and walked on. Yes, they'd come a long way.

∽∾

Outside Fort Kearny, the wagon train formed a wider circle than nights on the trail. The drovers moved the herd of livestock a distance away, where new grass was available. Since Whistler's train was one of the first to go through that spring, the emigrants were able to graze their animals within a mile of the fort without having to fight for the right to forage. They'd stay two days to bake, wash, and visit the fort. For the men, it would be a reprieve. For the women, it meant more work than usual, but they didn't mind. They'd anticipated this stop for weeks.

Wood was at a premium, as the fort's detachment and settlers and Indians in the vicinity had long since stripped the area of easily available fuel. On the morning after their arrival, Rob and Eb consulted with the men heading each family, reporting to them the advice of the fort's commanding officer. They drew lots for a detail of six men to cut wood in the hills a few miles away, and Rob sent them off with an empty wagon. Clean water was available from the well at the fort.

The women soon put their camps to rights and prepared to descend on the trading post. Eb and two of the Harkness boys were assigned to patrol the camp while the others were gone, so that nothing would be pilfered by the Indians that congregated to stare at the newcomers.

Elise and Anne were as eager to visit the post as the other women.

"I hope we can learn something about Uncle David here," Anne said as they dressed their hair in the tent, out of view of the curious.

"I hope so, too, but we have to keep in mind that this fort was built since your Uncle David came this way. Still, there's a chance one of the officers posted here met him in his travels." Elise coiled Anne's dark hair and pinned it firmly at the back of her head.

"What shall we wear?" Anne asked. "Should we get out better dresses than we've been wearing every day?"

"That would make us stand out. Do we want that?"

"Hmm. Perhaps not. The Indians are already quite bold. Rebecca said they wanted to touch her little Dorothy's hair." Anne shivered. "I hoped to shop for a new hat, but Mr. Whistler says the trader won't likely have anything like that. Staples and goods to trade to the Indians, that's what he said to expect."

"My dear, why do you need a new hat?" Surely Anne didn't want to replace the mourning bonnet she'd dismantled for the netting.

"The other women seem to take offense at our hats from the Bond Street milliner. Perhaps a straw hat or a poke bonnet would make them more accepting of us."

"Not a poke bonnet!" Elise moved around to where she could see Anne's face. "You wouldn't, my lady!"

"Hush, now," Anne whispered. "These tent walls are thin."

Elise nodded, ashamed of her lapse. Weeks had passed since she'd addressed Anne as her mistress.

"Pardon me. But really—one of those awful bonnets that hide the face?"

"But that's the idea—to hide it from the sun and this ceaseless wind. I fear my cheeks are chapping, despite my parasol and the lotion we brought, and my lips peel even if I use the emollient salve twenty times a day."

"I know," Elise said. "It's distressing, but I believe our remedies are better than what anyone else we're traveling with can offer."

"Perhaps the trader has something."

Thomas crouched behind the wagon wheel, listening. He could hear the women's conversation plainly. "My lady," indeed. He wasn't sure what to make of that exchange. Was the girl, Anne, some sort of upper crust? Both the women were high class, but now that he thought of it, Miss Finster seemed always to defer to Miss Stone. He'd thought it was because Miss Stone wasn't as strong as the older woman. But she was stouter now than when they'd left Independence. Walking all day beside the wagon train for more than a month had forced her to find a little stamina.

Once the ladies headed out for the fort, they'd be gone for hours. That was what he'd been waiting for—the time Peterson had told him to watch for. He'd been patient. With any luck, he'd have something to put in the report he'd send back East from the fort tomorrow. Troopers would take the mail out. Couldn't ask for better delivery service than that.

"Do you want your gray shawl?" Miss Finster said. "I'll fetch it for you when I get my reticule from the wagon."

Thomas dodged back and stood. Time to make himself scarce. If Miss Finster saw him, she'd order him to do some chores while they were gone. When he was sure they'd left, he'd come back. At least he hadn't been picked for the firewood detail. He'd have to watch out for Bentley and the Harkness boys, though. They'd be on guard. That was well and good—you needed a guard around Fort Kearny, especially since the Indian village seemed extra large this spring. Some of those braves had no conscience when it came to other folks' belongings.

He ambled off toward the barracks. The fort had a small garrison, but there was bound to be a card game later. He could line up some amusement for tonight and then come back to carry out his plan.

Elise hurried back to the encampment. She'd left Anne at the trading post with Rebecca Harkness, Lavinia, and Abby. Elise was determined to get some laundry done today, and Anne would be in good hands. The trader's prices had shocked her so much that Elise doubted she'd buy anything.

In an empty sugar sack, she carried her prize—two cans of beef stew. Anne didn't know of her purchase—she'd save it until they'd been out on the trail again for several days. When they were tired to death of bacon and the oysters were nearly gone, then she would open the first can of stew.

Now—where was Thomas? He'd disappeared this morning before she could ask him to fetch enough water to fill her big kettle and the washtub. She was determined to get this washing done, even if she had to haul the water herself—but that would be her last resort. Perhaps the promise of clean clothing for himself would be enough to motivate Thomas to haul the water.

As she came around Mr. Leonard's wagon and faced the small tent, she stopped short. The tent flap was loose. She and Anne had fastened it securely when they'd left camp an hour ago. She tiptoed forward and lifted the edge of the flap. Peering into the dim corners, she tried to determine if anything was missing or out of place. Their bedrolls and baggage inside looked undisturbed.

A rustling sound came from behind her. She turned toward the wagon. Had one of the Indians sneaked inside? Eb and Rob had warned all the travelers about the Indians—thieving savages, according to Thomas. The wagon master had set a guard. Still, with fifty wagons to watch, those men couldn't see everything at once.

The rustle came again, followed by a muffled thump. Elise shivered. Should she go for one of the guards or investigate herself? If she went for help, the thief might escape with his plunder. She looked around and saw Eb strolling just inside the perimeter of the loose wagon circle a hundred yards away. If she screamed, he would hear her. She decided to confront the intruder herself and get a good look at him.

She walked stealthily to the back of the wagon. The canvas flap was down, but it hung loose at one edge. Her hand trembled as she reached for it. Was she insane to do this? Whoever was in there might be armed.

She looked about for anything with which she could defend herself. The wooden paddle with which she stirred laundry leaned against the side of the wagon. She hefted it and rested it on one shoulder. Now, if she could just fling the canvas back and grip the paddle before the thief leaped on her.

The flap drew aside before she could touch it, and she found herself face-to-face with Thomas. He was stooped over, his head only inches above hers. He stared into her eyes for a moment. She wondered if he would simply let the curtain fall and hope she would go away.

Elise choked back the laughter that threatened. This situation was not amusing.

"Thomas."

"Miss Finster."

"You frightened me."

"Oh? I'm sorry."

"I thought an Indian was rifling our supplies."

He smiled and straightened a little. "Not at all, ma'am."

They stood gazing at each other for a long moment. Thomas's smile gradually faded and became more of an appraisal.

"What are you doing?" she asked at last.

"Well, I thought you'd want to do some wash today, ma'am. I was going to get things ready for you."

"The washtub is already out."

"Oh. Is it?"

"It is. There's nothing else in the wagon for you to get."

His eyes narrowed to slits. "My stuff is in here. Surely I have a right to get something out of my own pack."

"That's not what you said you were doing."

Thomas raised his chin. Footsteps claimed Elise's attention. Eb Bentley was nearly to their wagon. Should she tell him about the incident? Better to consult Anne first.

"I shall require a great deal of water for my washing."

"Oh yes, ma'am." Thomas climbed down from the wagon.

"Good morning, Miss Finster."

Elise managed a smile for Eb. "Mr. Bentley."

"Been to the fort?" he asked.

"Yes, but I'm about to begin my wash day."

"Very industrious of you." He eyed Thomas. "Costigan."

Thomas nodded to him and went to the side of the wagon where their buckets hung. "I'll bring all the water you need, Miss Finster." He walked off toward the well.

"Everything all right?" Eb asked quietly, after Thomas was out of earshot.

"I'm not certain. He gives me pause."

"Aha." Eb pressed his lips together and watched Thomas's retreating figure. "Don't hesitate to tell me or Rob if there's a problem."

"Thank you. He was rummaging about in the wagon, and I surprised him. It could be nothing, but I'll speak to Anne later. If she feels unsafe, we'll come to you."

"Do that."

Eb shouldered his rifle and strolled toward the next wagon.

# CHAPTER 16

W e certainly can't trust him," Anne said as they gathered in the last of the clean clothes that evening. "I can't see that anything is missing from the baggage though."

"Nor I." Elise quickened her steps as an Indian woman moved stealthily toward the farthest of their clothing. "Here! Leave that alone, you!" She ran and snatched the linen towel from the grass and walked back toward Anne, picking up Thomas's spare shirt and one of Anne's woolen petticoats as she went.

"Is that all of it?" Anne asked.

"I think so. Some of the woolens are still damp, but we'll lose them if we don't take them in now." Elise had stood guard over the laundry most of the afternoon. With only a short clothesline rigged between their wagon and Mr. Leonard's, she'd had to resort to laying out the rest of the items on the grass to dry. Within an hour, Indian women and children were hedging about the camp. A squeal from Lavinia had alerted the rest to beware of pilfering. Eb and several other men made continuous rounds, but they couldn't cover the whole perimeter of the camp at once.

"You look exhausted," Anne said, "and Mr. Whistler wants to move on tomorrow."

"I thought we were taking another day to rest."

"Apparently not. He says we should take advantage of the fine weather."

Elise let out a deep sigh.

"There'll be dancing tonight in the fort," Anne said.

"I'm too tired to dance."

"So am I."

"Wilbur Harkness will be disappointed, not to mention every other single man in our company and a fort full of soldiers."

Anne smiled. "They'll survive. But what shall we do about Thomas?"

"I'm certain he went through our bags."

"So am I."

"Let me think about it," Elise said. "He behaved very well for the rest of the day and hauled plenty of water. I even gave a bucket to Mrs. Libby."

They stopped beside their wagon, where they used the tailboard and an upended crate as work surfaces. "Let's fold these clothes and get supper started. I've had a pot of dry beans simmering all day." On most days they didn't keep a fire going long enough to cook beans, so this would be a change of diet.

"Here comes Mr. Bentley," Anne said.

The paint horse cantered toward them. Elise no longer felt apprehensive or annoyed at the sight of Eb Bentley. When had that happened?

He pulled up next to them in a small puff of dust and tugged at his hat brim. "Ladies."

"Oh," Anne gasped. "What is that?"

Elise noticed then that Eb had an animal carcass slung behind his saddle.

"I shot a pronghorn while I was scouting the back trail to see how far behind us the next train is. Would you ladies like a piece of venison after I butcher it?"

"That would be very nice," Elise said. Anne was still eyeing the dead animal with distaste. She would change her mind when she took her first bite, Elise was sure.

"I'll bring it by a little later."

"Thank you. And how far back *is* the next caravan?" Elise asked.

"If they push hard, they'll be here tomorrow night—they're camping where we were two nights ago." Eb touched his hat brim and trotted off.

"So that's why Mr. Whistler wants to pull out in the morning," Elise said. "He suspected another train was close behind us."

"Oh well. I suppose we're better off to stay ahead. The fresh meat will be a nice change," Anne said doubtfully. "As grateful as I am for the canned oysters, I admit I'm a bit tired of them."

Elise smiled, imagining how happy Anne would be next week when she produced her tinned stew. The oysters and bacon, along with cornbread and biscuits, had been their staple foods for more than a month. They'd rationed out the dried fruit and rice, but their few root vegetables, eggs, and canned soups were now gone.

"I was able to get two tins of peaches at the fort," Anne said, her head tilted down.

Elise arched her eyebrows. "I thought we agreed that prices were too high."

"I know, but when I heard the word *peaches*, I was suddenly ravenous. If I'd known Mr. Bentley would give us some of his game, I'd have held back."

"Why don't we save the peaches for when you get that feeling again and just enjoy the venison tonight?"

"That's reasonable. Spread out our treats." Anne chuckled. "Odd, isn't it? Three months ago we'd hardly consider tinned peaches a delicacy."

"It was very nice of Mr. Bentley to offer us part of his meat," Elise said. "It looked to be quite a small animal. There wouldn't be enough for everyone."

"He's sweet on you," Anne said. "One of many heartsick men on this wagon train."

"Oh stop."

While Anne put away their clean clothes, Elise set about preparing a double batch of biscuits so they'd have plenty for the next day. She'd just put the lid on the dutch oven when Eb returned with a sizable chunk of meat in a sack.

"I reckon you can roast it or stew it, whichever you please," he said.

"Thank you very much, Mr. Bentley." Anne expressed her gratitude but stood back and let Elise accept the gift.

"Oh, and I. . ." Eb shifted on his feet and scrunched up his face for a moment. "I saw this at the trading post and thought you might be able to use it."

From the crook of his arm he produced a flour sifter and held it out to Elise.

"Oh! How wonderful!" She laughed aloud and reached for it. Her gaze met Eb's, and suddenly she felt self-conscious. "I'm sure that trader charged you a pretty penny. Let me—"

"It's a gift," he said quickly.

Elise hesitated, uncertain what the social standard was for presents from frontier scouts. The venison she had no problem with—many of the wagon train families shared small portions of supplies with each other. But the sifter fell into a different category— Eb had spent money for it.

"Thank you," she said softly. "Perhaps I can salvage Miss Stone's veil." She glanced about, but Anne had disappeared.

"Would you ladies be going to the dancing tonight?" Eb asked.

"Oh, well. . .we thought not, since we're rolling out at dawn."

He nodded. "I'm not much of a dancer myself."

"Mr. Bentley. . ."

"Yes'm?"

It was on the tip of her tongue to invite Eb to eat supper with them, but what was she thinking? She'd never in her life been that bold with a man. Now, if David Stone stood before her, it might be different.

And how would Eb take it if she invited him? And what would their neighbors in the other forty-nine wagons think? They had at least four months of trail before them. She'd hate for Eb to think she liked him in *that* way and have to spend the entire summer correcting the notion.

"I wondered if you and Mr. Whistler could use a dozen biscuits. Thomas finds them quite palatable now."

"That'd be fine, ma'am. Thank you."

❧

"Independence Rock." Anne picked up her pace as they walked between the wagons and the low, muddy river.

"Yes, we're halfway now." Elise smiled. Both she and Anne could be proud of this accomplishment, and what tales they would have to tell when they returned to England.

Lavinia, Rebecca, and Abby walked with them today.

"We'll dance again tonight," Lavinia said eagerly. Her parents had allowed her to attend the revels at Fort Laramie, the second fort on the trail. Rebecca wouldn't permit her daughter to try on Anne's gowns, but she'd allowed the loan of a gauzy shawl from India, and Lavinia had gone to the dance walking as tall as a princess. Anne had worn a dress that wasn't a ball gown at all, but one she might wear to a country house dinner party. Even in that, a modest gray skirt and bodice, she'd caused a sensation at the fort.

Their friends in England would swoon from shock if they saw her now. Both Anne and Elise had lost weight, but they'd gained muscle and stamina. Despite their precautions, their faces had tanned. Their lips were chapped by the constant wind, and their hands had grown rough from hard labor. Even so, when Elise looked at Anne objectively, she thought her mistress was more beautiful than ever.

So, apparently, had the soldiers at Fort Laramie. Lavinia had coaxed the ladies into attending the dance. It was the first time Elise had danced in nearly a year, though Lady Anne had attended many parties and balls in last year's season. Elise accompanied her to most of them but did not always join in the dancing. Neither woman had found herself without partners all evening at Fort Laramie, however. Elise would recall the commanding officer's charming words to her for many a year.

"We get a lot of women traveling along the trail," he'd said as they waltzed about the parade ground in the moonlight and the regimental band played. "But we seldom see such beauties as we have here tonight." He'd gazed directly into her eyes as he spoke, and Elise had found herself blushing. Surely that statement was a bit bold for a man who had a wife present. But the commander's lady was off dancing with Rob Whistler and some of the higher-ranking officers. Elise decided to take it impersonally. "Yes, we've some lovely young ladies in the wagon train," she said.

Anne had been the center of a flock of officers and pioneer men. They cut in on each other furiously, and the poor girl had probably danced with more than fifty men. She returned to the camp exhausted but pleased that she had brought a bit of color into their lives. The only thing that could have made the evening better, Elise reflected, was if Thomas had stayed sober. He'd come and claimed her hand near midnight, and the whiskey on his breath was overpowering.

Eb Bentley hadn't danced, but he'd warned her that he didn't dance much. He was off guarding the wagons and livestock, a necessary precaution in view of the sizable Indian camp just outside the fort grounds. Eb always seemed to have guard duty when the musicians tuned up. Elise began to think it was his design. But what did it matter? He was only the scout, and his absence didn't disappoint her in the least.

They camped beneath the mammoth rock on the plains the last afternoon of June. Elise and Anne quickly raised their tent while Thomas unhitched the mules. They no longer expected him to put it up for them. What had once been a complicated and frustrating task was now another ten-minute chore.

Since they'd formed the wagon circle early, they had time to bake. Several of the men had gone hunting, and they rode into camp bringing quarters of buffalo and tales of the hunt. By the time Elise had built a fire, they were parting out chunks of meat to each family.

"What are you wearing tonight?" Anne asked as she filled the coffeepot.

Elise shrugged. "This dress. I promised Lavinia I'd fix her hair. By the time we're done with supper and cleaning up, I won't have time to change my clothes. But I'll help you dress if you wish to wear a gown."

"I thought perhaps my green promenade dress," Anne said, "but the evenings have been so warm of late that perhaps I'll wear the one I wore at Fort Laramie."

"It made a sensation with the soldiers," Elise said. "I'm sure everyone here would love to see it again—it's a beautiful dress."

"Funny how we're keeping our fanciest gowns in reserve," Anne noted.

Elise smiled. "I fear we'd be snubbed again if they saw you in your full finery, my dear. They'd all think we imagined ourselves above them."

"They already think that."

"Several of the ladies act friendly to us now." Elise didn't add that nearly all the gentlemen seemed to find excuses to help them out. When Thomas wasn't about, it didn't seem to matter anymore. Bachelors like the Adams brothers and Wilbur Harkness happened by their campfire morning and evening to ask whether the ladies had plenty of water and fuel. Most of them lingered to gaze at Anne as long as they could get away with it.

"Mr. Whistler promised us two days of rest," Anne said, "though I wouldn't exactly call laundry and baking rest."

Elise smiled at her. "I suspect he was referring to the livestock getting the rest. We'll work all day, for certain."

"At least we're capable of putting in two days of demanding labor now. I'd never have imagined it." Anne clamped the top on the coffeepot and brought it to the fire pit. "Shall I put the grate on now?"

"Yes, and I'll set the stew on that. Too bad we've no potatoes."

"No, but the dumplings Rebecca taught you to make are almost as good."

Elise heard a distant shout. She shielded her eyes and looked upward. "The boys are climbing the rock."

Anne stood beside her. "Do you want to go up?"

"I think not. I'll save my strength for this evening."

That night's gathering was held outside the wagon corral. The leaders felt there was little danger, but nevertheless three men were detailed to guard the encampment and make sure the livestock remained calm.

Elise and Anne walked to the bonfire with the Harkness family. The Adams brothers joined them, and Elise took note that Anne crossed the distance with Wilbur on her right and quiet Daniel Adams on her left. Lavinia had her own followers. Several of the young men watched her as the group neared the grassy expanse near the bonfire. As soon as the fiddler and the accordionist began to play, a fellow of about eighteen came to claim Lavinia. Wilbur took Anne's hand and swept her away, much to Daniel's chagrin. He wandered off toward a cluster of other single men. Mrs. Legity and Mrs. Libby came over to stand with Rebecca and Elise.

"That's Johnny Klein with Lavinia," Rebecca said. "He spends most days back with the herd, but he manages to see my Lavinia at least once a day. Wouldn't surprise me if she heard a proposal before this journey's over."

Mrs. Legity's lip curled. "So long as it's not that Daniel Adams. He's twice her age."

"I doubt he's much over thirty," Rebecca said placidly. "Besides, he'd probably be in a better position to take care of her than one of these young pups would. He seems like a steady man, and he and his brother have the wherewithal to set up a prosperous farm."

Rob Whistler, wearing a pale shirt that looked clean in the moonlight, strolled over to them. "Mrs. Legity, would you care to dance?"

The widow shed her arrogance and held out her hand. "Why, Mr. Whistler, it would be my pleasure."

"Rob's a good man," Rebecca said. "Always dances with the widows first."

Elise hadn't thought about it, but she saw that Rebecca was right.

"Agnes Legity was in a snit earlier, going on about how Rob shouldn't dance, since his wife isn't here." Rebecca smiled and shook her head. "She doesn't seem to think that matters now."

"Mr. Whistler is a man who can be trusted, I'm sure," Elise said.

"Yes, I'd say so. Now Eb, he's a different sort."

"What do you mean?" Elise wasn't sure whether to be shocked or not.

"Oh, not that he can't be trusted. He can. You won't likely see him out to dance though. That's all I meant. But he'll be right there in the morning, making sure everyone's got what they need. And while we mend our wagons and do our washing, he'll scout ahead for the next campsite and make sure the trail's safe for us."

"Well, Mrs. Harkness!"

Elise and Rebecca turned at the cheerful voice. Rebecca's husband, Orrin, had come up behind them.

"Be you looking for a dance partner?" he asked.

"Don't mind if I do since there aren't any army officers about to dance with."

Rebecca smiled at Elise and took Orrin's hand. Elise stood alone for only a moment before Hector Adams approached her with a shy smile.

"Miss Finster?"

"Yes, sir?"

"May I?"

"Delighted." She took his hand and stepped out with him in time to the music.

※

Eb walked slowly about the encampment, just within the circle of wagons. The oxen and mules were quiet tonight. Maybe the music coming from over near the bonfire soothed them. They'd made a big corral this time, with ropes tied between the wagons and boxes and gear piled up to discourage the animals from trying to get out.

Very few folks had stayed in camp. Even the young children were allowed to go over to watch the dancing for a while. Their parents would carry them back to their tents when they fell asleep.

Eb didn't mind watching the other folks' stuff while they played. He and Rob had a good company this time, and only a few troubles had beset them—small ones at that. A broken wheel, a child who burned his hand, a few cattle that wandered off but were soon recovered. But no one had complained about the rules, and all the heads of household cooperated with taking their turns in the lineup and participating in chores that benefited the entire outfit. He hoped the rest of the trip went as well.

Several times in his rounds, he crossed paths with Abe Leonard and Thomas Costigan, the other two guards. He wasn't sure Thomas was the best pick for the job, but he seemed alert each time Eb saw him. If he sneaked off and shirked his duty, Eb would make a note of it.

Two hours had passed when Rob entered the circle between two wagons and strolled toward Eb.

"They're winding down the party. You want to go have a dance or two?"

"Nah," Eb said.

"Aw, why not? I'll bet the ladies are disappointed." Rob laughed. "I had a turn earlier with Miss Finster, but I couldn't get near Miss Stone. The boys are lined up six deep every time the music changes."

"That right?"

"Yes. They all think she's unapproachable by daylight, but the moon and music give them courage."

"Hmm." Eb rested his rifle on his shoulder as Rob fell into pace with him.

"Whyn't you go over for a while?" Rob said.

Eb thought about it as they ambled past four more wagons. The moon was just past full, and it shed plenty of light on the enclosure. A rangy mule stood in their path, cropping what was left of the buffalo grass. Eb slapped it on the rump to make it get out of their way.

"Howdy," Abe called from up ahead.

"All quiet?" Eb asked.

Abe waved in assent. "How's the dancing going?"

"Fine and dandy," Rob said. "You want to go over? I'm trying to convince Eb, but he won't go."

"Oh, you ought to," Abe said. "A young feller like you should be dancing."

Eb laughed. True, Abe was ten years or so older, but Eb didn't consider himself a "young feller."

"Go on," Rob said. "Give me your gun and go kick up your heels."

Reluctantly, Eb surrendered the rifle. There was no reconsidering after that, but he felt exposed.

Rob scowled at him. "Git going!"

Eb slipped under the rope barrier between two wagons. In the dark expanse between the bonfire and the wagons, he walked alone. The warm breeze caressed his face. He'd kept shaving for three solid months on the trail. Didn't know why exactly. Maybe he'd skip it tomorrow. It would save time, and there wasn't any reason to keep on shaving.

The closer he got to the bonfire, the more alien he felt. The fiddle and the accordion blasted out a polka, and he hung back. He certainly wasn't going to make a fool of himself to that music. He stood in the shadows and looked over the twenty couples whirling about in the firelight. Miss Stone was dancing with Will Strother, a lad of about sixteen. They looked as though they were having fun. The Harkness sisters, Lavinia and Abigail, were out there with a couple of the Foster boys.

It took only half a minute to realize the one person he was looking for wasn't dancing. Eb looked about the edges of the circle. There she was, talking to Rebecca Harkness and "Ma" Foster. He edged toward them, staying behind the circle of watchers so he wouldn't catch their attention and have to stop and chat.

The riotous music ended, and the dancers caught their breath and swapped partners for another round. The musicians launched into "Jeanie with the Light Brown Hair," and some of the older men moved into the circle with their wives.

*Now or never,* Eb thought. His legs felt like sticks of firewood as he propelled himself toward her. Orrin Harkness had claimed his wife's hand, but Mrs. Foster still stood with Miss Finster, and Mrs. Libby had joined them. Eb took another step so that he was beside them and cleared his throat.

All three women looked over at him.

"Evening," Eb said. The music swelled.

"Well, hello, Mr. Bentley." Miss Finster sounded charmed to see him, which made his heart thrum annoyingly fast.

"Howdy, Eb," said Mrs. Foster.

Mrs. Libby just nodded, her eyebrows raised in apparent shock at seeing him.

"I wondered. . .well. . .uh. . .Miss Finster, you know I'm not much of a dancer, but. . .uh. . .well, if you'd care to. . ."

"Why, thank you. I'd be pleased." She put her hand in his.

Eb was surprised to find she wore gloves. Not knitted, keep-me-warm-in-January gloves, but soft, white cotton, I'm-a-lady gloves. He held her hand tenderly and placed his other hand tentatively on her waist. She smiled up at him and laid her left hand on his shoulder. Moonlight softened her features, and he could have believed she was in her twenties at that moment. Why didn't the men swarm her the way they did Miss Stone? They were crazy not to. Eb swallowed hard and made himself step in time to the music.

As they moved away from the older women, he was sure he heard Mrs. Libby say, "Well, did you ever?"

To which Mrs. Foster replied, "No, I never."

Elise knew her face was red, but she hoped no one could see that in the darkness. Of course, that almost-full cheese of a moon didn't aid her cause. It cast shadows almost as sharp as daytime ones.

Since her dance with Eb Bentley turned out to be the last of the evening, he'd been on hand to walk her back to the wagons. On her other side, Anne strolled along with Wilbur Harkness, who had vied with several other young men for the privilege. Anne kept up a bright chatter with Wilbur, which seemed to please him to no end. She described their panic as they tried to harness the mule team their first morning on the trail, making a comical anecdote out of it. Wilbur laughed so hard, Elise knew his heart was long gone.

She looked up at Eb's face. He was watching her, and his lips twitched when their gazes met.

"Nice evening," Eb said.

"Yes, I think everyone enjoyed it immensely."

He nodded slowly.

"You ought to be the hero of that story Anne's telling," Elise said.

"Oh, she just hasn't gotten to that part yet."

Elise smiled. Should she tuck her hand in his elbow? He hadn't offered his arm. She walked beside him, careful not to brush against his sleeve. Perhaps Eb was only seeing her "home" because he perceived it as his duty.

The white mounds of the wagon tops rested like puffs of cotton around the field. The little tent she shared with Anne stood pale against the grass. They'd left a path of about six feet between it and the wagon and built their fire to one side. The two couples stopped in the space between the prairie schooner and the tent, suspended between the bustle of the encampment and the vast quiet of the prairie. Eb seemed to feel it, too. Was he wishing for the ranch he owned? Rob had said this was Eb's last trip east. He wanted to stay on his land and not make another long trek. She could understand that. A cozy home waiting at the end of the trail. If only she and Anne could look forward to that.

"I guess you're glad we're halfway," she said.

Eb nodded. "I am. We've made good time and had few troubles. Though I can picture what you ladies are facing—staying in Oregon a short time and heading on back next spring."

Next spring. Elise hadn't allowed herself to contemplate it, but he was right—they'd have to spend the winter in Oregon. Maybe by spring they'd be ready to explore the option of sailing home. Wasn't a railroad being built across Panama? If they didn't have to sail around Cape Horn, the ocean journey might not be too arduous. She refused to even think about Anne's seasickness.

"Yes," she managed. "As soon as we locate Mr. Stone, I'm sure we'll be ready to turn homeward."

"Unless you fall in love with Oregon."

Her heart thudded. "Is it really as beautiful as they say?"

"You can't imagine, ma'am. You might not think much of it this winter—it rains a lot, at least where my ranch is. But come spring . . .well, it's about the prettiest place you'll ever see. It sets on the river, and there's mountains in the distance. Got some woods on my spread, but mostly it's open, and I'm going to run cattle on it."

"It sounds lovely." In a corner of her mind, she pictured a little cottage in a valley full of flowers—a place she and Anne could stay together comfortably, away from the constraints of England's society. She'd think about that. When they reached Oregon, if Anne seemed taken by the place, perhaps she'd suggest it—though at this point she was sure Anne had no plans beyond finding her uncle and returning with him to England. But if they couldn't find David. . .

A few steps away, Wilbur was saying, "Well, good night, Miss Anne. I sure did have fun."

"So did I, Wilbur. And thank you for walking me home."

Eb smiled at Elise, as though they were indulgent parents to the pair of energetic young people.

"Reckon I'd better go find Rob. Looks like things stayed quiet in camp though."

"Good night, all," Wilbur said. He turned and walked away.

Elise opened her mouth to bid Eb a good evening when a sharp cry came from Anne.

"Elise! Look. Someone's been in our tent."

# CHAPTER 17

Eb and Miss Finster hurried over to the tent. Eb eyed the little canvas structure closely. Miss Stone had already untied one side of the front door flap and raised it, but she had no illumination other than the moonlight. It shone bright, more than halfway across the sky in its circuit, but even so, the interior of the tent lay in darkness.

"How can you tell?" he asked.

"There's a clod of dirt on my bed, and the blanket is mussed."

Eb stooped and peered inside, careful not to block the moonlight. The two bedrolls in the tent were smoothed over, except for a couple of depressions on one, as if someone had knelt on the blankets. He could plainly see the clump of dirt she'd mentioned, too, on the foot end of the bedroll, near the opening.

"Anything else out of place?" he asked.

Miss Stone frowned and studied the dim interior. "Not that I can see."

Eb straightened. "Miss Finster, want to take a look?"

Miss Stone stood back and let her friend move closer. Miss Finster went to her knees at the tent door and sat motionless for a long moment. She turned her head and looked up at him.

"Anne's satchel has been moved. I tidied up before we left camp, and I'm sure it wasn't crooked like it is now."

Eb nodded. "Do you want to light a lantern and look through your things tonight?"

Miss Finster looked to Miss Stone for the decision.

"Yes," the young woman said. "This makes me cross. I wouldn't be able to sleep, wondering if anything's been taken."

"We've a small lantern in the tent," Miss Finster said. "There's another in the wagon."

"Let me get the one from the wagon," Eb said. "That way you'll

177

SUSAN PAGE DAVIS

be able to see everything without having to make a disturbance while you get the lantern." As an afterthought, he said, "Perhaps you'd best check the wagon, too, and see if it looks ransacked."

The women walked with him to the back of their wagon. A lantern hung just inside the back bow, and Eb took it out and lit it. He held it up so they could look inside. Miss Stone climbed up and surveyed the contents of the wagon for a minute.

"I think it's all right," she said.

Miss Finster gave her a hand, and she hopped down. Eb carried the lantern back to their tent.

Miss Finster crawled inside then turned and took the lantern from him. After a minute, she came back to the flap.

"I think both our satchels were gone through. I checked mine, and everything seems to be intact. Anne, here's yours."

She passed a large leather carryall through the opening. Eb took it and set it on the ground. He held the lantern while Miss Finster came out of the tent and Miss Stone opened the satchel.

After thoroughly inspecting the contents of the bag, which Eb decided he'd better not observe too closely, she caught her breath.

"The letter."

"Letter?" Eb asked.

"The last letter my uncle David sent from St. Louis. It's missing."

Eb thought about that. "Anything else?"

"No."

"Your marcasite necklace?" Miss Finster whispered.

"It's here."

Miss Finster turned to him. "She left most of her jewelry in a vault in England, but she brought a few less valuable pieces. The garnet necklace she's wearing is one. The marcasite pendant should have been attractive to a thief. I think that tells us something about him."

"What?" Miss Stone asked.

"He's more interested in your uncle than he is in your jewelry," Eb said.

Miss Finster nodded. "Precisely."

178

So many thoughts pummeled Eb's brain that he wanted to get away, off by himself under the stars, to think. Miss Stone had valuable jewels in England. Miss Finster apparently had none. Somehow that fit with the protective manner he'd observed in the older woman taking care of the younger. But it also reinforced little things he'd observed—Miss Stone held the purse strings on this expedition. Miss Finster might make most of the practical, everyday decisions, but the important questions rested with Miss Stone. And this missing uncle—who was he? Why would anyone outside his family care whether or not the ladies were able to locate him?

It was none of Eb's business of course. But thievery on the wagon train *was* his business—his and Rob's.

"I'd like to fetch Rob Whistler and discuss this with him, if you ladies don't mind."

As he'd half expected, Miss Finster looked to Miss Stone, who pressed her lips together, frowning. After a moment, she nodded.

"That's fine," Miss Finster said. "We'll wait here while you get him."

Eb strode toward his and Rob's campsite. Rob was spreading his bedroll a few feet from the fire ring.

"I need to talk to you," Eb said.

Rob looked up at him. He dropped the edge of the blankets and stood straight. "What is it?"

"Trouble at the English ladies' camp. Someone went in their tent while they were gone and took something."

"What?" Rob asked.

"You know that famous uncle of Miss Stone's that they're looking for?"

"Well, I dunno how famous he is," Rob said with a hint of a smile.

"He's famous enough that someone stole his letter out of Miss Stone's bag."

Rob whistled softly. "They're sure?"

"Yeah. I could see someone had been in there. Those ladies are neater than a pin, and their bedrolls were mussed a little. Miss Finster said her stuff had been looked through, too, but she didn't think anything was missing. I expect they fold every piece of ribbon just so, and they'd know if someone pawed through their baggage."

Rob nodded. "So...this letter. Why would someone take it?"

"I don't know, but I'm thinking we should take the ladies off a little ways, where no one else can hear us talking, and get the full story. Because there's more to it than we know."

"All right." Rob looked around. "I reckon we can go over near the bonfire. Most everybody's left there."

Eb could see that the big fire had burned down to embers just about right for roasting a prairie chicken, if anybody had one to roast.

"There's still enough firelight that everyone would see us."

"You think it's that important?"

"I do," Eb said. "We don't want to draw much attention to this."

"All right. I'll go out a hundred yards toward the river from their tent. You get them and meet me out there. Should I put another guard on to watch their camp?"

"Whoever did it got what he wanted."

"Right." Rob settled his hat more firmly and headed out onto the grassy expanse toward the river.

Eb hurried back to the ladies and led them to the meeting place. With the moon still high and bright, Rob's pale shirt made him easily visible if anyone was looking. The ladies' dresses were darker, and Eb had his leather vest over a chambray shirt. He placed himself between Rob and the wagons as a minor precaution.

"Evening, ladies," Rob said softly. "Eb's told me what happened. We thought maybe it's time we knew more about your uncle, Miss Stone, and why this letter would be valuable to someone outside your family."

Miss Stone looked at Miss Finster—an instinctive movement, Eb realized. She looked to her friend for advice, and Miss Finster looked to her for authority.

"First off," Eb said, "I don't mean any offense, but it might help us if we clear one thing up right now. You two aren't just friends, are you?"

After a pause during which those significant looks again cut the air, Miss Finster turned to face him squarely. "That is correct, Mr. Bentley. Miss Stone is my employer."

Eb nodded. He'd guessed it, but how many other people had? Not Rob, that was certain. He stood there staring at Miss Finster like a thunderstruck buffalo calf.

"Your employer?"

"That's right, Mr. Whistler," Miss Finster said. "I've worked for the Stone family for more than twenty years. First I was a housemaid at the earl of Stoneford's home. Then I was elevated to the position of lady's maid for the countess."

"Countess?" Rob's idiot expression grew more pronounced.

Miss Finster nodded toward Miss Stone. "Yes. Lady Anne's mother."

"Lady—" Rob caught a quick breath and whipped around to stare at Eb now. "You knew this?"

"Nope."

Miss Stone smiled and held out her hand in supplication. "Please, gentlemen, don't be concerned about that. This is exactly why we've kept quiet about my. . .connections."

"But why—I mean—they let you just—" Rob broke off and shook his head in bewilderment.

Miss Finster touched his sleeve and said softly, "Lady Anne's father passed away last October, and he had no male offspring to inherit his title. Lady Anne has no brothers, you see. But the earl did."

Miss Stone's sad smile was tragic in the moonlight. "That's correct. My father had two brothers, but one of them predeceased him. That leaves only Uncle David."

"And Uncle David is the new earl," Eb said slowly, thinking it out as he went.

"Yes, if we can find him," Miss Finster said. "He has to return to England to claim his title and Anne's father's estate."

Rob blew out a long breath. "I'm guessing this estate would be worth claiming."

"Oh yes."

The two ladies stood in silence while Eb and Rob absorbed the information.

"Do you have any idea who might have done this?" Rob asked at last.

"I have an idea," Miss Finster said. "I caught our hired man poking about in the wagon another time, and he claimed he was only getting something from his own bundle, but he'd changed his story, and I thought at the time he looked guilty."

"I remember," Eb said. "You've had some trouble with him shirking his chores, too, haven't you?"

"Some."

"What do you think we should do?" Rob asked Eb.

Eb thought for a moment. "Search him." It might cause trouble in the train if nothing turned up, but he didn't like the idea of a ne'er-do-well skulking about the ladies' camp.

"I'll do it," Rob said. "Where does he keep his bedroll?"

"In the back of our wagon," Miss Finster said. "I think he usually sleeps near the men who are tending the livestock."

"You ladies can retire," Eb said. "We'll make sure the guards pay close attention to your camp tonight."

"Thank you," Miss Stone said. "That will be a comfort."

She and Miss Finster headed off across the grass toward the encampment.

"Let me get Costigan," Eb said.

"No." Rob started walking.

It didn't take Eb long to catch up. "Why not?"

"You've got it in for him. If he's not forthcoming, I'll get one of the other men, and we'll search his person, like you said. But check his bedroll first, and any other gear he has. I don't want this to get personal."

"Why would it?" Eb growled.

"You tell me."

Eb grabbed his arm and stopped. "What are you talking about?"

Rob dropped his voice to a whisper. "Come on, Eb, you know

you've got it bad for Miss Finster. I don't want you giving Costigan a reason to hold a grudge. Don't worry—if he's got that letter, we'll get it. But if it's on him, I don't want you to be the one to take it off him."

Eb's jaw worked as he tried to decide whether to laugh or yell at his friend.

Rob laid a hand on his shoulder. "Take it easy. It's all right."

"Take back what you said."

Rob's face puckered in a frown. "What? That you like her? Don't be ridiculous. It's obvious."

"I don't treat her any different than I do the other ladies."

"Oh sure. Back in Independence, you wanted me to refuse to let them join us. You were positive those two would cause trouble. Well, guess what? They're not the ones causing trouble. I can't see that they've held us up any either—except maybe that first morning. But the first day is always chaos. And now, every night when you come in from scouting, you stop by their wagon to see if they're doing all right or if they need something. It's fine, Eb, but you might as well quit denying that you like her."

Eb had no reply. He glowered at Rob for a moment then turned on his heel.

Thomas tossed down his poker hand in disgust. He'd lost almost a dollar, and he'd only been playing for half an hour. This just wasn't his night.

"Costigan."

He glanced up. Rob Whistler was standing just outside their little circle of five. This couldn't be good. Probably he'd get ragged on for gambling with the boys. Some of the parents took exception to their kids playing cards.

"Yeah?" It was hard to stare Whistler down when you were sitting on the ground, so Thomas stood.

"Word with you," Whistler said and walked away.

Thomas sighed. "Deal me out, boys."

He followed the wagon master away from the drovers' camp. Whistler stopped and waited for him.

"What do you want?" Thomas asked.

"When you were on guard duty, did you see anything unusual?"

Thomas squinted at him. "No. Something happen?"

"Miss Stone says someone took something from a bag in her tent."

Not what he'd expected. Those English dames were sharper than he'd thought. He'd figured she might notice it tomorrow or the next day.

"I didn't see anyone nosing around."

Whistler held his gaze for a long moment. "In light of some other things that have happened, we'll need to check through your stuff."

"What things? You got no right."

"Yes, I do, Costigan. We've got no law out here except me. You and all the others agreed before we left Independence that what I say goes. Now, Miss Finster says you were snooping around in their wagon a while back."

"I was looking for her washtub. I didn't know she'd already set it out. Oh, good night!" He turned away.

"If I were you, I wouldn't make this difficult." Whistler's tone was icy. Funny, Thomas had always figured Bentley for the tough guy of the duo. Where was Bentley, anyhow?

"I'm telling you I didn't take anything of theirs."

"Then you don't mind us searching your stuff."

"Yes, I do mind. When those women hired me, I didn't expect to be accused of stealing. Listen, I put up with late meals—and burnt half the time at that—and those two not knowing a linchpin from a rattlesnake. If you think I'm going to stand for this—"

"You will stand for it if you want to stay with us," Whistler said.

"Rob!"

Thomas looked toward the voice. Eb Bentley and Wilbur Harkness were coming toward them from the drovers' campsite. Bentley waved something small and white in the moonlight. Thomas clenched his teeth.

"What have you got?" Whistler asked as they drew nearer.

"It's a letter addressed to Miss Stone's father, in England."

Whistler eyed Thomas narrowly. "Now isn't that a coincidence. That's the exact item Miss Stone told us was taken from her bag."

"You planted that," Thomas said to Bentley. "You haven't liked me since that first day, when I was late. That couldn't be helped, but you've held it against me ever since. You filched that while we were on watch, and now you're using it as an excuse to get me in trouble."

"Oh, be quiet," Bentley said.

Thomas turned to Whistler. "I'll bet those women don't want to pay me, that's it."

Whistler asked Bentley, "You got a witness?"

"Yes. Wilbur went with me to where Costigan's bedroll was stashed. He watched me go through his bundle."

"That's right," Wilbur said. "Eb found the letter rolled up inside a shirt."

"What's your interest in this letter?" Whistler asked Thomas.

"Nothing. I didn't take it."

Whistler shook his head. "You can't bluff your way out of this. I'll advise Miss Finster to pay you off, and you'll be leaving us at the next civilized place we come to. I reckon that'll be Schwartzburg. We'll be there in a few days. It's not much, but you'll be safe there until another train comes along, or you can go back East if you want. Now, I'm not going to do anything to you, so long as you behave yourself. One more stunt like this, and we'll confine you until we get to a place where we can turn you over to the authorities."

Thomas knew he was beat. He'd just have to send word to Peterson that he'd failed. He didn't like that idea. Maybe he could figure out a way around it. No time to think now. Whistler was jawing again.

"On second thought, I'll get your pay from the ladies and bring it to you. You keep clear of them while you're with us, you hear me, Costigan? Them and their belongings and their livestock."

"Oh, I hear you all right." Thomas walked away before he could say more.

# CHAPTER 18

The next morning, the ladies dressed in the dark tent and stepped into the cool daybreak in the shadow of the great rock.

"Our laundry is done up," Anne observed. "What have you planned for today?"

Elise walked toward the back of the wagon. "Baking. I want plenty ahead—maybe enough to last us all week. Although we won't need so much, since we're not feeding Thomas anymore."

"Yes. I won't be sorry to see him leave the company." Anne threw her a worried glance. "You don't think he'll bother us again, will he? Out of spite, I mean?"

"I hope not. We shall miss him when it's time to lug water."

"Perhaps someone else will help us."

Elise shrugged and reached into the wagon for her crate of pans and utensils. "We can survive on our own. We've proven that. But I shan't say no if Wilbur or one of the Adams brothers offers to help us."

"I wouldn't look for Daniel to come around," Anne said.

"Oh? Why's that?"

"I turned him down last night."

Elise paused with the crate in her arms. "Do you mean. . .for a dance, or. . ."

"He asked me to marry him."

As the sun sent its first rays over the prairie, the other travelers began to stir. Oxen lowed, and a man called to his son. Elise couldn't move. She just stared at Anne.

"When did this happen?"

"While we waltzed." Anne chuckled. "Oh Elise, don't look so stricken. I told him that I had no plans beyond finding Uncle David and returning to England. He asked if there was anything he could do to change my mind. I tried to let him down gently."

Elise sighed and set the crate on the ground. "Well, he's been pining over you for a month. I suppose I should have expected it. We're usually right ahead of them in line, except when we change to the back, and we see more of him and Hector than we do of a lot of others. And, Anne dear, he *is* a nice young man."

"But I don't think I wish to spend the rest of my life on a wheat farm. That's what he hopes to do, you know—raise wheat."

"It does sound a bit bland, yet—don't you think there's something appealing about it? A secure place with a man who adores you? Of course he wouldn't be able to afford a cook or a housemaid, I'm sure."

"I don't know if I'd care, if I met the right man," Anne said.

"Dan Adams isn't the one though?"

"That's right." Anne took the tinderbox from the crate.

The livestock in the wagon circle stirred and shifted. A horse snorted, and Elise looked toward the sound. Eb Bentley was slipping a headstall over his paint gelding's poll.

"Odd how the idea of marrying a commoner isn't nearly as repulsive as it was three months ago." Anne bunched up a handful of wood shavings and dry grass.

"It's because you're not in England now," Elise said.

Anne shook her head. "I even feel a bit guilty nowadays, knowing I would have thought of people like Rebecca Harkness and the Adams boys as beneath my notice." She hit the flint and steel together and blew on the sparks.

"I agree with you," Elise said. "When you get to know some of these folks, you realize they've a bit of regality about them."

Anne reached for the small store of kindling Thomas had left by the fireplace last night.

Elise ruminated on their change of perspective as she got out her butcher knife and sliced off a small bit of bacon fat to grease the spider with. Anyone in England who knew Lady Anne would be shocked to learn she would even consider marrying a plain American and living in what they would call obscure poverty. She tried to picture Anne visiting someone like the Blithes or the Cranfords and taking Dan Adams along to a dinner party. It wouldn't do at all. Anne would be snubbed in rare form. Yet she *could* picture Anne and Daniel living in quiet contentment if only Anne were bitten by love. *If I fell truly in love, class wouldn't matter one whit.*

Eb led his paint out of the corral between their wagon and Abe Leonard's and stopped to give the saddle's cinch strap one last tug. He looked over and nodded at them.

"Morning, ladies."

"Good morning, Mr. Bentley," Elise said. She couldn't seem to look away from him. His dusty hat, so worn and comfortable looking, was the perfect complement to his rugged features. It was an honest hat. And she believed he'd shaved this morning. How had he managed that before the sun was fully up? A man of unexpected talents.

"Lovely day," Anne sang out.

"Yes, it is." He hesitated a moment then led his horse closer to Elise. "I have to admit, you ladies have surprised me. I know you're going to have it rougher in some ways without Costigan, but I think you can make it."

"Why thank you, sir." Elise marveled at the warmth in her heart. "Coming from you, that is praise indeed."

"Well, if you need anything, you tell me or Rob. We'll see that you're taken care of."

"We'll do our best not to call on you too often."

He nodded, gazing at her with thoughtful brown eyes. "I reckon you will."

Elise resolved anew to prove that his faith in her and Anne was not misplaced.

Eb smiled and swung into the saddle. "Up, Speck." He touched his hat brim and trotted off to the west.

"Nothing common about that man," Anne said.

The next morning Rob Whistler blew his horn from the center of the wagon circle before it was light enough to see more than the snowy wagon covers. Elise and Anne were already dressed. They hurried out into the central corral to separate their mules from the other livestock. Elise nearly bumped into Nick Foster.

"I've got one of your wheelers here, ma'am."

"Thank you, Nick!" Elise took Challenger's halter from him and tugged the big mule toward her wagon. She tied him up and went back for another mule. Anne passed her, leading Chick, one of their leaders.

"Get the harness out," Elise called to her. "I'll bring Bumper and Blackie."

They had come nine hundred miles from Independence, Missouri, but the mules looked to be in good flesh to her untrained eye. The two days of leisure at Independence Rock had left them well rested. The men had taken the stock out of the camp during the day to let them graze along the river, and all of the animals seemed to have benefited from it. Bumper, at least, exhibited high spirits this morning, kicking out at another mule they passed.

They were ready to move out when the horn sounded again, and Elise took the reins. Anne sat beside her on the seat. They'd used enough provisions to more than offset her weight. Elise directed the four mules to move into line behind Mr. Leonard's wagon, with the Adams brothers behind them. She felt rather powerful, sitting up on the seat. An hour of staring at the mules' hindquarters and the water barrel fixed on the back of Mr. Leonard's wagon lessened that impression. After two hours, Anne climbed down to walk for a while with some of the other women and gather buffalo chips for their evening fire. Toward noon, she returned and clambered up beside Elise again.

"Would you like me to drive for a while?"

"That would be nice. My shoulders are tired."

Anne stood and braced herself while Elise slid over on the seat.

"The clouds look ominous," Anne observed as she took the reins.

Now that she was on the other side, Elise could see farther westward beyond the wagon ahead. The overcast sky had gone nearly black, and the clouds were low enough to obscure the distant mountains.

"I'd say we're in for a storm."

Experience as they'd crossed the Nebraska prairie had taught them how violent a thunderstorm could be out here, with no trees to break the wind.

The wind picked up, tossing whirlwinds of dust high. Some of the drivers took their wagons to one side of the rutted trail so they wouldn't breathe so much of the roiling dust. Gusts tore at Elise's skirt and made the canvas wagon cover pop. The tall prairie grasses rippled like sea waves. Thunder rumbled over them, and lightning crackled in the distance.

Rob cantered his chestnut along the line as the first raindrops spattered down.

"Circle the wagons," he shouted. "Hobble your teams if you can and turn them loose in the middle. Circle now so the drovers can drive the loose herd inside. Storm's a-coming!" Elise's heart caught then raced. They'd never hobbled the mules without Thomas. She doubted they could unhitch and hobble them all in time. Anne thrust the reins into her hands, slapping them against the wheelers' haunches. "Get up, Bumper! Up, Challenger!"

Anne clung to the edge of the wagon seat, but Elise had to brace herself with her feet as the mules followed Mr. Leonard's wagon. They lurched out of the rutted trail into the tall grass, plowing it down as they went.

As the rain increased to a downpour, the wagon ahead stopped. Others had lumbered into a lopsided oval. Elise hauled back on the reins, and the mules stopped just behind Abe's water barrel.

"Quick, Anne! The hobbles."

Elise leaped down into the wet grass as Anne dove into the wagon. Every traveler dreaded a stampede, and the storm could be more than enough to set one off.

Elise's fingers fumbled as she worked to unhitch the leather traces from the whiffletrees near the wagon tongue. Anne appeared, carrying an armful of short leather straps. Her calico dress was already soaked and clung to her frame. Elise decided to try to hobble the mules first then unhitch them.

"Work on Blackie first," she yelled over the wind. Blackie, the near leader, was the most placid of their mules and would probably allow Anne to work on his legs without a fuss. Challenger, on the other hand, pawed at the ground, throwing his head and snorting. "Oh, you'd love to get loose, wouldn't you?" Elise muttered.

Each rawhide strap had a loop in one end. This had to be slipped over the mule's elevated foot and pulled tight. The other end was then buckled around the other front leg. With great difficulty, she got the loop around his right cannon. She wasn't sure she could hook the other end around his left leg. Still in harness, Challenger was bound to Bumper, and she couldn't get between them.

"Let me help."

She looked up into Eb Bentley's brown eyes. His hat was pulled low over his brow, and his clothes were drenched, too. The rain pummeled them mercilessly.

Elise surrendered the end of the hobble to him.

"Unhook him from the wagon," Eb yelled.

She managed it at last. Eb had the strap in place by the time she released the toggle. Eb unbuckled him from the rest of the team. Still in his collar and harness, Challenger crow-hopped away from his teammates into the center of the circle.

Out of nowhere, Dan Adams appeared. "Give me some of the hobbles. Get under the wagon."

She'd expected him to say "in the wagon," but as she processed his command and handed over the remaining hobbles, she realized that hailstones the size of peas, and some as large as grapes, now pelted them. She ran to the side of the wagon and threw herself down, rolling the grass flat as she gained the shelter beneath the wagon bed. She stretched out, parallel to the box above her. If the mules still hitched should begin to move, she didn't want to be run over.

A moment later, Anne joined her, wild eyed and shivering. "The cattle are panicking. The men are trying to close the gaps between the wagons."

Elise crawled to the front of the wagon and peered out. All

of their mules were unhitched. She could see the wheels of Abe Leonard's wagon thirty feet away. Over the wind, the noise of hailstones hitting the ground rivaled the thunder. She could hear the screams of mules and urgent lowing of the oxen. Animals shifted about and bumped the side of the wagon. Outside their shelter, everything moved and roared.

Anne lay on the ground and covered her head with her arms. Elise moved closer and wrapped an arm around her. Anne's body convulsed with shivering.

"So c–cold," she cried.

Between the rear wheels, Elise saw someone's feet. A big wooden box plopped down on the sodden grass and accumulation of ice balls. Still the man kept working. *He's tying ropes between the wagons to keep the animals in,* she thought. *Dear God, help them!*

A fearsome ripping came from above them. Anne jerked her chin up and stared at Elise.

"The wagon cover," Elise said. Everything in the wagon would get soaked.

Anne threw her arms around Elise's neck and clung to her. Elise held her and stroked her back and shoulders. It reminded her of the night Anne's mother had died. The girl had wept for hours, inconsolable.

At last the roaring lessened. Elise relaxed her hold on Anne and crept to the edge of the wagon. Rain still fell, but softly now. The hail had collected in rows along the ground beside the wagons. Some of the stones were as large as eggs. Many of the canvas tops had split or shredded. Men moved slowly among the herd of livestock, speaking quietly to the animals. Others stood in gaps between wagons with sticks or guns in their hands, ready to drive back a mule or ox that wanted to escape.

How badly damaged was their own wagon? They had a spare cover. If only she could get at it now and spread it over the bows before all their foodstuffs were ruined.

Eb Bentley came and hunkered down next to the wagon. "You ladies all right?"

"Yes. But our wagon top is torn, isn't it?"

"Not as bad as some," Eb said. "And we've lost a few animals."

"Lost them?"

"Two are dead from the hailstones. Half a dozen more got past us and ran off."

"Are any people hurt?" she asked.

"Nothing serious. I think all your mules are safe, but I'm not sure. We'll stay here until tomorrow. The stock needs to calm down and warm up again. Some of them were so shocked by the storm and the cold that they could die just from that."

"Really?"

He nodded. "I've seen it before. We'll build fires as soon as we can, just to take the chill off. If I hitch your mules to the side of your wagon, can you rub them all over with a sack or something?"

"Yes, I can do that."

"That'll help warm them up. Tell me where your coat is in the wagon, and I'll try to get it out for you."

Anne poked her head out beside Elise. Her face was streaked with tears. "I can help, too, Mr. Bentley."

He eyed her for a moment then nodded. "We can use you."

Elise thought her arms would drop off before she stopped rubbing the mules. Eb and Daniel found all six of their team—the four they'd released and their two spares in the loose herd. They rotated the ones they rested, and this morning Prince and Zee had been left in the drovers' care. Those two seemed less traumatized than the others. Chick and Blackie were the worst. They stood trembling while Elise and Anne brushed them and rubbed them with the sacks.

At last the sun peeked through holes in the clouds. When the mules' hair was dry, Elise threw down her gunnysack. Eb had used the dry chips they'd collected yesterday and started a fire. She filled the coffeepot from the small rain barrel on the side of the wagon.

"There's still a little ice inside the wagon," Anne said. "If you think the mules are all right now, I'll toss the ice in a bucket and see what needs to be aired."

"Good. I expect some of those men could use a cup of coffee."

Elise found on a quick inspection that their food containers were unharmed. Some of their bedding was sodden with rainwater and melted hailstones, and the extra harnesses should probably be taken out and oiled. Most other things would survive the wetting.

A half hour later, when Dan Adams came over and asked if they had an extra wagon cover to replace their torn one, she held up the steaming coffeepot.

"We do, sir, and we have hot coffee. Are you interested?"

"Oh Miss Finster." Dan grinned at her, his teeth gleaming in his mud-streaked face. "If you give me a cup of hot brew, I reckon I'll feel fit enough to put your new wagon cover on all by myself."

"That's impressive, sir, but you needn't. Miss Stone and I will be happy to help. But drink your coffee first."

Other men appeared as if by magic—Dan's brother Hector, Abe Leonard, and even young Nick Foster. Elise kept an eye on Anne as she moved among them, smiling equally on them all. No trace of tears remained on her flushed cheeks. Dan watched the lovely dark-haired girl with a mournful gaze but managed a smile when Anne offered him a cold biscuit.

Eb arrived at last, trudging slowly with his chin low on his chest. Elise went to the fire and lifted the coffeepot.

"I've about one cup of coffee left in this pot, Mr. Bentley," she called to him. "I can't guarantee you won't get some grounds."

"I don't care if I have to chew it to swallow it," he said.

She smiled and poured the dregs into the tin cup Nick had emptied.

Anne took the pot from her. "I'll start a new batch."

Eb took a long sip and sighed. "Thank you kindly, ma'am. That hits the spot." He eyed her over the rim as he took another drink. "I've got some news for you," he said a moment later.

Elise's stomach clenched. "What sort of news?"

"Costigan's gone."

"Gone?" She stared at him. "How do you mean?"

"He lit out this morning, shortly after we broke camp. One of the drovers told me. He took Rob's extra saddle horse."

Elise had to concentrate to keep her jaw from dropping. "He stole Mr. Whistler's horse?"

"That's the word. Ralph Libby saw him leading the mare out. He said Costigan claimed Rob told him he could use the mare today to do some hunting. But he had his bedroll with him."

"And Mr. Whistler knew nothing of it."

Eb shook his head.

"I'm so sorry."

"Not your fault."

"Perhaps not, but Anne will feel responsible. If she hadn't told you about the letter—"

"We're better off without him," Eb said.

"Anne will want to reimburse Mr. Whistler for the horse."

Eb shook his head. "Don't even suggest it. Rob wouldn't hear of it, and there's no need to cause Miss Stone more distress. I'm just surprised he didn't take my other mount. Anyway, we'll report him as a horse thief to the authorities the next time we have a chance. If some troopers pass us, Rob will send a letter back to Fort Laramie to alert them."

"It's so evil. Anne paid him every cent she'd promised him, even though he'd only gone halfway with us."

"I figured." Eb sipped his coffee.

"She wanted to be sure he wouldn't be stranded out here. Do you think he'll make it to Schwartzburg on his own?"

"Likely, unless this storm caught him bad."

"He's obviously resourceful," Elise mused.

"That's one way of putting it. He knows the country, and we're only a day's ride out from the trading post at Schwartzburg. Oh, it'll take the wagons four or five days more, but he'll be there tomorrow, I reckon, if he keeps moving."

Elise let out a long breath. "So."

Anne came back with the coffeepot. "I'll put this on the fire. You gentlemen come back in a while, and we'll give you another round." She came over to stand beside Elise. "Dan's looking over our wagon cover."

Eb handed Elise his empty cup. "I'm heading out with a couple of men to look for the missing stock. Dan will take care of you though."

Elise went to front of the wagon, where Daniel was standing on the seat, peering over the wagon top.

"How bad is the damage?" she called up to him.

"Could be worse. It's mostly the front end that tore. I'm thinking if your extra cover will fit, we could put it right over this one. That would give you extra strength on the part that's still good, and it would be less work in the long run."

Anne came to stand beside Elise. They looked up into the front opening and could see the sky through the large gashes in their "roof."

"Do you think we could mend this one?" Anne asked. "If so, maybe we should take it off now and work on it in the evenings."

Dan shook his head doubtfully. "It's pretty extensive. I think I'd leave it on. You can baste some of the tears together from inside at your leisure."

"How is your wagon, and Hector's?" Elise asked.

"Hec's is all right. Mine's got one rip. For some reason, we didn't get it as bad as you did—or maybe our cloth was stronger, I don't know." Dan hopped down beside them.

"I'd be happy to stitch yours up this evening," Elise said. "Maybe we can take a piece off this one where it's torn worst and use it for a patch."

"You don't need to do that," Dan said.

"You've helped us a lot. I'd be glad to do something for you."

Daniel nodded. "All right. Now, let's get your extra cover out."

"I know right where it is," Anne said. She and Dan walked to the back of the wagon. Elise decided to leave them alone to do it. If anything needed to be said between them, she didn't want to hinder them by her presence.

"Miss Finster."

She whirled and smiled as Rob approached her. "Hello, Mr. Whistler. I'm so sorry about your horse."

"Don't fret about it, ma'am. How are you and Miss Stone faring?"

"Well, thanks to the gentlemen of this company. Daniel Adams is helping Anne get out our spare wagon cover now."

Rob looked up at the still-damp canvas. Ragged edges fluttered in the breeze.

"Good. We're going to stay right here until morning. The stock needs time to settle down. We're a ways from water, but most folks have enough to last a day."

"We can all use the afternoon to make repairs and dry out, I expect."

He nodded. "And at daybreak, we'll move on."

"I wish we could do something about your horse," Elise said.

Rob pushed his hat back and squinted up at the sky. The clouds were higher and sparser now, and the wind carried them along eastward.

"Well, she was a good mare, but. . .I hope we've seen the last of Costigan."

<hr />

Elise had hoped for a town or at least a small settlement at Schwartzburg. What she got was a small trading post and livestock dealer. Schwartz had begun the post where a large creek flowed into the Platte, as a place to capitalize on the trade with wagon trains and Indians. He also collected horses and mules, which he traded to the army. Wagon trains were not allowed to camp within two miles of the post so that Schwartz's livestock could have the grass within that distance.

Whistler's company, as they were known along the way, camped just after noon as close as they could—two miles east of the post, where the grass grew lush and a line of elm trees edged the river. The Harkness men emptied their farm wagon and offered to drive up to a dozen ladies to the trading post so they could shop.

"You go ahead," Elise told Anne. "There's no need for us both to go, and I'll catch up on things here."

"If you're sure."

Elise smiled. "I am. Mr. Whistler says prices are exorbitant here, and I doubt there's anything I'd want to purchase."

"All right." Anne opened her purse and took out a roll of American bills. "Here, I'll leave this with you so I won't be tempted. If it can't be bought for a few coins, we'll do without it."

Elise tucked the money deep in her pocket and looked around to check if anyone was watching. With Thomas gone, they were probably safe. No more problems had surfaced in the last few days beyond weary livestock and leaking wagons. Some of their fellow travelers had seen their osnaburg or canvas coverings damaged beyond easy repair in the hailstorm and hoped to buy more fabric at Schwartzburg.

Elise busied herself with baking gingerbread by Rebecca's recipe, mending, and washing out a few underthings. She felt quite domestic. Perhaps there was hope for her as a housewife someday. Several men in their company had taken to coming 'round in the evening and chatting with the ladies, and not all of them goggled at Anne. Their attention made Elise feel feminine, and she longed to wear a pretty gown again. Her two calico dresses had faded and hung shapelessly.

There was talk of dancing that evening. On a whim, she opened Anne's largest trunk and looked over her mistress's gowns. If they didn't overdo it, perhaps they could wear something a little dressier this evening than they had since Independence. If she could persuade Anne, the battle was won. She laid out a modest brown plaid walking dress with an ecru underskirt for her mistress and opened her own trunk to find something suitable for herself.

She took the gingerbread out of the dutch oven at the perfect moment. Now for some biscuits. As she worked the handle of her sifter, she thought about Eb Bentley. He was nothing like David Stone, yet he embodied many of the qualities she'd always considered essential in a man—in a husband. There. How shocking was this admission? She peered into the sifter and found only a small mound of worms and a couple of beetles. She tipped them into the fire and scooped another pint of flour into the sifter.

"Elise!"

Her name came from a distance, borne by the wind, but it was Anne's voice that called. She squinted westward. Eb's pinto pounded toward her along the trail from Schwartzburg and—could it be? Anne was perched behind the saddle, peeking around Eb's shoulder and waving her handkerchief, her skirts billowing above her knees.

Elise plunked the sifter down beside the bowl of flour, lifted her skirt, and ran to meet them.

Eb stopped the pinto so quickly that Speck almost sat down on the trail. Anne slid off the horse's rump and was standing up beside Elise before Speck got his feet under him again, as though Anne and Eb had practiced the maneuver and performed it on purpose.

"Elise! There's news!"

By now alarm had seized Elise. When Anne threw herself into her arms, Elise clutched her fiercely. A quick glance up at Eb's face revealed nothing.

"What is it? Tell me."

Anne sobbed. "Uncle David. They say he's buried in the graveyard near the trading post."

# CHAPTER 19

Anne collapsed in Elise's arms. Eb jumped off the pinto's back as she swooned and helped Elise lower her gently to the grass beside the dusty trail.

"Anne? Anne, my dear." Elise patted the girl's face. She hadn't any smelling salts nearby, though there was a vial buried deep in one of Anne's trunks. They hadn't needed them since St. Louis.

"It's a shock," Eb said. "I could see she was stunned when she heard it, and I told her she should wait for you to come. She insisted on telling you herself, so I brought her back here."

"Thank you," Elise said. "I'm not sure what to do."

"I can carry her to your tent."

His intent eyes and evident concern made her heart clutch for an instant. "Perhaps that's best. We've smelling salts, and I'll make her a strong cup of tea."

Anne's eyelids fluttered, and she blinked up at them. "Oh dear. Have I swooned?"

"Yes, but don't distress yourself. You'll be fine." Elise brushed a tendril of fine, dark hair back beneath Anne's hat brim. If Eb weren't hovering, she'd loosen the poor thing's corset strings.

"The trader," Anne said faintly. "He's German."

Elise wondered if Anne had temporarily lost her senses. Of course the trader was German, with a name like Schwartz. Anne's eyes widened suddenly and focused on Elise once more. "Uncle David. He died here. The trader said so."

Elise frowned. "Did he say when? Or how it happened?"

"A few years ago. He wasn't just sure when, but he was certain it was Uncle David. He says there's a marker in the cemetery." Anne sat up and grasped Elise's wrist. "We have to go and see it."

"Of course." Elise glanced at Eb. "I hate to ask, but would

you go with us?"

"Sure. I'll get my other horse. Can one of your mules go under saddle?"

"I believe Thomas rode Chick a few times."

He nodded. "I'll see if I can borrow a couple of saddles."

Elise almost insisted on sidesaddles, but that might be a bit optimistic.

Eb stood. "Miss Stone, may I carry you to the camp?"

"I should say not. I'm perfectly capable of walking." Anne reached for Elise, and together they rose. Anne inhaled deeply and straightened her shoulders. "I shall be fine."

Elise smiled at Eb. Anne's spirits were back to what they should be.

"At least let me put you up on Speck, and I'll lead him," Eb said.

Anne consented and let him boost her into the saddle. When they reached camp, she slid down with a steadying hand from Eb. She looked into the tent and stopped halfway under the flap.

*The dresses,* Elise thought. She'd left them laid out on their bedrolls.

"I don't believe I shall dance tonight," Anne said.

Elise feared Anne would faint again. "I'm sorry, dear. It was presumptuous of me."

"You didn't know about—" Anne sobbed.

Elise looked over her shoulder at Eb. "Give us a few minutes."

He nodded. "I'll get the other mounts."

An hour later, they rode toward the trading post together. Eb had scrounged up one sidesaddle without Elise mentioning it. Mrs. Libby, who was past sixty, had come up with it. Anne insisted Elise use it on Eb's spare horse, a solid brown gelding that Eb inexplicably called "Pink." Anne rode Chick astride, with the voluminous skirt of her riding habit cascading about the mule's flanks in waves of blue velvet. It held enough yardage to cover her ankles, to Elise's relief. The last thing they needed was trappers and Indians ogling her ladyship's limbs.

Elise had only ridden a few times, and for the first mile she was too terrified to think of anything but maintaining her balance and gripping the pommels between her knees. By the time they could see the buildings, her confidence had marginally returned. Although Eb claimed he hadn't ridden Pink for a couple of days, the gelding moved calmly and seemed willing to follow Speck anywhere.

The trading post was made of mud brick—adobe, Eb called it. "Those walls are a couple of feet thick," he told them. "They'll stop a lot of bullets."

"Is there need for such protection?" Elise asked.

"Oh yeah. Schwartz sells livestock to the army. The Indians will try to run off the herd every chance they get."

Anne seemed lost in her own thoughts, paying no attention to the conversation.

"Now remember, Schwartz is a shrewd one," Eb said as they tied up the horses. "He'll squeeze the last penny out of a traveler."

"He's dishonest?" Elise asked.

"Hasn't been proven, but likely. Last summer when we got here, another wagon train had lost thirty head of livestock while they camped nearby. The wagon master said it wasn't Indians that stampeded their herd, but Schwartz denied any knowledge of it."

Elise patted her pocket where Anne's hoard of money still lay. She fully intended to return to camp without parting with a cent.

"Now, I see Rob's horse, Bailey, tied up yonder," Eb said. "Why'n't I go in and see if he's inside? I'll tell him what's up, and he can go with us, too."

Eb must distrust the trader deeply to want his friend's support for something as innocuous as a visit to the graveyard. Elise nodded. "We'll wait here for you."

He went into the building. Elise and Anne walked over and stood in the shadow of the eaves. The heat was oppressive, but at least they were out of the direct rays of the sun. A couple of other buildings sat nearby—one no more than a hovel, which Elise hoped was a storage shed, not a dwelling. The larger structure appeared to be a barn, and she could see several men moving between it and a fenced pasture east of it.

A cluster of people from the wagon train came out of the trading post.

"Hello," Mrs. Legity called. "You been inside yet?"

Elise shook her head. "No. Did you find any bargains?"

Mrs. Legity snorted. "Not what I'd call bargains." She pulled up suddenly and looked Anne over from head to toe. "That outfit looks a mite hot for this weather."

"Perhaps you're right," Anne said with a sweet smile.

Elise noted the beads of perspiration on her mistress's brow. As soon as the others had walked on toward the Harkness wagon, she pulled out a handkerchief.

"Allow me." She patted at Anne's forehead. "I'm so sorry. Mrs. Legity is right—that habit is far too heavy for this sun."

"It was a choice between modesty and comfort, I fear. For once, I wish I'd been less proper."

Elise held back a laugh. "My dear, if your friends knew all the rules of propriety you've broken in the last three months, they would never receive you again. I can only hope that you don't suffer heatstroke for the sake of convention."

"Yes. I should have just leaped on the mule wearing my calico. Lavinia would have done it."

"I daresay she would." Elise was glad Anne could laugh about the wardrobe situation, but would she go back to her mourning weeds soon?

The door to the trading post opened, and Rob and Eb came out together.

"What's this all about?" Rob asked the scout. Eb quickly told him about Anne's earlier visit to the trading post and what Schwartz had told her.

"There's another fellow behind the counter now," Eb told the ladies. "He says Schwartz is out at the corral. Binchley hoped to trade in his oxen here for some better ones, and Schwartz is showing him what he's got."

"Shall we go out there and speak to him?" Anne asked.

203

Rob offered Anne his arm. "Let me escort you, Miss Stone. We'll find out where this graveyard is."

Elise walked beside Eb in their wake. The enormity of Anne's news hit her. If David was dead, their mission was ended. She would never again see the man whose memory she'd treasured all these years. They could return to Fort Laramie with the next cavalry detachment or train of freighters' wagons that came through heading eastward—and thence on to Independence and eventually New York and London. Was she ready to return home?

More important, perhaps, was the question of the earldom. Would the authorities in England accept whatever evidence they could collect? Elise doubted a death certificate existed.

Schwartz greeted them and left Mr. Binchley with instruction to think over his offer.

"I'm so sorry that I had to bear you such sad news, miss," he said to Anne in heavily accented English. He glanced at Elise, Eb, and Rob. "I see you've brought your friends to support you. You'd like to see Mr. Stone's grave of course."

"Yes, sir, I would. At once, please."

Rob patted Anne's hand and addressed the trader. "Where is this graveyard of yours, Schwartz? We'll take Miss Stone there to view her uncle's grave."

"I'll show you. It's beyond that grove yonder." He pointed toward a distant clump of trees.

Rob frowned down at Anne. "Shall we get the horses? Or perhaps we can borrow the Harknesses' wagon."

Eb looked toward the road. "Wilbur's left to go back to camp."

"I can walk that far," Anne said.

It was a stroll of a quarter mile, and had their purpose been less grim and the sun's rays less intense, it might have proved a pleasant stroll. Though the path was not well worn, someone had recently gone before them through the grass that nearly reached Elise's waist.

In a few minutes, they arrived beneath several spreading willows, which gave a welcome respite from the sun. Schwartz paused in the shade and pointed to where the path continued.

"It's just down there a few steps more. Mr. Stone is buried on the left side of the lot. It's marked with a wooden cross, as are most of the graves."

"His name is on it?" Eb asked.

"Oh yes."

"We'll find it."

Schwartz gazed at Anne for a moment. "An Englishman, wasn't he?"

She nodded. "My father's brother."

"I am sorry."

"Can you tell me how it happened?" she asked.

Schwartz inhaled deeply and looked toward the river. "He came by with a company of other travelers in the summer. This time of year or a bit later."

"How did the man die?" Eb's gaze bore into the German.

"He was sick when he got here. Asked if he could lay up a few days and then catch up to the others. I let him sleep in the cabin with my men—wish I hadn't though. He got worse, and they were all afraid they'd catch his disease. It wasn't cholera though. I made sure of that before I let him stay on. He died the third day, I think it was."

"What about his things?" Eb asked. "His wagons, saddle horse, and any personal effects."

"Wagons?" Schwartz seemed surprised at that.

"We were told he took three wagons full of goods," Anne said. "He planned to open a store in Oregon."

Schwartz stroked his beard. "I didn't know that. I suppose he had other men driving the wagons for him. The captain of the company left him here with a horse, saddle, and bedroll. That's all I know about."

"And what became of those?" Eb asked.

Schwartz spread his hands in supplication. "We had no way of knowing whom to contact, and I kept the horse as payment for the care he received. There was nothing else."

"Nothing?" Anne asked bleakly.

"I think not."

"Surely the wagon master gave you a way to contact him or Stone's drivers," Rob said.

"No, sir." Schwartz glanced toward the trading post. "I left my nephew in the store, and his English is not so good. I should go and check on him."

Rob and Eb exchanged a dark glance. "You must compensate Miss Stone for her uncle's horse, saddle, and other gear," Rob said.

Schwartz glowered at him. "I told you—"

"We know what you said," Rob replied. "It didn't sound as though he received much care. A horse and saddle is too much payment for digging a grave. I don't expect the man stayed without some cash in his pockets either."

"He had no valuables on him when he came here." Schwartz's harsh tone softened when he glanced at Anne again. "Of course we had to burn his bedroll. You understand. The sickness. . ."

"Leave us," Eb said.

Schwartz nodded and strode quickly toward the trading post.

Anne raised a gloved hand to her lips and closed her eyes. Elise put an arm around her.

"Are you all right, my dear?"

Anne nodded. "Let us go on."

They stepped out of the copse into the harsh sunlight. A short distance away, several weathered crosses stuck up out of the tall grass. Rob took Anne's hand and threaded it through the crook of his arm again.

"The left side," Anne said softly. The grass was bent over in several paths among the markers, and they veered to the left edge of the little cemetery.

A moment later they located the cross made of two short boards nailed together. DAVID STONE was carved rudely into the horizontal piece. They all stood gazing at it for a moment.

Anne sobbed. "It's too awful." She wiped tears from her pale cheeks with her delicate white handkerchief.

"I know." Elise stepped closer to her, on the other side from Rob.

Tears flooded her eyes. "But if you hadn't inquired at the trading post, we might never have known of this. We might have passed by and never learned his fate."

"Yes. We could have gone all the way to Oregon on a fruitless errand."

"I wonder what became of his wagons full of goods," Elise said.

Rob looked over Anne's head at her. "Shall we say a few words?"

"I would like that," Anne said.

"Is the Twenty-Third Psalm all right?"

"Yes."

Rob started to recite the psalm, and Elise took Anne's hand. Together they whispered the words in unison with Rob. From behind them, Eb's quiet voice joined in.

"'. . .And I will dwell in the house of the Lord for ever. Amen.'"

After a moment's silence, Rob began to pray. "Dear heavenly Father, we ask that You would comfort Miss Stone's heart. We pray also that You would give her wisdom and guide her footsteps as she has some decisions ahead of her. For David Stone, we thank You for his time on this earth, and that he was a man people loved and respected. Please comfort his family in England when they receive this news. Amen."

Elise opened her tear-filled eyes. This crude resting place was completely inadequate for David.

Eb cleared his throat. "The inscription looks mighty fresh."

Elise stared at the boards for a moment before his words penetrated her numbness. The cross of wind- and rain-battered boards looked as though it might well have stood there for several years, but the letters on the crosspiece left yellowish wood exposed.

"Yes, it does," she said.

Eb walked around them and bent over the marker. "No dates, just the name. What do you think, Rob?"

"I'm not sure." Rob looked about. "It's a mite trampled here, wouldn't you say?"

Eb surveyed the grass around the grave. He went to his knees and spread back the stalks at the base of the cross. He picked up something small between his fingertips and held it close to his eyes. He held it out to Rob and dropped it into his hand then burrowed into the grass again, searching carefully.

"What is it?" Elise asked.

Rob held out his palm. "A wood shaving. A fresh one."

Eb rocked back on his knees and held out more.

"Looks like we need to talk to Mr. Schwartz again," Rob said.

Eb stood. "No need for you ladies to get into it. We'll get the truth out of him."

"But I don't understand," Anne said. "Why would he lie about a grave?"

"Maybe he's not telling the truth about how Mr. Stone died," Rob said.

Eb shook his head. "In that case, why did he even offer the information that there was a grave here? When Miss Stone asked at the trading post, he could have simply said he'd never heard of the man."

"And why carve his name on the cross now?" Elise asked.

Rob frowned. "Maybe to make it look as though they took better care of him than they really did?"

A thought leaped to Elise's mind. "Mr. Hoyle."

"Who?" Eb asked.

"A man I met in Independence. He was forming a wagon train. He's the one who told us David Stone traveled west with him in 1850. And also the one who mentioned the three wagons full of merchandise."

"What else did he say?" Eb asked.

Elise frowned in concentration. "He said David originally planned to move to California, but on the trail he changed his mind. He went to Oregon instead. At least, Mr. Hoyle said he left their company with a group of other wagons at the cutoff."

Eb looked at Rob. "If he stuck with them to the cutoff, he would have been alive when they passed here."

"Yup."

Anne looked from Rob to Eb and back again. "So either Mr.

208

Hoyle or Mr. Schwartz lied. How do we know which?"

Rob pushed his hat back. "I've known Ted Hoyle for at least three years. Never heard anything bad about him. He's generally considered reliable. But Schwartz. . ." He shook his head.

"Sounds like we'd better have that talk with the trader," Eb said.

Rob nodded. "You ladies go back to the trading post and wait for us. Eb and I will see if Schwartz is out near the barn again."

Elise took Anne's elbow. "Come. These two gentlemen will get to the bottom of this."

Anne sniffed and wiped her damp eyes with her handkerchief. "Yes, I trust Mr. Whistler and Mr. Bentley implicitly."

They walked back through the willows and toward the buildings. Elise steered Anne away from the barnyard to avoid the men working there. They neared the trading post from the back.

"If we wait here, we can see when Mr. Bentley and Mr. Whistler leave the barn," Elise said. "I'd just as soon be out of sight of the wagon train people entering and leaving the post, too."

Anne concurred, and they stood quietly beneath the eaves. A back door was open, and somewhere inside, two men were talking. Elise pricked up her ears and leaned toward the open doorway.

"Elise. . ."

Anne stopped speaking when Elise held up an urgent hand. She was almost certain. . . Yes, it was true.

"One of the men inside is speaking German," she whispered to Anne.

"It must be Mr. Schwartz, but to whom is he speaking?"

"I don't know. None of the other folks in our company speak German that I know of." Elise tiptoed closer to the doorway.

One man said quite clearly in German, "I think they're buying it."

She held her breath. It had been so long since she'd had a conversation in her native tongue, she had to listen closely. Although she disliked Schwartz based on what Eb and Rob had said, she would find it satisfying to go around to the front room of the trading post and have a chance to speak to him in German.

209

As this flashed through her mind, the second man laughed. "That's good, if they believe you. Amazing how trusting some people are."

Elise frowned. What were they talking about? Not a literal transaction, it seemed. Anne was waiting a few steps away, eyeing her curiously. Elise put a finger to her lips, and Anne nodded.

"...The young woman, she is distraught, but what can I say? If we can fool her, we will get a good payoff. That and the livestock will make this a profitable encounter, I think."

The other man laughed. "They'll never be able to prove it wasn't Indians, not with the evidence we'll give them."

"Enough," Schwartz said, louder than before. "Now go back to work."

Elise stepped quickly away from the door, grabbed Anne's wrist, and pulled her around the corner of the building.

"What's going on?" Anne hissed.

"A good question." Elise held her close to the side wall as footsteps clumped out into the cleared area behind the post. A moment later Schwartz came into view, walking away from them. He headed straight for the barn and corral without looking back. Elise exhaled.

"There are Mr. Bentley and Mr. Whistler." Anne nodded toward the barn. Apparently Eb and Rob had unsuccessfully searched for Schwartz in the outbuildings. They now met him outside near the corral and stood talking for a minute.

"What I heard sounded suspicious," Elise said softly. "I want to tell those two gentlemen and see what they say—but definitely not in front of the trader."

# CHAPTER 20

D o you have witnesses?" Eb asked Schwartz.

"Witnesses?" The big man repeated. "To Stone's death, you mean?"

"Yes." Eb didn't blink.

Schwartz shrugged. "My hired men. Let's see. . .one of them is dead now. Drowned crossing the river. Another went hunting last fall and never returned. My hired hands come and go. I'm not sure I can produce anyone else who was here when this regrettable incident happened."

"I'll just bet," Eb said.

Schwartz's eyes narrowed. "What are you driving at?"

Rob stepped forward. "Here, now, gentlemen, no need to get upset. Mr. Schwartz, is there anything else you can tell us about Mr. Stone's final days? For instance, who was captain of the wagon train he traveled with?"

Schwartz spread his hands, palms up. "You ask me to remember, after so long a time?"

"If it was someone you knew. . .someone you'd dealt with before. . ." Rob eyed him closely.

"I think the emigrants had elected a captain from their company. They were traveling by the book, as we say. Using one of those handbooks that tell you where the next watering place is."

Rob glanced at Eb. They both knew better than to suggest Ted Hoyle had captained Stone's train.

"We'll bring Miss Stone into the store in a few minutes," Rob said. "I expect you to give her a hundred dollars for the horse and saddle."

"A hundred dollars?" Schwartz stared at him. "You want to drive me out of business, is that it? I hardly make a penny on the supplies

I sell here. Every grain of corn must be hauled across the plains. I can't pay her a hundred dollars."

Eb opened his mouth and closed it again. He was going to ask why Schwartz had altered the grave marker, but he already knew something wasn't right. The whole business stank. If he'd lied about the grave, he'd probably lied about the rest, too. Maybe he'd laid claim to all of David Stone's goods—wagons, merchandise, livestock, and all.

"I think that would be the least you could do," Rob said. "I'll bring her in shortly." He nodded to Eb, and Eb followed him toward the trading post.

"I don't like it," Rob said.

"Me either." Eb nudged him. "The ladies are waiting for us. Miss Finster looks fit to tear into somebody."

Rob doffed his hat as they approached the women. "Well, ladies, I'm not thoroughly satisfied with the outcome, but I told Schwartz I'd take Miss Stone into the store, and that I expected him to compensate her. We'll see what happens."

"Do you think he really got Uncle David's horse?" Miss Stone asked. "I don't believe he's telling us the whole truth, but if he's a liar, why not lie about that?"

"I'm not sure what he's up to, but the scoundrel ought to at least feel it a little in his pocketbook." Rob looked over his shoulder. "He's coming up from the barn. Do you feel ready to face him again, Miss Stone?"

"I suppose so, but I'm not sure it would be right for me to take money from him."

"You go on," Miss Finster said. "Trust Mr. Whistler's judgment. Meanwhile, I'll speak to Mr. Bentley about what I heard just now."

Eb studied her face. "What's that?"

"Elise heard Herr Schwartz talking to someone in German a few moments ago," Miss Stone said.

Miss Finster flushed and looked down. "It may be nothing, but I thought I should tell you."

"Perhaps I should hear it before we go inside," Rob said.

"All right."

Eb glanced around and saw that Schwartz had veered off toward the back of the building. Miss Finster waited until he was out of sight. She lowered her voice and stepped closer to Eb and Rob than she normally would, and Eb felt her sense of urgency.

"He told the other person—and I've no idea who that may be, except it seemed to be someone working for him—that 'the young woman is distraught.' I wondered if he might be speaking about Anne. Then he said that if they can fool her, they will be paid well. What was I to think, other than that he must be lying to us about David's death? Though how on earth he could profit from that, I have no idea."

Rob's face wrinkled as he thought about it. "If he's lying, he certainly won't want to part with a hundred dollars for a horse he never took possession of."

"That's true," Eb said. "On the other hand, if he does agree to pay Miss Stone, that wouldn't necessarily mean he's telling the truth. It might be a sign that he's deep into it for something. The question is, what?"

"Do you really think my uncle survived the trip west?" Miss Stone asked. Her tear-streaked face and reddened eyes presented a pathetic picture, and Eb wanted badly to comfort the young woman.

"I wish I could tell you what all of this means, miss. Personally, I'm leaning toward thinking that grave yonder is a fake—or else it belongs to someone else. Seems to me Schwartz or one of his cronies carved the name on the cross today because they saw that it might benefit them. Whether your uncle is actually resting in that plot is questionable."

"Let's go in and see what he says to you," Rob suggested.

Miss Finster nodded. "Go, Anne. I'll wait out here with Mr. Bentley."

Rob and Miss Stone walked toward the front of the trading post. As soon as they rounded the corner, Miss Finster looked up at Eb.

"There was more I didn't want to tell you in front of Anne.

I don't think it will affect Mr. Whistler's conversation with the trader—in fact, it may be better that he doesn't know it yet, so he won't inadvertently give away anything."

"Oh? What's up?"

She inhaled sharply and glanced toward the barn as though marshaling her thoughts. Eb couldn't help noticing how pretty she looked. She wore a fetching brown hat he didn't believe he'd ever seen before, and her golden hair just showed around her forehead and ears. Her skin glowed with good health, and she looked less fragile than she had when they'd set out in April. Not that she and Miss Stone were ever sickly, but they'd both grown stronger on the trail.

"He said something about livestock to the other man. I didn't hear much, but when he mentioned Anne—that is, the 'young woman'—he said something about how some people are so trusting, in a detrimental way."

Eb frowned. He thought he understood what that meant—just.

"And then he said what I told you before about being well paid if they could fool her. But it was what he said next that really caught my attention."

"Which was?"

"He said—in German, you understand—that between that and the livestock, this should be a profitable encounter, and the other man said 'they'll blame it on Indians.' He mentioned leaving some evidence."

"What did you take that to mean?" Eb asked. "What encounter was he talking about?"

"I thought at first he meant with Anne. But Anne hasn't anything to do with livestock, except our poor little team of six mules. Unless he meant her uncle's livestock, that pulled his three wagons. But that was years ago, so why would he refer to it in the same breath as 'this encounter'? Or 'this meeting?'" She sighed and touched his sleeve lightly. "Mr. Bentley, I'm of German birth, but I've lived in England since I was sixteen."

"I never would have guessed. You speak English just about perfectly, ma'am."

"Thank you."

"In fact, I was surprised when you said you could speak German. I thought you were English all this time."

She smiled. "My name should have given me away. *Finster* means 'dark or brooding' in German."

He appraised her for a moment and then shook his head. "You're not like that."

"That's kind of you. My point is, it's been decades since I regularly conversed in the German language. But I'm wondering if perhaps he meant this encounter with our wagon train."

Eb inhaled slowly through his nose. "Our herd."

"Yes. When he said that about Indians. . ." She frowned and nodded slowly. "Yes, I'm certain that is what he said. They would leave evidence, and we would blame the Indians."

He huffed out his breath. "We'll increase our guard tonight."

"A wise precaution, I'd say."

"Yes. But will it be enough?" Eb took a few steps away from the adobe building, and Miss Finster walked with him, her face anxious. "What would his thieving ways have to do with Miss Stone?" he asked. "Why bother to fool her into thinking her uncle died here if he didn't? And if he did, why go to the trouble of carving the name on the cross all of a sudden?"

"And why would Mr. Hoyle say David continued with his company to the cutoff for Oregon? He seemed to remember Mr. Stone perfectly. I believe he liked him, and it sounded as though they got to be friends. I don't think he was mistaken."

Eb nodded. "Ted Hoyle's a sharp customer. He wouldn't have told you all that if it wasn't true."

"What can we do, then? Is there any way to prove whether or not that is truly David Stone's grave?"

"Short of digging him up, I don't see how. And even that might not prove anything. Could be someone's buried there, and they stuck the marker with Stone's name on it over the remains. Unless there was something in the grave that would positively identify the body. . ." He shook his head. "Not worth distressing

Miss Stone further, I'm thinking."

"But if the grave were empty. . ." Miss Finster looked up at him so hopefully Eb wanted it to be true and to prove it to her instantly.

"I doubt Schwartz would chance it. And he had plenty of old graves to choose from."

"I suppose you're right. But I have another question."

Eb's heart stirred, and not only for Miss Stone's predicament. For some ridiculous reason, he wondered how many becoming hats Miss Finster had in her wagon. "Yes, ma'am?" he managed.

"If Schwartz is lying, how did he know about David Stone?"

"That's easy. Miss Stone told him herself when she went into the trading post this morning. She showed him that portrait of her uncle that she carries around in her handbag."

Miss Finster nodded. "I'm sure she did. She inquires of everyone we meet. But still. . .assuming Schwartz thought quickly and concocted this story of David's illness while she stood there, do you think he'd have time to prepare the grave marker?"

Eb scratched his chin. "It took more than an hour for me to take her back to camp, get the horses ready, and fetch you two back here. He or one of his men could have done it in that amount of time. I think the shavings prove it was done recently. Very recently. And it points to someone standing there in the cemetery to do the carving, not preparing the cross in the barn or someplace else. A quick job on a marker that was already in place, if you ask me."

"I suppose you're right. But I still wonder if he only learned it when Anne inquired."

"He's shrewd. When a company of people comes to his store, he'll spot someone who might be easy to trick, and then he'll figure how to get that person's money. I was in the post when Miss Stone asked about her uncle. She reacted so strongly—he might have conceived the whole plan right then and there."

"How did he react to her distress?"

Eb shrugged. "He seemed concerned, but I wasn't really watching him closely. Maybe I should have, but I was more worried about her. Mrs. Harkness and I took her outside for some fresh air, and Miss Stone asked me to take her back to the wagons so she could tell you."

"Here they come." Miss Finster moved her chin just a bit in the direction of the trading post.

Eb waited until Rob and Miss Stone reached them. "What happened in there?"

"Not much," Rob said. "Schwartz refused to pay Miss Stone anything. I asked if he'd sign a statement saying David Stone had died here and when, but he wouldn't. He said he didn't personally witness the death, and he didn't want to get in trouble."

Eb grimaced. "Getting awfully honest all of sudden, isn't he?"

"Seems like it. Finally he offered Miss Stone a few groceries," Rob said.

"I wasn't sure I wanted to take them." Miss Stone's pert chin rose in defiance. "Wouldn't that be like admitting he's telling the truth?"

Rob smiled. "I told him she'd think on it, and we'd come back later if she wanted the things."

"How much did he offer?"

"Ten dollars' worth of goods, but at his prices that wouldn't amount to much."

"Elise, he wants a dollar a pound for flour. And they have a few fresh eggs—at two dollars apiece. Can you imagine?" The young woman's brown eyes fairly sparked.

"No, I can't," Miss Finster said. "Shall we go back to camp?"

Elise tossed and turned that night, hearing the guards every time they passed the tent on their rounds. Rob and Eb had met with the men of the company and told them they suspected the camp might be raided, emphasizing the need for watchfulness. They'd tightened the wagon circle before sunset and made certain every mule, ox, milk cow, and saddle horse was safe inside. Because of the tight quarters and shortage of grass, the animals were fretful all night. Frequent bouts of kicking, squealing, braying, and snorting kept the travelers in a restless, intermittent doze.

An hour before dawn the camp began to quicken. The guards woke the men who were to relieve them.

"Mr. Whistler insisted on keeping a double guard while we break camp," Anne remarked as she led Chick over to be harnessed. "So far everything is going smoothly."

"Yes, almost too well," Elise said. "Maybe there was no danger after all."

"Or maybe they saw our vigilance and decided not to risk a raid."

As they worked together to get the mules harnessed, Eb rode up on Pink and dismounted near them.

"You ladies all right this morning? Need anything?"

"We're fine, thank you," Elise said. She was glad they had the wheelers already hitched and were nearly done with the leaders. "We'll be ready to pull out in five minutes."

"Great. We're not far from where the Sweetwater flows into the Platte. I think you'll find the change in terrain pleasant, but we will be climbing steadily now." Eb cast an appraising eye over their two near mules. "Your team looks in pretty good shape. Better than some."

"Thank you," Elise said. "We pamper them a bit, I'm told, but I think men and animals work better when they're well fed."

He smiled. "You've done well. A lot of folks have run out of grain."

Anne's head popped up over Blackie's back, from where she'd been fastening a buckle on the other side. "We determined at the outset to bring plenty of oats for them. I can't stand to see a hungry animal."

Elise said, "She'd pick up stray cats, too, if there were any out here."

Eb chuckled and laid a hand on Chick's withers. "I don't know how you ladies do it, but you have the smartest wardrobes and the fittest livestock of the company."

"Thank you." Elise dropped her voice. "I guess we worried for nothing yesterday."

"I'm not so sure," Eb said. "We'll keep a double guard again tonight."

"You think they might follow us, then?" Elise glanced Anne's way, but she was busy with Blackie's harness.

"You may have mistaken their intentions," Eb conceded. "But Rob and I would rather be safe than sorry."

"I admit I'll feel better when we have another day's journey between us and Herr Schwartz."

"Yes. This morning I'll ride ahead and scout our stopping place for nooning, and after that I'll scout our back trail, rather than farther ahead of us."

"Probably wise."

Eb smiled at her. "Don't fret, Miss Finster. We'll soon be out of Schwartz's territory."

Beyond the river, the banks rose in bluffs that cut off their view, but on the other side, they could see a fair distance. The mountains loomed, snowcapped and daunting. Every time Elise surveyed the rugged peaks, her chest ached. Nothing like this could be found in England. She must encourage Anne to make more drawings. Since Thomas left them and their labor had increased, Anne hadn't taken out her sketchbook.

"If you hadn't told me we can cross this mountain range fairly easily, I'd never believe it," Elise said.

Eb grimaced slightly. "I didn't mean to give you the impression that it will be simple. It's a rough road, and up north in the Oregon Territory it can be even rougher. But a lot of people have gone before us and improved the road. I think you and Miss Stone will do just fine. Mrs. Harkness, on the other hand, may have to part with some furniture and books."

Elise drove most of the morning, with Anne beside her on the seat. Rob had warned all of the travelers to stay close together.

"We don't want any stragglers today. I'll have the drovers keep the herd of loose stock within sight of the last wagons, too."

The herdsmen wouldn't like that. They ate enough dust when they kept the animals back half a mile or so. But for one day, they could stand it, Elise supposed.

Everyone seemed a little on edge. Abe Leonard barked at his oxen more sharply than usual, and the Adams brothers hadn't stopped by to offer their assistance in the morning. When her son-in-law didn't bring water quickly enough, Mrs. Legity had railed at him so loudly that the entire camp heard every word.

Elise fretted at the slowness of their pace. Her mules could outdistance the ox teams in short order, but they had to keep their place in line. Where the terrain allowed it, they could spread out in several columns, but when they had to go single file, they still had to resume their assigned position.

They rode the two miles to the trading post and crawled past it at the oxen's gait. A few people stopped to buy one or two items they'd decided they needed no matter what the price, but most of the wagons plodded steadily on.

After another hour on the trail, Elise handed the reins to Anne and got out her knitting bag. She was determined to master Rebecca Harkness's sock pattern before they reached Oregon, and her third attempt looked promising.

She peeled off her gloves. Already her hands were sweating. This would be a searing hot day unless she was mistaken. She patted her forehead with a handkerchief and picked up her partly made sock.

"Do you think we're doing the right thing?" Anne asked a minute later.

Elise stopped stitching and looked over at her. Anne's wide-brimmed hat shadowed her sober face.

"How do you mean that?"

Anne gave a half shrug, keeping her gloved hands and the lines steady. "Going on."

"As opposed to turning back?" Elise asked.

"Yes. I can't help thinking that perhaps Uncle David *is* buried back there at Schwartzburg, and we're going farther and farther from him and home."

"Herr Schwartz was lying. We all agreed on that."

"Yes, but what if he wasn't lying about all of it? What if the grave part is real?" Anne looked at her anxiously.

"I don't see how it can be," Elise said. "And I don't trust that man any further than I could throw an ox. You must keep your faith strong. God will bring this odyssey to the conclusion that pleases Him, and I trust Him."

"I know you're right. And with that aside, part of me keeps saying, 'We can't leave the wagon train now.' Tearing ourselves away from this company would be traumatic, don't you think?"

"Well, yes." Elise began to knit again. "It's come to seem a bit like a family, hasn't it? But we'll all part when we reach Oregon."

"Oh, I know that day is coming. But it seems to me we've got unfinished business now, beyond finding Uncle David."

"Whatever are you talking about?"

Anne smiled. "This is as much about your future as it is about mine."

"Dear Anne, I'm sure we can build a future together, whatever happens."

"That's not the future I'm talking about."

"Then whatever *are* you talking about?"

"Why, you and Mr. Bentley of course."

The blood rushed to Elise's cheeks, and she put her hands to her face. "Oh dear."

"Yes," Anne said. "You care for him."

"You know me so well, I can't deny it. I suppose I do care, but that doesn't mean anything will ever come of it." Elise lowered her hands and stared piteously at Anne. "He's not at all what I imagined in a. . .in a husband."

"No, I expect not. Yet doesn't he embody everything a woman desires? Everything she needs in a man?"

Elise's embarrassment climbed even higher at Anne's intimate, wistful tone.

"Please, I. . ."

"What? You mean to say you don't think about it?"

"About what?"

"Marrying him of course."

"No. Yes. I mean, it's out of the question."

"That depends on what the question is."

They rode in silence for several minutes.

"Besides," Elise said, as though their conversation had not lapsed. "I wouldn't leave you now. Not when you need me so much."

"Thank you, my dear friend. But once this journey is over—when we've found Uncle David—though I love you, I shan't need you so much. If an opportunity arose. . ."

Elise shook her head. "Put that notion aside, my dear. Eb Bentley has shown no indication of such a possibility. He's an independent man. I've heard him mention his ranch in Oregon, and he wants to get back to it and stock it with cattle. He never intends to leave Oregon again."

"That doesn't mean he wouldn't take a wife to share that life with him."

"I have no hope of it. Just because a man treats you civilly doesn't mean he has matrimonial designs on you."

"Mr. Whistler has a wife, you know."

"I've heard him mention her."

"Yes, and he thinks his best friend would be much happier if he had one, too. He told me so." Anne drove along placidly, adjusting the reins when needed and calling to the mules now and then. Elise knit half a sock while her thoughts soared over the plains to Oregon.

# CHAPTER 21

**E**b rode slowly back to meet the wagon train. It was too hot to ask Pink to go any faster. He would switch his saddle over after eating and ride Speck this afternoon. He spotted the dust of the train long before he could see the lead wagons. They'd only made about four miles. He hated to suggest it to Rob, but if they took a long nooning, the animals would be fresher in the evening, when the sun headed down and the earth cooled.

Rob rode up to the head of the column to meet him.

"Everything quiet?" Eb asked.

"So far."

Eb turned Pink and rode alongside Rob, heading west again. It was the best way to let Rob catch him up on the train's progress that morning without being overheard by any of the others.

"You still planning to ride back to Schwartzburg when we stop?" Rob asked.

"I don't suppose it would do any good."

Rob turned in the saddle and looked back through the sea of dust, at the long line of wagons. "I don't like the idea of you going back."

"It'll only be four or five miles."

"I know. But you're likely to get in a tight spot if you go nosing around."

"Nah," Eb said. "There's another wagon train close behind us. Likely they'll reach Schwartzburg today. I can mingle with their people."

"Yes, but if Schwartz spots you, he'll figure something's up. I think you should stay clear of the place."

"All right, I won't go. But I'd still like to scout the trail behind us a ways."

"If you think it will help. We've an invitation to eat supper tonight with Miss Finster and Miss Stone if we've a mind to."

"I was thinking we ought to take a long nooning and move on in the evening. Let the stock rest while it's hottest and move out once the sun's mostly down."

Rob nodded. "I expect that would be a good plan today. I hoped we'd be farther from Schwartzburg when we stopped though."

"So did I." Eb looked ahead at the road he'd ridden that morning. "It's almost two miles to the spot where I thought we'd stop. Think they can go on that long?"

"Probably. Binchley's got an ox that's about done in. He really should have traded with Schwartz, but he said he didn't have enough cash."

Eb sighed. "We'll probably get some tough, stringy beef tomorrow."

"Yeah. Well, we may as well push on. You talking about that spot with the trees and grass down in the bottom?"

"That's the one."

"They'll make it that far. Especially if we tell everybody we'll take a long rest once we get there."

"All right. It's a good spot to water the livestock after folks draw the water they want to use."

"I remember it. Let's spread the word." Rob turned Bailey around but paused. "Shall I tell the ladies we'll eat supper with them?"

"Do you want to?" Eb asked.

"Of course. They're not the best cooks on the train, but the company can't be beat. And it'll give you a good chance to get better acquainted with Miss Finster's sterling qualities."

"Oh, you know so much about her?" Eb eyed his friend skeptically.

"I know it's time you got married again, and I haven't seen a prospect as pleasing for many a year."

"Get off that hobby horse, Rob."

"Not until you're married."

Rob urged Bailey into a trot. They rode back to the wagons, and

Rob told the first driver to stop when he got to the place Eb had described. Together they rode back along the lines, telling families to expect a long nooning. Most of the people expressed gratitude.

Eb smiled when he came in sight of the Englishwomen's wagon. Miss Stone sat straight as a flagpole on the seat, holding the lines like they were made of spun sugar. Miss Finster sat beside her, wearing a wide-brimmed straw hat with a cluster of pheasant feathers and knitting away lickety-split. They made a charming picture of both competence and domesticity—and beauty, though Eb wasn't much to comment on that, especially with Rob watching like a hawk for something to tease him about.

He rode up close and doffed his hat. "Long nooning today. We'll set out again when the sun's past its hottest."

"That sounds good, Mr. Bentley," Miss Stone called with a smile.

Miss Finster nodded. "Please God there'll be some shade where we stop."

"There's a few willows near the river, ma'am."

"Good. Will you and Mr. Whistler eat with us? If we're having a long rest stop, we'll prepare our big meal then, instead of in the evening."

Eb turned Pink around, so the horse moved along beside the wagon at the mules' pace. "That would be a pleasure, ma'am."

"We'll be pleased, Mr. Bentley," Miss Stone called over the clopping of hooves and the creaking of harness. She smiled so large Eb wondered if he'd made a mistake in accepting the invitation. Between Rob and Miss Stone, he felt like a rabbit with its neck in a snare.

Later, when they sat in the meager shade, it didn't seem like such a bad idea. The ladies served their plain dinner graciously, and Eb couldn't think of any other wagonside he'd rather eat at. The wagons were loosely circled, with the livestock in the middle as usual, but they constantly tried to stray out through the gaps. The ten men on guard spent as much energy keeping the livestock in as they did watching for intruders. Miss Finster had tied her clothesline in two passes at knee and waist height between her wagon and Abe

Leonard's, and Dan Adams had rigged a similar arrangement with his wagon, behind the ladies', so while they ate their dinner no oxen nosed out into their eating area.

Both ladies wore dresses that looked fine enough for a fancy funeral. They hadn't ever given in to the droopy bonnets most of the women wore out here, even when the wind blew strong across the prairie. That suited Eb just fine—he liked the way Miss Finster's elegant hats framed her face. And Miss Stone would look good in anything, with her youth and beauty. She looked healthy now, much healthier than she had in St. Louis. He was glad she was smiling again. Seeing her weep yesterday when she stood at the grave was hard—but her spirits seemed to have lifted.

The biscuits were a little tough, but Miss Finster had cooked the bacon to perfection, and Miss Stone had baked a cake of sorts. It was doughy and sweet, and chunks of tinned peaches hid in its depths.

"Miss Anne, I don't know if I've ever had anything that hit the spot like this," Rob said. He sat on the ground with his long legs stretched out before him and his back to their rear wagon wheel.

"It's tasty, all right," Eb said.

"Why, thank you, gentlemen," Miss Stone said. "I modified Mrs. Harkness's cobbler recipe. Elise thought we'd best use up most of our canned goods before we go much farther."

"They're heavy," Miss Finster said, and the two men nodded.

"Now's the time to use up anything you won't need later on," Rob said.

"Has Orrin thrown out that big cupboard yet?" Eb asked.

"Nope. Rebecca says she won't go to Oregon without it. I reckon she'll toss the schoolbooks first."

Miss Finster rose and took the coffeepot off the fire grate. "Gentlemen?"

"Thank you." Rob held out his cup. The ladies had four china cups with saucers, unlike the tin cups most of the people carried. They didn't seem to mind having cups that were a little heavier and a little more fragile.

She filled Rob's cup and came over to Eb. He held his out for her. Nice, how the handle didn't get hot when she poured the steaming brew into it.

He took a cautious sip. It was hot all right, but he also knew by now that Miss Finster's coffee was a bit hit-or-miss.

She looked anxiously from him to Rob. "Well? Have I poisoned you?"

"Mighty good," Rob said.

Eb had to agree. She'd hit it right. Either she was getting better at cooking on the trail or today was an exceptionally good random draw. He nodded at her.

"Well, good." She took the pot back to the fire and lifted a small, steaming kettle. "The tea water is hot, Anne."

Miss Stone got up and fussed around for a minute or two, measuring tea leaves into a round, pierced tea ball. The ladies carried a teapot. The first time Eb had seen it, he'd laughed aloud. Now he thought it was nice. They'd come a thousand miles and hadn't busted it. He guessed they'd proven their right to make tea the way they wanted it.

Miss Finster poured the pot of hot water into the teapot. "Too bad we haven't any milk." She glanced toward the wagon. "I guess I'd better fetch another bucket of water, or we won't be washing dishes."

"Let me get it for you." Eb set his cup and saucer on the ground and pushed himself to his feet.

"No need," Miss Finster said. "I wasn't hinting."

Still trying to prove her competence.

"I know." He looked her straight in the jay-blue eyes, something he'd avoided doing too often. "I'd like to get it for you."

She hesitated then handed over the wooden bucket. "If you've no objection, I'll bring the small pail and fill it, too."

Eb could have carried them both without breaking a sweat, but something kept him from protesting. He just nodded. His face felt like it was on fire.

"We shan't be five minutes, Anne," Miss Finster said.

"Take your time." Miss Stone poured a little of the tea from the teapot into her cup and eyed it critically then set the pot down. "You'll keep a close eye on her, won't you, Mr. Bentley?"

"Aw, call me Eb. And yes, of course I will." It came out a bit gruffly, but Miss Stone's smile told him she forgave any shortness on his behalf. Rob just leaned back against the wagon wheel and sipped his coffee, not looking at him, but Eb suspected he was smirking behind that cup.

Next thing Eb knew, they were walking away from the wagon circle, toward the river. The cattle had stirred up the already muddy river at the most accessible place, but there was a path a little way upstream, and Eb led her there. Miss Finster peered up at him from under that outlandish hat. How did she keep it from crushing in the wagon, anyway?

"I thought Miss Anne looked happier today," he said.

"Yes. We talked this morning. She wants to go on. She and I both trust your instincts—yours and Mr. Whistler's."

"About Schwartz, you mean?"

"Yes. I've no doubt he lied to us. It was hard for Anne to leave, wondering if her uncle was really buried there, but she's decided to believe he's not and to trust God to see us through to the end of our journey."

"That's the right way to think."

"I believe Anne has handled this entire thing well." She smiled, and he thought again what a picture she made—a refined lady out here in the wilderness, keeping her dignity and her daintiness, but not afraid to pitch in and do the heavy work herself.

Eb paused where the path led down the riverbank. "I think you're a lot like Miss Anne yourself. And I daresay you've helped her along on her journey."

She gazed up into his eyes. "Thank you, Mr. Bentley."

Should he offer his hand to assist her down the few steep steps? "I don't suppose you could call me Eb?"

She glanced away, down at her bucket first and then toward the river. "Habits are difficult to break, but I shall try. My given name is Elise."

He shifted his bucket to the other hand and reached out to her. "May I help you down this spot in the path, Miss Elise?"

Her dainty fingers grasped his rough hand with a surprisingly strong grip.

On the way back to the campsite, Elise wondered how she'd gotten herself into this situation. She'd willingly agreed—no, if the truth be told, she had initiated—going on this walk to the river along a secluded path with a man she knew only superficially.

Even as she thought how improperly she was behaving, she knew that was silly. Rules from British high society did not apply here.

The quiet scout walking beside her carried both pails of water. He wouldn't give up the smaller one, though she'd protested. There came a point where she could see that his pride would be hurt if she persisted, and so she gave up.

Edwin Bentley—Eb—had become a bigger distraction than the snowcapped mountains looming before them or the vague fear that a band of wild Indians would suddenly appear over a ridge. She couldn't hold one rational thought in her head with him walking beside her.

"I expect we should let the livestock loose to graze," he said. "There's not enough grass in the wagon circle to last them long."

"We don't want to take any chances this close to Schwartzburg."

He nodded. "Probably I'm overly suspicious. I just can't help thinking Schwartz was up to something. And what you heard about them blaming the Indians. . .well, that can't be good."

"I didn't see many Indians around his place."

"There were a few in the trading post when I went in yesterday morning. Not many. They're mostly out hunting buffalo now, I reckon."

As Elise looked up at his resolute profile, she knew he would give his life to protect the people in the wagon train. Eb Bentley was a man she could trust, and one she could admire without regret.

"Anne asked me today if we were right to go on," she said.

Eb paused on the path and looked down at her. "What do you think?"

"I should hate to wait at Schwartzburg for a company heading east. But beyond that, yes. I think we should continue our search."

"So do I."

Her heart swelled. "Thank you. It helps to have a rational man support our decision. I admit I had second thoughts."

Eb studied her for a moment. "What will you do if you get to Oregon and don't find him?"

"I suppose we'll go home. Though Anne will be crushed."

"I suppose her family wants her back. They must be worried about the two of you."

Elise gave him a wry smile. "Her family is small—smaller than it used to be. Those remaining are not so doting as you might suppose."

"Her friends. . . ?"

"Yes. Well, you see, friends aren't always faithful. Anne has had a comedown in position since her father died. Her loss of fortune. . . I'm sure some of her friends truly care about her, but right now she is depending very much upon finding her uncle so that he can set things to rights for her. If that doesn't happen. . ."

"Does she have a plan?"

"Oh yes." Elise looked away from his direct stare. "The two of us will probably settle in a quiet corner of England and live out our lives together. I will gladly serve her, though she treats me more as a friend than a servant."

"I haven't seen any hoity-toity ways from her since I've known her."

"No. She isn't like that. We decided to act as friends on this trip, and it has become true. She is my dearest friend now. If God wills us to live humbly together as spinsters for the rest of our lives, I shall not be discontent. Though I can't imagine that for Anne. With her beauty and her gentle spirit, even though she'll have only a meager allowance, I would think some fair-minded man would fall in love with her."

"Yes, one would think so. In fact, I'd say several have."

Elise smiled. "Yes, the young men in our company adore her. Several are head over heels, but she tells me she hasn't found one she can love with all her heart, and so she keeps them at arm's length. She tries to treat them all equally, and I think she's done a good job."

Eb cleared his throat. "And yourself? You wouldn't consider marrying unless she was settled?"

Elise glanced at him sharply. His open expression brought a flush to her cheeks. "I must think of her first. It is my duty to her and to her parents. But if she should find the protection of a good man she can love, I suppose anything is possible. With God, I mean. . ."

"Oh yes," Eb said. "Anything at all."

"Even at my age."

He chuckled, and she realized she'd said the words aloud. Her already warm cheeks flamed.

"Forgive me, Mr. Bentley—Eb. That was a private thought gone renegade."

He looked as though he would speak, but footsteps approaching from the encampment stopped him. They both looked up the path. Mrs. Legity and her son-in-law, Josiah Redman, approached carrying water pails.

Eb gestured for her to precede him, and Elise resumed walking.

Mrs. Legity came even with them, and Elise stepped out of the path for her.

"Miss Finster," Mrs. Legity said in a high-pitched tone that bespoke rampant speculation.

"Hello," Elise said as cheerfully as possible. She smiled at Josiah, who nodded.

"Mr. Bentley." Mrs. Legity drew out his name.

"Ma'am."

After the two had passed, Elise looked over her shoulder at Eb. He winked at her. Elise whirled toward camp in confusion, certain that her beet-red face would confirm any rumors Mrs. Legity fancied to start.

They set out as the sun threw its last rays from behind the mountains onto the wisps of cloud above. The array of color filled Elise's heart with a yearning she didn't understand.

"We need to hurry," Anne called over Bumper's withers. "We're leading tonight."

Holding first place in the line of wagons was an honor not to be taken lightly. They'd only had the privilege twice so far, and Elise was determined to be ready when the moment came to form up. For once she wouldn't be staring over the mules' ears at the back of Abe Leonard's wagon. Instead she'd see the vast openness before them, and perhaps Rob's back, or even Eb's if he didn't ride off miles ahead to scout. That prospect spurred her on as she tugged at the harness straps.

A moment later Anne again called her to earth with a low cry of distress.

"What's the matter?" Elise asked.

"There's a buckle missing from Bumper's breeching."

"Is the strap broken?"

"No, I don't think so. How could this have happened?"

"All too easily, I'm afraid. I'll look around in the wagon."

"I'll check here in the grass. Perhaps we dropped it when we unhitched." Anne knelt and began to pat the trampled stalks near the mules' feet.

Elise fumbled about in the empty crate where they kept the harness during their stops. It was empty. For the first time, they were hitching all six mules to the wagon. Hector Adams had come while they were packing up and told them Rob said they would have a harder pull than they'd yet experienced, and to put their full teams in the lineup.

Anne came to the back of the wagon. "Find anything?"

"No. I may need to light the lantern."

"I'll do it."

"Do we have any extra buckles?" Elise stuck her hand into a crack between the crate and the dish box and willed her fingers to find the missing item.

"Shoe buckles," Anne said with a laugh.

Elise frowned. "Get ready to drive, and make sure we haven't left anything out that should be packed. I'll see what I can find."

Ten minutes later they took their place at the front of the line with Elise driving. "Go straight on," Rob told her. "There's not much of a moon, but there's plenty of starlight tonight, and the road should be clear and obvious for the first hour or two." She slapped the reins on Challenger's and Blackie's hindquarters. With Zee and Prince in the swing position, between the leaders and the wheelers, the elongated team seemed to stretch for miles before her in the eerie starshine.

Anne sat beside her, gazing ahead as they rumbled into the foothills and left the river below them.

"Too bad we have to waste this romantic moonlit ride."

Elise laughed. "It won't be wasted if it brings us closer to South Pass."

They rode along peacefully, with Rob checking in on them every thirty minutes or so and reporting that all was calm in their wake. The temperature had cooled significantly, and with the ever-present breeze, the evening made for comfortable traveling.

Two hours into their trek, a lone horseman rode toward them out of the west. The mules were leaning into their collars and straining a bit as they climbed toward the pass.

Anne nudged Elise with her elbow. "Here comes Eb. He'll ride up and put a finger to his hat brim and say, 'Ladies.'"

Elise laughed. "Probably."

"Nice to have a dependable man around, isn't it?"

Before she could answer, Eb trotted up on Speck and touched his hat. "Ladies."

"Good evening, Eb," Elise said, quite loudly in hopes of covering Anne's unladylike giggle. "How does the road look ahead?"

He swung Speck around and let him walk slowly beside the

wagon. "Smooth as glass—uphill glass, that is. No trouble from behind, I take it."

"We've heard nothing untoward."

"Good. We'll stop and rest in a little while. Then we'll continue on for a ways. You'll come eventually to a highland meadow that will make good grazing for the stock. It's about three miles ahead. But I'll see you again before then." He nodded and wheeled the spotted horse away.

"Three miles ahead," Anne said. "So—another three or four hours at ox pace?"

"Maybe more, with this incline." Elise had barely spoken when they heard a shout behind them—not the usual shout of an ox driver to his team or a parent to a child. "What was that?"

In the distance a series of loud bangs erupted, followed by more shouting. Anne grabbed Elise's arm. "Gunfire. Should we stop? We can't circle the wagons here on this uphill grade."

Elise's stomach clenched. "Maybe that's what they planned on. Waiting for us to get into an indefensible position."

"Keep going, then," Anne said. "We should keep on unless Rob or Eb tells us otherwise."

Elise slapped the wheelers with the lines. "Up! Chick, Bumper, move along!" The mules perked up their ears and stepped a little faster.

A closer voice reached them, from two or three wagon lengths behind.

"Any men who can, ride back to the herd."

"Should I hop down and run back to ask Dan what's happening?" Anne asked.

"No! Don't you dare leave me up here alone."

After what seemed forever, they heard hoofbeats coming up the line fast.

"Keep going," Rob's steady voice shouted. "Keep your teams moving along."

"Is there trouble back there?" Dan Adams called.

"A bit. Eb and some others went back to help. The best thing we can do is keep everyone moving until we get to a spot where we can circle. We're vulnerable all strung out like this."

Elise kept driving, but for the first time she wished she wasn't leading tonight. Driving in first position in daylight as they rolled across the empty prairie was one thing, but her heart seemed to have climbed into her throat and taken residence there.

"How far?" she asked as Rob cantered up alongside her perch.

"I believe there's a more level spot up ahead—perhaps a quarter mile. I'll go on and see, but I won't go too far."

He rode forward, and Elise flicked the reins again. "Keep going, boys! It's not far now."

"Thank God we've got all six of our mules hitched tonight," Anne said.

"Yes, they can pull harder."

"And we won't lose our reserves."

Minutes later, Rob cantered back down the trail and reined in next to Elise. "It's not far. Keep going up there about as far as you can see now, and the trail will open out in a grassy area. Pull off to the left and start the circle as best you can. I'll ride down the line now, but if possible I'll get back up there to guide you."

# CHAPTER 22

**H**e's not an Indian." Eb stared at the prisoner in the moonlight. Will Strother and Josiah Redman stood by, guarding the young man while the rest of the drovers tried to calm the livestock and move them up the trail behind the wagon train.

"Wish we coulda got them all," Will said. "They shot Nicky."

"I saw him," Eb said. "It's not serious. Nick's mama will fix him up in no time." He deliberately made light of Nick's wound to soothe the boy. Bad enough the Foster boy had been grazed by one of the raiders' bullets. He didn't need the rest of the young men getting all hotheaded and eager to retaliate. "What we need to do is get the wagons to where they can circle and run the rest of the stock inside. Then we'll see how many head are missing and decide what to do about this."

"We should maybe go after them now," Josiah said.

Eb shook his head. "We're in their territory. They have the advantage in the dark. Our top goal is safety. Recovering a few head of livestock isn't worth losing one of our people."

"All right, so what do we do with him?" Josiah jerked his head toward the young man who sat on the ground with his wrists and ankles bound. He watched them closely as they talked.

Eb lifted his right foot and nudged the prisoner's foot with his boot. "Who are you?"

The young man just blinked up at him.

"When he talks, it ain't English," Josiah said.

Eb nodded. "Schwartz's nephew, I'm thinking." He hunkered down next to the prisoner. "I got a feeling you understand more English than you let on. But that's all right. I've got someone who can speak your lingo."

He stood and looked at Josiah. "Abe Leonard's got the last

236

wagon in line tonight. Walk this fella up there and tell Abe I want him tied up in the back of the wagon. Then one of you ride along behind and make sure he stays in it. Once we get the wagons circled again, I'll deal with him."

"Yes, sir," Will said.

Josiah nodded.

Eb mounted Speck and rode to where James Binchley was overseeing the herdsmen.

"How you doing, James?"

"Good, considering. They came out of nowhere, Eb. Guess we'd let the herd lag behind a little too far, and they figured they could run off some stock before the rest of you would get down to help us."

"Yeah, that's what I figured. I guess moving after dark wasn't such a bright idea."

"Seemed logical, with it so hot in the daytime."

Eb nodded, appreciative of the man's support. "Live and learn."

"At least we had a double guard on the herd tonight." Binchley gave a short bark of a laugh. "Some of the boys complained. But you expect that from boys. They won't question the orders from here on."

"Not for a while, anyway. I'm sorry Nick Foster got hurt."

"Yeah, that's too bad. He's young and tough though. It hit his arm, but I don't think it broke the bone."

"Nope, it didn't."

"He's a lucky young man," Binchley said. "And so are we all— I don't think we lost more than six or eight mules. No cattle."

"We'll take a count as soon as we get camped."

"Hey, Eb!" Elijah Woolman, the eighteen-year-old son of a farmer, rode up holding out what looked at first like a stick. "Look at what we found!"

Eb took it from Elijah and studied it. "It's a Lakota arrow. Where'd you get it?"

"Down in the flat yonder. We think the thieves were hiding there in the brush by the river and rode out as we passed by. Mr. Clark and I went to look around and see if we could learn anything, and we found this lying on the ground."

Eb stuck the arrow into his scabbard, alongside his rifle. "They planted it to make us think Indians attacked."

He rode forward, up the gradual slope. When he reached Abe's wagon, he found Josiah Redman riding behind with his rifle across the pommel of his saddle.

"Prisoner's quiet so far," Josiah called with a casual salute.

Eb went on up the line until he found Rob at the small meadow, directing the first wagons into formation. He rode over and halted Speck next to Bailey.

"Everything all right yonder?" Rob asked.

"As well as you could expect, maybe better."

"Just the one kid hit?"

"Yup. He'll be fine. Keep him off herd duty for a week or two though. You know they caught one of the raiders?"

"Heard it but didn't know if it was true."

"It is. We've got him tied in Leonard's wagon at the end of the line."

"What are you going to do with him?"

"Thought I'd ask Miss Finster to talk to him."

Rob jerked his head around. "Are you crazy?"

"No. It's a white man, but he speaks another language. I figure it's German. Schwartz's nephew, maybe. I never saw him at the trading post, but. . ."

"I did. I'll come with you after we get the circle formed."

❧

Elise wiped her brow with her sleeve. Uncouth, she thought, but she didn't bother to look for a handkerchief. She and Anne worked as quickly as they could to take the harness off the six mules. Rob had instructed them to unhitch, as they would wait for daylight to move on. The immediate goal was to pen all the livestock inside the wagon circle and wait for morning, with every able-bodied man armed and on watch.

She finally released the wheelers into the circle as Abe Leonard's wagon pulled into the spot ahead of hers. To her surprise, two mounted men rode just behind Abe's wagon. The rearguard of the train, she supposed.

She walked over to them and recognized Josiah Redman, Mrs. Legity's son-in-law, as the closer rider.

"Shall we tie up our clothesline to the wagon and unpack boxes and such to fill the gap, Mr. Redman?" she asked.

Redman hesitated and measured the distance between her wagon and Leonard's with his eye. "Tie the clothesline on your end and bring me the other. And you don't need to pile up your bundles. We'll keep a couple of men here all night."

"Oh." That was odd, but Elise did as he'd said. She wasn't averse to having a couple of armed men close to her station, but she wasn't sure she and Anne would want to put up the tent and crawl inside. An air of expectancy hovered over the temporary camp.

As she finished tying the end of the rope through the iron ring at the front of the wagon bed, Eb rode up. She could tell it was him, though the moon had gone behind the clouds, because Speck's white patches stood out clearly.

He dismounted and walked over to her. "Miss Elise, I wondered if you'd do us all a favor."

"I? What could I possibly do for the company?"

"Come speak to the prisoner and see if he understands German."

"Prisoner?" She stared at him.

Quickly Eb sketched out for her what had happened on the trail behind them while she drove her team up the slope to the meadow.

"Are you willing?" he asked.

"Yes, I suppose so. Will I have to get into Mr. Leonard's wagon with him?"

"I'll have the boys bring him out."

A few minutes later a young man bound with ropes sat on the tongue of her wagon. Elise and Anne stood together next to the wagon, clutching hands.

"I had no idea," Anne whispered. "While we were tending to the team, they had him in there, just a few feet away."

"Yes." Elise swallowed hard. Why hadn't she asked Eb to take him somewhere else, where Anne didn't have to see him? "Stay back, my dear. I'm sure they've disarmed him, but it wouldn't do to draw the attention of an unsavory character to you."

Eb came over to her. "Are you ready?"

"What shall I say to him?" Elise asked.

"Don't tell him your name or anything else about you and Miss Anne. I think he speaks English, or at least understands it some, but he doesn't want us to know that. Just see if you can tell if he understands your lingo. If he does, you can ask him if he's one of Schwartz's men and what they were up to." He extended his hand to her.

Elise tried to quell her trembling as she placed her hand in his. Eb drew her over to where the prisoner sat. The men had brought a lantern, and she could see his face clearly. But if he was bluffing about his linguistic skills, how could she make him betray himself?

"You are right," she said in clear German, looking toward Eb. "I think your decision to hang him is the correct one." She turned back to watch the prisoner's face. "He is definitely one of the thieves and worthy of execution. As soon as possible."

The young man's face blanched. He stirred as though he would leap up, but his bonds held him in place.

"*Nein, frau!* Nein!" In German, he blurted, "What have I done to you? You mustn't let them kill me!"

She glared at him fiercely. "If you want to be spared, you had better tell these men what you were doing and who was involved. They would just as soon hang you as not. And you can stop pretending that you don't speak English."

He shook his head and raised his tied hands. "Please, madam," he said in German, "my English is not good. If you will tell them— please—I did not want to do anything to them. It was not my fault, but they made me go with them."

"Who?" she asked. "Who made you do this?"

His whole body wilted and his chin drooped. "Herr Schwartz."

"Your uncle?"

His head snapped up. "He is not kin to me. He brought a couple of us over to work for him, and he tells people we are his family, but it isn't true."

Elise glanced at Eb. He was watching her keenly. "He says Schwartz was behind it all, and he forced his workers to take part in the raid. This man claims he's not related to Schwartz and didn't want to do it."

"How long has he been with Schwartz?"

Elise asked the man.

"A little more than a year. He said he couldn't trust the Americans he had working for him before. He brought me and Franz over last year. He paid our passage and said we could work it off in six months. But he doesn't treat us well. I've been saving my pay so that I can leave him and strike out on my own, but it's hard. He pays us next to nothing."

Elise relayed this information, and Eb directed her to ask what Schwartz would do with the livestock he had stolen.

When she did, the man replied, "He has a place to hide them for a while—a canyon in the rocks. He takes them feed. And after a while he will bring them out a few at a time and sell them."

"Can you show our men where it is?" Elise asked.

"No! He would certainly kill me."

Elise laughed and said harshly, "You care now who kills you? All right, it's your choice. I will tell these men to go ahead and do it."

"What's he saying?" Eb asked.

"He will tell you where Schwartz hides livestock he has stolen."

Eb gazed at Elise with new admiration. "I don't know what you told him, but thank you."

"Only that you would hang him at once if he didn't cooperate."

Eb suppressed a smile. "At dawn we'll take the wagons on to the place I originally planned for us to camp. There's better grazing and access to the river. Then we'll leave a dozen men with the camp. The rest of us will ride back to the trading post and settle things with Schwartz."

"What will you do with this man?" Elise asked.

"I don't know yet. Ask him where the hiding place is, please."

Elise turned back to the prisoner and spoke to him in German. Eb tried to pick out a word or two, but he couldn't. The young man seemed to understand perfectly, however. He grimaced and rattled off a lengthy explanation, during which Elise nodded periodically.

"*Danke,*" she said at last. She turned and took Eb's arm, leading him a short distance away.

"I'm sure he understands you, so be careful what you say in front of him. Tell your guards as well."

"All right."

"He says the animals will be in a canyon—a sort of ravine or steep valley, I take it, up Willow Creek."

"How far?"

"About two miles. The way is rocky at first, which hides their hoofprints. A large rock juts out over the water. If you go behind this rock, you should be able to locate the trail easily."

"We'll find it." Eb realized she still held on to his arm lightly. He dared to pat her fingers for a moment. "You've done well, ma'am. Danke."

She smiled and squeezed his arm just a little. "You're welcome. Need I remind you to be careful, whatever you do? Herr Schwartz is a rogue."

"That and a few other things." Reluctantly, Eb released her hand and walked over to Josiah. "Put him back in Leonard's wagon and tie him down. Keep at least two men guarding him all night."

He walked around the outside of the circle. Rob was helping Orrin Harkness and his boys close the gaps between the wagons in the barricade.

"We'll only stop here until sunup," Eb said.

"Yes, but we don't to want to make it easy for them to start a stampede if they come back." Rob lifted his hat and wiped his brow. "What's going on in your head, Eb?"

"We take most of the men at daybreak and ride back to Schwartzburg. The prisoner says Schwartz forced his employees to steal for him. Not sure I believe him about the coercion, but we need to meet him with a show of force and be ready for resistance."

"Spoken like an old soldier."

"Watch who you're calling old."

Rob smiled. "All right, you'll be in charge."

"I think you should stay here with the company," Eb said.

"Why?"

"If things don't go well, they'll need you."

Rob squinted at him in the near darkness. "How many men do you think Schwartz has?"

"Not that many, but he's foxy."

Wilbur, his father, and his younger brother Ben came over to stand beside them. "We going down and teach that trader a lesson?" Wilbur asked.

"Not until we move the wagons to a better place at daylight," Eb said. "Then we'll split up the men. Leave a dozen here. The rest will go with me."

"As near as we can tell, they only got about eight mules at the most," Orrin said.

"They would have gotten more if our men hadn't been on the lookout for them," Wilbur added.

"Well, eight is too many," Rob said. "But they're not worth killing over."

"I don't intend to kill anyone unless it's necessary." Eb gazed levelly into his eyes. "We'll be fine, Rob. I won't shame you."

"It's not you I'm worried about. Some of these young fellas are mad as sin."

<hr />

When Elise awoke, the sun was beating mercilessly on the tent and the interior felt uncomfortably warm. She stirred to lift the tent flap a bit, hoping for a breeze off the river. Drumming hoofbeats grew louder. She listened for a moment. Shouts of exultation greeted the riders.

"Anne! Wake up, dear."

Anne stirred and blinked at her. Perspiration stood in beads on her forehead.

"The men are back," Elise said.

"Help me with my corset—quickly!"

A few minutes later, they crawled out of the tent and brushed their skirts down. The travelers had gathered near the Harkness wagons, so Elise and Anne made their way around the circle to stand on the fringe of the crowd. Eb stood on a crate between two of the wagons.

"Mr. Harkness has volunteered his smallest wagon for use as a temporary jail," Eb was saying to the listeners.

Elise peered around and spotted a group of men standing a ways off, holding four men at gunpoint. Among them was Schwartz.

"We'll keep the prisoners in there until we get to the next place that has some legal authorities," Eb said.

"Whyn't we send them back to Fort Laramie and be rid of them?" asked Mr. Libby.

"I'll let Mr. Whistler answer that."

Eb hopped down from the crate, and Rob climbed up to take his place. "If we sent off a detachment of our men to deliver these prisoners, we'd have to send quite a few, just to make sure our men were safe and couldn't be overpowered. That in turn would weaken our force with the wagons. I don't know about you, but with the rugged terrain ahead of us, not to mention possible trouble with the Indians north of here along the Snake, I don't like the idea of having fewer men where the women and children are."

"How long would it take 'em to ride back to Laramie?" Hector Adams called.

"Well, they'd need to take the wagon, unless you want to put the prisoners on horses, and that, to my way of thinking, is asking for trouble." Rob shook his head. "I think the safest way is to take them along with us."

"Did you recover all our livestock?" Mr. Binchley asked.

"I'm happy to say our delegation did that. However, they also found a few oxen and a couple of horses that didn't belong to our company in the canyon. And of course, back at Schwartz's trading post, there was quite a bit of stock in his pens. We can't just leave all those animals with no one to care for them."

"So what are we going to do?" Abe asked.

"I'd buy one of the oxen," Binchley said.

"Who would you pay?" asked Nick Foster's father, James.

"You should just take it," Wilbur said. "They stole from us. That's restitution."

"Now, folks, let's not let go of our morals and common sense." Rob looked out over their heads. "Eb, can you speak to this issue, please?"

Rob got down, and Eb climbed back up on the box.

"We figure we'll release the first man we captured and leave him in charge of the trading post."

"But he's a thief," James Foster shouted.

Eb raised both hands. "Folks, hear me out. There are other wagon trains behind ours. One of them is camped two miles east of Schwartzburg. Their scout came to the trading post this morning while we were there. We told him what was going on and that we'd have someone there by noon to open the store for his people. He gave his word that they'd do things in an orderly manner. Now, that's a good thing. They could take advantage of this situation. But we're not that kind of people, and neither are they."

A murmur ran through the gathering, and Elise shivered.

"Hear me out," Eb said. Although he didn't shout, people quieted to listen. "The young man we caught last night is as close as we've got to an honest man from Schwartzburg. I believe that if we go with him today and open the store, he'll behave himself. Mr. Whistler will get behind the counter with him, and he'll sell goods and livestock to all of you at fair prices. I'm talking fair—enough to allow that young man to restock the trading post after we leave. We're not going to steal from him. And then the folks in the next wagon train can come in and buy from him."

"That sounds all right to me," Dan Adams called.

Eb nodded in his direction. "Thanks, Dan. Folks, as near as

I know, we're all Christian people. We don't want to turn around and steal from anyone. We'll see that Schwartz and the other three men who stood against us this morning are turned over to a marshal or an army officer, and we'll leave the young man who's in Abe Leonard's wagon to run the post. Rob and I will write out statements for him to keep by him in case the law wants proof later that he has a right to be there. And we'll also give statements when we turn the prisoners over, telling exactly what happened and how that one fellow helped us get back our own livestock."

He stood still for a moment while the people absorbed what he'd said.

"All right. Let's get the prisoners accommodated, and then anyone who wants to trade can ride back with us. Mr. Harkness won't be able to haul folks in his farm wagon like he's done before, so you'll have to ride or take another wagon, but I reckon we can get our business done by noon and leave Schwartzburg to the next company of emigrants. We'll get on our way this afternoon and push on into the evening."

He jumped to the ground before anyone could raise more questions.

Anne grabbed Elise's arm. "I'm going to see if I can use Mrs. Libby's saddle on Chick."

"You want to go back to Schwartzburg?"

"Yes! I'm going to get a few of those eggs if I have to raid the henhouse myself. I'll ask Eb how much it would be fair to pay for them."

She hurried away.

"Do you want to go back and trade?"

She whirled to find Eb at her elbow. "Oh, no thank you."

"This may be your last opportunity before we get to Oregon. It's chancy along the Snake these days."

Elise smiled. "Take Anne. She wants an egg or two. Since we're going to stay here several more hours, I think I'll do some baking."

"All right. We found Rob's horse in the canyon, you know."

She stared at him. "You mean. . ."

"Yes. The one Costigan stole."

"Thomas wasn't with them, was he?"

"No. I asked Schwartz, but he won't talk to me."

She thought about their options. "I'd like to know where he is."

"Me, too," Eb said. "Always better to know where your adversary is."

"I could ask the young man before you release him."

He nodded. "I was going to see if you'd talk to him anyway, so we'd be sure he understood what we're going to do. I want him to realize we're putting him in a position of trust. We'll give him papers, like I said, in case the law comes out here. But he'll be alone for a while. It could be dangerous for him. Indians or some other no-good like Schwartz could come and try to take over."

"He may not want to stay here alone."

"That's true. If he wants to go with us, he can, but that would mean abandoning the post and taking the extra stock with us. Still, I want him to know what he's up against if he stays. Maybe he can get someone to help him before too long. I just can't think of a better plan."

Neither could she.

"Eb, have you thought any more about digging up that grave?"

He hesitated. "I'll ask Miss Anne if she wants us to."

"Thank you."

Eb rode out to the cemetery with Hector Adams. He'd left Rob in the store with the young German man, who Elise had learned was named Georg Heinz.

"You think that young fella will be all right here?" Hector dismounted and unstrapped a shovel from his saddle.

"There'll be enough traffic along the trail for the next couple of months that he should be," Eb said. "If someone who wants a job comes by, he'll make out."

"If that someone is honest."

"Right." Eb let Speck's reins fall and reached for his own

shovel. "Let's get this done. I don't want to hold up the train, and I don't want to keep Miss Anne wondering any longer than needed." He looked back toward the buildings. "I was afraid she was going to insist on watching."

"Dan will take care of her while we do it. He'll make sure she stays up yonder."

Eb strode to the board cross marked DAVID STONE. He looked at it for a long moment. Hector gave a long sigh and removed his hat.

Eb took his hat off, too, and looked skyward. "Lord, we mean no disrespect. I'm asking that You let us know for sure if this grave belongs to Mr. Stone."

After a moment's silence, Hector said, "Amen."

Eb grasped the crossbar of the grave marker and pulled it from the ground. He laid it aside in the grass. Hector put the blade of his shovel to the earth and stepped down on it hard.

# CHAPTER 23

**E**lise carried the two plates carefully, mindful of her calico skirt swirling in the wind. At least it wasn't so hot up here on the mountainside.

"What've you got there, Miss Finster?" called Charles Woolman, who had drawn one of the first watches over the prison wagon.

"Dinner for the prisoners. I've got two plates here, and I'll bring two more."

The second guard, Landon Clark, lowered his gun from his shoulder and walked toward her. "What are you giving them?"

"Mr. Whistler didn't say nothing about feeding them," Woolman said.

"It's very plain food. Just beans, cornbread, and a few dried apple slices."

"That's better'n what I'll likely get," Clark said.

Elise frowned at them. "You have to feed them. I wasn't sure the men had thought about it before they rode off, so I decided to provide their dinner today. Someone else can contribute at suppertime."

Woolman shook his head. "I'm not sure we can let you give that to 'em, Miss Finster."

"Why ever not? You've got to treat them humanely. We can't haul them all the way to Fort Dalles or someplace in between and hand them over malnourished."

Clark shrugged. "Don't see why not. They stole from us, and they'd have killed any one of us they had a chance to kill. They shot the Foster boy, you know."

Elise winced. "Yes, I know."

"I think we should hold off until the captain gets back." Woolman looked at Clark, and his companion nodded.

249

Elise hovered between tearing into them and retreating meekly. A shout from the other side of the camp drew her gaze.

Rebecca Harkness waved toward the trail. "They're coming back."

Elise hurried to her fireside and set down the two plates. She gathered her skirts and hurried to where Rebecca and several others had gathered to meet those returning from the trading post.

Anne rode in on Chick at Dan Adams's side. Elise waved, and they veered toward her.

Dan hopped to the ground, but before he could reach Chick's side, Anne had slid off the saddle, carefully balancing a small basket.

"Elise! It's not him."

"Not David?"

"No. It's someone else," Anne said.

Elise folded her into her embrace. Dan caught Chick's reins as Anne let go of them.

"I'll take care of the mule," he said.

Elise drew Anne toward their wagon. "Where are Rob and Eb?"

"They're talking to the leaders from the next train. They said there's at least two more companies behind them. Rob told that young German fellow to be polite and treat them fairly. He seemed to understand. Oh, and Rob made out a price list for him to use while he trades." Anne laughed. "You should have seen him, wearing an apron and measuring out groceries."

"Rob Whistler is a good man," Elise said.

"Yes, he is. He saved out half a dozen eggs for me. I paid a dollar for the lot." Anne held out her basket.

"How delightful! We can make a cake next time we stop if you'd like."

"Or feed them at breakfast time to the men who've helped us so much."

"Whatever you wish, my dear."

Anne's face sobered. "And Eb and Hector dug up the cemetery plot."

"What did they find?"

"They wouldn't tell me, but Eb says he's positive it's not Uncle David." Anne drew in a deep breath. "So. We're going onward, as we planned."

Elise squeezed her shoulders. "We'll trust God to bring us to David in Oregon."

Anne nodded and glanced about. "Oh, you have dinner ready."

Elise grimaced. "I made those plates for two of the prisoners."

"That was kind of you."

"The guards wouldn't let me give it to them."

"What? That's awful." Anne glowered toward the prison wagon. It was drawn apart from the circle, and the two guards stood talking near the tailboard. "Well, when Rob gets back, you take it up with him."

"I shall. I suppose you and I might as well eat in the meantime."

Elise fed Dan Adams, too. Afterward he hovered about Anne so closely as she washed the dishes that Elise decided he would soon wear out his welcome. She handed him a bucket and asked him to bring more water. Finally the wagon master rode up with Eb and Hector.

After a quick consultation with the guards, Rob came to Elise's fireside.

"I understand you're willing to feed the four prisoners."

"Yes, if Mr. Woolman and Mr. Clark will let me."

"That's good of you. Of course we have to meet the prisoners' basic needs until we turn them over to the law." Rob noticed Dan approaching with the water. "Dan, will you give me a hand, please? We'll get some of this food over to the prisoners."

Quickly Elise filled the plates she had. "We only have three," she explained. "I can borrow another, or they can take turns eating."

"I'll get you another one," Dan said.

He hurried off to his wagon and returned a moment later with a tin plate. Elise loaded on the beans and apples, and she added an extra slice of cornbread to each plate, partly out of spite to the two unsympathetic guards.

"I'll ask another family to pitch in tonight," Rob said. He and

Dan took the meals to the prison wagon.

As Elise began to wipe out the pans, Eb strolled over.

"Good day, Mr. Bentley," she said.

He eyed her for a moment, and she couldn't decipher the odd look on his face. At last he pushed back his hat and said, "Good day, *Miss Elise.*"

Her cheeks grew warm. So that was it. She busied herself with rinsing out the bean pot. "Eb. I understand things went in Anne's favor at the cemetery."

"Yes. We've eliminated the possibility that her uncle is buried in that grave."

"Do I want to know how you are so certain?"

He hesitated. "Probably not."

"She said it was someone else." Elise glanced up at him. "So the grave wasn't empty?"

"Oh, it had an occupant, all right. But unless Mr. Stone was . . .shall we say, of unusually small stature. . .then it most certainly wasn't him."

"A child," Elise whispered, staring down at her hands.

"That or a small woman. The bits of clothing contribute to the evidence that the unfortunate soul was female."

She nodded. "Mr. Stone was as tall as yourself, sir. A well-proportioned man."

"You knew him well?" Eb asked.

Again she flushed. "Yes. As well as one might when working in his brother's home. I saw him frequently before he left England." She turned away and carried the pot to her dish crate.

Eb followed her. "I'm sorry we had to go through this, but it seemed to relieve Miss Anne's mind."

"It must have been a chilling experience for you and Hector. Thank you for doing it."

Eb nodded. "Elise. . ."

"Yes?" She wiped her hands on her apron and looked up at him.

He didn't say anything for a long moment. They stood looking at each other, and though she couldn't fathom why, she felt her heart was near breaking.

"You think young Heinz will be all right?" she said at last, to break the silence.

"Yes, I do." Eb shifted and looked away. "Rob said there was a family in the next wagon train who'd been sick and were worn out. They wanted to rest for a while. Their captain suggested the man might work with Heinz for a while, to pay for their keep while they stay there, and they could move on with a later company when they were ready."

"That makes me feel a little better." She glanced toward the fire. "I've a bit of cornbread left. I'm afraid I gave away all the beans. I ought to have kept some over for you and Rob."

"No matter. I'll find something."

"And you've no more word on Thomas Costigan?"

"No. He's gone on, I'm guessing. We may hear of him farther along the trail. I'm glad Rob got his spare horse back. Binchley got a stout pair of oxen, too. We're in pretty good shape now, I think."

Elise pried the last pieces of cornbread from the pan. "Here. If you take this, it will save me putting it away."

"Much obliged."

He ambled away, chewing the meager offering. Elise hoped some other woman would take pity on him and give him something more substantial to eat.

He was back a half hour later, when Rob had blown the horn and passed the word to hitch up the teams.

"Can I help you ladies?"

"Thank you, but we're just about ready," Elise told him. She ran her hand over Zee's flanks as she visually checked all the straps and buckles on the near side of his harness.

"What's that?" Eb asked.

"Hmm?" She looked where he was pointing.

"That sparkly buckle."

Elise chuckled. As usual, he'd found her out, but this time she felt no embarrassment. "That, sir, is a buckle off a bejeweled evening purse. We were lacking one buckle when we needed to harness all six of our mules, and I found that amongst our things."

Eb shook his head. "I don't know how you do it—you and Miss Anne both. You seem to go at everything sideways, but it works." He bent over and peered more closely at the buckle.

"They're not real jewels, if that's what you're wondering."

"It did enter my mind. If I'd have known, I could have brought you a buckle from the trading post."

"Yes, or Anne could have, if she'd thought of it. Don't you worry, Eb. We'll get by."

He straightened and smiled at her. "Yes, I reckon you will."

∿

Eb rode Pink ahead of the wagon company as far as South Pass. Their train had made good time since Schwartzburg, and none of the other groups had caught up to them. One band of freighters had passed them, and he'd seen a couple of Indians from a distance, but the trail seemed quiet compared to last year.

He sat for a while on his horse, scanning the western horizon. If only he were heading home to Jeanie.

He lifted his gaze to the cloudless sky. Up here, the breeze was cool. Tonight they'd need their wool blankets, even in mid-July.

Rob would need him today to encourage more folks to lighten their wagons, so he turned eastward. This slope was not the steepest they would encounter, but the long, steady climb would take its toll on the livestock. So far Elise and Anne's team seemed to be holding up well. Most of their heavy supply of feed was gone now, but the extra rations they'd used had stood them in good stead.

Odd how his thoughts could leap so quickly from Jeanie to Elise.

"Elise." He said the musical name aloud. He no longer felt guilty. That had to be good. Rob would think so.

He met Rob at the head of the company. So far they'd lost two wagons. One family had turned back early in the trek, and another had broken an axle beyond repair. The owners had no spare, so now the young couple rode muleback, with what little gear they'd kept on their other two mules. They'd get to Oregon with a few threadbare clothes and little besides, but they were sturdy and hopeful. They'd make it.

Rob's first words confirmed Eb's feelings about the weight of some of the wagons.

"I've been working on the Harkness family, but Rebecca's stubborn. She won't give up the furniture. And now that their third wagon is hauling the prisoners, their tools are in the family wagons, too."

"They may want to take back their loan of the wagon," Eb said.

"I'm afraid they might."

"Well, we can make the prisoners walk more."

"I suppose it's fitting. I don't want to lose them, is all." Rob sighed and looked ahead. "How's the trail look?"

"Same as always at the pass. Not much traffic. There's nobody else at the camp spot."

"Good." Rob looked behind him. "There's a gap behind Binchley's wagon. Guess we'd better go see what's holding up the Fosters."

Most of the day, Rob persuaded folks to be reasonable while Eb and the Adams brothers helped unload heavy items. They sent the drovers with the herd of loose stock on ahead, to give the animals more time to graze. By sunset, all forty-eight wagons had topped the pass, albeit some with reluctant owners.

Eb followed the last wagon—Landon Clark's—over the almost imperceptible summit of the pass and found Elise standing alone at one side of the broad trail, gazing west.

Eb rode Pink up beside her and dismounted. "Long thoughts?"

"Yes. As long as the shadows. This is the watershed, isn't it?"

"Yes, ma'am. They call it the Great Divide. All the rivers from here on flow west."

She turned and looked back, but they were past the top, and you couldn't see far. She gave a great sigh and faced west again.

"Miss Anne must be driving."

"Yes. I told her I wanted to walk for a while."

"Don't blame you, but you don't want to linger back here alone. There's bears and cougars in these parts." He didn't mention that there might be two-legged vermin as well.

Elise began to walk slowly downhill. "I've been thinking about Rob Whistler's horse."

"Oh? Bailey's a good mount."

"Not Bailey," she said. "The other one."

"I see." And he should have. She was a thinker, and no doubt she'd been turning over the implications in her mind since he told her they'd found Rob's stolen horse.

"It was Thomas Costigan who told Schwartz about David Stone."

"That seems likely." He walked along beside her, leading Pink.

"He traded his horse at Schwartzburg."

"I expect he's gone on ahead of us now," Eb said.

She nodded. "Georg Heinz barely remembered his visit, but that's what he thought happened. I believed Georg when he said he didn't know anything about Mr. Stone though."

Eb considered that. He had only what Elise told him to go on so far as what the young German man had said.

"But for some reason," she continued, "Thomas thought it would be to his advantage to tell the trader about the Stone family. He either prepared that cross or had Schwartz do it."

They walked on for a minute, with only Pink's steps and the distant rumbling, creaking, and shouting from the wagon train breaking the silence.

"Has to be some money in it for him," Eb said at last. "Can't see it any other way."

"Yes. That means either he hopes to find David and get some money out of him—which doesn't make a lot of sense to me, since David hasn't claimed the estate of Stoneford yet—or someone else is paying him."

"Can't argue with you there."

"I think he hoped we'd give up and go back to England."

"Yes. But he went on."

"That troubles me," Elise said. "I must tell Anne."

"She may have thought it out."

Elise nodded. "She might have. She's an intelligent girl. I worry about her running headlong into something she doesn't understand."

"Like someone wanting to take advantage of her uncle?"

"Perhaps. I wish I knew."

"Elise." He stopped walking. Pink stopped, then Elise.

She turned to face him. "Yes?"

"If there's anything I can do to help you...you or Miss Anne... well, you can count on me. You know that, don't you?"

She smiled a bit sadly, and he thought it was a pity she had to know sadness and unease out here. She reached up hesitantly and touched his cheek. Warmth flowed through him. In that second, he wished he could find Thomas G. Costigan and thrash him—and set the world to rights for Elise.

"Yes, Eb," she said. "I know."

# CHAPTER 24

Elise wandered farther from the wagons while Anne drove. Even buffalo chips were scarce now. Finding fuel grew harder each day. She could see wooded hills in the distance, but they were too far away to do her any good.

Lavinia walked toward her, pushing her chip barrow. Abby trailed her sister's steps.

"Find anything?" Lavinia called.

"No. Did you?"

"Just a little dried dung, but it's not buffalo. Ma won't be happy."

"Ma's never happy since she had to leave Great-Grandmother's cupboard," Abby said.

"I'm sorry." Elise had already expressed her sympathy to Rebecca, but the girls seemed to need a little extra encouragement. "It must have been hard for your mother to part with so many things that held memories for her."

"I know you're right." Lavinia fell into step with her.

Elise headed back toward the line of wagons on a diagonal course, watching the ground as she walked. The bunch grass was heading up, and it was hard to spot much that was useful down between the stalks.

"Maybe we'll have a cold dinner tonight." She gave the girls a rueful smile and patted her empty chip sack.

"And tomorrow night." Abby kicked at a tuft of milkweed. "We're running out of stuff we can eat without cooking it though."

"Ma says if we can get her enough fuel, she'll make a big batch of beans tonight, and biscuits, too," Lavinia said. "Enough to last three or four days. Of course, we'd have to give some of it to the prisoners."

"Wish we had some meat," Abby said.

258

"I believe some of the men went hunting." Elise determined to steer the conversation away from the prisoners. The Harkness family had given the most by providing the wagon. They also took a rotation for providing the men's meals. How deeply did Rebecca and the rest of the large family resent that? Eb had told Elise that they couldn't haul their heavy furniture over the Blue Mountains and the Cascades anyway, but the Harkness clan might not see it that way. "Didn't your brothers go off with Mr. Bentley this morning?"

"Yes," Lavinia said. "Wilbur and Ben both went. Pa wanted to go, but we needed him to drive."

As they neared the file of wagons, they came abreast of a small group of women who were walking together.

"Hello, ladies," Elise called. "Are you finding anything to burn?"

"Precious little," Agnes Legity said, "and it's our turn to feed the thieves."

"They should have hung 'em all back at Schwartzburg," Mrs. Strother said. "I told Mr. Whistler we have barely enough to get us through to Oregon without giving any of our food to those rascals."

Elise turned to Lavinia and touched her arm. "Let's take what you have to your mother, shall we?"

Lavinia and Abby seemed happy to leave the other women. Elise saw them to their family's place in line. Rebecca was walking near the wagon her husband drove, with one of the young children on each side of her. She shook her head when Lavinia showed her their meager findings.

"I don't know what's to do for fuel."

"Maybe we can twist up dry grass," Abby said. "I heard Ben say some people are trying to make little logs out of dried-up grass."

Rebecca frowned. "Wouldn't burn long. We'll see if the boys find anything. I told 'em when they rode out this morning to bring me anything that looks combustible."

Late in the afternoon after they'd formed their circle and released the teams, the hunters returned. Word spread quickly that they had killed two antelope. The animals weren't very large but would provide a taste for any families who wanted it.

"Perhaps we could get a soup bone," Anne said. "With rice and a bit of that dried corn, it would make a passable stew."

"We can ask," Elise said. The meat wouldn't stretch far among the company, and she knew several families were reaching the end of their supplies. Dan Adams had confided to Anne that he and Hector were down to beans and cornmeal. If they had no fire to cook it on, they'd go hungry.

Eb came by half an hour later carrying a haunch of fresh meat.

"Miss Anne, can I slice off a steak for you ladies?"

Anne, who would have cringed at the sight four months ago, fairly drooled over the raw meat. "That would be wonderful!"

"You're too generous," Elise said. "So many are hungrier than we are!"

Anne frowned. "She's right, and to be honest, we've nothing to cook it with."

"Tell you what. I'll give you a slice now, along with a few sticks I picked up this afternoon. Cook your supper and heat a kettle of water. After we're done the butchering and rationing, I'll bring you some meaty bones you can stew. You can let it simmer over what's left of your fire. I believe you're in line to feed the prisoners tomorrow."

"That sounds good, but shouldn't you and the other hunters get a good share of the meat first?"

"Don't you worry about us. The Harkness family's got a whole quarter, and I left a good portion with Rob for him and me. Say—" He stopped as though a new idea had hit him. "What if we bring it over, and we have one cook fire tonight? If you'll cook for Rob and me, that'd give you extra wood for the stewing."

Anne grinned. "And maybe we could do a batch of biscuits. Sounds like a good bargain to me!"

"I can't say no," Elise said. "But, Eb, don't put it about that I'm making stew for the prisoners."

"Oh? I thought other ladies would be glad to hear you were doing it."

"Some of them resent those men eating at all." She told him of the murmuring she'd heard earlier. "If their husbands feel the same way. . ."

Eb nodded. "It could get ugly. Guess I'll suggest to Rob that we double the guard on the prisoners tonight."

"Mr. Bentley. Eb."

Something nudged Eb's leg, and he sat up, reaching for his pistol.

"It's me, Eb."

"Miss Anne?" He squinted at her in the shadows. The camp was quiet but for the restless movement of the animals inside the wagon corral.

"Elise told me to get you. Some of the men are planning to attack the prison wagon."

Eb threw off his blanket and grabbed his left boot. "How do you know this?"

"We were baking extra johnnycake and Elise wanted to get more water."

"This late?" He frowned up at her as he tugged on the boot.

"Yes. We wanted plenty, and the coals were still hot. We might not have another chance to bake for days. Elise was going to see if any of the Harkness men would escort us to the creek. She overheard Mr. Foster and some of the others talking about rushing the wagon and—and getting the prisoners out. They want to kill them."

Eb pulled on the other boot and picked up his gun belt as he stood. "Where's Elise?"

"She went out to the prison wagon to tell the guards."

Eb gritted his teeth. Rob was out there with three other men that they'd judged could be trusted. What if one or more of them was in on this plot? He quickly ticked them off in his mind. Abe, Wilbur, and Dan. Shouldn't be any trouble there.

"Go back to your wagon and stay there," he said to Anne.

"What about Elise?"

"If she's still at the prison wagon, I'll make sure she gets back safely."

Anne lingered as he strapped on his holster and stooped to get his rifle. "You care about her, don't you, Eb?"

He jerked his chin up and eyed her cautiously. "I suppose I do."

"I suppose you more than suppose."

Eb grunted. "I'll take care of her."

Anne headed off toward the orange embers of her cook fire, and he strode toward the prison wagon. From twenty yards away he saw a wispy, pale figure to one side of the white-shrouded wagon. A few more steps and he could see that it was Elise, in a light-colored dress, talking to someone.

"Who's there?" Rob's shout didn't slow Eb down.

"It's me."

Abe Leonard stood beside Rob and Elise, with a long gun resting on his shoulder.

"We may have trouble," Rob said quietly. He was wearing his holstered pistol, and Eb was glad. Rob usually left it in his saddlebag.

"Miss Anne told me." Eb nodded at Elise. "You'd best get back to your camp, ma'am. May I escort you?"

Before Elise could answer, the tramp of many boots approaching reached them.

"Who's there?" Rob called.

"Charles Woolman."

Eb seized Elise's arm and drew her behind him.

Woolman and six other men walked over and stopped a few feet in front of Rob. Eb glanced around and saw Wilbur Harkness, one of the other guards on duty, peering around the edge of the prison wagon. Dan Adams must be somewhere nearby, too. Eb wanted to think Dan, Wilbur, and Abe would stand with him and Rob no matter what, but how could a man know for certain?

"What do you fellows want?" Rob asked.

"Thought we'd relieve the guard," Woolman said affably, but the tension in his companions' posture belied his tone. Eb shifted his rifle to his left hand and rested his right on the butt of his pistol.

"We've only been on duty an hour," Rob said.

Charles Woolman smiled. "We thought we'd lighten your duties some."

"I don't think so."

The smile disappeared. "Come on, Whistler," Woolman said. "You know those men will all hang if we get them to where there's law. All we aim to do is speed up the process and relieve the burden they're placing on this company."

"Forget it," Rob said.

"They're eating our food," James Foster said.

Eb looked over the small company of men. "Elijah, James, are you sure you want to be in on this? Josiah, I'm really surprised to see you here."

Josiah Redman's head drooped. "It's not my idea, Eb. But they've got a point."

"Oh, come on," Eb said. "Did your mother-in-law send you over here?"

Josiah glared at him.

Rob held up a hand. "All right, boys, just calm down. Charles, there's not going to be any violence done to these prisoners. You hear me?"

Woolman didn't answer but held Rob's stare in the starlight.

Dan Adams's deep voice came from behind Eb. "We've got five guns against you men, and all of them ready to fire. I suggest you go back to your wagons."

Eb wondered if Woolman or any of his friends had seen Elise. He didn't let his gaze waver from the group before him, but he wished he'd given her his pistol. Maybe Dan had pulled her back behind the wagon.

From inside the canvas cover came a guttural plea.

"Whistler! You won't let them harm us, will you?"

"Be quiet, Schwartz," Rob said. "Everything's under control."

"Are you sure about that?" James Foster took a step forward. "My boy was shot. He could have been killed. Now you're pampering those thugs. They eat better than the rest of us, and they only walk on the steepest parts of the trail. We're starving, Whistler."

"It may be weeks before we can turn them over to anyone," James Binchley said. "Think about it, Rob. We can't sustain them that long."

"It's not fair to expect us to," Woolman said.

Someone touched Eb's back lightly and he stiffened. A figure swished past him. He reached to stop her, but it was too late.

Elise planted herself nose to nose with Charles Woolman.

# CHAPTER 25

**H**ow dare you speak to the captain that way?" Elise could barely control the urge to slap him.

Woolman eyed her coolly. "Well, now. We've got lady guards, have we?"

Elise hiked her chin up. "You don't have to worry about your stash of dry beans, Mr. Woolman. Miss Stone and I will feed the prisoners from here on." She looked over the others in his little group. "Mr. Redman, Mr. Binchley, Mr. Foster. I thought better of you gentlemen. Don't tell me your wives want you here, because I don't believe it. You're all married to decent women."

She strode past them and made a beeline for her wagon. The absolute nerve of those men. She'd seen James Binchley dump a good forty pounds of bacon a week ago to lighten his wagon. Now he begrudged the prisoners a little food.

Anne met her at the edge of the glow cast by their dying fire.

"What happened? I was terrified, Elise."

"They're a bunch of bullies. I'm going straight to the Harknesses' wagons and tell Orrin what's going on. Wilbur's out there with Rob and Eb, along with Dan and Mr. Leonard, but they could use some reinforcements." She bunched up her skirt and prepared to go but turned back for a moment. "Oh, and I just told that horde of riffraff that we'd feed the prisoners from now on, so they don't have to give up their precious supplies."

Anne's jaw dropped. "Can we do that?"

"For a while." Remorse hit Elise, and she walked back to Anne and laid a hand on her sleeve. "I'm sorry. I shouldn't have said it without asking you."

"No, we'll get by." Anne smiled at her. "Look at the sacrifice Rebecca made. She gave up that furniture she loves so we'd have a prison wagon. We'll be fine."

Elise nodded and squeezed her arm gently. "Thank you." She hurried to the Harkness family's camp. Orrin sat by the smoldering remains of a very small fire.

"Mr. Harkness, there's trouble over the prisoners. Dan and Rob and the others may need help."

Orrin jumped up. "I was afraid something would happen, the way Woolman was talking." He reached into the nearest wagon and pulled out a rifle. He bent down and looked under the wagon. "Get up, Ben. Bring your shotgun."

Rebecca's head popped out between the flaps of a small tent nearby. She blinked. "Elise, is that you? What's happened?"

Orrin and Ben hurried off into the darkness, and Elise tiptoed closer to Rebecca. "I think things will be fine, but some of the men were making a fuss over the prisoners."

"Should we raise a few of the others?"

"I don't think it would hurt. Who else will support the wagon master?"

Rebecca crawled out of the tent. "Well, there's Mr. Libby. He's close by."

They thought of two other men who had always seemed fair minded. After alerting them, Rebecca walked Elise back to her wagon. Anne had poked up the coals enough to heat water for tea.

"I've heard them talking and arguing some"—Anne said, nodding in the direction of the prison wagon—"but nothing that sounded badly out of hand. And I saw your husband and Ben go by. I hope things will settle down soon." She smiled at Rebecca. "May I pour you some tea?"

"Land, if you ladies ain't the beatingest. You know I'll not turn down anything served in a china cup." Rebecca accepted her tea, and they sat down on boxes to talk quietly.

Elise limited herself to one cup of tea and took out her knitting. She'd gotten used to working in near darkness in the evenings, and the second sock was nearly finished.

Fifteen minutes later, Orrin, Ben, and Eb appeared out of the shadows.

"Come on, Becca," Orrin growled. "I reckon we can get some sleep now."

Rebecca stood and handed her cup and saucer to Elise. "Thank you, ladies. I had a delightful time."

"Good night," Elise and Anne called as the Harknesses left.

Eb lingered next to their wagon, and Elise turned to him for news.

"Things should be all right," he said softly.

Elise nodded. "Thank you."

"And you."

"I hope we've heard the last of their nonsense," Anne said. "Elise, I shall retire now."

"Good night, dear." Elise watched her go into the tent and looked back at Eb. "They backed down, then?"

"Right after you left, Josiah came over to our side. When Orrin and Ben showed up, I think that clinched it, but then we got Libby and Bishop, too. You must have told them."

She nodded.

"We owe you and Anne a great debt. Everything calmed down when Woolman and his bunch saw they were solidly outmanned."

"Good. Will you be able to rest tonight?"

"For a while. I'm scheduled to relieve one of the guards in a few hours."

"Go and sleep, then. Come by for breakfast if you can before we break camp."

Eb nodded gravely. "Thank you. And what about you? Will you be able to sleep?"

Elise sighed. "I think I will. I admit I was so worked up that I fretted a bit this evening. But I picked up my knitting while Rebecca was here, and I actually finished my project. Knitting is calming to the nerves."

"That so?" Eb's smile brought a vague yearning to her heart.

"Yes, it is, and I'd like to give you the result, if you're of a mind to take it."

He arched his eyebrows. She went to the rear of the wagon and reached inside for her knitting bag.

"Here you go. Gray woolen socks. They're not perfect, but they'll keep your feet warm in the mountains." She held them out, suddenly nervous. What if he read too much into the gesture—or not enough? She'd used the finest yarn she could find in St. Louis, and the finished product was nothing to be ashamed of. In fact, Anne and Rebecca had praised her work highly as they waited for the men to return.

"I hardly know what to say." Holding the socks close, he inspected them in the dimness. "I allow I could use some new socks. Thank you very much."

She let her breath out. "You're welcome. I was afraid—"

"What?"

"Nothing." Her face flushed, but she hoped he couldn't see it. Eb smiled. "Good night, then."

They stood looking at each other for a long moment. At last he stirred and resettled his hat before turning away.

The wagons rattled on for the next few weeks as they headed north toward the Snake River. More trees lined the trail, and wild game increased. Between Eb and the Adams brothers, Elise and Anne had more meat in their stew pot than they'd had the first half of the journey. Several other families continued to contribute to the prisoners' meals, so Elise and Anne were not unduly burdened.

Eb came by nearly every morning to check on them before the wagons moved out. Sometimes he came early enough to help harness the mules. On other days, he stopped for a minute and spoke to them from the saddle before he rode out to scout. Elise treasured the moments he spent with her—even more those evenings when he sat by their campfire and shared their meal.

Sometimes Rob or Wilbur joined them, and now and again Dan Adams and his brother walked over, but Dan still seemed a bit wary around Anne. Elise wondered if he still hoped she'd change her mind and accept him as a suitor, or if he'd reconciled himself to the generous friendship Anne shared with all the young men. Even

Nick Foster, who was recovering from his wound, and Will Strother vied for the privilege of walking with Anne in the cool mornings, though she was several years older than they were.

Elise was happy with her one admirer. As the miles and the days passed, her heart became firmly attached to Eb Bentley. It worried her mildly, when she allowed herself to think about it. Mostly she told herself how blessed she was to have a dependable man like Eb for a friend.

They'd had the prisoners in custody for nearly three weeks when Eb rode back from scouting late one morning, accompanied by a dozen cavalry troopers. Word soon spread through the company that the troopers were headed for Fort Laramie and would take the prisoners.

Elise sought out Rob and took him aside.

"I've spoken to Anne and Rebecca. We'll collect cold food for a lunch for the prisoners and the troopers if you wish. Or if you want to stop longer, we'll prepare something hot."

"Well, we're trying to work out some details," Rob said. "I guess we should have taken enough mules from Shwartz's stock for the prisoners to ride on."

"Oh dear. I'd offer one of our mules, but Eb tells me we'll need them all in the Blue Mountains."

"You surely will. Don't worry—the lieutenant said he can offer compensation if Harkness will sell him the wagon and team. If not, they have a few packhorses along and may be able to redistribute their supplies. Or maybe some of our other folks will sell their extra mounts."

An hour later the cavalrymen were off with the prisoners riding two of their pack mules and two purchased from the company. The Adams brothers helped the Harkness men repack their three wagons, and Rob blew his horn to alert the travelers to prepare to move.

"I feel so free," Anne said as she hefted their dish box over the wagon's tailboard. "No more cooking for prisoners or worrying about their safety."

"Do you suppose we can remember how to cook for two?" Elise asked.

"Oh, some of the boys will still come around, I expect."

Elise smiled. "Yes, and often as not they bring us something for the kettle." She looked northward, over the beautiful hills. "We're not far from the Snake River. Just think, Anne. In a month, we'll be in Oregon City."

"And we'll find Uncle David."

Elise grasped her hand. "I pray it is so."

That evening Eb didn't get back to camp until dark, and he heard music from a mile away in the still night. As he drew closer, he could see couples dancing by firelight. He took care of Speck and washed his face and hands then wandered over to the revelry.

He sidled up to Hector Adams and watched the dancers bounding about to a lively tune. As usual, when the music stopped, Anne Stone was the center of a flurry of hopeful young men. Mr. Libby began to play another tune, and the couples reformed. The disappointed fellows looked about for available girls while Anne sprang off with Elijah Woolman.

Her choice of partners surprised Eb mildly, but then, Anne never did show partiality among the boys. He was glad she didn't hold it against Elijah that his father had led the men bent on a lynching a few weeks ago.

Hector glanced his way. "Howdy, Eb."

"Hec."

"She's yonder."

"Who?"

"Miss Finster," Hector said. "Who else?"

Eb tried not to smile, but he couldn't help it. He looked where Hector's chin was pointing and spotted Elise a third of the way around the circle of watchers.

"Much obliged." He left Hector and ambled slowly toward her. When he stepped up near her, he could smell her light fragrance.

She must have brought something with her that smelled good. Most days he didn't notice it—they all smelled of smoke and sun and perspiration. Couldn't help it. But sometimes of an evening, he caught a faint whiff of that scent. Lilacs, maybe? Something his mother had grown.

"Good evening, Eb."

"Hello."

She smiled large, and Eb's stomach clenched. Seemed like every night it was more and more important that he see her face.

"You're late getting back tonight," she said.

"I rode on to the river."

"Will we make it tomorrow?"

"The next day, I think."

She nodded, with the sweet smile still hovering on her lips. Should he ask her to dance? He'd like to hold on to her again, to feel her warmth and softness. Dancing allowed him to touch her. But it was so public.

"It's a fine night," she said.

"Yes."

They stood side by side, watching the movement of the dancers. Rob wasn't out there. He must be on guard. Dan Adams was dancing with Lavinia Harkness. She looked about to swoon, she was so happy. Her brother Wilbur cut in on Elijah Woolman and stole Anne right out of his arms.

Eb turned to Elise on impulse. "Would you walk with me?"

Her eyes widened, but she slipped her hand through the bend of his arm.

"I'd be delighted."

He led her quickly away from the circle and out away from the wagons, hoping no one had noticed. When they reached the trail, he slowed his steps and walked languidly with her northward.

After a hundred yards, he started to hear the crickets over the distant fiddling and the drumming of his heart. "I've been thinking a lot," he said.

She stopped walking. "Oh? What about?" The half-moon's light showed him her face, clear as day and dearer than life.

"You," he dared to say.

She caught her breath, and his heart tore off again, fast and loud. He felt it in his throat and wondered if she could feel it where she held his arm. He reached over and enclosed her fingers in his hand.

"Elise, I . . ."

She waited, expectant, maybe a little cautious.

"I sure do think a heap of you."

He saw the surprise in her eyes, quickly replaced by humor.

"That didn't come out very well, did it?" He cleared his throat. "What I mean is, I admire you. A great deal."

"Thank you, Eb. That means a lot to me."

Before he could think too deeply about it, he pulled her into his arms. She didn't resist but raised her hands to his collarbone and up around his neck. He didn't have to bend far to touch his lips to hers. How long had he craved this warm embrace? Since Jeanie died. He held her close, and she hung on to him, not a desperate clinging, but she rested in his arms as though this was her spot, and she belonged.

He released her with a sigh. The stars flared brighter, and the music swirled about them in a slow, dreamy melody.

"I love you," he said.

Her face glowed as she smiled up at him. "And I love you, Edwin Bentley."

He drew her toward him again. She kissed back, and he never wanted to let her go. Finally he lifted his head and held her close against his chest.

"I've got a ranch. It needs a lot of work, but I plan to tear into it this fall. If I thought you'd be there with me . . ."

She stirred and ran her hand lightly up and down his sleeve. Her warm touch tantalized him.

"I don't know what to say."

"Say you'll marry me, Elise. I'm not a wealthy man, but I can take care of you. We can have a good life together."

She exhaled deeply and rested her head against the front of his shirt. They stood for a long time in silence with the crickets chirping. The fiddle broke into a riotous polka and people clapped in time.

"It sounds wonderful," she said at last. "I've always dreamed of having my own home."

"It's a pretty place. I bought the land the first time I made this journey. Didn't have the heart to live there alone at first. My. . .my wife died on the trail. Maybe you knew that."

"No, I didn't." Elise raised her head and looked up at him with glittering eyes.

"Long time ago." He touched her hair and gently pressed her head back onto his shoulder where it belonged now. "Anyway, the next year I built a small house and settled in there. Then I got the barn built. It just took me some time."

"It must have been hard to be alone like that."

"That's pretty much why I kept helping Rob with his business. He likes bringing people west. It gave me a chance to get away from. . .from the memories and the loneliness, I guess. But this is my last wagon train. I'm ready now, and I don't want to keep traveling. Rob's quitting, too. Dulcie wants him to stay put, and I don't blame her."

"I don't really have a choice," Elise said softly. "I'm sorry, Eb. I have an obligation to Anne."

"But once we get to Oregon. . ."

"I don't see how I could leave her until she's found her uncle."

Eb was quiet for a long time. The music stopped, and he could hear some loud talk. The party must be breaking up for the night.

"I pray she'll find David quickly," Elise said. "But until her quest is ended, I am bound to her. You do understand?"

Eb's chest hurt. Slowly he loosened his hold on her and stepped back.

"Sure. I understand."

# CHAPTER 26

Eb didn't come by the wagon the next morning.

Elise went over their conversation in her mind a thousand times. He was hurting, she was sure. But her heart ached, too. That didn't mean she would avoid him.

She made extra coffee, hoping he'd show up before they broke camp, and ended up giving it to the Adams boys. Late that evening, she and Anne unhitched alone. Elise was exhausted from driving most of the day and walking the rest. Anne scrounged a few sticks and made them each a couple of flapjacks, but the fire wasn't hot enough and the cakes were pale and doughy.

"I'm sorry," Anne said. "I should have tried harder to find more wood."

"Never mind. I'm not very hungry."

"I haven't seen Eb all day. He was late last night, too."

"Yes," Elise said.

"But you saw him last night."

Elise pressed her lips together. She wished Anne wouldn't persist.

Wilbur, Ben, and Lavinia Harkness came over, laughing and swinging the family's buckets.

"We're going for some water," Wilbur said. "Want to come?"

Anne hurried to grab a pail. "Yes, thank you. Elise? Coming?"

Elise shook her head. "I'll stay."

"Want your knitting bag?" Anne asked.

"No. I think I'll retire early tonight."

"All right." Anne hesitated. "I'll see you later."

As the young people walked away, Lavinia said, "Is Miss Elise feeling poorly?"

"I think she's just tired," Anne said.

Elise sat in the flickering shadows for a full ten minutes. If she moved, her heart would shatter. At last she forced herself to stand and rake the embers together then cover them with ashes. She glanced around the little camp. The coffeepot sat on a rock by the fire, where she'd left it when Hector brought it back. Other than that, all their belongings were in the wagon or the tent.

She went to the little tent and crawled inside. In the pitch darkness, she removed her dress, stockings, and corset. She took down her hair and lay down on her bedroll.

What had she done?

Eb was a good, kind man, and she loved him. Had she flung away her one chance at a happy life?

*No*, she told herself. *I can be happy with Anne.*

Tears rolled down her cheeks. She scrubbed them away with the backs of her hands. She closed her eyes and sobbed.

*Lord, I love him. I can't stop. So is this the way I'll feel for the rest of my life? Please take away the hurt. I'd rather not have loved him than to feel this way.*

She remembered his kisses. Putting a finger to her lips, she knew the pain was worth it. And yet... She buried her damp face in the pillow slip and hoped her spasms of weeping would pass before Anne returned.

*✺*

"Send it by ship," said the quartermaster at Fort Dalles. "That's the surest way this time of year."

Thomas G. Costigan scowled at him. "By ship? That will take months. And what if the ship goes down?"

The quartermaster shrugged. "If you send it overland, it won't reach New York until next spring. Maybe high summer. And the shipping route is quite reliable now. If it's a really important message, you might want to do both. One is bound to get through."

"That would be expensive." Thomas considered his limited resources. How important was it that he get a message to Peterson, anyway? He supposed he wouldn't be paid until he got back East.

Why not just go on to the Willamette Valley, finish the job, and then report in person? He could hop a ship as fast as he could put a letter on one.

He slapped the desk and straightened.

"Well?" asked the quartermaster.

"Changed my mind. Thank you."

Thomas walked out onto the parade ground and looked over the town below him and the Columbia River beyond. He didn't need any more instruction or communication. It didn't matter whether the two women had given up or continued their journey. He just needed to get on down to Oregon City before Rob Whistler's wagon train came through and make sure David Stone was dead— one way or another.

For nearly two weeks, the company progressed slowly to the Snake River and then along its winding banks. Eb never came to their wagon. Most days, he was gone as long as the daylight lasted. Any news was relayed by Rob.

Anne confronted Elise one morning as they moved into line behind Abe Leonard.

"What happened between you and Eb?"

"Why do you think anything did?" Elise asked. She'd begun knitting again, but not socks this time. She was determined to produce a knitted jumper for the baby Josiah Redman's wife was expecting.

"I haven't seen him in ages. Up, you!" Anne slapped Bumper and Challenger with the reins then turned to gaze at Elise. "I thought he liked us, and I know *I* didn't quarrel with him."

Elise's cheeks grew warm. "We didn't quarrel."

"Then what?"

After several seconds of silence, Anne reached over and clasped one of Elise's hands. "Tell me, dear. I know you care for him, and you've been dragging around camp for a fortnight. It's depressing to see you so unhappy."

Elise gasped an involuntary sob. Tears sprang into her eyes.

"Oh dear." Anne produced a fine handkerchief, still pretty and soft despite their harsh laundry conditions.

Elise dabbed at her eyes. "Thank you. I daresay it won't seem like much to you, since you've had so many marriage proposals—"

"Only four," Anne said. "Well, five if you count Wilbur's second one. But from four gentlemen."

Elise smiled though she didn't feel like it. "Darling, that's splendid. Haven't you given any of them serious consideration?"

"I don't see how I could, not knowing what my future holds. Do you?"

"No." Elise faltered and gazed down at the ball of wool in her lap. "No, I don't. And that's just what I told Eb."

"You told—oh Elise." Anne lowered her hands and the reins. Her shoulders sagged.

"Here now, you're letting the mules slow down." Elise reached for the whip.

Anne sat up and adjusted the reins. She took the whip from Elise but didn't use it.

"So, he proposed to you."

Elise nodded.

"The night of the last dancing?"

"Yes."

"I was so happy for you that night. He kept you out late, walking in the moonlight."

Elise sighed. "It started out a happy time. But I had to tell him."

"Tell him what?"

"That I couldn't."

Anne was quiet for a minute, watching the mules. "You wanted to say yes."

Elise's lips trembled so that she couldn't answer. She sniffed and raised the handkerchief to her eyes.

Anne looked over at her. "My dearest Elise, I'm so sorry! You must tell him you were mistaken."

"How can I?"

"You mean because he's nowhere to be found, or because you were not mistaken?"

For some reason, this question made Elise's tears spill faster. To her surprise, she saw that Anne was crying, too.

"Anne, do you think you could love Dan Adams?"

Anne arched her eyebrows then shook her head. "I...don't think so. Not that way, though he's a very good man. And Wilbur is a dear. But no, I don't think I want to marry either of them. Wilbur's not settled enough in his character. And as to the others, why Mr. Shelley is too old, and Wally is just a boy."

Elise managed a watery smile. "You've quite a litany of suitors. But I agree on all of them, except possibly Dan."

"Perhaps if things were different. With Uncle David, I mean. But I never aspired to marry a farmer, you know."

"Yes, I know." Though a quiet farm life sounded alluring to Elise, Anne had become quite adventurous, and her youthful spirit would want variety and a bit of unpredictability. "This trip should have soured you on travel and adventure, but I can't see that it has."

"Quite the opposite," Anne said. "I'm ready to dive into it with Uncle David, if he's willing."

Elise nodded. "That would be lovely for you. You'd have his protection."

"And you could marry Eb and go off to become ranchers."

Anne's eager smile almost drew Elise into her fairy tale, but she knew it couldn't be. "We must find your uncle." *And by then, Eb will have forgotten me,* she thought.

"You mustn't throw away what he's offering because of me," Anne said earnestly.

Elise feared no answer would satisfy her. As she tried to find an explanation that could not be argued against, Rob cantered up on Bailey and slowed to pace the horse with Elise's mules. They had veered off westward from the Snake, where a sweeping bend curved the river northward.

"Say good-bye to the Snake, Miss Elise. That's the Farewell Bend. We'll see it no more."

"So we're heading into the mountains now."

"Yes. The Blue Mountains. Beautiful, but treacherous."

He cantered off up the line. Elise gazed over at the winding river.

"We're nearing the end of the trail," Anne said.

"Yes. But they say the hardest part is yet to come." They rode on in silence, each deep in her own thoughts. Parting from Eb would be the most difficult part of this entire adventure, Elise mused. But he had already begun the separation. Could it be any worse than this? Anne might open the subject again if she looked at her, and so when Elise could no longer see the river, she looked straight ahead.

The Blue Mountains proved worthy of their reputation. Eb stayed with the company more, as the people worked together to get every wagon up each brutal slope and down the other side. Some families combined the strength of their livestock, double-teaming and even triple-teaming their wagons upward.

Elise and Anne's six mules managed, after they'd jettisoned another of Anne's trunks, a few more clothes, three books they'd both read several times, and one of their kettles. They took turns walking up the inclines, so that the team had only one of them to pull.

Eb and Rob seemed to be everywhere, giving advice, throwing their shoulders to the load when needed, and helping repair wagons that were damaged in the cruel passage.

And yet Eb never came near. Elise saw him at dawn one morning with Anne, carrying an armful of wood for her. But he stopped and passed the bundle to Anne before they came within hailing distance. He wouldn't place himself where Elise could speak to him, or where he couldn't avoid greeting her without being rude. Her chest tightened and she clenched her teeth. She turned her back as Anne approached with the wood and prayed for grace.

Anne dropped the sticks and began to build up the fire. Elise filled the kettle with water, not speaking. She got out dishes and bacon and cornmeal for mush.

"I saw Eb," Anne said when she took the kettle from the grate fifteen minutes later.

"Did you?" No matter how she tried, Elise couldn't feign disinterest with Anne.

"I asked him plainly why he stays away."

"Oh."

Anne turned and faced her with brooding brown eyes. "He said you wouldn't have him, and he doesn't wish to distress you by hanging about."

"Hanging about?" Elise set the kettle down with a thump that slopped a little hot water. "Is that what he calls it? I'd thought he was courting me." She sobbed and realized how ridiculous that sounded, when she had abruptly ended the courtship. Hanging about indeed.

"Well, yes." Anne had tears in her eyes as she walked to Elise and placed her arms around her. "Dear Elise. I know you love him."

"So does he. I told him so." Elise sniffed and pulled away. "Excuse me."

She went to the tent and blew her nose. Hastily she rolled up their bedding and set it and their satchels outside.

Anne had their breakfast plates ready, and Elise accepted hers.

"Thank you. We can strike the tent as soon as we finish."

The journey to the Columbia and Fort Dalles stretched out, uneventful yet full of everyday crises. Elise did what she did best— she coped. Scorched food could be salvaged, torn clothing mended, and broken straps could be sewn. Her heart was another matter. She'd pined over David Stone for many years, imagining herself heartbroken, but she had never imagined the pain she felt now.

When they struck the river, ten wagons left them. The owners had decided to ferry down the Columbia to Vancouver. The rest were bound for Oregon City by way of the Mount Hood Toll Road, Barlow's route. Rob's tales of the dangers to come scared Elise a bit. Yet they'd come through so much she felt she ought to have more confidence. They were tough now. They could deal with what lay ahead.

Eb stood at the edge of Summit Meadows, his head bowed and his hat in his hand. After several minutes, he went to his knees in the long grass. He prayed silently, tears running down his cheeks and into his beard stubble. The wind blowing through the pass had a bite to it. He hoped snow wouldn't arrive before the wagon train.

After a long time, he got up and went to where he'd tied Speck. He took his coat from the back of the saddle and pulled it on. He would camp tonight near Jeanie's grave. He always did when he came across the Barlow Road. It had cost him a dollar to ride through with Speck. The wagons' owners would pay five dollars each. It was worth it though, to avoid the perils of the Columbia in autumn. So long as the wagons didn't crash, that was.

He inhaled carefully and tried not to think about the chute on Laurel Hill. Every year he dreaded going there. He hated snubbing wagons down the chute. Every year he told Rob he wouldn't do it again. Rob could go without him. But he'd only stayed away one year—that first year after he lost Jeanie.

One thing was for certain—if Elise's wagon was going down Laurel Hill, he'd be there to make sure it landed safely at the bottom. He fumbled in his saddle bag with chilled hands for his gloves and pulled out the socks she'd knitted for him. He stared down at them. This would be a good time to start wearing them.

He carried his gloves and the gray woolen socks to a stump and sat down. He used the toe of his right boot to lever off the left one. Peeling down his worn sock, he scowled at the hole in the heel. The new ones were so fine, he almost hated putting them on.

"Hey!"

He jerked his head up and listened. Was it just the wind, or had he really heard a shout?

Nothing. Maybe it wasn't a human shout. Maybe there was a catamount in these parts.

He put the boot back on and pulled off the right one. He'd just got it back in place, solidly on his foot, and picked up the ragged socks he'd discarded when he heard it again.

"Help!"

Now, that was human.

He dropped the socks and hurried toward the trail, where he stopped and listened.

"Hello," he shouted.

"Hey!"

It wasn't very loud, but it came from the other side of the trail, where the ground dropped off perilously. He hurried over the wagon ruts and through the tall weeds. At the edge of the precipice, he looked down.

"Anybody down there?"

"Help me!"

"Where are you?" he called, scanning the rocks and brush below.

"Here!"

A bush moved, off to his right and at least fifty feet down. Eb caught his breath. A buckskin horse was lying motionless on its side near the sheer wall, about five yards from the bushes. It would be a difficult climb down. How on earth would he get the fellow up?

"I need to find a path down."

The bush moved again, but the man didn't reply.

Eb dashed back to Speck and took his rope from the saddle. He wasn't sure it was long enough to get him over the cliff, and he surely couldn't carry a man up a rope. He led Speck across the meadow.

"Come on, boy. We've got to find a safe way down that drop."

It took him twenty minutes to find a place where he was certain he could get down without losing his footing. He tied Speck at the top and shouldered the coil of rope and his canteen. He checked his revolver and knife and headed down.

A harrowing climb down brought him into the ravine he'd surveyed. He picked his way over rocks, brush, and debris toward where he thought the man lay.

He spotted the dead horse first and headed for the bushes nearby.

"I'm here."

A bush shimmied, and Eb walked forward.

"You hurt bad?" He drew his pistol, just on principle.

"My leg's busted," the man gasped. "Can you get me out of here? I've been down here three days. Maybe four."

"I'll sure try." Eb parted the bushes and stared down into the strained face of Thomas G. Costigan.

# CHAPTER 27

Elise drove when they left Fort Dalles, and Anne walked most of the morning with some of the other women. The desolate, arid land they crossed held no appeal for the emigrants. All were eager to push on to the lush Willamette Valley they'd heard so much about.

Rob's horse came trotting along the line, and Elise seized the rare chance to speak privately with the wagon master.

"Mr. Whistler!"

"Yes, ma'am."

"I haven't seen Eb for several days now."

Rob's face fell into grave lines. "No, he's gone on ahead."

"Doesn't he every day?"

"Mostly, but we won't see him for a while now."

"I don't understand," she said.

Rob pulled his hat off, wiped his brow, and settled the hat on his head again. "We're nearing the place where Jeanie died."

"Ah."

Jeanie. Elise had never heard her name before, but she didn't have to ask who Jeanie was. Even Rob spoke the name with reverence.

"What happened to her, if I may ask?"

"You may. There's a place coming up. Not for a few days, but it's a very steep grade going down a mountain. We'll have to snub the wagon wheels to trees and lower them with ropes down a chute of sorts."

Elise stared at him. "You mean—?"

"Eb didn't want her to drive, but she insisted she could do it if he and the other men tended the ropes." Rob shook his head. "The rope gave way, and their wagon crashed on down the slope. Jeanie . . . Jeanie was killed instantly. At least she didn't suffer."

"He told me she died on the trail, but I had no idea."

"It was pretty bad," Rob said.

"And they were so close to their destination."

"Yes." He sighed. "We don't try to drive wagons down there anymore. It's one of my rules. We rope them all down, with no people inside." He looked ahead toward the mountains. "Eb will be there when we need him. But every trip he goes on alone and camps near that place. I expect he spends some time at her graveside."

Elise drew in a shaky breath. What had she done to Eb, turning him down when he was so near this emotion-filled place? It must have taken great courage for him to declare himself to her, knowing he'd have to pass his wife's grave soon.

"Oh dear," she whispered.

Rob eyed her keenly. "Are you all right, Miss Elise?"

She couldn't lie, but if she said no, he would feel he needed to do something to help her. She gazed at him, unable to speak.

"He told me about your conversation the night of the dancing," Rob said quietly.

Elise looked down at her hands, holding the reins. "I've been cruel to him."

"That's not the way he sees it. He said you were being kind to Anne—being a mother when she has none of her own. He thought that was upstanding of you."

"Did he?" Her voice caught. "I thought he was angry with me."

"No, ma'am. Don't think that. He is grieving a bit though. For you, I mean."

They rode along, and Rob didn't flit off to check on another wagon. Elise decided he had more on his mind, and she was right.

"This is the first time I've seen him take to a woman since Jeanie died," Rob said. "I had hopes that you'd marry him. Eb needs a good woman by his side."

Her cheeks felt warmer than the cool sun of September warranted. "I also had hopes, sir. And yet, I can't help feeling it was wrong of me to raise his expectations."

"Now don't go all guilt ridden on us. You know where God wants you. Right now, it's on this wagon train. And if we get to the end of the trail and you feel He still wants you with Miss Anne, then that's where you should be. Neither Eb nor I would fault you for that."

"But I've disappointed him horribly."

"Yes."

She wished he hadn't agreed so readily. The heaviness that had plagued her since she'd rejected Eb pushed down on her now, so weighty she thought it might crush her lungs.

"Let the Lord work things out," Rob said.

"That's sound advice."

He nodded and touched his hat brim. "Good day, Miss Elise." He urged his mare into a trot and rode up the line of wagons. Elise settled in to watch the mules. They were climbing, and ahead lay the forested slopes of the Cascades.

"Dear God, whatever You want for me, I'll accept," she whispered. "Just please, don't let me be the one to leave Eb heartbroken by the trail again."

Thomas was hanging over a cliff, tied to a framework of tree limbs. Eb Bentley thought he could get him up over the rim of the drop-off by having his horse pull the travois contraption up. It had seemed like a reasonable idea at the time, but now it seemed insane. Every step that horse took raised him higher off the bottom of the ravine and shook the travois until Thomas was sure it would go to pieces. Pain lanced through his leg and up his entire body.

They must be almost to the top. He could hear Eb talking to the horse.

"Easy, Speck. Just a little more."

The strain on the rope increased, pulling the branches up and away from the edge. Thomas ground his teeth together to keep from screaming. He was helpless, strapped to this thing. A moan escaped through his teeth.

Eb said something low to the horse. All movement stopped, with Thomas suspended vertically over the edge, fifty feet above his dead horse.

"You all right, Costigan?" Eb yelled.

"Yeah. Just get on with it."

Eb's horse snuffled, and the frame shivered again. It inched upward, a bit at a time, then a big jump. At last it crashed backward, and Thomas was lying on his aching back, staring up at the sky and gasping for breath. The pain in his leg nauseated him.

"Good boy." Footsteps approached and then Eb was beside him. "Costigan? You with me?"

"Yeah. Lost my hat."

"I ain't going to get it."

"Didn't think you would. Just get me off these sticks."

"I'll have Speck pull you over to my camp spot first."

Thomas swore. Eb had used another short rope, his dead horse's reins, and both their belts to secure him to the travois, and he wanted nothing better than to have the straps removed.

Eb walked away and made some adjustments to the rope. He lifted the ends of the branches so that Thomas's head was higher than his feet. Excruciating pain washed over him.

"My leg!"

Eb lowered the travois to the ground. "Sorry about that. We'll have to drag you over the ground. That'll be rough."

"Can't you just camp here?"

"Too close to the edge."

Before they'd gone ten yards, Thomas let himself fall into blackness.

When he woke up, stars shone overhead. He heard snapping and turned his head. Eb was crouched near a small campfire.

"Musta passed out," Thomas muttered.

"Good thing we splinted your leg before I moved you, I reckon." Eb raked at his fire and set a small coffeepot on the coals. "If nobody comes along by morning, I'll take you down off this mountain. Don't want to, but I will if I have to."

Costigan grunted. How long would it take to get him to the nearest house? He was sure Eb wouldn't take him farther than that.

"You still with the wagon train?" Thomas asked.

"Yup. They'll be here day after tomorrow."

"Why'n't you just keep me here until they come?"

"Oh no." Eb opened a little cloth bag and peered into it. Coffee, Thomas surmised. "Your leg's bad. I looked at it while you were unconscious. Other than that, I'd say it's mostly bruises. But you need to see a doctor—someone who can set it right, or you might never walk on it again."

Thomas grimaced.

"Be thankful you didn't break your neck," Eb said. "Look, I've got jerky and some crackers and a couple of biscuits. I'll make us some coffee. Wish I had something to kill the pain for you, but I don't."

Thomas nodded. "I appreciate it, Bentley." A cool breeze blew over him and he shivered. "You got a blanket?"

"Yeah. I brought your bedroll and saddlebags up earlier." He walked out of the small circle of firelight and returned a moment later with a dark wool blanket. He draped it gently over Thomas.

"All right?"

"Yup." Thomas didn't tell him how even the weight of the blanket made his leg scream with pain. What was the use?

"I'll tell you now," Eb said, "I'm turning you over to the law."

"What for?" Thomas knew he was at Eb's mercy, but it didn't seem fair.

"Where should I start? Horse stealing?"

Thomas said nothing.

"And then there's the little matter of Mr. Stone."

"What about him?"

"I figure you heard about him in Independence from conversations between Miss Stone and Miss Finster. Just bits and pieces, but everywhere they went, they were asking about him. You got curious and followed them. You signed on with them under false pretenses—told them I'd recommended you, but I hadn't. And somehow you came to understand that Miss Anne's uncle might be worth some money. You stole her letter to see if you could piece together the story."

Well, he had it partly right. Thomas closed his eyes and tried not to think about the pain.

"At first I thought you were just a petty thief looking for an opportunity. But you made a mistake at Schwartzburg."

"What was that?" Thomas asked.

"More than one mistake, actually. First, you told Schwartz about Miss Stone. Bad business. Schwartz is slipperier than a greased eel. Then you got him to help you try to convince Miss Anne her uncle was dead. You hoped she'd turn back so you could find David Stone on your own."

He was close to the truth. But Bentley thought he was on his own mission and had no clue about Peterson.

"Then there's Rob's horse. Taking that mare was a big mistake. We might have overlooked it if you'd stolen a mule. Not one of the wagon master's horses." Eb came over and held out a piece of jerky. "Can you eat?"

"I'm starving." Thomas took the jerky and held it to his mouth. He wasn't sure he had the strength to take a bite.

Eb sat down and chomped off a piece of his own strip. He chewed for a minute. "You wanted to get to Stone before anybody else did. I'm not sure how that would help you. Not yet, but I'll figure it out. I mean, David Stone doesn't have any money to speak of. Not now."

Thomas chewed on the tough jerky until it began to soften. Just let him talk. Maybe he'd reveal something useful.

Eb froze with his strip of meat partway to his mouth. He sat perfectly still for a moment then scowled down at Thomas.

"You were going to kill him, weren't you? Because he might not be worth anything right now, but to somebody he's worth a whole lot if he's dead."

# CHAPTER 28

Eb stood on the mountainside, watching the wagon train approach. The sun was still low behind them, barely peeking over the next row of hills. The oxen looked as small as mice. He could easily pick out Elise and Anne's wagon by ticking off the teams in the order they always used, minus the families who had left them at The Dalles. Between Abe Leonard, with his ox team, and the Adams boys with their two wagons, were the ladies and their six-mule team.

It was going to be hard seeing her again, but he wouldn't let anyone else take her over this mountain. He thought about riding down to meet them, but he hated to make Speck climb back up here again.

Instead he walked back to his camping spot. Speck grazed in the meadow. The pinto had had a good rest and plenty to eat the last few days, without having to fight for it. Eb went to the fire pit and poured the bottom half of his morning coffee into his tin cup. He'd cut it close on provisions. Hadn't counted on having to feed Costigan for a day. But he'd have something good tonight, he was sure. The ladies on the first few wagons down the chute would start baking for the men who would work long into the night.

He felled a couple of medium-sized trees at the top of chute to use as drag anchors behind the wagons and hiked back to his lookout. The wagons were much closer now, nearly to the steepest part of the upgrade. He left his gear at the campsite and headed down the mountain, carrying only his rifle.

Rob spotted him and waved his hat. Eb raised his hand and went on down. Landon Clark's wagon was first in line, with a double team of oxen. Rob was checking over the wheel hubs and fittings as Eb approached.

"I think you'll be all right, Landon. We'll get you up, let all the cattle rest awhile, then bring them back down to take the Binchleys' wagon up."

"Where do you need me most?" Eb asked.

"I'm still trying to convince Mrs. Libby to lighten her load. And Dan and Hector won't give up any of their tools. They're both planning to pack a few loads up on their backs, but still. . ."

"We could use them better to help other people."

"I know, but they think they've pared down to the barest necessities. Oh, and the Redmans and Strothers are going to double up their teams. They might need help."

Eb gazed down the line of wagons and nodded.

"They're number twelve today," Rob said.

Eb didn't have to ask who. He'd already figured that out from his lookout. He'd have to pass Elise and Anne's wagon to get to Josiah Redman's.

Anne was inside the wagon, handing a wooden box down to Elise. Eb sprang forward and took it from her.

Elise stared at him with eyes big and round. They were bluer than the tranquil sky above. He couldn't look away.

"Eb."

"Elise."

"We missed you." She looked down then, her coral lips pressed into a thin line.

"Thanks. Where do you want this stuff?"

"Anywhere. We'll likely leave it."

He glanced at the contents. Another kettle, four china cups and saucers, two more books, five pounds or so of bacon, and something made of green cloth.

"I'm sorry."

She shrugged. "We cooked up a lot of bacon last night and gave away most of it."

"Wish I'd had some yesterday."

She smiled at that. "I'm glad you're back."

With the six mules pulling and Anne driving, Elise got behind the wagon and pushed, with four strong men helping.

"Go on, Miss Elise," Hector Adams said, scowling at her as he shoved his shoulder against the frame below the tailboard.

"I'll do my bit, so long as I'm able."

They'd agreed that morning—Elise would drive up the first part of the slope, and Anne would walk. Anne took the reins halfway up. It took three hours in all to get up the mountain. When they finally reached the crest, Elise flopped against a tall fir near the trail and panted, not caring if she ever stood again.

"Elise, dear, eat this."

She opened her eyes. Anne hovered over her with a cup of water and a slab of johnnycake.

"Have you looked down the chute?" Elise asked.

"Not yet." Anne's face betrayed her anxiety.

Elise took the cup and the cornbread. "Thank you. Get some for yourself."

Eb found them a few minutes later. He hunkered down beside them and cast a critical eye over both women. "We'll take your wagon down in about ten minutes."

Elise set down her cup and arranged her skirts so she could rise modestly. "I'll help."

"No, the other men and I will take it down. There's a path you ladies can walk down that's away from where we'll be working. It's steep, but you should be all right if you go slow and help each other. You can take your tinderbox if you want and go down to the meadow and start a cook fire. When we bring you your wagon, you'll have a nice bed of coals ready for baking."

Elise met his gaze steadily. "What about the mules? I can drive the team down."

"You will not." He spoke quietly, but he stared down at her with eyes of steel.

Elise's heart tripped. Was this too much like the conversation he'd had with Jeanie a few years back? She drew in a deep breath. "All right."

He held the gaze a moment longer then nodded. "Thank you." He glanced over at Anne. "Might as well tell you ladies now. Some freighters came through here yesterday."

"They passed us on the trail," Anne said. "Seemed in a big hurry, and they muddied the water at the creek."

"They're a brash bunch," Eb said. "But they seemed like honest men. I...entrusted them with a man I'd found injured near the trail."

"An injured man?" Elise asked. "What happened?"

"His horse went off the edge of a bluff in the dark. His leg was broken." Eb hesitated and added, "It was Thomas G. Costigan."

Anne gasped.

"Thomas?" Elise eyed Eb closely.

"Yup. He said he'd been lying there three or four days when I came along. Heard him yelling. I got him up to my camp. Those freighters came the next day, and I asked them to get him to a doctor if they could. They had a ledger, and they let me use a sheet of paper from it to write out a letter to Marshal Nesmith in Oregon City. They'll give it to him when they get there. I put in it what I know about Costigan, and what I suspect."

"What do you suspect?" Elise asked.

Eb gritted his teeth and looked at Anne. "I believe he was out to murder your uncle."

"What?" Anne's face went white.

Elise reached for her hand. "Why would he do that?"

"Well, I don't like to say it or even think it, but you told me once that if David Stone was proved dead, somebody else in England would profit."

Elise and Anne stared at each other.

"It's true," Elise said. "But how—"

"I don't know how, but Costigan was going to get something out of it. He'd told Schwartz he'd get paid to fool you two into giving up hunting for Stone, didn't he?"

"Something along those lines."

Eb nodded. "I think someone paid Costigan to find out if Stone was still alive, and if so to. . .to change that."

"It makes me ill to think of it," Elise said.

"It makes *me* furious." Anne balled her hands into fists. "Are you sure he won't get away again?"

"His leg was busted up pretty bad, and I think infection had set in. But I put all I knew down on the paper and impressed on the freighting captain that it was vital to get that to the marshal."

"Thank you," Elise said.

"Just doing what seemed right. Maybe the marshal can make him tell who really employed him." Eb stood. "Now, let's get your wagon ready. We'll tie four ropes to the frame and loop them around trees. Four men will let the ropes out slow. Shouldn't be any problems."

Elise swallowed hard. Suddenly she was sure she didn't want to watch. She was glad Eb had given her other instructions.

"Let's get a few things out of the back, Anne. We'll go down and bake some biscuits."

After a harrowing descent along a rudely blazed path through the woods, they came into a pleasant meadow where the first eight wagons were already aligned to make the beginnings of a circle. Anne carried their tinderbox, mixing bowl, and a jar of sourdough starter in a bucket, while Elise brought the flour and other ingredients for their biscuits in a sack. They hurried to Mrs. Foster, who had a fire going.

"There's good water not far away, ladies," Mrs. Foster called.

They left their supplies near the Fosters' wagon and hurried along another path, to the little stream spilling down over the rocks.

"You need to speak to Eb tonight," Anne said as they started back to the camp.

"What about? Thomas?"

"No. About your future."

Elise pulled up and stared at her. "Whatever do you mean?"

"You need to tell him that you'll marry him as soon as we locate

Uncle David—which I've no doubt we'll do within a few days. Thanks to Thomas's accident, I expect we'll find him in good health."

"We've no assurance—"

Anne cut her off with a sweep of her hand. "No, we've none whatsoever, but if God wills, you and Eb Bentley can have a happy life together. The sooner you tell him that, the better."

"But, my dear! What will you do?"

"Do? Why, go back to Stoneford with Uncle David of course. While I shall miss you, my heart will warm each time I think of you and Eb on your ranch. And you will write me long, news-filled letters, telling me about the cattle and the weather and what you've baked for your husband's dinner."

"I can't just go and tell him. . .that."

"And why not? If you need a little assistance, I could tell him for you. Elise, you love him. This is your chance for happiness. Don't let him go off again without knowing you'll have him. Please don't do that to him."

<hr />

Eb came into camp with the Harkness men, driving their last wagon—the small one that had been their prison wagon. Elise watched as they maneuvered into place and completed the circle. The boys who had been guarding the livestock bustled to help them close the gaps.

Anne came to stand beside her, holding Elise's shawl.

"Go tell him. I'll have a plate of hot beans and biscuits ready when you bring him here after."

"But—"

"No buts." Anne laid a hand on her arm. "Don't fail me, Elise."

Elise frowned at her. Their relationship had changed so drastically in the last six months that she knew she could argue with her mistress now, and she could probably browbeat Anne until she won. But she didn't want to.

She walked toward the Harkness camp, around the big circle. The men were still unhitching the teams.

"I've got everything ready," Rebecca shouted.

"Good, 'cause we're hungry," Orrin said.

Elise sneaked past him and Ben as they worked on the first team of mules. Wilbur saw her as she passed him and called, "Hello!"

Elise nodded to him but didn't stop. Eb was peeling the harness off the last team. She stood back for a moment, watching his swift, efficient movements. When he turned away with the harness in his arms, he spotted her and stopped in his tracks.

"Evening."

"Hello." She stepped forward. "May I speak to you?"

"Certainly." He took the harness to the wagon and bundled it inside. When he faced her, he offered his arm. "Shall I take you back to your wagon, or would you like to take a shortcut?"

She smiled at that. There was no shorter way to her wagon than the way she'd come, unless they went directly across the circle seething with oxen and mules.

"Is there such a thing as a long-cut?"

"I think we could find one."

They walked away from the wagons, toward the verge of the forest. She pulled her shawl close without releasing his arm. It felt good to be near him again, to be touching him and knowing he enjoyed it.

His pinto was picketed near the edge of the meadow. Nearby, a fire pit held cold ashes, and a small pile of gear lay tumbled on the grass.

"Rob and I are camping here. Care for a chair?"

Eb steered her toward a fallen log. She sat down, careful to leave him plenty of space, and he sat beside her.

"What can I do for you?"

She drew a deep breath and gazed out over the sloping meadow. "It's lovely here."

"That it is."

"I imagine it's even more beautiful in the valley." She sneaked a glance at him. Eb was watching her intently. "I want to stay here in Oregon, Eb." She held her breath.

His eyes widened, and he reached over to enclose her hand in both of his. "You mean that?"

"Yes."

He squeezed her hand.

"If you can just wait a little bit until I deliver Anne to Mr. Stone, why then. . ."

"You'll marry me?" he asked softly.

She nodded, unable to trust her voice.

"I know you can't leave her yet," he said.

"But you'll wait? You won't forget me or. . .or be angry?"

"The only thing I'll be is waiting. When you say the word, I'll be there."

"Oh Eb, I love you."

He pulled her into his embrace, and she squeezed him. He smelled of pitch and sweat and horses, but she didn't care.

"If it takes awhile, I'll be getting the ranch into shape," he said. "Just let me know."

"I will."

He kissed her, and Elise let him hold her for a long time before she remembered her instructions.

"Oh! Anne is fixing our dinner."

He didn't move. "There's one more thing."

"What?" She didn't want to leave their spot either, although she felt vaguely wicked for staying out here with Eb.

"What will you do if her uncle has passed away?"

Elise sighed. "I refuse to think about that."

"But you should."

She pulled away from him. "I don't know. I suppose I'll try to talk her into staying with us—if you're agreeable to that."

"I am."

She smiled. "Thank you. That means a lot."

He pulled her back against his shoulder. She rested her head against him for a moment.

"We really should go."

"Huh." Eb stroked her hair. "It's a tough choice. Of course, I haven't had much of a meal for three days now."

Elise laughed and stood, brushing her skirt into place. "Come, Mr. Bentley. You need to keep up your strength."

She took his arm and walked with him toward the wagons.

Eb sniffed. "Somebody's burning something."

"Likely it's Anne."

"I expect you're right."

# CHAPTER 29

Oregon City knelt on the eastern bank of the Willamette River, beckoning to Elise's heart like paradise. After six months on the trail, sleeping in the little tent and eating the plainest of provisions, caring for their mules, and driving the wagon over every inch of the inhospitable trail, she and Anne had arrived.

"I can scarcely believe it," Anne said, clutching her hat with one hand as though it would fly off and sail onward to the Pacific. "We've done it, Elise!"

"Yes, we have. Now we've only one more task to accomplish."

They were twentieth in line, more than halfway back on their depleted train. Anne leaned out to the side, gulping in the sight of the businesses and solidly built houses that made up the town.

"Rob said this was the first city incorporated west of the Mississippi," Elise said.

"The Mississippi—that crossing seems like another life."

Elise smiled. "It was. We're pioneer women now, not the two fine ladies who left England last spring."

Anne's musical laugh burbled out, lifting Elise's spirits to new heights. "I wouldn't trade this journey for anything. When Uncle David and I get back to London, we'll be the most popular party guests in town."

"Everyone will want to hear your tales." Elise had let the team slow as she scanned the signboards on the shops. She snapped the reins on the wheelers' rumps to make them quicken their pace and close the distance between them and Mr. Leonard's wagon.

Eb rode up beside Elise. "The store Mr. Stone kept is on the next street. Turn right up yonder. Folks filing land claims will keep on going straight. I'll show you where you want to be though."

"Oh dear, I haven't said good-bye to everyone." Anne's stricken face mirrored Elise's confusion.

They'd camped ten miles out last night, and everyone had visited other people's campfires, jolly and hopeful for the morrow. Elise had learned how to send letters to families who had no address as yet. The Harknesses hoped to settle near Oregon City and would pick up mail sent to them there in care of general delivery. The Adams boys had plans for farming near Champoeg, twelve miles to the south. The Libbys hoped to join their son and his family up the Clackamas River.

But still, she'd expected somehow that they would all be together one last time, not flake off one by one as the train progressed.

"Where will you and Rob be?" she asked.

"I'll stick with you for a while," Eb said. "Rob will go as far as the land claims office to help anyone who needs it. After you ladies are settled, I'll go and find him and help out wherever I'm needed. But I hope to leave for my ranch by tomorrow."

Elise's heart dropped. Eb would leave them, and she and Anne would be alone again. Unless they found David. And then?

"You've got my instructions on how to find me," Eb said.

She nodded. His ranch was south of Oregon City, a few miles outside the flourishing town of Corvallis. He and Rob had both bought land there several years back. She could send Eb a message at Corvallis, or make her way up the river to that town. But the prospect of doing that alone after so long with the close-knit wagon company frightened her.

Eb's eyes narrowed. "You send me word, and I'll come back here for you."

She nodded, her mouth so dry she couldn't speak.

He reached out and touched her shoulder just for a moment. "All right, here's where you turn off. I'll go ahead and scout you a spot near the haberdashery—six mules and a schooner need space."

He and Speck trotted off and rounded the corner.

"Gee," Elise called. She tugged on the reins, pulling the mules' heads to the right. The leaders swung around, and the swing team and wheelers followed.

"Good-bye! Good-bye!" Anne shouted, leaning far out over the side of the seat, so she could wave to the Adams brothers. "Thank you! You, too!"

She settled back beside Elise and smoothed down her skirt. "I shall miss them."

"Yes." Elise glanced at her. Anne was dabbing at her eyes with a handkerchief. "Are you sorry you let Dan get away?"

"No. I don't think so." She sighed.

Buggies, farm wagons, pack mules, and saddle horses filled the street. Elise guided the mules while trying to keep track of Speck's brown-and-white rump ahead of them. Footsteps pounded up from behind, and Ben Harkness's head appeared on Anne's side of the wagon.

"Ma said to give you this!" He thrust something into Anne's hand.

"Oh, thank you," Anne said. "Give her my best."

"And remember, if you ladies need anything, we won't be far away."

"Bless you, Ben," Elise called.

Anne leaned out over the street again and waved. "Good-bye!"

Elise squinted ahead. "I've lost Eb."

"He can't be far." Anne unrolled the cloth Ben had given her. "Oh, look. It's one of Rebecca's knitted dishcloths."

Elise glanced over at it. "She was knitting that last night, bless her heart." Ahead, one of the larger buildings sported a sign reading VALLEY MERCANTILE.

"That must be it." As she spoke, she glimpsed Speck. Eb was still in the saddle, waving to her.

The mules lumbered past the store, which seemed to be a popular shopping place. Eb gestured for her to pull around to the far side of the building. Two minutes later, Elise and Anne stood on the front porch of the store. Elise's lungs burned. How must Anne be feeling now? She looked over her shoulder. Eb was right behind them.

"Are you ready, Miss Anne?" he asked.

Anne nodded. "Yes, though I wish I had changed into a promenade dress."

Elise smiled. Last night they'd discussed what they would wear on their arrival at Oregon City. They'd decided not to cast aside their calico dresses, out of deference to the many women in the company who had nothing better.

"You mean you've still got all your gowns?" Eb eyed her with amusement.

"Not all, but several, and not much else. We got rid of just about everything but the mules' rations, enough food to get us here, the harness, and our clothing. Our wagon is really quite empty," Anne said.

Unfortunately, her purse was, too, Elise knew. If David was inside this building, all would be well. If not. . .well, they could sell the team and wagon.

Anne squared her shoulders and stepped to the door. Eb held it for them, and the ladies entered the dim building.

A woman stood behind the counter. Anne walked directly to her.

"Excuse me. I'm looking for David Stone. Would he happen to be here?"

The woman looked at her for a moment then turned her head and yelled in a rusty screech, "Nathan!"

Elise jumped. Anne glanced at her and smiled. They waited in silence until a dark-haired man of about thirty, wearing a long, white apron, emerged from among the shelves of groceries.

"What is it, Nancy?"

Elise exhaled. She hadn't admitted how much she was counting on finding David—at once, while Eb was still at her side.

"This woman wants to find Mr. Stone. She talks like him."

The young man turned to Anne. His eyebrows lifted, and a gleam lit his eyes. "Well, now. Mr. Stone? Mr. David Stone?"

"Yes." Anne sounded a bit flustered. "Is he about?"

"No. I'm sorry, he's not."

"But. . ." Anne swung around with tears threatening to spill from her eyes and looked to Eb.

"David Stone used to own this store, I believe," Eb said gruffly.

"Yes, he did." The man smiled. "I'm Nathan Daley. I bought out Mr. Stone about a year ago."

"A year ago?" Anne sagged against her, and Elise slipped an arm about her.

"Do you know where he's gone?" Elise asked.

Daley shrugged. "It's my understanding he bought a spread down near Eugene. He sold out to me, lock, stock, and pickle barrel, you might say." He chuckled, but Elise couldn't raise a smile.

"Do you have an address or directions to his property?" she asked.

"Can't say as I do, but I expect you could reach him through the post office at Eugene. It's quite a ways south of here. . . ."

"I know where it is," Eb said.

Anne opened her handbag. "Just to be certain, this is a miniature of David Stone. It was made when he was about twenty."

Daley took it and carried over to the nearest window. "Yup, that's him." He turned and grinned at Anne. "He looked like you, miss."

"Yes." Anne took the picture back, somber faced. "As far as you know, then, he's in good health?"

"He was when he left here. I'm sorry I can't tell you anything more recent."

"It's all right."

Eb drew them aside. "What do you ladies want to do? Eugene is a far piece."

"Perhaps we should take rooms for the night," Anne said doubtfully.

Elise couldn't help noticing the bins of cabbages, carrots, beets, and other fresh vegetables at the front of the store.

"Should we buy a few supplies?"

"The sight of those cabbages makes my mouth water," Anne said. "But unless we have a place where we can cook. . . We don't want to go on camping, do we?"

Elise hesitated, not sure how much cash Anne had left.

"There's a boardinghouse or two," Eb said.

The door opened and a tall, thin man strode in, heading straight for the counter. Daley had gone to aid a customer, and the woman behind the counter eyed the newcomer.

"May I help you, sir?"

"Yes. I understand this establishment is owned by David Stone."

Elise grabbed Anne's arm. "It's the mustache man."

Anne caught her breath. "Are you sure?"

"Yes." Elise took Eb's arm and hustled the two of them behind a rack of harness. "Eb, that man was on our train out of New York, and our steamship across the Mississippi. Anne spotted him watching us near the dock in St. Louis."

"And you think he followed you all the way out here?" Eb's face looked less than credulous.

"I don't know how," Elise said, "but I'm sure it's him."

Eb walked to the end of the aisle and stood watching the man at the counter.

"Wonderful," the man said with great sarcasm. "And how far away is Eugene?"

"You'll have to ask Mr. Daley," the woman said. "He was just explaining it to someone else."

"Someone else?" the man asked. "Not a Mr. Thomas G. Costigan?"

"Why, no. I've never heard of that person. This was two women."

"Two women?" the man snapped. "Two *English* women?"

"Yes, I'd say so. Very pretty accents." The clerk nodded toward where they stood, partially concealed by the racks of merchandise. "They're still in the store."

As the man turned in their direction, Elise squeezed Eb's arm.

"Can you talk to him and detain him?" Eb whispered. "I'll go for the marshal."

Anne strode to the open area before the counter and planted herself before the man with the mustache.

"Who *are* you?"

"I beg your pardon." The man darted a glance toward the door as though looking for escape. Eb was just closing in behind him.

304

"You followed my companion and me halfway across this country to St. Louis," Anne said, "and now we arrive here in Oregon City after an arduous journey and find you here—inquiring for my uncle."

"Aha." The man gulped and looked her up and down.

Elise stepped up beside Anne and glared at him. "You'd best explain yourself, sir. Start with your name."

"I. . .er. . .Charles Peterson."

"And how did you get here?"

He seemed relieved at that question. "I came by ship. Most of the way, that is."

"Why?" Elise asked.

He hesitated then said with an air of confession, "I was employed to search for Mr. Stone."

"By whom?"

"That is a private matter."

"Is it?" Anne asked. "Because my family's solicitor told me the trustees of my father's estate would not spend any more money looking for my uncle. If they are not paying you, I demand to know who is."

"I am not at liberty to say, miss. Now, if you will excuse me—"

"No! I will not excuse you." Anne held his stare, and Elise slipped around the man and stood solidly in front of the door.

"Nathan," screeched the woman behind the counter.

Mr. Daley hurried toward her, wiping his hands on his apron. "What is it?" He looked at Anne and Peterson. "May I be of some assistance?"

"We would like the marshal to question this man," Anne said.

"Oh dear. The marshal? Whatever for?" Daley glanced at Nancy. "What's this about?"

"This man inquired about my uncle," Anne said. "In practically the same breath, he asked for a man we know is a criminal."

"What are you talking about?" Peterson asked. "I did no such thing."

"Yes, you did. Thomas G. Costigan is now in the marshal's

custody. If you're an acquaintance of his, then you should speak to the marshal as well."

"I don't know what you think you know, but I shan't be a part of this scandalous scene." Peterson backed toward the door and bumped into Elise. "Oh excuse me, ma'am." He looked at her and gave a start. "Oh, my."

"Yes," said Elise. "We'll all wait here until the marshal arrives."

Daley looked in dismay at the crowd of customers gathering to watch. "Please, ma'am, if you could just take this dispute elsewhere..."

"I'm afraid we can't," Elise said.

She felt a shove on the door behind her, and then someone knocked.

"It's Eb!" Anne was looking out the window. "He's got Rob and some of the boys with him."

Elise opened the door. Eb strode in and gave Peterson a stern look. "Stay where you are, mister. I've sent a young man to fetch the marshal. Dan, watch the door."

Dan Adams took up his place next to Elise. Hector Adams, along with Rob Whistler, Wilbur Harkness, and Eb, formed a ring around Peterson. The store seemed very small and crowded. Anne edged over to Elise and groped for her hand.

"I'm sorry for the inconvenience, folks," Mr. Daley called to his customers. "Just continue your shopping. I'm sure this misunderstanding will be clarified soon."

The shoppers drifted back to the displays of wares. Within minutes, Ben Harkness came to the door with another man.

"Here's Marshal Nesmith," Ben said.

The marshal nodded to Eb. "Bentley. That the fella?"

"Yes, sir."

The marshal walked over to Peterson. "Who are you?"

"The name is Peterson, sir. I just came by ship, all the way from New Orleans, and before that down the Mississippi."

"You know Thomas Costigan?"

"Well, I..."

"That's good enough for me." Nesmith nodded at Eb. "If you and Whistler say he's a bad'un, I'll take him in for questioning."

"I think that would be wise," Rob said.

They sent the Adams and Harkness brothers on their respective ways with hearty thanks. Rob treated the ladies to tea and a sandwich at a café while Eb accompanied Nesmith and Peterson to the marshal's office.

An hour later, Anne and Elise went to tell the marshal their story with only Eb and Rob present. Anne explained her family's situation in detail, and Elise added what she knew of Peterson's and Costigan's activities.

"Well, it's starting to add up," the marshal said. "Costigan's in a bad way. The doctor thinks he might not make it."

"Oh dear," Elise said. "It's that bad?"

"Well, his leg's infected, and he won't let the doc take it off. It might kill him. So I told him, whatever he knows, he'd best tell me. And he said this Peterson hired him in St. Louis just to follow the ladies around and see if they learned anything about David Stone's whereabouts. Costigan gathered that someone in England wanted to find the man and was hoping the ladies would lead him to Stone. When he heard them tell someone they had decided to join the wagon train, he told Peterson, and Peterson told him to hire on with them if he could, or to join the train some other way. Peterson offered him a lot of money to come overland with the ladies and see if they found Stone. What he didn't tell Costigan, it appears, is that he would set out by ship and try to get here first."

"I may be a little slow," Rob said, "but why do they want to find Miss Anne's uncle so badly?"

"He's the new earl," Eb said, "and he'll be worth millions if he claims the title."

"So they hoped to extort money from him?"

"The way I see it—" Eb glanced at Anne.

She nodded. "Go ahead, Mr. Bentley. Your theory makes as much sense as anything else I can think of, probably more."

"Peterson was going to kill David Stone," Eb said. "That way, if the concerned parties in England could get a valid death certificate proving Stone was deceased, the next in line could claim the estate. Be the new earl."

Anne sighed. "I'm afraid it's true. Thomas must have figured it out when he saw the letter addressed to my father—the earl of Stoneford. Marshal, will you prepare a letter to my family's solicitor, Andrew Conrad? He must learn of this as soon as possible. It will be months before it reaches him, I know, but action must be taken in England."

"Who is this person who would get your uncle's money and title?" Nesmith asked.

Anne put her hand to her forehead and drew in a deep breath. "I've no proof, but I fear my cousin is behind all of this. He's in line for the earldom, but he can't inherit a penny unless Uncle David's death is proven."

"I see. Once we sort this all out, I'll write that letter for you, ma'am."

"Thank you. I'll need to go to Eugene as soon as possible to find my uncle and tell him all that has happened."

"I have a man down there," the marshal said. "I'll send him word to look into Mr. Stone's whereabouts. I wouldn't want any more trouble out of this business."

"Miss Anne, you could go as far as Marysville with Eb and me," Rob said. "Corvallis, they call it now. You'd be more than halfway to Eugene, and we'd be happy to escort you that far."

"That's generous of you," Elise said.

Anne smiled at the two men. "It sounds wonderful."

They wrote out statements of the events leading up to their encounter with Peterson, and Rob and Eb took them to a boardinghouse.

"This place has a good reputation," Rob said. "If you want, you can keep your wagon and drive it to Corvallis. Or there's a stagecoach that takes mail that far."

"It would probably be more economical to drive ourselves, if you don't mind our slow pace," Elise said.

Rob nodded. "Fine with me. I was thinking you might want to send a letter right away. If Mr. Stone is set up in Eugene like Mr. Daley said, then you could go on down there. But if he's not, I'd hate to see you go all that way for nothing."

"That might be wise," Anne said.

Elise smiled up at Rob. "I regret that you've delayed getting home to Dulcie on our account."

"So do I," Eb said.

"She'll understand if I take another day or two." Rob eyed his friend for a moment. "So, you want to sleep in a bed here at the boardinghouse tonight?"

"I might get used to luxury then," Eb said.

"Fair enough. We'll camp by the boat landing." Rob said to Anne, "We'll help you get a letter on the steamer in the morning before we set out. If you tell your uncle to write to you at the post office in Corvallis, you might not have long to wait after you get there."

# CHAPTER 30

Four days later, Elise and Anne were quite comfortable in their rooms at the City Hotel, a rambling, wood-frame building on the corner of Madison and Second Streets in the bustling town of Corvallis. Rob and Eb had left them two days earlier and returned to their ranches a few miles outside town.

Elise rose early on Monday and donned her best remaining morning dress and matching bonnet. The warm weather prompted her to choose a shawl instead of an overcoat, even though October was nearly upon them.

A light tap on her door announced Anne's arrival.

"Good morning! Ready for breakfast?"

They went down to the dining room, where Anne attacked the generous breakfast with relish. Elise also savored the food, thankful they could eat eggs and toast with jam and butter, and even more thankful that someone else had prepared it all. Immediately afterward they set out for their daily walk to the post office.

"Are you sure we can afford the hotel?" Elise asked, not for the first time.

"My dear, we've settled this," Anne said. "I have a bit left, though not a large bit. It's true that we'll be out of funds soon, no matter what happens. Until we know whether Uncle David is alive and able to help us, we have to live."

"Yes, but we could live more frugally."

"How? By camping in the wagon? No, I'm glad we sold it," Anne said. "The money from that will allow us to continue staying here several more weeks if we must, or to find transportation south to Eugene."

As they entered the post office, the postmaster looked up from his business of sorting mail.

"Ah, Miss Stone. Happy news, I hope." He held out an envelope.

"Oh, thank you!" Anne seized it. "God bless you, sir!"

She and Elise hurried outside and found seats on the front porch of a nearby store. Anne examined the front of the envelope. Her name and "General Delivery, Corvallis" were scrawled across it.

Elise could hardly breathe while she waited for Anne to remove the paper inside and unfold it. The young woman read the message silently then looked at her.

"Well?" Elise asked.

"It says, 'Come on to Eugene. David.' That's all."

"But it's enough," Elise said. "We must send word to the marshal."

"Yes. And to Eb. Elise, listen to me." Anne took her hand and looked earnestly into her eyes. "I want you to marry Eb now. I'll go up the river myself and find Uncle David. It's only two days' journey, or one if I press on at a good pace."

"It's almost fifty miles. You can't do that in one day, even with a good, fast horse and buggy."

"I think I could."

"Well, stop thinking it."

"You don't need to go with me."

Elise looked away. "David should come here to get you. I find it very odd that he didn't say more in his letter." Elise shook her head. "No, I can't let you go alone."

Anne glowered at her. "I should be perfectly safe. We're in civilized territory now."

"That is a matter of opinion."

"Well, let us send our messages and see what arrangements I can make for travel."

They stopped at a store, where Anne purchased several sheets of paper and two envelopes, and continued on to the post office. While she wrote a brief message to the marshal, Elise, at her insistence, penned a note to Eb:

*Dear Eb,*

*We've heard from Anne's uncle and he urges her to go to Eugene. She insists she can travel alone, but I can't let her. I hope we shall make the journey in less than a week.*

Elise reread what she had written and then, with blushing cheeks, added, "Surely within a week or two, my errand will be completed and I shall return to Corvallis."

"Don't seal Eb's letter yet," Anne said. "I want to write him a note as well."

"All right."

"Here, can you address this to the marshal for me?" Anne passed her the message she had written and grabbed another sheet of paper.

A minute later, Anne placed both their notes to Eb in an envelope, sealed it, and took their two letters to the counter.

"How long will the one to Mr. Bentley take?" she asked the postmaster.

He squinted down at the address. "Oh, it's only five miles or so out there. Somebody will take it today."

"Wonderful." Anne turned and took Elise's arm. "Come, my dear. Let's go and inquire about boats and buggies and all that sort of thing."

Eb hitched his horse outside the City Hotel and brushed off his clothes. He was wearing a new shirt, and he was careful not to let Speck slobber on it. The sun was sinking, and he hoped he'd find the ladies inside. If they'd headed out this morning, he would be hard pressed to catch them.

He walked into the lobby and ambled to the desk. "Howdy."

"Hello," said the clerk.

"I'm here to see Miss Finster and Miss Stone."

"I believe they're at supper." The clerk nodded to his left, and Eb headed in that direction. He came into a dining room with four long tables. Seated at one of them were Anne, Elise, and six men.

Anne saw him first. She nudged Elise and spoke in her ear. Elise looked up, and her face broke into a beautiful smile. She rose and came to meet him.

"Eb! How wonderful to see you. You didn't have to come."

"Didn't I? Miss Anne seemed to think I should."

"Really?" Elise looked back at Anne, but her friend was deep in conversation with two of the men seated at the table. "We're nearly done eating. Can I get you a cup of coffee? There's an unoccupied table over there—you see?"

She pointed to a smaller table in a corner.

"Sure."

He went to it, and a moment later Elise came over carrying two ironstone mugs.

"Is Miss Anne coming?" he asked.

"She says she will in a minute. One of the gentlemen is quizzing her about London."

Eb held Elise's chair while she slid into it. He sat down. For a moment, he stayed still, looking at her. She sipped her tea and watched him over the rim of her cup.

"You're a sight for sore eyes," Eb said.

"Thank you. I've missed you terribly."

"Have you?" Her words emboldened him to reach for her hand.

"Yes. How is everything at the ranch?"

"Not too bad. A bit overgrown. I've bought twenty head of stock. Planning to get some more next week. And I've. . .fixed up the house a little."

She smiled. "Anne's uncle answered her letter—a bit tersely, but he told her to come."

"So you said in your note."

Elise nodded. "So we're going. We hope to leave tomorrow morning." She lowered her voice. "If we go upstream a ways, we may be able to get a riverboat as far as Eugene."

"Oh, I don't know. It's pretty shallow above here."

"Well, if we must, we'll hire a wagon and horse."

"Elise, stay here."

"What? I can't."

Eb pulled in a deep breath and let it out again. "Anne says you can."

"She can't go by herself. I can't let her."

"Rob says you can, too."

"What?" She eyed him as if he were crazy. "What does Rob have to do with it?"

"He's coming in the morning. Him and Dulcie."

Elise brightened. "We'll get to meet Dulcie at last?"

"That's right. I showed her and Rob your letter and Anne's last night. They both want to come. Elise, they'll take Anne to Eugene."

"What? You're not serious."

"I'm dead serious. They want us to. . .well, you know. To be together. To get married. Now, while Anne's still here. And then they'll take her to Mr. Stone. It will be a nice outing for them, Dulcie says. Rob's been gone all year, and she's been stuck at home by herself. I'll take care of their livestock, and they'll get to have an adventure together. Dulcie's wild to do it."

She seemed to weigh his words carefully. "That's. . .wonderful of them to offer, but I feel obligated to finish what I started. When I've left Anne with David, I'll come back here."

Eb sank back in his chair. He didn't want her to go, but he didn't want to argue either. She was right about Anne—the girl was too young and pretty to travel alone in this country. Why had he let Anne get his hopes up with her silly message? *I think you should come to town now and marry Elise at once.* What did a girl like Anne know about marriage and obligations, anyway? She was only spinning dreams.

But what if they went off and something happened to keep Elise in Eugene? Supposing one of them got injured or became ill? And what about David Stone? Eb had the feeling there was something between him and Elise twenty years ago. She blushed every time his name came up. What if they saw each other again and Elise didn't *want* to come back to Corvallis?

"So. . .you don't know any more about Stone. Whether he's got a family or anything?"

"No, we don't. The message was very short, but I suppose he was in a hurry to get it off quickly."

Eb thought about that. Maybe Elise was right to be cautious. But he hoped that once she met Dulcie, she'd give in. Everyone loved Dulcie, and she was so sensible and efficient. Elise couldn't say no to her. And Anne's suggestion in her letter of a wedding here in Corvallis before she parted from Elise could come true. That's all he had to do—bide his time. Tomorrow Elise would be his bride.

"Eb! How delightful." Anne stood beside him, beaming down at them.

Eb stood and greeted her. The supper crowd was thinning out.

"Won't you join us, Miss Anne?" he asked.

"Yes, thank you."

Eb pulled out a chair for her.

"I've been thinking," she said, smiling brightly at Elise. "Marshal Nesmith said he has a deputy in Eugene. If I go down there and find this deputy, he can go with me to Uncle David's property. I shall be perfectly safe."

"You don't need to worry about your safety," Eb said. "Rob and Dulcie will go with you."

"What?" Anne stared at him.

"They'll be here in the morning," Eb said. "They want to ride down to Eugene with you. Rob's bringing a wagon, and you can ride together. They'll take you safely to your uncle. Dulcie's looking forward to it."

Anne smiled in triumph at Elise. "It's perfect."

"It does sound. . .fortuitous." Elise shot Eb a glance that seemed almost shy for someone so self-sufficient.

"And you can have the wedding before we set out," Anne said.

Elise raised a hand. "I'm not sure. . . ."

"What?" Anne asked. "If the Whistlers will travel with me, we can have the ceremony right away. Come on, Elise. You can't disappoint me after all these months of planning."

"Who's been planning?" Elise asked.

"I have of course."

Eb swallowed hard. What if she said no again?

"Elise?" he asked softly.

She turned and looked at him with those blue eyes that melted him. "Will you?"

She hesitated a moment.

"I know the preacher pretty well," Eb said.

"This is so sudden."

"A mite, but. . ."

"But you both know you want to be married," Anne said.

Eb raised his eyebrows and waited, barely able to breathe.

Elise clasped his hand. "When will Rob and Dulcie get here?"

"In the morning. I could go around tonight and speak to the preacher."

She pressed her lips together and smiled, blushing to her hairline. "All right, I will."

Something tight let go in Eb's chest. If they'd been alone, he'd have kissed her for sure.

"My dear ladies!" The small, auburn-haired woman hopped down from the wagon before Rob could get around to help her. "I'm so thrilled to meet you. I'm Dulcie."

Elise warmed to her at once and drew her into an embrace. "We're pleased to meet you, too."

Anne kissed her cheek. "Your husband did so much for us on the trail. And now you're both going to help me get to Uncle David."

"I'm looking forward to it more than you can imagine."

"Well, hey there!"

At Rob's warm greeting, Elise looked toward the street. Eb was driving up in another wagon, and another man rode beside him on a chestnut horse.

"Anne," Elise said. "Anne! It's—"

Anne turned and stared. "Oh my." She walked over to the newcomers. "Dan? What are you doing here?"

Eb laughed. "I ran into him when I got into town. He was riding up Madison Street, looking lost."

Dan Adams dismounted and gazed longingly down at Anne. "I couldn't stop wondering if you'd found your uncle. Finally Hector got sick of it and told me to ride on down here and see. I figured if you'd left already, I could ask Mr. Whistler, and he'd know."

"Sure enough, I know!" Rob slapped Dan on the back. "You might as well come to the wedding, Dan."

"Wedding?"

"That's right. Eb and Miss Elise. We're about to walk over to the church. Come along."

On the way, Rob told Dan the details. Anne walked with Dulcie, chattering away about their upcoming trip, and Elise found herself behind them, with Eb at her side.

"Didn't get a chance to say hello, Miss Finster."

She eyed him cautiously. "Miss Finster, is it?"

"I won't get to call you that much longer."

She smiled and slipped her hand through his arm. "Hello, yourself."

"I don't believe I've seen you looking quite this beautiful before."

Elise felt she might explode into a million glittering shards. "Not even in St. Louis, before the wind and the mules and the campfire took their toll?"

He gazed down at her as they walked and squinted up the corners of his eyes. "Not even then. And you were a sight then."

They reached the church, and Dulcie waited for her at the door. "Here, dear Miss Elise. I nearly forgot to give you these." She folded back the muslin cover over a bundle she'd carried. In the crook of her arm lay a plump bouquet of hawkweed and black-eyed susans. "I don't have many tame flowers yet."

"These are lovely," Elise said.

Inside the church, the minister met them with his Bible in his hand.

"Morning, folks." He shook Eb's hand and Rob's.

Rob said, "You know Dulcie. This is the bride, Miss Elise

Finster. And this is her friend, Miss Anne Stone, and a friend of us all, Daniel Adams."

The minister greeted each one. "Are you ready to begin?"

Eb nodded.

"Reckon we should," Rob said. "We've got a trip ahead of us."

"Then come this way."

They followed the minister to the front of the little church. Eb and Elise stood before him, with Anne next to Elise and the others close in a half circle.

*This is it,* Elise thought. *I'm an American now. I shall never go back to England. I shall never see Stoneford again or wait on Lady Anne.*

She looked up at Eb. He must have seen some flicker in her expression. He took her hand and tucked it through his arm then stood facing the minister but caressing her hand.

She passed the wildflowers to Anne. The minister pronounced the vows, and she and Eb repeated them. When he asked for a ring, Rob surprised her by producing one from his pocket. She looked up at Eb, and he smiled at her. So he'd bought a ring yesterday, too. What else had he done while she basked in blissful ignorance with Anne last evening?

Whatever it was, she knew it was for her peace and comfort.

"I pronounce you man and wife," said the minister.

Eb bent to kiss her, and Elise clung to him for a moment.

Her girlhood dreams couldn't have conjured up this moment if she'd tried. Elise Finster, well-trained lady's maid, marrying a roughhewn rancher in the Oregon Territory.

Eb pulled away slightly and whispered, "Hello, Mrs. Bentley."

Elise smiled. God had reached across two continents to bring her and Eb together. She had never been so happy.

# About the Author

Susan Page Davis is the author of more than thirty novels in the historical romance, mystery, romantic suspense, contemporary romance, and young adult genres. A history and genealogy buff, she lives in Kentucky with her husband, Jim. They are the parents of six terrific young adults and are the grandparents of six adorable grandchildren. Visit Susan at her Web site: www. susanpagedavis.com.

---

## Other Books by
## Susan Page Davis

### Ladies' Shooting Club Series

*The Sheriff's Surrender*
*The Gunsmith's Gallantry*
*The Blacksmith's Bravery*